The Cat who Walks through Walls:

A Comedy of Manners

By Robert A. Heinlein and published by
New English Library

The Cat who Walks through Walls:
A Comedy of Manners

Robert A. Heinlein

NEW ENGLISH LIBRARY

Copyright © 1985 by Robert A. Heinlein

First published in the United States of America by
G. P. Putnam's Sons in 1985

First published in Great Britain in 1986 by
New English Library, Mill Road, Dunton Green, Sevenoaks, Kent.
Editorial office: 47 Bedford Square, London WC1B 3DP.

Typeset by Rowland Phototypesetting Ltd,
Bury St Edmunds, Suffolk

Printed in Great Britain by
Biddles Ltd, Guildford and King's Lynn

British Library C.I.P.

Heinlein, Robert A.
   The cat who walks through walls: a comedy
of manners.
   I. Title
813'.54[F]   PS3558.E458/

ISBN 0-450-06149-3

To

Jerry and Larry and Harry
Dean and Dan and Jim
Poul and Buz and Sarge
(Men to have at your back)

R.A.H.

Ah Love! could you and I with Him conspire
To grasp this sorry Scheme of Things entire,
Would we not shatter it to bits – and then
Re-mould it nearer to the Heart's Desire!

RUBÁIYÁT OF OMAR KHAYYÁM
Quatrain XCIX, Fifth Edition
(as rendered by Edward FitzGerald)

BOOK ONE—

Indifferent Honest

I

'Whatever you do, you'll regret it.'

ALLAN MCLEOD GRAY 1905–1975

'WE NEED you to kill a man.'

This stranger glanced nervously around us. I feel that a crowded restaurant is no place for such talk, as a high noise level gives only limited privacy.

I shook my head. 'I'm not an assassin. Killing is more of a hobby with me. Have you had dinner?'

'I'm not here to eat. Just let me—'

'Oh, come now. I insist.' He had annoyed me by interrupting an evening with a delightful lady; I was paying him back in kind. It does not do to encourage bad manners; one should retaliate, urbanely but firmly.

That lady, Gwen Novak, had expressed a wish to spend a penny and had left the table, whereupon Herr Nameless had materialized and sat down uninvited. I had been about to tell him to leave when he mentioned a name, Walker Evans.

There is no 'Walker Evans.'

Instead, that name is or should be a message from one of six people, five men, one woman, a code to remind me of a debt. It is conceivable that an installment payment on that ancient debt could require me to kill someone – possible but unlikely.

But it was not conceivable that I would kill at the behest of a stranger merely because he invoked that name.

While I felt obliged to listen, I did not intend to let him ruin my evening. Since he was sitting at my table, he could bloody well behave like an invited guest. 'Sir, if you don't want a full dinner, try the after-theater suggestions. The lapin ragout on toast may be rat rather than rabbit but this chef makes it taste like ambrosia.'

3

'But I don't want—'

'Please.' I looked up, caught my waiter's eye. 'Morris.'

Morris was at my elbow at once. 'Three orders of lapin ragout, please, Morris, and ask Hans to select a dry white wine for me.'

'Yes, Dr Ames.'

'Don't serve until the lady returns, if you please.'

'Certainly, sir.'

I waited until the waiter had moved away. 'My guest will be returning soon. You have a brief time to explain yourself in private. Please start by telling me your name.'

'My name isn't important. I—'

'Come, sir! Your name. Please.'

'I was told simply to say "Walker Evans".'

'Good as far as it goes. But *your* name is not Walker Evans and I do not traffic with a man who won't give his name. Tell me who you are, and it would be well to have an ID that matches your words.'

'But – Colonel, it's far more urgent to explain who must die and why you are the man who must kill him! You *must* admit that!'

'I don't have to admit anything. Your name, sir! And your ID. And please do not call me "Colonel"; I am Dr Ames.' I had to raise my voice not to be drowned out by a roll of drums; the late evening show was starting. The lights lowered and a spotlight picked out the master of ceremonies.

'All right, all right!' My uninvited guest reached into a pocket, pulled out a wallet. 'But Tolliver must die by noon Sunday or we'll all be dead!'

He flipped open the wallet to show me an ID. A small dark spot appeared on his white shirt front. He looked startled, then said softly, 'I'm very sorry,' and leaned forward. He seemed to be trying to add something but blood gushed from his mouth. His head settled down onto the tablecloth.

I was up out of my chair at once and around to his right side. Almost as swiftly Morris was at his left side. Perhaps Morris was trying to help him; I was not – it was too late. A four-millimeter dart makes a small entry hole and no exit wound; it explodes inside the body. When the wound is in the torso, death follows abruptly. What I was doing was searching the crowd – that and one minor chore.

4

While I was trying to spot the killer, Morris was joined by the head-waiter and a busman. The three moved with such speed and efficiency that one would have thought that having a guest killed at a table was something they coped with nightly. They removed the corpse with the dispatch and unobtrusiveness of Chinese stagehands; a fourth man flipped up the tablecloth, removed it and the silver, was back at once with a fresh cloth, and laid two places.

I sat back down. I had not been able to spot a probable killer; I did not even note anyone displaying a curious lack of curiosity about the trouble at my table. People had stared, but when the body was gone, they quit staring and gave attention to the show. There were no screams or expressions of horror; it seemed as if those who had noticed it thought that they were seeing a customer suddenly ill or possibly taken by drink.

The dead man's wallet now rested in my left jacket pocket. When Gwen Novak returned I stood up again, held her chair for her. She smiled her thanks and asked, 'What have I missed?'

'Not much. Jokes old before they were born. Others that were old even before Neil Armstrong was born.'

'I like old jokes, Richard. With them I know when to laugh.'

'You've come to the right place.'

I too like old jokes; I like all sorts of old things – old friends, old books, old poems, old plays. An old favorite had started our evening: *Midsummer Night's Dream* presented by Halifax Ballet Theater with Luanna Pauline as Titania. Low-gravity ballet, live actors, and magical holograms had created a fairyland Will Shakespeare would have loved. Newness is no virtue.

Shortly music drowned out our host's well-aged wit; the chorus line undulated out onto the dance floor, sensuously graceful in half gravity. The ragout arrived and with it the wine. After we had eaten Gwen asked me to dance. I have this trick leg but at half gee I can manage the classic slow dances – waltz, frottage glide, tango, and so forth. Gwen is a warm, live, fragrant bundle; dancing with her is a Sybaritic treat.

It was a gay ending to a happy evening. There was still the matter of the stranger who had had the bad taste to get himself killed at my table. But, since Gwen seemed not to be aware of the unpleasant incident, I had tabled it in my mind, to be dealt with later. To be sure I was ready any moment for that

5

tap on the shoulder . . . but in the meantime I enjoyed good food, good wine, good company. Life is filled with tragedy; if you let it overwhelm you, you cannot enjoy life's innocent pleasures.

Gwen knows that my leg won't take much dancing; at the first break in the music she led us back to our table. I signaled Morris for the check. He produced it out of midair; I dialed my credit code into it, set it for standard gratuity plus half, added my thumbprint.

Morris thanked me. 'A nightcap, sir? Or a brandy? Perhaps the lady would enjoy a liqueur? Compliments of Rainbow's End.' The owner of the restaurant, an ancient Egyptian, believed in good measure – at least to his regulars; I'm not sure how tourists from dirtside were treated.

'Gwen?' I queried, expecting her to refuse – Gwen's drinking is limited to one glass of wine at meals. One.

'A Cointreau would be pleasant. I would like to stay and listen to the music a while.'

'Cointreau for the lady,' Morris noted. 'Doctor?'

'Mary's Tears and a glass of water, please, Morris.'

When Morris left, Gwen said quietly. 'I needed time to speak with you, Richard. Do you want to sleep at my place tonight? Don't be skittish; you can sleep alone.'

'I am not all that fond of sleeping alone.' I clicked over the possibilities in my mind. She had ordered a drink she did not want in order to make me an offer that did not fit. Gwen is a forthright person; I felt that had she wished to sleep with me she would have said so – she would not have played get-away-closer about it.

Therefore she had invited me to sleep in her compartment because she thought it to be unwise or unsafe for me to sleep in my own bed. Therefore—

'You saw it.'

'From a distance. So I waited until things quieted down before returning to the table. Richard, I'm not sure what happened. But if you need a place to lie doggo – be my guest!'

'Why, thank you, my dear!' A friend who offers help without asking for explanations is a treasure beyond price. 'Whether I accept or not, I am in your debt. Mmm, Gwen, I too am unsure what happened. The total stranger who gets himself

6

killed while he's trying to tell you something – A cliché, a tired cliché. If I plotted a story that way today, my guild would disown me.' I smiled at her. 'In its classic form you would turn out to be the killer . . . a fact that would develop slowly while you pretended to help me search. The sophisticated reader would know from chapter one that you did it, but I, as the detective, would never guess what was as plain as the nose on your face. Correction: on my face.'

'Oh, my nose is plain enough; it's my mouth that men remember. Richard, I am not going to help you hang this on me; I simply offered you a hideout. Was he really killed? I couldn't be sure.'

'Eh?' I was saved from answering too quickly by Morris's arrival with our liqueurs. When he left, I answered, 'I had not thought about any other possibility. Gwen, he was not wounded. Either he was killed almost instantly . . . or it was faked. Could it be faked? Certainly. If shown on holo, it could be done in real time with only minor props.' I mulled it over. Why had the restaurant staff been so quick, so precise, in covering it up? Why had I not felt that tap on the shoulder? 'Gwen, I'll take you up on that offer. If the proctors want me, they'll find me. But I would like to discuss this with you in greater detail than we can manage here, no matter how carefully we keep our voices down.'

'Good.' She stood up. 'I won't be long, dear.' She headed for the lounges.

As I stood up Morris handed me my stick and I leaned on it as I followed her toward the lounges. I don't actually have to use a cane – I can even dance, as you know – but using a cane keeps my bad leg from getting too tired.

When I came out of the gentlemen's lounge, I placed myself in the foyer, and waited.

And waited.

Having waited long past what is reasonable I sought out the maître d'hôtel. 'Tony, could you please have some female member of your staff check the ladies' lounge for Mistress Novak? I think that it is possible that she may have become ill, or be in some difficulty.'

'Your guest, Dr Ames?'

'Yes.'

'But she left twenty minutes ago. I ushered her out myself.'

7

'So? I must have misunderstood her. Thank you, and good night.'

'Good night, Doctor. We look forward to serving you again.'

I left Rainbow's End, stood for a moment in the public corridor outside it – ring thirty, half-gravity level, just clockwise from radius two-seventy at Petticoat Lane, a busy neighborhood even at one in the morning. I checked for proctors waiting for me, halfway expecting to find Gwen already in custody.

Nothing of the sort. A steady flow of people, mostly groundhogs on holiday by their dress and behavior, plus pullers for grimp shops, guides and ganders, pickpockets and priests. Golden Rule habitat is known systemwide as the place where anything is for sale and Petticoat Lane helps to support that reputation insofar as fleshpots are concerned. For more sober enterprises you need only go clockwise ninety degrees to Threadneedle Street.

No sign of proctors, no sign of Gwen.

She had promised to meet me at the exit. Or had she? No, not quite. Her exact words were, 'I won't be long, dear.' I had inferred that she expected to find me at the restaurant's exit to the street.

I've heard all the old chestnuts about women and weather, *La donna è mobile*, and so forth – I believe none of them. Gwen had not suddenly changed her mind. For some reason – some *good* reason – she had gone on without me and now would expect me to join her at her home.

Or so I told myself.

If she had taken a scooter, she was there already; if she had walked, she would be there soon – Tony had said, 'Twenty minutes ago.' There is a scooter booth at the intersection of ring thirty and Petticoat Lane. I found an empty, punched in ring one-oh-five, radius one-thirty-five, six-tenths gravity, which would take me as close as one can get by public scooter to Gwen's compartment.

Gwen lives in Gretna Green, just off Appian Way where it crosses the Yellow Brick Road – which means nothing to anyone who has never visited Golden Rule habitat. Some public relations 'expert' had decided that habitants would feel more at home if surrounded by place names familiar from dirtside. There is even (don't retch) a 'House at Pooh Corner.'

What I punched in were coordinates of the main cylinder: 105, 135, 0.6.

The scooter's brain, off somewhere near ring ten, accepted those co-ordinates and waited; I punched in my credit code and took position, crouched against acceleration pads.

That idiot brain took an insultingly long time to decide that my credit was good – then placed a web around me, tightened it, closed the capsule and *whuff! bing! bam!* we were on our way . . . then a fast float for three kilometers from ring thirty to ring one-oh-five, then *bam! bing! whuff!* I was in Gretna Green. The scooter opened.

For me such service is well worth the fare. But the Manager had been warning us the past two years that the system does not pay its way; either use it more or pay more per trip, or the hardware will be salvaged and the space rented out. I hope they work out a solution; some people need this service. (Yes, I know; Laffer theory will always give two solutions to such a problem, a high and a low – except where the theory states that both solutions are the same . . . and imaginary. Which might apply here. It may be that a scooter system is too expensive for a space habitat at the present state of engineering art.)

It was an easy walk to Gwen's compartment: downstairs to seven-tenths gravity, fifty meters 'forward' to her number – I rang.

Her door answered, 'This is the recorded voice of Gwen Novak. I've gone to bed and am, I hope, happily asleep. If your visit is truly an emergency, deposit one hundred crowns via your credit code. If I agree that waking me is justified, I will return your money. If I disagree – laugh, chortle, chuckle! – I'll spend it on gin and keep you out anyhow. If your call is not an emergency, please record a message at the sound of my scream.'

This was followed by a high scream which ended abruptly as if a hapless wench had been choked to death.

Was this an emergency? Was it a hundred-crown emergency? I decided that it was not any sort of emergency, so I recorded:

'Dear Gwen, this is your fairly-faithful swain Richard speaking. Somehow we got our wires crossed. But we can straighten it out in the morning. Will you call me at my digs when

9

you wake up? Love and kisses, Richard the Lion-Hearted.'

I tried to keep my not-inconsiderable irk out of my voice. I felt badly used but underlying it was a conviction that Gwen would not intentionally mistreat me; it had to be an honest mixup even though I did not now understand it.

Then I went home *whuff! bing! bam! . . . bam! bing! whuff!*

I have a deluxe compartment with bedroom separate from the living room. I let myself in, checked for messages in the terminal – none – set it for sleep conditions both for door and terminal, hung up my cane, and went into the bedroom.

Gwen was asleep in my bed.

She looked sweetly peaceful. I backed out quietly, moved noiselessly in undressing, went into the 'fresher, closed the door – soundproof; I said it was a deluxe setup. Nevertheless I made as little noise as possible in refreshing myself for bed, as 'soundproof' is a hope rather than a certainty. When I was as sanitary and odorless as a male hairless ape can manage short of surgery, I went quietly back into my bedroom and got most cautiously into bed. Gwen stirred, did not wake.

At some hour when I was awake in the night, I switched off the alarm. But I woke up about my usual time, as my bladder can't be switched off. So I got up, took care of it, refreshed for the day, decided that I wanted to live, slid into a coverall, went silently into the living room, and opened the buttery, considered my larder. A special guest called for a special breakfast.

I left the connecting door open so that I could keep an eye on Gwen. I think it was the aroma of coffee that woke her.

When I saw that her eyes were open, I called out, 'Good morning, beautiful. Get up and brush your teeth; breakfast is ready.'

'I did brush my teeth, an hour ago. Come back to bed.'

'Nymphomaniac. Orange juice or black cherries or both?'

'Uh . . . both. Don't change the subject. Come here and meet your fate like a man.'

'Eat first.'

'Coward. Richard is a sissy, Richard is a sissy!'

'An utter coward. How many waffles can you eat?'

'Uh . . . decisions! Can't you unfreeze them one at a time?'

'These are not frozen. Only minutes ago they were alive and singing; I killed 'em and skun 'em myself. Speak up, or I'll eat all of them.'

'Oh, the pity and the shame of it all! – turned down for waffles. Nothing left but to enter a monastery. Two.'

'Three. You mean "nunnery."'

'I know what I mean.' She got up, went into the refresher, was out quickly, wearing one of my robes. Pleasant bits of Gwen stuck out here and there. I handed her a glass of juice; she paused to gulp twice before she spoke. 'Gurgle, gurgle. My, that's good. Richard, when we're married, are you going to get breakfast for me every morning?'

'That inquiry contains implied assumptions I am not willing to stipulate—'

'After I trusted you and gave all!'

'– but, without stipulation, I will concede that I would just as lief get breakfast for two as for one. Why do you assume that I'm going to marry you? What inducements do you offer? Are you ready for a waffle?'

'See here, mister, not all men are fussy about marrying grandmothers! I've had offers. Yes, I'm ready for a waffle.'

'Pass your plate.' I grinned at her. '"Grandmother" my missing foot. Not even if you had started your first child at menarche, then your offspring had whelped just as promptly.'

'Neither one and I am so. Richard, I am trying to make two things clear. No, three. First, I'm serious about wanting to marry you if you'll hold still for it . . . or, if you won't, I'll keep you as a pet and cook breakfast for you. Second, I am indeed a grandmother. Third, if, despite my advanced years, you wish to have children by me, the wonders of modern microbiology have kept me fertile as well as relatively un-wrinkled. If you want to knock me up, it should not be too much of a chore.'

'I could force myself. Maple syrup in that one, blueberry syrup in this. Or maybe I did so last night?'

'Wrong date by at least a week . . . but what would you say if I had said, "Jackpot!"'

'Quit joking and finish your waffle. There's another one ready.'

'You're a sadistic monster. And deformed.'

'Not deformed,' I protested. 'This foot was amputated; I

wasn't born without it. My immune system flatly refuses to accept a transplant, so that's that. One reason I live in low gravity.'

Gwen suddenly sobered. 'My very dear! I wasn't speaking of your foot. Oh, heavens! Your foot doesn't matter . . . except that I'll be more careful than ever not to place a strain on you, now that I know why.'

'Sorry. Let's back up. Then what is this about me being "deformed"?'

At once she was again her merry self. 'You should know! When you've got me stretched all out of shape and no use to a normal man. And now you won't marry me. Let's go back to bed.'

'Let's finish breakfast and let it settle first – have you no mercy? I didn't say I wouldn't marry you . . . and I did *not* stretch you.'

'Oh, what a sinful lie! Will you pass the butter, please? You're deformed all right! How big is that tumor with the bone in it? Twenty-five centimeters? More? And how big around? If I had seen it first, I would never have risked it.'

'Oh, piffle! It's not even twenty centimeters. I didn't stretch you; I'm just middlin' size. You should see my Uncle Jock. More coffee?'

'Yes, thank you. You surely did stretch me! Uh . . . is your Uncle Jock actually bigger than you are? Locally?'

'Much.'

'Uh . . . where does he live?'

'Finish your waffle. Do you still want to take me back to bed? Or do you want a note to my Uncle Jock?'

'Why can't I have both? Yes, a little more bacon, thank you, Richard, you're a good cook. I don't want to marry Uncle Jock; I'm just curious.'

'Don't ask him to show it to you unless you mean business . . . because he always means business. He seduced his Scout-master's wife when he was twelve. Ran away with her. Caused considerable talk in southern Iowa because she didn't want to give him up. That was over a hundred years ago when such things were taken seriously, at least in Iowa.'

'Richard, are you implying that Uncle Jock is over a hundred and still active and virile?'

'A hundred and sixteen and still jumping his friends' wives, daughters, mothers, and livestock. And has three wives of his own under the Iowa senior-citizen cohabitation code, one of them – my Aunt Cissy – being still in high school.'

'Richard, I sometimes suspect that you are not always entirely truthful. A mild bent toward exaggeration.'

'Woman, that is no way to talk to your future husband. Behind you is a terminal. Punch it for Grinnell, Iowa; Uncle Jock lives just outside. Shall we call him? You talk to him real pretty and he might show you his pride and joy. Well, dear?'

'You are just trying to get out of taking me back to bed.'

'Another waffle?'

'Quit trying to bribe me. Uh, a half, maybe. Split one with me?'

'No. A whole one for each of us.'

'"Hail, Caesar!" You're the bad example I've always needed. Once we're married I'm going to get fat.'

'I'm glad you said that. I had hesitated to mention it but you *are* a bit on the skinny side. Sharp corners. Bruises. Some padding would help.'

I'll omit what Gwen said next. It was colorful, even lyrical, but (in my opinion) unladylike. Not her true self, so we won't record it.

I answered, 'Truly, it's irrelevant. I admire you for your intelligence. And your angelic spirit. Your beautiful soul. Let's not get physical.'

Again I feel that I must censor.

'All right,' I agreed. 'If that's what you want. Get back into bed and start thinking physical thoughts. I'll switch off the waffle iron.'

Somewhat later I said, 'Do you want a church wedding?'

'*Coo!* Should I wear white? Richard, are you a church member?'

'No.'

'Neither am I. I don't think you and I really belong in churches.'

'I agree. But just how do you want to get married? So far as I know there isn't any other way to get married in the Golden Rule. Nothing in the Manager's regulations. Legally the institution of marriage does not exist here.'

'But, Richard, lots of people do get married.'

'But how, dear? I realize they do but, if they don't do it

through a church, I don't know how they go about it. I've never had occasion to find out. Do they go to Luna City? Or down dirtside? How?'

'Whatever way they wish. Hire a hall and get some VIP to tie the knot in the presence of a crowd of guests, with music and a big reception afterwards . . . or do it at home with just a few friends present. Or anything in between. It's your choice, Richard.'

'Huh uh, not mine. Yours. I simply agreed to go along. As for me, I find that a woman is at her best if she is a bit tense through being unsure of her status. Keeps her on her toes. Don't you agree? *Hey!* Stop that!'

'Then stop trying to get my goat. If you don't want to sing soprano at your own wedding.'

'You do that once more and there ainta gonna be no wedding. Dear one, what sort of a wedding do you want?'

'Richard, I don't need a wedding ceremony, I don't need witnesses. I just want to promise you everything a wife should promise.'

'You're sure, Gwen? Aren't you being hasty?' Confound it, promises a woman makes in bed should not be binding.

'I am not being hasty. I decided to marry you more than a year ago.'

'You did? Well, I'll be – Hey! We met less than a year ago. At the Day One Ball. July twentieth. I remember.'

'True.'

'Well?'

'"Well" what, dear? I decided to marry you before we met. Do you have a problem with that? I don't. I didn't.'

'Mmm. I had better tell you some things. My past contains episodes I don't boast about. Not exactly dishonest but somewhat shady. And Ames is not the name I was born with.'

'Richard, I will be proud to be addressed as "Mrs Ames." Or as . . . "Mrs Campbell" . . . Colin.'

I said nothing, loudly – then added, 'What more do you know?'

She looked me firmly in the eye, did not smile. 'All I need to know. Colonel Colin Campbell, known as "Killer" Campbell to his troops . . . and in the dispatches. A rescuing angel to the students of Percival Lowell Academy. Richard, or Colin, my oldest daughter was one of those students.'

'I'll be eternally damned.'

'I doubt it.'

'And because of this you intend to marry me?'

'No, dear man. That reason sufficed a year ago. But now I've had many months to discover the human being behind the storybook hero. And . . . I did hurry you into bed last night but neither of us would marry for that reason alone. Do you want to know about my own tarnished past? I'll tell.'

'No.' I faced her, took both her hands. 'Gwendolyn, I want you to be my wife. Will you have me as your husband?'

'I will.'

'I, Colin Richard, take thee, Gwendolyn, to be my wife, to have and to hold, to love and to cherish, as long as you will have me.'

'I, Sadie Gwendolyn, take thee, Colin Richard, to be my husband, to care for and love and cherish for the rest of my life.'

'Whew! I guess that does it.'

'Yes. But kiss me.'

I did. 'When did "Sadie" show up?'

'Sadie Lipschitz, my family name. I didn't like it so I changed it. Richard, the only thing left to make it official is to publish it. That ties it down. And I do want to tie it down while you're still groggy.'

'All right. Publish it how?'

'May I use your terminal?'

'*Our* terminal. You don't have to ask to use it.'

'"Our terminal." Thank you, dear.' She got up, went to the terminal, keyed for directory, then called the *Golden Rule Herald*, asked for the society editor. 'Please record. Dr Richard Ames and Mistress Gwendolyn Novak are pleased to announce their marriage this date. No presents, no flowers. Please confirm.' She switched off. They called back at once; I answered and confirmed.

She sighed. 'Richard, I hurried you. But I had to. Now I can no longer be required to testify against you in any jurisdiction anywhere. I want to help in any way that I can. Why did you kill him, dear? And how?'

II

'In waking a tiger, use a long stick.'

MAO TSE-TUNG 1893–1976

I STARED thoughtfully at my bride. 'You are a gallant lady, my love, and I am grateful that you do not want to testify against me. But I am not sure that the legal principle you cited can be applied in this jurisdiction.'

'But that's a general rule of justice, Richard. A wife can't be forced to testify against her husband. Everyone knows that.'

'The question is: Does the Manager know it? The Company asserts that the habitat has only one law, the Golden Rule, and claims that the Manager's regulations are merely practical interpretations of that law, just guidelines subject to change – change right in the middle of a hearing and retroactive, if the Manager so decides. Gwen, I don't know. The Manager's Proxy might decide that you are the Company's star witness.'

'I won't do it! I won't!'

'Thank you, my love. But let's find out what your testimony would be were you to be a witness in – what shall we call it? Eh, suppose that I am charged with having wrongfully caused the death of, uh, Mr X . . . Mr X being the stranger who came to our table last night when you excused yourself to visit the ladies' lounge. What did you see?'

'Richard, I saw you kill him. I saw it!'

'A prosecutor would require more details. Did you see him come to our table?'

'No. I didn't see him until I left the lounge and was headed for our table . . . and was startled to see someone sitting in my chair.'

'All right, back up a little and tell me exactly what you saw.'

'Uh, I came out of the ladies' room and turned left, toward our table. Your back was toward me, you'll remember—'

16

'Never mind what I remember; you tell what you remember. How far away were you?'

'Oh, I don't know. Ten meters, maybe. I could go there and measure it. Does it matter?'

'If it ever does, you can measure it. You saw me from about ten meters. What was I doing? Standing? Sitting? Moving?'

'You were seated with your back to me.'

'My back was toward you. The light wasn't very good. How did you know it was I?'

'Why – Richard, you're being intentionally difficult.'

'Yes, because prosecutors are intentionally difficult. How did you recognize me?'

'Uh – It was *you*, Richard, I know the back of your neck just as I know your face. Anyhow, when you stood up and moved, I *did* see your face.'

'Was that what I did next? Stand up?'

'No, no. I spotted you, at our table – then I stopped short when I saw someone seated across from you, in my chair. I just stood there and stared.'

'Did you recognize him?'

'No. I don't think I ever saw him before.'

'Describe him.'

'Uh, I can't, very well.'

'Short? Tall? Age? Bearded? Race? How dressed?'

'I never saw him standing up. He wasn't a youngster but he wasn't an old man, either. I don't think he wore a beard.'

'Moustache?'

'I don't know.' (I did know. No moustache. Age about thirty.)

'Race?'

'White. Light skin, anyhow, but not blond like a Swede. Richard, there wasn't time to catch all the details. He threatened you with some sort of weapon and you shot him and you jumped up as the waiter came over – and I backed up and waited until they took him away.'

'Where did they take him?'

'I'm not sure. I backed into the ladies' lounge and let the door contract. They could have taken him into the gentlemen's room just across the passage. But there's another door at the end of the passage marked "Employees Only."'

'You say he threatened me with a weapon?'

'Yes. Then you shot him and jumped up and grabbed his weapon and shoved it into your pocket, just as our waiter came up on the other side.'

(Oho!) 'Which pocket did I put it in?'

'Let me think. I have to turn myself that way in my mind. Your left pocket. Your left outside jacket pocket.'

'How was I dressed last night?'

'Evening dress, we had come straight from the ballet. White turtleneck, maroon jacket, black trousers.'

'Gwen, because you were asleep in the bedroom, I undressed last night here in the living room and hung the clothes I was wearing in that wardrobe by the outer door, intending to move them later. Will you please open that wardrobe, find the jacket I wore last night, and get from its left outside pocket the "weapon" you saw me place in it?"

'But –' She shut up and, solemn-faced, did as I asked.

In a moment she returned. 'This is all there was in that pocket.' She handed me the stranger's wallet.

I accepted it. 'This is the weapon with which he threatened me.' Then I showed her my right forefinger, bare. 'And this is the weapon I used to shoot him when he pointed this wallet at me.'

'I don't understand.'

'Beloved, this is why criminologists place more faith in circumstantial evidence than they do in the testimony of eyewitnesses. You are the ideal eyewitness, intelligent, sincere, cooperative, and honest. You have reported a mixture of what you did see, what you thought you saw, what you failed to notice although it was in front of you, and what your logical mind fills in as necessities linking what you saw and what you thought you saw. This mixture is now all solidly in your mind as a true memory, a firsthand, eyewitness memory. But it didn't happen.'

'But, Richard, I *did* see—'

'You saw that poor clown killed. You did not see him threatening me; you did not see me shoot him. Some third person shot him with an explosive dart. Since he was facing you and it hit him in the chest, that dart must have come right past you. Did you notice anyone standing?'

'No. Oh, there were waiters moving around, and busmen, and the maître d' and people getting up and sitting down. I mean I didn't notice anyone in particular – certainly not anyone shooting a gun. What sort of a gun?'

'Gwen, it might not look like a gun. A concealed assassin's weapon capable of shooting a dart short range – It could look like anything as long as it had one dimension about fifteen centimeters long. A lady's purse. A camera. Opera glasses. An endless list of innocent-appearing objects. This gets us nowhere as I had my back to the action and you saw nothing out of the way. The dart probably came from behind your back. So forget it. Let's see who the victim was. Or whom he claimed to be.'

I took out everything from all the pockets of that wallet, including a poorly-concealed 'secret' pocket. This last held gold certificates issued by a Zurich bank, equivalent to about seventeen thousand crowns – his get-away money, it seemed likely.

There was an ID of the sort the Golden Rule issues to each person arriving at the habitat's hub. All it proves is that the 'identified' person has a face, claims a name, has made statements as to nationality, age, place of birth, etc., and has deposited with the Company a return ticket or the equivalent in cash, as well as paying the breathing fee ninety days in advance – these latter two being all the Company cares about.

I do not know as certainty that the Company would space a man who, through some slip, has neither a ticket away nor air money. They might let him sell his indentures. But I would not count on it. Eating vacuum is not something I care to risk.

This Company ID stated that the holder was Enrico Schultz, age 32, citizen of Belize, born Ciudad Castro, occupation accountant. The picture with it was that of the poor slob who got himself killed through bracing me in too public a place . . . and for the steenth time I wondered why he hadn't phoned me, then called on me in private. As 'Dr Ames' I am in the directory . . . and invoking 'Walker Evans' would have got him a hearing, a private hearing.

I showed it to Gwen. 'Is that our boy?'

'I think so. I'm not sure.'

'I am sure. As I talked to him face to face for several minutes.'

The oddest part about Schultz's wallet was what it did not contain. In addition to the Swiss gold certificates it held eight hundred and thirty-one crowns and that Golden Rule ID.

But that was all.

No credit cards, no motor vehicle pilot's license, no insurance cards, no union or guild card, no other identification cards, no membership cards, nit. Men's wallets are like women's purses; they accumulate junk – photos, clippings, shopping lists, et cetera without end; they need periodic house-cleaning. But, in cleaning one out, one always leaves in place the dozen-odd items a modern man needs in order to get by. My friend Schultz had nothing.

Conclusion: He was not anxious to advertise his true identity. Corollary: Somewhere in Golden Rule habitat there was a stash of his personal papers . . . another ID in a different name, a passport almost certainly not issued by Belize, other items that might give me a lead to his background, his motives, and (possibly) how he had invoked 'Walker Evans.'

Could these be found?

A side issue niggled at me: that seventeen thousand in gold certificates. Instead of its being get-away money could he have expected to use so fiddlin' a sum to hire me to kill Tolliver? If so, I was offended. I preferred to think that he hoped to persuade me to make the kill as a public service.

Gwen said, 'Do you want to divorce me?'

'Eh?'

'I hustled you into it. My intentions were good, truly they were! But it turns out I was stupid.'

'Oh. Gwen, I never get both married and divorced on the same day. Never. If you really want to shuck me off, take it up with me tomorrow. Although I think that, to be fair, you ought to try me out for thirty days. Or two weeks, at least. And permit me to do the same. So far, your performance, both horizontally and vertically, has been satisfactory. If either becomes unsatisfactory, I'll let you know. Fair enough?'

'Fair enough. Although I may beat you to death with your own sophistries.'

'Beating her husband to death is every married woman's privilege . . . as long as she does it in private. Please pipe down, dear; I've got troubles. Can you think of any good reason why Tolliver should be killed?'

'Ron Tolliver? No. Although I can't think of any good reason why he should be allowed to live, either. He's a boor.'

'He's that, all right. If he were not one of the Company

20

partners, he would have been told to pick up his return ticket and leave, long ago. But I didn't say "Ron Tolliver," I just said "Tolliver.'''

'Is there more than one? I hope not.'

'We'll see.' I went to the terminal, punched for directory, cycled to 'T.'

'''Ronson H. Tolliver, Ronson Q.'' – that's his son – and here's his wife, "Stella M. Tolliver." Hey! It says here: "See also Taliaferro.'''

'That's the original spelling,' said Gwen. 'But it's pronounced 'Tolliver'' just the same.'

'Are you sure?'

'Quite sure. At least south of the Mason and Dixon Line back dirtside. Spelling it "Tolliver" suggests poh white trash who can't spell. Spelling it the long way and then sounding all the letters sounds like a Johnny-come-lately damyankee whose former name might have been "Lipschitz" or such. The authentic plantation-owning, nigger-whupping, wench-humping aristocrat spelled it the long way and pronounced it the short way.'

'I'm sorry you told me that.'

'Why, dear?'

'Because there are three men and one woman listed here who spell it the long way, Taliaferro. I don't know any of them. So I don't know which one to kill.'

'Do you have to kill one of them?'

'I don't know. Mmm, time I brought you up to date. If you are planning to stay married to me at least fourteen days. Are you?'

'Of course I am! Fourteen days plus the rest of my life! And you are a male chauvinist pig!'

'Paid-up lifetime membership.'

'And a tease.'

'I think you're cute, too. Want to go back to bed?'

'Not until you decide whom you intend to kill.'

'That may take a while.' I did my best to give Gwen a detailed, factual, uncolored account of my short acquaintance with the man who had used the name 'Schultz.' 'And that's all I know. He was dead too quickly for me to learn more. Leaving behind him endless questions.'

I turned back to the terminal, keyed it to shift to

wordprocessing mode, then created a new file, as if I were setting up a potboiler:

THE ADVENTURE OF THE MISSPELLED NAME
Questions To Be Answered

1. Tolliver or Taliaferro?
2. Why does T have to die?
3. Why would 'we all be dead' if T is not dead by noon Sunday?
4. Who is this corpse who called himself 'Schultz'?
5. Why am I the logical hatchet man for T?
6. Is this killing necessary?
7. Which one of the Walker Evans Memorial Society sicked this thumb-fingered bubblehead on me? And why?
8. Who killed 'Schultz'? And why?
9. Why did the staff of Rainbow's End move in and cover up the killing?
10. (Omnibus) Why did Gwen leave before I did and why did she come here instead of going home and how did she get in?

'Do we take them in order?' asked Gwen. 'Number ten is the only one I can answer.'

'That one I just chucked in,' I answered. 'Of the first nine I think that, if I find answers to any three, I could then deduce the rest.' I went on putting words up on the screen.

POSSIBLE ACTIONS
'When in Danger or in Doubt,
Run in Circles, Scream and Shout.'

'Does that help?' asked Gwen.

'Every time! Ask any old military man. Now let's take it one question at a time.'

Q. 1 – Phone each Taliaferro in the directory. Learn preferred pronunciation of name. Strike out any who use the every-letter pronunciation.

Q. 2 – Dig into background of whoever is left. Start with the *Herald* back files.

Q. 3 – While checking Q2, keep ears spread for anything scheduled or expected for noon Sunday.

22

Q. 4 – If you were a corpse arriving at Golden Rule space habitat and you wanted to conceal your identity but had to be able to get at your passport and other documents for departure, where would you stash them? Hint: Check when this cadaver arrived in Golden Rule. Then check hotels, lockers, deposit box services, poste restante, etc.

Q. 5 – postpone

Q. 6 – postpone

Q. 7 – Reach by phone as many of the 'Walker Evans' oath group as possible. Keep going till one spills. Note: Some jelly brain may have talked too much without knowing it.

Q. 8 – Morris, or the maître d', or the busman, or all of them, or any two, knows who killed Schultz. One or more of them expected it. So we look for each one's weak point – liquor, drugs, money, sex (*comme ci ou comme ça*) – and what was your name back dirtside, chum? Any paper out on you somewhere? Find that soft spot. Push it. Do this with all three of them, then see how their stories check. *Every* closet has a skeleton. This is a natural law – so find it in each case.

Q. 9 – Money (Conclusive assumption until proved false.)

(Query: How much is all this going to cost me? Can I afford it? Counter query: Can I afford *not* to pursue it?)

'I've been wondering about that,' said Gwen. 'When I poked my nose in, I thought you were in real trouble. But apparently you are home free. Why must you do anything, my husband?'

'I need to kill him.'

'*What?* But you don't know which Tolliver is meant! Or why he should be dead. If he should be.'

'No, no, not Tolliver. Although it may develop that Tolliver should be dead. No, dear, the man who killed Schultz. I must find him and kill him.'

'Oh. Uh, I can see that he should be dead; he's a murderer. But why must *you* do it? Both are strangers to you – both the victim and whoever killed him. Actually it's not your business. Is it?'

'It *is* my business. Schultz or whatever his name is was killed while he was a guest at my table. That's intolerably rude. I won't put up with it. Gwen my love, if one tolerates bad manners, they grow worse. Our pleasant habitat could decay into the sort of slum Ell-Five is, with crowding and unmannerly behavior and unnecessary noise and impolite language. I must find the oaf who did this thing, explain to him his offense, give him a chance to apologize, and kill him.'

III

'One should forgive one's enemies, but not before
they are hanged.'

HEINRICH HEINE 1797–1856

MY LOVELY bride stared at me. 'You would *kill* a man? For
bad manners?'

'Do you know of a better reason? Would you have me ignore
rude behavior?'

'No but – I can understand executing a man for murder;
I'm not opposed to capital punishment. But shouldn't you
leave this to the proctors and the management? Why must you
take the law into your own hands?'

'Gwen, I haven't made myself clear. My purpose is not to
punish but to weed . . . plus the esthetic satisfaction of retaliation for boorish behavior. This unknown killer may have had
excellent reasons for killing the person who called himself
Schultz . . . but killing in the presence of people who're eating
is as offensive as public quarreling by married couples. Then
this oaf capped his offense by doing this while his victim was
my guest . . . which made retaliation both my obligation and
my privilege.'

I went on, 'The putative offense of murder is not my concern.
But as for proctors and the management taking care of that
matter, do you know of any regulation forbidding murder?'

'What? Richard, there *must* be one.'

'I've never heard of one. I suppose the Manager might
construe murder as a violation of the Golden Rule—'

'Well, I would certainly think so!'

'You do? I'm never certain what the Manager will think.
But, Gwen my darling, killing is not necessarily murder. In
fact it often is not. If this killing ever comes to the Manager's
attention, he may decide that it was justifiable homicide. An
offense against manners but not against morals.

25

'But –' I continued, turning back to the terminal, '– the Manager may already have settled the matter, so let's see what the *Herald* has to say about it.' I punched up the newspaper again, this time keying for today's index, then selecting today's vital statistics.

The first item to roll past was 'Marriage – Ames – Novak' so I stopped it, punched for amplification, keyed for printout, tore it off and handed it to my bride. 'Send that to your grandchildren to prove that Granny is no longer living in sin.'

'Thank you, darling. You're so gallant. I think.'

'I can cook, too.' I scrolled on down to the obituaries. I usually read the obituaries first as there is always the happy chance that one of them will make my day.

But not today. No name I recognized. Especially no 'Schultz.' No unidentified stranger. No death 'in a popular restaurant.' Nothing but the usual sad list of strangers dead from natural causes and one by accident. So I keyed for general news of the habitat, let it scroll past.

Nothing. Oh, there were endless items of routine events, from ships' arrivals and departures to (the biggest news) an announcement that the newest addition, rings 130–140, were being brought up to spin and, if all went by schedule, would be warped in and its welding to the main cylinder started by 0800 on the sixth.

But there was nothing about 'Schultz,' no mention of any Tolliver or Taliaferro, no unidentified cadaver. I consulted the paper's index again, punched for next Sunday's schedule of events, found that the only thing scheduled for noon Sunday was a panel discussion assembled by holo from The Hague, Tokyo, Luna City, Ell-Four, Golden Rule, Tel Aviv, and Agra: 'Crisis in Faith: The Modern World at the Crossroads.' The co-moderators were the president of the Humanist Society and the Dalai Lama. I wished them luck.

'So far we have zip, zero, nit, swabo, and nothing. Gwen, what is a polite way for me to ask strangers how they pronounce their names?'

'Let me try it, dear. I'll say, "Miz Tollivuh, this is Gloria Meade Calhoun f'om Savannah. Do you have a cousin, Stacey Mae, f'om Chahlston?" When she corrects my pronunciation of her name, I apologize and switch off. But if she – or he – accepts the short form but denies knowing Stacey Mae, I say,

26

"I wonduhed about that. She said it, Talley-ah-pharoh . . . but I knew that was wrong." What then, Richard? Work it up into a date or switch off by "accident"?'

'Make a date, if possible.'

'A date for you? Or for me?'

'For you, and then I'll go with you. Or keep the date in your place. But I must first buy a hat.'

'A *hat?*'

'One of those funny boxes you sit on the flat part of your head. Or would if you were dirtside.'

'I know what a hat is! I was born dirtside same as you were. But I doubt if a hat has ever been seen off Earth. Where would you buy one?'

'I don't know, best girl, but I can tell you why I need one. So that I can tip my hat politely and say, "Sir or madam, pray tell me why someone wishes you dead by noon Sunday." Gwen, this has been worrying me – how to open such a discussion. There are accepted polite modes for almost any inquiry, from proposing adultery to a previously chaste wife to soliciting a bribe. But how does one open *this* subject?'

'Can't you just say, "Don't look now but somebody's trying to kill you"?'

'No, that's the wrong order. I'm not trying to warn this bloke that someone is gunning for him; I'm trying to find out *why*. When I know why I might approve so heartily that I would just sit back and enjoy it . . . or even be so inspired by the purpose that I would carry out the intent of the late Mr Schultz as a service to mankind.

'Contrariwise, I might disagree so bitterly that I would enlist for the duration, volunteer my life and services to the sacred cause of keeping this assassination from happening. Unlikely if the intended target is Ron Tolliver. But it's too early to choose sides; I need to understand what is going on. Gwen my love, in the killing business one should never kill first and ask questions afterwards. That tends to annoy people.'

I turned back to the terminal, stared at it without touching a key. 'Gwen, before we make any local calls I think I should place six time-delay calls, one to each of the Friends of Walker Evans. That's my basic clue anyhow, that Schultz could mention that name. Some one of that six gave him that name

27

. . . and that one should know why Schultz was in such a sweat.'

'"Time-delay"? Are they all out-far?'

'I don't know. One is probably on Mars, two others may be in the Belt. Could even be one or two dirtside but, if so, under phony names just as I am. Gwen, the debacle that caused me to give up the merry profession of arms and caused six of my comrades to wind up as my blood brothers . . . well, it smelled nasty to the public. I could say that media reporters who didn't see it happen could not possibly understand why it happened. I could assert truthfully that what we did was moral in context – that time, that place, those circumstances. I could – Never mind, dear; let it stand that my band of brothers are all in hiding. Tracing them all down could be a tediously long chore.'

'But you want to talk to just one, don't you? The one who was in touch with this Schultz.'

'Yes, but I don't know which one that is.'

'Richard, would it be easier to backtrack Schultz to find that one than it would be to locate six people all in hiding, some under assumed names, and scattered all over the Solar System? Or even outside it.'

I stopped to consider it. 'Maybe. But how do I backtrack Schultz? Do you have an inspiration, my love?'

'No inspiration. But I do remember that, when I arrived here in Golden Rule, they asked me at the hub not only where I lived, and checked it against my passport, but also where I had come from that trip – and checked that against my visa stamps. Not just that I had come from Luna – almost everyone arrives here from Luna – but how I got to Luna. Weren't you asked that?'

'No. But I was carrying a Luna Free State passport showing that I was born in the Moon.'

'I thought you were born on Earth?'

'Gwen, Colin Campbell was born dirtside. "Richard Ames" was born in Hong Kong Luna – it says here.'

'Oh.'

'But attempting to backtrack Schultz is indeed something I should try before I try to locate all six. If I knew that Schultz had never been out-far, I would look first close to home – Luna, and dirtside, and all habitats ballistically coupled to

28

Terra or Luna. Not the Asteroid Belt. Or even on Mars.'

'Richard? Suppose that the purpose is to – No, that's silly.'

'What's silly, dear? Try it on me anyhow.'

'Uh, suppose this – whatever it is – conspiracy, I suppose – isn't aimed at Ron Tolliver or any other Tolliver, but is aimed at you and your six friends, the "Walker Evans" people. Could the purpose be to get you to take strong measures to get in touch with all the others? And thereby get you to lead them, whoever they are, to all seven of you? Could it be a vendetta? Could whatever happened cause a vendetta against all seven of you?'

I had a cold feeling at the pit of my stomach. 'Yes, that could be. Although not, I think, in this case. As it would not explain why Schultz was killed.'

'I said it was silly.'

'Wait a moment. Was Schultz killed?'

'Why, we both saw it, Richard.'

'Did we? I thought I saw it. But I admitted that it could have been faked. What I saw appeared to be death by explosive dart. But – Two simple props, Gwen. One makes a small dark spot appear on Schultz's shirt. The other is a small rubber bladder he holds in his cheek; it contains fake blood. At the right instant he bites the bladder; "blood" comes out of his mouth. The rest is acting . . . including the strange behavior of Morris and other staff members. That "dead" body has to be removed quickly . . . through that "Employees Only" door . . . where he is given a clean shirt, then hustled out the service door.'

'You think that is the way it happened?'

'Uh – No, damn it; I don't! Gwen, I've seen many deaths. This one happened as close to me as you are this minute. I don't think it was acting; I think I saw a man die.' I fumed to myself. Could I be mistaken on such a basic point?

Of course I could be! I'm no supergenius gifted with *psi* powers; I could be wrong as an eyewitness quite as easily as Gwen could be.

I sighed. 'Gwen, I just don't know. It looked to me like death by explosive dart . . . but if the intention was to fake it and if it was well prepared, then of course it would look like that. A planned fakery does account for the swift cover-up. Otherwise the behavior of the staff of Rainbow's End is almost

unbelievable.' I brooded. 'Best girl, I'm not sure of anything.
Is somebody trying to drive me out of my skull?'

She treated my question as rhetorical, which it was – I hope.
'Then what do we do?'

'Uh . . . we try to check on Schultz. And not worry about
the next step until we have done that.'

'How?'

'Bribery, my love. Lies and money. Lavish lies and a parsi-
monious use of money. Unless you are wealthy. I never thought
to ask before I married you.'

'*Me?*' Gwen's eyes went wide. 'But, Richard, I married *you*
for *your* money.'

'You did? Lady, you've been swindled. Do you want to see
a lawyer?'

'I suppose so. Is that what they call "statutory rape"?'

'No, "statutory rape" is carnal knowledge of a statue . . .
although why anyone should care I have never understood. I
don't think it's against regulations here.' I turned back to the
terminal. 'Do you want that lawyer? Or shall we look for
Schultz?'

'Uh . . . Richard, we're having a very odd honeymoon. Let's
go back to bed.'

'Bed can wait. But you can have another waffle while I try
to look up Schultz.' I keyed the terminal again for directory,
scrolled for 'Schultz.'

I found nineteen listings for 'Schultz' but no 'Enrico
Schultz.' Small wonder. I did find 'Hendrik Schultz,' so I
keyed for amplification:

'The Reverend Doctor Hendrik Hudson Schultz, BS, MA,
DD, DHL, KGB, Past Grand Master Royal Astrological
Society. Scientific Horoscopy at moderate prices. Weddings
solemnized. Family counseling. Eclectic and holistic
therapy. Investments advice. Bets accepted at all hours at
track odds. Petticoat Lane at ring ninety-five, next to Madame
Pompadour.' Over this was his picture in holo, smiling and
repeating his slogan: 'I'm Father Schultz, your friend in need.
No problem too large, no problem too small. All work guaranteed.'

Guaranteed to be *what?* Hendrik Schultz looked just like
Santa Claus minus the beard and not at all like my friend
Enrico, so I keyed him out – reluctantly, as I felt kinship with

30

the Reverend Doctor. 'Gwen, he's not in the directory, or not in it by the name on his Golden Rule ID. Does that mean he was never in it? Or that his name was removed last night before his body was cold?'

'Do you expect an answer? Or are you thinking aloud?'

'Neither one, I guess. Our next move is to query the hub – right?' I checked the directory, then called the office of immigration at the hub. 'This is Dr Richard Ames speaking. I'm trying to locate a habitant named Enrico Schultz. Can you give me his address?'

'Why don't you look him up in the directory?' (She sounded just like my third-grade teacher – not a recommendation.)

'He's not in the directory. He's a tourist, not a subscriber. I just want his address in Golden Rule. Hotel, pension, whatever.'

'Tut, tut! You know quite well that we don't give out personal information, even on marks. If he's not listed, then he paid fair and square not to be listed. Do unto others, Doctor, lest ye be done unto.' She switched off.

'Where do we ask now?' inquired Gwen.

'Same place, same seatwarmer – but with cash and in person. Terminals are convenient, Gwen . . . but not for bribery in amounts of less than a hundred thousand. For a small squeeze, cash and in person is more practical. Coming with me?'

'Do you think you can leave me behind? On our wedding day? Just try it, buster!'

'Put some clothes on, maybe?'

'Are you ashamed of the way I look?'

'Not at all. Let's go.'

'I give in. Half a sec, while I find my slippers. Richard, can we go via my compartment? At the ballet last night I felt very chic but my gown is too dressy for public corridors at this time of day. I want to change.'

'Your slightest wish, ma'am. But that brings up another point. Do you want to move in here?'

'Do you want me to?'

'Gwen, it has been my experience that marriage can sometimes stand up against twin beds but almost never against twin addresses.'

'You didn't quite answer me.'

'So you noticed. Gwen, I have this one nasty habit. Makes me hard to live with. I write.'

The dear girl looked puzzled. 'So you've told me. But why do you call it a nasty habit?'

'Uh . . . Gwen my love, I am not going to apologize for writing . . . anymore than I would apologize for this missing foot . . . and in truth the one led to the other. When I could no longer follow the profession of arms, I had to do something to eat. I wasn't trained for anything else and back home some other kid had my paper route. But writing is a legal way of avoiding work without actually stealing and one that doesn't take any talent or training.

'But writing is antisocial. It's as solitary as masturbation. Disturb a writer when he is in the throes of creation and he is likely to turn and bite right to the bone . . . and not even know that he's doing it. As writers' wives and husbands often learn to their horror.

'And – attend me carefully, Gwen! – there is *no* way that writers can be tamed and rendered civilized. Or even cured. In a household with more than one person, of which one is a writer, the only solution known to science is to provide the patient with an isolation room, where he can endure the acute stages in private, and where food can be poked in to him with a stick. Because, if you disturb the patient at such times, he may break into tears or become violent. Or he may not hear you at all . . . and, if you shake him at this stage, he bites.'

I smiled my best smile. 'Don't worry, darling. At present I am not working on a story and I will avoid starting one until we arrange such an isolation chamber for me to work in. This place isn't big enough and neither is yours. Mmm, even before we go to the hub, I want to call the Manager's office and see what larger compartments are available. We'll need two terminals also.'

'Why two, dear? I don't use a terminal much.'

'But when you do, you need it. When I'm using this one in wordprocessing mode, it can't be used for anything else – no newspaper, no mail, no shopping, no programs, no personal calls, nothing. Believe me, darling; I've had this disease for years, I know how to manage it. Let me have a small room and a terminal, let me go into it and seal the door behind me, and it will be just like having a normal, healthy husband who goes to the office every morning and does whatever it is men do in offices – I've never known and have never been much interested in finding out.'

'Yes, dear. Richard, do you enjoy writing?'

'No one enjoys writing.'

'I wondered. Then I must tell you that I didn't quite tell you the truth when I said that I had married you for your money.'

'And I didn't quite believe you. We're even.'

'Yes, dear. I really can afford to keep you as a pet. Oh, I can't buy you yachts. But we can live in reasonable comfort here in Golden Rule – not the cheapest place in the Solar System. You won't have to write.'

I stopped to kiss her, thoroughly and carefully. 'I'm glad I married you. But I will indeed have to write.'

'But you don't enjoy it and we don't need the money. Truly we don't!'

'Thank you, my love. But I did not explain to you the other insidious aspect of writing. There is no way to stop. Writers go on writing long after it becomes financially unnecessary . . . because it hurts less to write than it does not to write.'

'I don't understand.'

'I didn't either, when I took that first fatal step – a short story, it was, and I honestly thought I could quit anytime. Never mind, dear. In another ten years you will understand. Just pay no attention to me when I whimper. Doesn't mean anything – just the monkey on my back.'

'Richard? Would psychoanalysis help?'

'Can't risk it. I once knew a writer who tried that route. Cured him of writing all right. But did not cure him of the need to write. The last I saw of him he was crouching in a corner, trembling. That was his good phase. But the mere sight of a wordprocessor would throw him into a fit.'

'Uh . . . that bent for mild exaggeration?'

'Why, Gwen! I could take you to him. Show you his gravestone. Never mind, dear; I'm going to call the Manager's housing desk.' I turned back to the terminal—

– just as the durn thing lit up like a Christmas tree and the emergency bell chimed steadily. I flipped the answer switch. 'Ames here! Are we broached?'

Words sounded while letters streamed across the face of the

CRT, and the printer started a printout without my telling it to – I hate it when it does that.

'Official to Dr Richard Ames: The Management finds that the compartment you now occupy designated 715301 at 65-15-0.4 is urgently needed. You are notified to vacate at once. Unused rent has been applied to your account, plus a free bonus of fifty crowns for any inconvenience this may cause you. Order signed by Arthur Middlegaff, Manager's Proxy for Housing. Have a Nice Day!'

IV

'I go on working for the same reason a hen goes on
laying eggs.'

H. L. MENCKEN 1880–1956

My eyes grew wide. 'Oh, goody goody cheesecakes! Fifty
whole crowns – golly! Gwen! Now you can marry me for my
money!'

'Do you feel well, dear? You paid more than that for a bottle
of wine just last night. I think it's perfectly stinking. Insulting.'

'Of course it is, darling. It is intended to make me angry,
in addition to the inconvenience of forcing me to move. So I
won't.'

'Won't move?'

'No, no. I'll move at once. There are ways to fight city
hall but refusing to move is not one of them. Not while the
Manager's Proxy can cut off power and ventilation and water
and sanitary service. No, dear, the intention is to get me angry,
ruin my judgment, and get me to make threats that can't be
carried out.'

I smiled at my darling. 'So I won't get angry and I'll move
right out of here, meek as a lamb . . . and the intense anger
that I feel down inside will be kept there, out of sight, until
it's useful to me. Besides, it changes nothing, as I was about
to apply for a larger compartment – one more room, at least
– for us. So I'll call him back – dear Mr Middlegaff, I mean.'

I keyed for directory again, not knowing offhand the call
code of the housing office. I punched the 'execute' key.

And got a display on the screen of 'TERMINAL OUT OF
SERVICE.'

I stared at it while I counted ten, backwards, in Sanskrit.
Dear Mr Middlegaff, or the Manager himself, or someone,
was trying hard to get my goat. So above all I must not let it

35

happen. Think calm, soothing thoughts, suitable for a fakir on a bed of nails. Although there did not seem to be any harm in thinking about frying his gonads for lunch once I knew who he was. With soy sauce? Or just garlic butter and a dash of salt?

Thinking about this culinary choice did calm me a bit. I found myself unsurprised and not materially more annoyed when the display changed from 'TERMINAL OUT OF SERVICE' to 'POWER AND POWER-DEPENDENT SERVICES WILL TERMINATE AT 1300.' This was replaced by a time display in large figures: 1231 – and this changed to 1232 as I looked at it.

'Richard, what in the world are they doing?'

'Still trying to drive me out of my skull, I surmise. But we won't let them. Instead we'll spend twenty-eight minutes – no, twenty-seven – clearing out five years of junk.'

'Yessir. How can I help?'

'That's my girl! Small wardrobe out here, big one in the bedroom – throw everything on the bed. On the shelf in the big wardrobe is a duffel bag, a big jumpbag. Stuff everything into it as tightly as possible. Don't sort. Hold out that robe you wore at breakfast and use it to make a bundle out of anything that you can't jam into the duffel bag; tie it with its sash.'

'Your toilet articles?'

'Ah, yes. Plastic bag dispenser in buttery – just dump 'em into a bag and shove them in with the bundle. Honey, you're going to make a wonderful wife!'

'You are so right. Long practice, dear – widows always make the best wives. Want to hear about my husbands?'

'Yes, but not now. Save it for some long evening when you have a headache and I'm too tired.' Having dumped ninety percent of my packing onto Gwen I tackled the hardest ten percent: my business records and files.

Writers are pack rats, mostly, whereas professional military learn to travel light, again mostly. This dichotomy could have made me schizoid were it not for the most wonderful invention for writers since the eraser on the end of a pencil: electronic files.

I use Sony Megawafers, each good for half a million words, each two centimeters wide, three millimeters thick, with

36

information packed so densely that it doesn't bear thinking about. I sat down at the terminal, took off my prosthesis (peg leg, if you prefer), opened its top. Then I removed all my memory wafers from the terminal's selector, fed them into the cylinder that is the 'shinbone' of my prosthesis, closed it and put it back on.

I now had all the files necessary to my business: contracts, business letters, file copies of my copyrighted works, general correspondence, address files, notes for stories to be written, tax records, et cetera, and so forth, ad nauseam. Before the days of electronic filing these records would have been a tonne and a half of paper in half a tonne of steel, all occupying several cubic meters. Now they massed only a few grams and occupied space no larger than my middle finger – twenty million words of file storage.

The wafers were totally encased in that 'bone' and thereby safe from theft, loss, and damage. Who steals another man's prosthesis? How can a cripple forget his artificial foot? He may take it off at night but it is the first thing he reaches for in getting out of bed.

Even a holdup man pays no attention to a prosthesis. In my case most people never know that I am wearing one. Just once have I been separated from it: An associate (not a friend) took mine away from me in locking me up overnight – we had had a difference of opinion over a business matter. But I managed to escape, hopping on one foot. Then I parted his hair with his fireplace poker and took my other foot, some papers, and my departure. The writing business, basically sedentary, does have its brisk moments.

The time on the terminal read 1254 and we were almost through. I had only a handful of books – bound books, with words printed on paper – as I did my research, such as it was, through the terminal. These few Gwen stuffed into the bundle she had made from my robe. 'What else?' she demanded.

'I think that's all. I'll make a fast inspection and we'll shove anything we've missed out into the corridor, then figure out what to do with it after they turn out the lights.'

'How about that bonsai tree?' Gwen was eyeing my rock maple, some eighty years old and only thirty-nine centimeters high.

'No way to pack it, dear. And, besides, it requires watering several times a day. The sensible thing is to will it to the next tenant.'

'In a pig's eye, chief. You'll carry it by hand to my compartment while I drag the baggage along behind.'

(I had been about to add that 'the sensible thing' has never appealed to me.) 'We're going to your compartment?'

'How else, dear? Certainly we need a bigger place but our urgent need is any sort of roof over our heads. As it looks like snow by sundown.'

'Why, so it does! Gwen, remind me to tell you that I'm glad I thought of marrying you.'

'You didn't think of it; men never do.'

'Really?'

'Truly. But I'll remind you, anyhow.'

'Do that. I'm glad you thought of marrying me. I'm glad you did marry me. Will you promise to keep me from doing the sensible thing from here on?'

She did not commit herself as the lights blinked twice and we were suddenly very busy, Gwen in putting everything out into the corridor while I made a frantic last go-around. The lights blinked again, I grabbed my cane, and got out the door just as it contracted behind me. '*Whew!*'

'Steady there, boss. Breathe slowly. Count ten before you exhale, then let it out slowly.' Gwen patted my back.

'We should have gone to Niagara Falls. I told you so. I told you.'

'Yes, Richard. Pick up the little tree. At this gee I can handle both the bag and the bundle, one in each hand. Straight up to zero gee?'

'Yes but I carry the duffel bag and the tree. I'll strap my cane to the bag.'

'Please don't be *macho*, Richard. Not when we're so busy.'

'"*Macho*" is a put-down word, Gwen. Using it again calls for a spanking; use it a third time and I beat you with this here cane. I'll damn well be *macho* anytime I feel like it.'

'Yes, sir. Me Jane, you Tarzan. Pick up the little tree. Please.'

We compromised. I carried the duffel bag and used my cane to steady myself; Gwen carried the bundle with one hand, the bonsai maple with the other. She was unbalanced and kept shifting sides with the bundle. Gwen's proposed arrangement was, I must admit, more sensible, as the weight would not have been too much for her at that acceleration and it fell off steadily as we climbed up to zero gee. I felt sheepish, a touch ashamed . . . but it is a temptation to a cripple to prove, especially to women, that he can so do everything he used to do. Silly, because anyone can see that he can't. I don't often give in to the temptation.

Once we were floating free at the axis we moved right along, with our burdens tethered to us, while Gwen guarded the little tree with both hands. When we reached her ring, Gwen took both pieces of luggage and I did not argue. The trip took less than a half hour. I could have ordered a freight cage – but we might still be waiting for it. A 'labor-saving device' often isn't.

Gwen put down her burdens and spoke to her door.

It did not open.

Instead the door answered, 'Mistress Novak, please call the Manager's housing office at once. The nearest public terminal is at ring one-hundred-five, radius one-thirty-five degrees, acceleration six-tenths gravity, next to the personnel transport facility. That terminal will accept your call free of charge, courtesy of Golden Rule.'

I cannot say that I was much surprised. But I admit that I was dreadfully disappointed. Being homeless is somewhat like being hungry. Maybe worse.

Gwen behaved as if she had not heard that dismal announcement. She said to me, 'Sit down on the duffel bag, Richard, and take it easy. I don't think I'll be long.'

She opened her purse, dug into it, came up with a nail file and a bit of wire, a paper clip, I believe. Humming a monotonous little tune she started to work on the compartment's door.

I helped by not offering advice. Not a word. It was difficult but I managed it.

Gwen stopped humming and straightened up. 'There!' she announced. The door opened wide.

She picked up my bonsai maple – our bonsai maple. 'Come in, dear. Better leave the duffel bag across the threshold for now, so that the door won't pucker up. It's dark inside.'

I followed her in. The only light inside was from the screen on her terminal:

ALL SERVICES SUSPENDED

She ignored it and dug into her purse, brought out a finger torch, then used its light to get into a drawer in her buttery, took out a long, slender screwdriver, a pair of Autoloc tweezers, a nameless tool that may have been homemade, and a pair of high-pot gloves in her slender size. 'Richard, will you hold the light for me, pretty please?'

The access plate she wished to reach was high up over her microwaver and was locked and decorated with the usual signs warning tenants against even looking cross-eyed at it, much less touching it, with incantations of 'Danger! Do Not Tamper – Call Maintenance,' etc. Gwen climbed up, sat on the oven top, and opened the access plate with just a touch; the lock apparently had been disabled earlier.

Then she worked very quietly save for that monotonous little hum, plus an occasional request for me to move the torch light. Once she produced a really spectacular fireworks display which caused her to cluck reprovingly and murmur, 'Naughty, naughty. Mustn't do that to Gwen.' She then worked most slowly for a few more moments. The compartment's lights came on, accompanied by that gentle purr of a live room – air, micromotors, etc.

She closed the access plate. 'Will you help me down, dear?'

I lifted her down with both hands, held on to her, claimed a kiss for payment. She smiled up at me. 'Thank you, sir! My, my, I had forgotten how nice it is to be married. We should get married more often.'

'Now?'

'No. Lunchtime now. Breakfast was hearty but it is now past fourteen. Feel like eating?'

'It's good exercise,' I assented. 'How about the Sloppy Joe on Appian Way near ring one-oh-five? Or do you want haute cuisine?'

'A Sloppy Joe is okay; I'm not a fussy eater, dear. But I don't think we should go outside for lunch; we might not be able to get back in.'

'Why not? You do a slick job of bypassing a change in a door combo.'

'Richard, it might not be that easy again. They simply haven't noticed, as yet, that locking me out didn't work. But when they do – They can weld a steel plate across the doorway if that is what it takes. Not that it will, as I shan't fight being moved any more than you did. Let's eat lunch; then I'll pack. What would you like?'

It turned out that Gwen had salvaged from my buttery gourmet items I had in freeze or in sterile pack. I do stock unusual viands. How can you know ahead of time, when working on a story in the middle of the night, that you are going to suffer a craving for a clam sundae? It is merely prudent to have materials on hand. Otherwise you could be tempted to stop work and leave your monastic seclusion in order to find an item you must have – and that way lies bankruptcy.

Gwen laid out a buffet of her supplies and mine – ours, I should say – and we ate while discussing our next move . . . for move we must. I told her that I intended to call dear Mr Middlegaff as soon as we finished lunch.

She looked thoughtful. 'I had better pack first.'

'If you wish. But why?'

'Richard, we have leprosy; that's evident. I think it must be connected with the killing of Schultz. But we don't know. Whatever the cause, when we stick our heads outside, I had better have my things ready just as yours are; we may not get back in.' She nodded at her terminal, still shining with the message: ALL SERVICES SUSPENDED. 'Putting that terminal back into service would be more than a matter of wheedling a few solenoids, since the computer itself is elsewhere. So we can't beard Mr Middlegaff from this compartment. Therefore we must do everything we need to do here before we go out that door.'

'While you pack, I can duck out to call him.'

'Over my dead body!'

'Huh? Gwen, be reasonable.'

'Reasonable I emphatically am. Richard Colin, you are my brand-new bridegroom; I intend to get years and years of wear out of you. While this trouble is going on, I am not letting you out of my sight. You might disappear like Mr Schultz. Beloved, if they shoot you, they are going to have to shoot me first.'

I attempted to reason with her; she put her hands over her ears. 'I won't argue it, I can't hear you, I'm not listening!' She uncovered her ears. 'Come help me pack. Please.'

'Yes, dear.'

Gwen packed in less time than I had taken, yet my help consisted mostly of keeping out of her way. I'm not too used

41

to living with females; military service is not conducive to homelife and I tended to avoid marriage, aside from short-term contracts with Amazon comrades – contracts automatically canceled by orders for change of duty. After I reached field grade I had had female orderlies a couple or six times – but I don't suppose that relationship is much like civilian marriage, either.

What I'm trying to say is that, despite having written many thousands of words of love-confession stories under a hundred-odd female pen names, I don't know much about women. When I was learning the writing scam, I pointed this out to the editor who bought from me these sin, suffer, and repent stories. The editor was Evelyn Fingerhut, a glum middle-aged man with a bald spot, a tic, and a permanent cigar.

He grunted. 'Don't try to learn anything about women; it would handicap you.'

'But these are supposed to be true stories,' I objected.

'They *are* true stories; every one of them is accompanied by a sworn statement: "This story is based on fact."' He jerked a thumb at the manuscript I had just brought in. 'You've got a "Fact" slip clipped to that one. Are you trying to tell me it ain't so? Don't you want to get paid?'

Yes, I wanted to be paid. To me the acme of prose style is exemplified by that simple, graceful clause: 'Pay to the order of –' I answered hastily, 'Well, as a matter of fact that story is no problem. I didn't actually know the woman but my mother told me all about her – it was a girl she had gone to school with. This girl did indeed marry her mother's younger brother. She was already pregnant when the truth was discovered . . . and then she was faced with that horrible dilemma just as I've told it: the sin of abortion, or the tragedy of an incest baby with a possibility of two heads and no chin. All fact, Evelyn, but I trimmed it a bit in telling it. It turned out that Beth Lou was no blood relation to her uncle – and that's the way I wrote it – but also her baby was no relation to her husband. That part I left out.'

'So write it again and leave that part in and the other part out. Just be sure to change the names and places; I don't want any complaints.'

At a later time I did so and sold that version to him also, but never did get around to telling Fingerhut that it hadn't happened to a schoolmate of my mother, but was something I had cribbed from a book belonging to my Aunt Abby: the librettos of *The Ring Cycle* by Richard Wagner, who should have stuck to composing music and found himself a W. S. Gilbert to write his librettos; Wagner was a terrible writer.

But his preposterous plots were just right for the true confessions trade . . . toned down a little, not quite so hard core – and, of course, different names and locales. I didn't steal them. Or not quite. They are all in the public domain today, copyrights expired, and besides, Wagner stole those plots in the first place.

I could have made a soft living on nothing but Wagnerian plots. But I got bored with it. When Fingerhut retired and bought a turkey ranch, I quit the confession business and started writing war stories. This was more difficult – for a time I almost starved – because military matters I do know something about, and that (as Fingerhut had pointed out) is a handicap.

After a while I learned to suppress what I knew, not let it get in the way of the story. But I never had that trouble with confession stories as neither Fingerhut, nor I, nor Wagner, knew anything at all about women.

Especially about Gwen. Somewhere I had acquired the conviction that women need at least seven pack mules to travel. Or their equivalent in big suitcases. And of course women are by nature disorganized. So I believed.

Gwen moved out of her compartment with just one large case of clothes, smaller than my duffel bag, with every garment neatly folded, and one smaller case of – well, non-clothes. Things.

She lined up our chattels – duffel bag, bundle, large case, small case, her purse, my cane, bonsai tree – and looked at them. 'I think I can work out a way,' she said, 'for us to handle all of them at once.'

'I don't see how,' I objected, 'with only two hands apiece. I had better order a freight cage.'

'If you wish, Richard.'

'I will.' I turned toward her terminal . . . and stopped. 'Uh—'

Gwen gave full attention to our little maple tree.

'Uh –' I repeated. 'Gwen, you're going to have to loosen up. I'll slide out and find that nearest terminal booth, then come back—'

'No, Richard.'

'Huh? Just long enough to—'

'No, Richard.'

I heaved a sigh. 'What's your solution?'

'Richard, I will agree to any course of action that does not involve us being separated. Leave everything inside this compartment and hope that we can get back in – that's one way. Place everything just outside the door and leave it, while we go to order a freight cage – and call Mr Middlegaff – that's another way.'

'And have it all disappear while we are gone. Or are there no two-legged rats in this neighborhood?' I was being sarcastic. Every habitat in space has its nightwalkers, invisible habitants who cannot afford to remain in space but who evade being returned to Earth. In Golden Rule I suspect that the management spaced them when they caught them . . . although there were darker rumors, ones that caused me to avoid all sorts of ground pork.

'There is still a third way, sir, adequate for moving us as far as that terminal booth. That being as far as we can go until the housing office gives us a new assignment. Once we know our new address we can call for a cage and wait for it.

'The booth is only a short distance. Sir, earlier you said you could carry both your bag and your bundle, with your cane strapped to your bag. For this short distance I agree to that. I can carry both my cases, one in each hand, with the strap of my purse let out so that I can sling it over my shoulder.

'The only problem then is the little tree. Richard, you've seen pictures in *National Geographic* of native girls carrying bundles on their heads?' She didn't wait for me to agree; she picked up the little potted tree, placed it atop her head, took her hands away, smiled at me, and sank down, bending only her knees, spine straight and bearing erect – picked up her two cases.

She walked the length of her compartment, turned and faced me. I applauded.

'Thank you, sir. Just one thing more. The walkways are

sometimes crowded. If someone jostles me, I'll do this.' She simulated staggering from being bumped, dropped both cases, caught the bonsai as it fell, put it back on top her head, again picked up her luggage. 'Like that.'

'And I'll drop my bags and grab my cane and beat him with it. The jerk who jostled you. Not to death. Just a reprimand.' I added, 'Assuming that the miscreant is male and of mature years. If not, I'll make the punishment fit the criminal.'

'I'm sure you will, dear. But, truly, I don't think anyone will jostle me, as you will be walking in front of me, breaking trail. All right?'

'All right. Except that you should strip to the waist.'

'Really?'

'All pictures of that sort in *National Geographic* always show the women stripped to the waist. That's why they print them.'

'All right if you say to. Although I'm not really endowed for that.'

'Quit fishing for compliments, monkey face; you do all right. But you're much too good for the common people, so keep your shirt on.'

'I don't mind. If you really think I should.'

'You're too willing. Do as you please but I am not, repeat *not*, urging you to. Are all women exhibitionists?'

'Yes.'

The discussion ended because her door signal sounded. She looked surprised. I said, 'Let me,' and stepped to the door, touched the voice button. 'Yes?'

'Message from the Manager!'

I took my finger off the voice button, looked at Gwen. 'Shall I open up?'

'I think we must.'

I touched the dilator button; the door spread open. A man in a proctor's uniform stepped inside; I let the door snap back. He shoved a clipboard at me. 'Sign here, Senator.' Then he pulled it back. 'Say, you *are* the Senator from Standard Oil, ain't you?'

V

'He is one of those people who would be enormously improved by death.'

H. H. MUNRO 1870–1916

I SAID, 'You have that backwards. Who are *you?* Identify yourself.'

'Hunh? If you ain't the Senator, forget it; I got the wrong address.' He started to back out and bumped his behind against the door – looked startled and turned his head, reached for the dilator button.

I slapped his hand down. 'I told you to identify yourself. That clown suit you're wearing is no identification; I want to see your credentials. Gwen! Cover him!'

'Right, Senator!'

He reached for a hip pocket, made a fast draw. Gwen kicked whatever it was out of his hand; I chopped him in the left side of the neck. His clipboard went flying and down he went, falling with the curiously graceful leisureliness of low gravity.

I knelt by him. 'Keep him covered, Gwen.'

'One second, Senator – watch him!' I pulled back and waited. She went on, 'Okay now. But don't get in my line of fire, please.'

'Roger wilco.' I kept my eyes on our guest, collapsed loosely on the deck. His awkward posture seemed to say that he was unconscious. Nevertheless there was a chance that he was shamming; I had not hit him all that hard. So I applied my thumb to the left lower cervical pressure point, jabbing hard to cause him to scream and claw at the ceiling if he were awake. He did not move.

So I searched him. First from behind, then I rolled him over. His trousers did not quite match his tunic, and they lacked the braid down the sides that a proctor's uniform

46

trousers should have. The tunic was not a good fit. His pockets held a few crowns in paper, a lottery ticket, and five cartridges. These last were Skoda 6.5mm longs, unjacketed, expanding, used in pistols, tommies, and rifles – and illegal almost everywhere. No wallet, no IDs, nothing else.

He needed a bath.

I rocked back and stood up. 'Keep your gun on him, Gwen. I think he's a nightwalker.'

'I think so, too. Please look at this, sir, while I keep him covered.' Gwen pointed at a pistol lying on the deck.

Calling it a 'pistol' dignifies it more than it deserves. It was a lethal weapon, homemade, of the category known traditionally as 'rumble gun.' I studied it as thoroughly as I could without touching it. Its barrel was metal tubing so light in gauge that I wondered whether or not it had ever been fired. The handgrip was plastic, ground or whittled to conform to a fist. The firing mechanism was concealed by a metal cover held in place by (believe me!) rubber bands. That it was a single-shot weapon seemed certain. But with that flimsy barrel it could turn out to be a one-shot as well; it seemed to me to be almost as dangerous to the user as to his target.

'Nasty little thing,' I said. 'I don't want to touch it; it's a built-in booby trap.'

I looked up at Gwen. She had him covered with a weapon quite as lethal but embodying all the best in modern gunsmith's art, a nine-shot Miyako. 'When he pulled a gun on you, why didn't you shoot him? Instead of taking a chance on disarming him? You can get very dead that way.'

'Because.'

'Because what? If someone pulls a gun on you, kill him at once. If you can.'

'I couldn't. When you told me to cover him, my purse was 'way over there. So I covered him with *this*.' Something suddenly glinted in her other hand and she appeared to be a two-gun fighter. Then she clipped it back into her breast pocket – a pen. 'I was caught flat-footed, boss. I'm sorry.'

'Oh, that I could make such mistakes! When I yelled at you to cover him, I was simply trying to distract him. I didn't know you were heeled.'

'I said I was sorry. Once I had time to get at my purse I got out this persuader. But I had to disarm him first.'

I found myself wondering what a field commander could do with a thousand like Gwen. She masses about fifty kilos and stands not much over a meter and a half high – say one hundred sixty centimeters in her bare feet. But size has little to do with it, as Goliath found out a while back.

On the other hand there aren't a thousand Gwens anywhere. Perhaps just as well. 'Were you carrying that Miyako in your purse last night?'

She hesitated. 'If I had been, the results might have been regrettable, don't you think?'

'I withdraw the question. I think our friend is waking up. Keep your gun on him while I find out.' Again I gave him my thumb.

He yelped.

'Sit up,' I said. 'Don't try to stand up; just sit up and place your hands on top of your head. What's your name?'

He urged on me an action both unlikely and lewd. 'Now, now,' I reproved him, 'let's not have rudeness, please. Mistress Hardesty,' I went on, looking directly at Gwen, 'would you enjoy shooting him just a little bit? A flesh wound? Enough to teach him to be polite.'

'If you say so, Senator. Now?'

'Well . . . let's allow him that one mistake. But no second chance. Try not to kill him; we want him to talk. Can you hit him in the fleshy part of a thigh? Not hit the bone?'

'I can try.'

'That's all anyone can ask. If you do hit a bone, it won't be out of spite. Now let's start over. What is your name?'

'Uh . . . Bill.'

'Bill, what is the rest of your name?'

'Aw, just Bill. That's all the name I use.'

Gwen said, 'A little flesh wound now, Senator? To sharpen his memory?'

'Perhaps. Do you want it in your left leg, Bill? Or your right?'

'Neither one! Look, Senator, "Bill" actually is all the name I've got – and make her not point that thing at me, will you, please?'

'Keep him covered, Mistress Hardesty. Bill, she won't shoot you as long as you cooperate. What happened to your last name?'

'I never had one. I was "Bill Number Six" at the Holy Name Children's Refuge. Dirtside, that is. New Orleans.'

'I see. I begin to see. But what did it say on your passport when you came here?'

'Didn't have one. Just a contractor's work card. It read "William No-Middle-Name Johnson." But that was just what the labor recruiter wrote on it. Look, she's wiggling that gun at me!'

'Then don't do anything to annoy her. You know how women are.'

'I sure do! They ought not to be *allowed* to have firearms!'

'An interesting thought. Speaking of firearms – That one you were carrying: I want to unload it but I'm afraid that it might explode in my hand. So we will risk your hand instead. Without getting up, turn around so that your back is toward Mistress Hardesty. I am going to push your zapgun to where you can reach it. When I tell you to – not before! – you can take your hands down, unload it, then again put your hands on your head. But listen closely to this:

'Mistress Hardesty, when Bill turns around, take a bead on his spine just below his neck. If he makes one little suspicious move – kill him! Don't wait to be told, don't give him a second chance, don't make it a flesh wound – kill him instantly.'

'With great pleasure, Senator!'

Bill let out a moan.

'All right, Bill, turn around. Don't use your hands, just will power.'

He pivoted on his buttocks, scraping his heels to do so. I noted with approval that Gwen had shifted to the steady two-handed grip. I then took my cane and pushed Bill's homemade gun along the deck to a point in front of him. 'Bill, don't make any sudden moves. Take your hands down. Unload your pistol. Leave it open with its load beside it. Then put your hands back on your head.'

I backed up Gwen with my cane and held my breath while Bill did exactly what I had told him to do. I had no compunction about killing him and I felt sure that Gwen would kill him at once if he tried to turn that homemade gun on us.

But I worried over what to do with his body. I didn't want him dead. Unless you are on a battlefield or in a hospital, a corpse is an embarrassment, hard to explain. The management was bound to be stuffy about it.

So I breathed a sigh of relief when he finished his assigned task and put his hands back on his head.

I reached out with my cane, reversed, and dragged that nasty little gun and its one cartridge toward me – pocketed that cartridge, then ground a heel down onto its tubing barrel, crushing the muzzle and ruining the firing mockup, then said to Gwen, 'You can ease up a little now. No need to kill him this instant. Drop back to flesh-wound alert.'

'Aye aye, Senator. May I give him that flesh wound?'

'No, no! Not if he behaves. Bill, you're going to behave, aren't you?'

'Ain't I been behaving? Senator, make her put the safety on that thing, at least!'

'Now, now! Yours didn't even have a safety. And you are in no position to insist on terms. Bill, what did you do with the proctor you slugged?'

'Huh?'

'Oh, come now. You show up here in a proctor's tunic that does not fit you. And your pants don't match the coat. I ask to see your credentials and you pull a gun – a rumble gun, for the love of Pete! And you haven't bathed in – how long? You tell me. But tell me first what you did with the owner of that tunic. Is he dead? Or just sapped and stuffed into a closet? Answer quickly or I'll ask Mistress Hardesty to give you a memory stimulant. Where is he?'

'I don't know! I didn't do it.'

'Now, now, dear boy, don't lie to me.'

'The truth! On my mother's honor it's the simple truth!'

I had doubts about his mother's honor but it would have been unmannerly to express them, especially in dealing with so sorry a specimen. 'Bill,' I said gently, 'you are not a proctor. Must I explain why I am certain?' (Chief Proctor Franco is a System-class martinet. If one of his stooges had shown up for morning roll call looking – and stinking – the way this poor slob did, the delinquent would have been lucky merely to have been shipped dirtside.) 'I will if you insist. Did you ever have a pin stuck under a fingernail, then the outer end of the pin heated? It improves one's memory.'

Gwen said eagerly, 'A bobby pin works better, Senator –

more mass to hold the heat. I've got one right here. Can I do it to him? Can I?'

'You mean, "May I," do you not? No, dear girl, I want you to continue to keep Bill under your sights. If it becomes necessary to resort to such methods, I won't ask a lady to do it for me.'

'Aw, Senator, you'll get soft-hearted and let up on him just when he's ready to spout. Not me! Let me show you – please!'

'Well . . .'

'Keep that bloodthirsty bitch away from me!' Bill's voice was shrill.

'*Bill!* You will apologize to the lady at once. Otherwise I will let her do to you whatever she wishes.'

He moaned again. 'Lady, I apologize. I'm sorry. But you scare it right out of me. *Please* don't use a bobby pin on me – I seen a guy once had that done to him.'

'Oh, it could be worse,' Gwen assured him pleasantly. 'Twelve-gauge copper wire conducts the heat much better and there are interesting places in the male body to use it. More efficient. Quicker results.' She added thoughtfully, 'Senator, I've got some copper wire in my small case. If you'll hold this pistol for a moment, I'll get it for you.'

'Thank you, my dear, but it may not be needed; I think Bill wants to say something.'

'It's no trouble, sir. Don't you want me to have it ready?'

'Perhaps. Let's see. Bill? What did you do with that proctor?'

'I didn't, I never saw him! Just two skins said they had a cash job for me. I don't make 'em, never seen 'em, they ain't with it. But there are always new ones and Fingers said they passed. He—'

'Hold it. Who is "Fingers"?'

'Uh, he's mayor of our alley. Okay?'

'More details, please. Your alley?'

'Man's got to sleep somewhere, ain't he? VIP like you has got a compartment with his name on it. I should be so lucky! Home is where it is – right?'

'I think you're telling me that your alley is your home. Where is it? Ring, radius, and acceleration.'

'Uh . . . that's not exactly how it is.'

'Be rational, Bill. If it's inside the main cylinder, not off in one of the appendages, its location can be described that way.'

'Maybe so but I can't describe it that way because that's not how you get there. And I won't lead you the way you have to go because –' His face screwed up in utter despair and he looked about ten years old. 'Don't let her hotwire me and don't let her shoot me a little bit at a time. Please! Just space me and get it over with – okay?'

'Senator?'

'Yes, Mistress Hardesty?'

'Bill's afraid that, if you hurt him enough, he will tell you where he hides to sleep. Other nightwalkers sleep there, too; that's the point. I suspect that the Golden Rule isn't big enough to hide him from those others. If he tells you where they sleep, they'll kill him. Probably not quickly.'

'Bill, is that why you're being stubborn?'

'Talked too much already. Space me.'

'Not while you're alive, Bill; you know things I need to know and I intend to squeeze them out of you if it takes copper wire and Mistress Hardesty's most whimsical notions. But I may not need the answer to the question I asked you. What happens to you if you tell me or show me where your alley is?'

He was slow in answering; I let him take his time. At last he said in a low voice, 'Nosies caught a skin six seven months ago. Cracked him open. Not from my alley thank Jesus. His alley was a maintenance space near a hundred ten and down at full gee.

'So the nosies gassed it and a lot of skins died . . . but this skin they turned loose. Cold help that was to him. He hadn't been walking twenty-four hours when he was grabbed and locked in with rats. Hungry ones.'

'I see.' I glanced at Gwen.

She gulped and whispered, 'Senator, no rats. I don't like rats. Please.'

'Bill, I withdraw the question about your alley. Your hide-out. And I won't ask you to identify any other nightwalker. But I expect you to answer anything else fully and quickly. No more stalling. No waste of time. Agreed?'

'Yes, sir.'

'Go back. These two strangers offered you a job. Tell me about it.'

'Uh, they tell me just a few minutes of razzle-dazzle; nothing to it. They want me to wear this jacket, make like a nosie.

52

Bong the door here, ask for you. "Message from the Manager," that's what I have to say. Then the rest like we did – you know. When I say, "Hey? You ain't the Senator! Or are you?", they are supposed to close in and arrest you.'

Bill looked at me accusingly. 'But *you* messed it up. You fouled it, not me. You didn't do *anything* like you was supposed to. You clamped the door on me – and you shouldn't uh. And you turned out to be the Senator after all . . . and you had *her* with you.' His voice was especially bitter when he referred to Gwen.

I could understand his resentment. How is a sincere criminal, trying hard, going to get ahead in his profession if his victim fails to cooperate? Almost all crime depends on the acquiescence of the victim. If the victim refuses his assigned role, the criminal is placed at a disadvantage, one so severe that it usually takes an understanding and compassionate judge to set things right. I had broken the rules; I had fought back.

'You've certainly had a run of bad luck, Bill. Let's check this "Message from the Manager" you were supposed to deliver. Keep him covered, Mistress Hardesty.'

'Can I take my hands down?'

'No.' The clipboard was still on the deck, between Gwen and Bill but a bit toward me; I could reach it without crossing her line of fire. I picked it up.

Clipped to the board was a receipt form for messages, with a place for me (or someone) to sign. Clipped beside it was the familiar blue envelope of Mackay Three Planets; I opened it.

The message was in five-letter code groups, about fifty of them. Even the address was in code. Written in longhand above the address was 'Sen. Cantor, St Oil.'

I tucked it into a pocket without comment. Gwen queried me with her eyes; I managed not to see it. 'Mistress Hardesty, what shall we do with Bill?'

'Scrub him!'

'Eh? Do you mean, "Waste him"? Or are you volunteering to scrub his back?'

'Heavens, no! Both. Neither. I am suggesting that we shove him into the refresher and leave him there until he's sanitary. Bathed, hot water and lots of suds. Hair shampooed. Clean fingernails and toenails. Everything. Don't let him out until he whiffs clean.'

53

'You would let him use *your* 'fresher?'

'Things being the way they are, I don't expect to use it again. Senator, I'm tired of his stink.'

'Well, yes, he does put one in mind of rotten potatoes on a hot day in the Gulf Stream. Bill, take off your clothes.'

The criminal class is the most conservative group in any society; Bill was as reluctant to strip down in the presence of a lady as he had been to divulge the hideout of his fellow outcasts. He was shocked that I would suggest it, horrified that a lady would go along with this indecent proposal. On the latter point I might have agreed with him yesterday . . . but I had learned that Gwen was not easily daunted. In fact I think she enjoyed it.

As he peeled down, Bill gained a bit of my sympathy; he looked like a plucked chicken, with a woebegone expression to match. When he was down to undershorts (gray with dirt), he stopped and looked at me. 'All the way,' I said briskly. 'Then duck into the 'fresher and take the works. If you do a poor job, you'll do it over. If you stick your nose outside in less than thirty minutes, I won't bother to check you; I'll simply send you back in. Now get those drawers off – fast!'

Bill turned his back to Gwen, took off his shorts, then scuttled sideways to the refresher in a futile effort to retain a fraction of his modesty. He sealed the door behind him.

Gwen put her pistol into her purse, then worked her fingers, flexing and extending them. 'I was getting stiff from holding it. Beloved, may I have those cartridges?'

'Eh?'

'The ones you took from Bill. Six, wasn't it? Five and one.'

'Certainly, if you wish.' Should I tell her that I too had use for them? No, data of that sort should be shared only on a 'need to know' basis. I got them out, handed them to her.

Gwen looked them over, nodded, again took out her sweet little pistol – slid out its clip, loaded the six confiscated rounds into it, replaced the clip, jacked one into the chamber, locked the weapon and returned it to her purse.

'Correct me if I'm wrong,' I said slowly. 'When I first called on you to back me, you covered him with a pocket pen. Then, after you disarmed him, you held him with an empty gun. Is that correct?'

'Richard, I was taken by surprise. I did the best I could.'

54

'I was not criticizing. On the contrary!'

'There never seemed to be a good time to tell you.' She went on, 'Dear, could you spare a pair of pants and a shirt? There are some right on top in your duffel bag.'

'I suppose so. For our problem child?'

'Yes. I want to shove his filthy clothes down the oubliette, let them be recycled. The stench won't clear out of here until we get rid of them.'

'So let's get rid of them.' I shoved Bill's clothes down the chute (all but his shoes), then washed my hands at the buttery's fountain. 'Gwen, I don't think I have anything more to learn from this lunk. We could leave him some clothes and simply leave. Or . . . we could leave right away and *not* leave him any clothes.'

Gwen looked startled. 'But the proctors would pick him up at once.'

'Exactly. Dear girl, this lad is a born loser; the proctors will grab him before long anyhow. What do they do with nightwalkers today? Have you heard any gossip?'

'No. Nothing with the ring of truth.'

'I don't think they ship them down to Earth. That would cost the Company too much money, thus violating the Golden Rule the way it is interpreted here. There is no jail or prison in Golden Rule; that limits the possibilities. So?'

Gwen looked troubled. 'I don't think I like what I'm hearing.'

'It gets worse. Outside that door, perhaps not in sight but somewhere near, are a couple of hoodlums who mean us no good. Or who mean me no good, at least. If Bill leaves here, having flubbed the job he was hired to do, what happens to him? Do they feed him to the rats?'

'Ugh!'

'Yes, "ugh." My uncle used to say, "Never pick up a stray kitten . . . unless you've already made up your mind to be owned by it." Well, Gwen?'

She sighed. 'I think he's a good boy. Could be, I mean, if anyone had ever bothered with him.'

I echoed her sigh. 'Just one way to find out.'

VI

'Don't lock the barn after it is stolen.'

HARTLEY M. BALDWIN

It is difficult to punch a man in the nose through a terminal.

Even if one does not intend to use such direct persuasion, discussion via computer terminal can be less than satisfactory. With the flick of a key your opponent can shut you off or turn you over to a subordinate. But if you are physically present in his office, you can counter his most reasonable arguments simply by being more stupidly stubborn than he is. Just sit tight and say no. Or say nothing. You can face him with the necessity of either assenting to your (oh so reasonable) demands or having you thrown out bodily.

The latter probably will not fit his public *persona*.

For these reasons I decided to skip calling Mr Middlegaff, or anyone at the housing office, and went directly to the Manager's office, in person. I had no hope of influencing Mr Middlegaff, who clearly had had a policy handed to him, which he was now carrying out with bureaucratic indifference ('Have a Nice Day' indeed!). I had little hope of getting satisfaction from the Manager – but, at least, if the Manager turned me down, I would not have to waste time going higher. The Golden Rule, being a privately-owned company not chartered by any sovereign state (i.e. being itself sovereign) had no authority higher than the Manager – God Almighty Himself was not even a minority partner.

Decisions by the Managing Partner might be utterly arbitrary . . . but they were utterly final. There was no possibility of years of litigation, no way a higher court could reverse his decision. The 'Law's Delays' that so blemished the workings of 'justice' in democratic states down dirtside could not exist here. I recalled only a few capital cases in the five years I had

56

lived here . . . but in each case the Manager had sat as magistrate, then the condemned had been spaced that same day.

In such a system the question of miscarriage of justice becomes moot.

Add to that the fact that the profession of law, like the profession of prostitution, is neither licensed nor forbidden and the result is a judicial system having little resemblance to the crazy ziggurat of precedent and tradition that passes for 'justice' dirtside. Justice in the Golden Rule might be astigmatic if not totally blind; it could not be slow.

We left Bill in the outer foyer of the Manager's offices, with our baggage – my duffel bag and bundle, Gwen's cases, the bonsai maple (watered before we left Gwen's compartment) – with instructions to Bill to sit on the duffel bag, guard the bonsai with his life (Gwen's phrasing), and watch the rest. We went inside.

There we each, separately, left our names at the reception desk, then found seats. Gwen opened her purse, got out a Casio game board. 'What'll it be, dear? Chess, cribbage, backgammon, go, or what?'

'You're expecting a long wait?'

'Yes, I am, sir. Unless we build a fire under the mule.'

'I think you're right. Any ideas about how to build that fire? Without setting fire to the wagon, I mean. Oh, what the devil! – go ahead and set fire to the wagon. But how?'

'We could use a variation on the old standard: "My husband knows all." Or "Your wife has found out." But our variation would have to be quite novel, as the basic ploy has long white whiskers.' She added, 'Or I can go into labor pains. That is always good for attention.'

'But you don't look pregnant.'

'Want to bet? So far no one has taken a good look at me. Just give me five minutes alone in that ladies' lounge across there and you'll be certain I'm nine months gone. Richard, this ploy I learned years ago when I was a claims investigator for an insurance company. It will always get one inside, anywhere.'

'You tempt me,' I admitted, 'as it would be such fun to

57

watch you work it. But the ploy we use not only has to get us inside, but also must keep us inside under circumstances in which the bloke will listen to our arguments.'

'Dr Ames.'

'Yes, Mrs Ames?'

'The Manager isn't going to listen to our arguments.'

'Please amplify.'

'I applauded your decision to go straight to the top because I saw that it would save time and tears to get all the bad news at once. We have leprosy; what has already been done to us makes that clear. The Manager intends not merely to force us to move; he means to kick us right out of Golden Rule. I don't know why but we don't have to know why – it simply is so. Realizing that, I am relaxed to it. Once *you* realize it, too, dear man, we can make plans. To go dirtside, or to Luna, or to Promised Land, Ell-Four, Ceres, Mars – wherever you wish, beloved. "Whither thou goest—"'

'To Luna.'

'Sir?'

'For now, at least. Luna Free State isn't bad. Currently it is moving from anarchy to bureaucracy but it is not yet completely musclebound. It still has quite a lot of freedom for people who know how to deal with it pragmatically. And there is still elbow room on Luna. And in Luna. Yes, Gwen, we must leave; I suspected it earlier and know it now. Save for one thing, we could go straight to the spaceport. I still want to see the Manager. Damn it, I want to hear it from his own lying lips! Then with a clear conscience I can turn on the poison.'

'You intend to poison him, dear?'

'A figure of speech. I plan to place him on my list, then quick Karma will do him in.'

'Oh. Perhaps I can think of a way to help it along.'

'Not necessary. Once on the list, they never last long.'

'But I would enjoy it. "Vengeance is mine, sayeth the Lord." But the Revised Version reads: "Vengeance is Gwen's . . . then Mine only if Gwen leaves Me any."'

I clucked at her. '*Who* was saying that I should not take the law into my own hands?'

'But I was talking about *you*, sir; I didn't say a word about *me*. I delight in making quick Karma even quicker – it's my pet hobby.'

'My darling, you are a nasty little girl, I am happy to say. Going to kill him with hives? Or with hangnails? Maybe hiccups?'

'I'm thinking of keeping him awake till he dies. Lack of sleep is worse than anything you listed, dear, if pushed far enough. The victim's judgment goes to pieces long before he stops breathing. He hallucinates. Including all his worst phobias. He dies in his own private hell and never escapes from it.'

'Gwen, you sound as if you had used this method.'

Gwen did not comment.

I shrugged. 'Whatever you decide, let me know how I can help.'

'I will, sir. Mmm, I think highly of drowning in caterpillars. But I don't know how to get that many caterpillars other than by having them shipped up from Earth. Except – Well, one can always arrange for them through the insomnia method. Toward the end you can cause the condemned to create his own caterpillars just by suggesting it to him.' She shivered. '*Schrecklich!* But I won't use rats, Richard. Never rats. Not even imaginary rats.'

'My sweet and gentle bride, I'm glad to know you draw the line at *something*.'

'Certainly I do! Beloved, you startled me with the notion that bad manners could be judged a hanging offense. My own concern is for evil, rather than for bad manners. I think evil deeds should never go unpunished. God's arrangements for punishing evil are too slow to suit me; I want it done *now*. Take hijacking. Hijackers should be hanged on the spot as soon as they are caught. An arsonist should be burned at the stake on the site of the fire he started, if possible before its ashes grow cold. A rapist should be killed by—'

I did not learn then what complex way of dying Gwen favored for rapists because a polite bureaucrat (male, gray, dandruffy, built-in *risus*) stopped in front of us and said, 'Dr Ames?'

'I am Dr Ames.'

'I am Mungerson Fitts, Assistant Deputy Administrator for Superrogatory Statistics. I'm helping out. I'm sure you understand how terribly busy the Manager's office is just now with the new addition being brought up to spin – all the temporary relocations that have to be made and all the disruptions to routine that have to be accommodated before we can all settle down in a larger and greatly improved Golden Rule.' He gave me a winning smile. 'I understand you want to see the Manager.'

'That's right.'

'Excellent. Because of the present emergency I am helping here in order to maintain the proud quality of Golden Rule service to our guests during alterations. I have been fully empowered to act for the Manager; you can think of me as his alter ego . . . because to all intents and purposes I *am* the Manager. This little lady – she is with you?'

'Yes.'

'Honored, ma'am. Delighted. Now, friends, if you will please come with me—'

'No.'

'Excuse me?'

'I want to see the Manager.'

'But I explained to you—'

'I'll wait.'

'I don't think you understood me. Please come with—'

'No.'

(At this point Fitts should have grabbed me with a come-along and tossed me out on my arse. Not that it is easy to do this to me; I trained with the Dorsai. But that is what he should have done. However, he was inhibited by custom, habit, and policy.)

Fitts paused and looked baffled. 'Uh – But you must, you know.'

'No, I don't know.'

'I'm trying to tell you—'

'I want to see the Manager. Did he tell you what to do about Senator Cantor?'

'Senator Cantor? Let me see, he's the Senator from, uh, from . . .'

'If you don't know who he is, how do you know what to do about him?'

'Uh, if you will just wait a moment while I consult.'

'You had better take us along – since you don't seem to be "fully empowered" on this critical issue.'

'Uh . . . please wait here.'

60

I stood up. 'No, I had better get back. The Senator may be looking for me. Please tell the Manager that I'm sorry I could not arrange it.' I turned to Gwen. 'Come, Madam. Let's not keep him waiting.' (I wondered if Mungerson would notice that 'him' was a pronoun without a referent.)

Gwen stood up, took my arm. Fitts said hastily, 'Please, friends, don't leave! Uh, come with me.' He herded us to an unmarked door. 'Wait just one moment, please!'

He was gone more than a moment but nevertheless only a short time. He returned with his face wreathed with smiles (I think that is the expression). 'Right this way, please!' He took us through the unmarked door, down a short passage, and into the Manager's inner office.

The Manager looked up from his desk and inspected us, not with the familiar, fatherly expression of the too-frequent 'Word from the Manager' announcements that come over every terminal. On the contrary Mr Sethos looked as if he had found something nasty in his porridge.

I ignored his chilly demeanor. Instead I stood just inside the door, Gwen still on my arm, and waited. I once lived with a fussy cat (is there another sort?) who, when faced with an offering of food not perfectly to his taste, would stand still and, with dignified restraint, look offended – a remarkable bit of acting for one whose face was completely covered with fur; however, he did it mostly by body language. I now did this to Mr Sethos, primarily by thinking about that cat. I stood . . . and waited.

He stared at us . . . and at last stood up, bowed slightly and said, 'Madam . . . will you please be seated?'

Whereupon we both sat down. Round one to us, on points. I could not have done it without Gwen. But I did have her help and once I got my butt into his chair he was not going to get it out – until I got what I wanted.

I sat still, kept quiet, and waited.

When Mr Sethos's blood pressure reached triggering level, he said, 'Well? You've managed to bull your way into my office. What's this nonsense about Senator Cantor?'

'I expect you to tell me. Have you assigned Senator Cantor to my wife's compartment?'

'Eh? Don't be ridiculous. Mistress Novak has a one-room efficiency compartment, the smallest size in first class. The

Senator from Standard Oil, if he came here, would be in a deluxe suite. Of course.'

'Mine, perhaps? Is that why you evicted me? For the Senator?'

'What? Don't put words in my mouth; the Senator isn't aboard. We've been forced to ask a number of our guests to shift around, you among them. The new section, you know. Before it can be welded on, all compartments and spaces adjacent to ring one-thirty must be evacuated. So we have to double up temporarily to make room for our displaced guests. Your compartment will have three families in it, as I recall. For a short while, that is.'

'I see. Then it was just an oversight that I was not told where to move?'

'Oh, I'm sure you were told.'

'I surely was not. Will you please tell me my new address?'

'Doctor, do you expect me to carry housing assignments in my head? Go wait outside and someone will look it up and tell you.'

I ignored his suggestion/order. 'Yes, I do think you carry them in your head.'

He snorted. 'There are more than one hundred eighty thousand people on this habitat. I have assistants and computers for such details.'

'I'm sure you do. But you have given me strong reason to think that you do have such details in your head ... when they interest you. I'll give an example. My wife was not introduced to you. Mungerson Fitts did not know her name, so he could not have told you. But *you* knew without being told. You knew her name and what compartment she lived in. Did live in, I mean, until you had her locked out. Is that how you apply the Golden Rule, Mr Sethos? By kicking out your guests without even the courtesy of warning them ahead of time?'

'Doctor, are you trying to pick a fight?'

'No, I'm trying to find out why you have been hassling us. Bullying us. Persecuting us. You and I both know that it has nothing to do with the temporary dislocations caused by bringing the new section up to spin and welded on; that's certain ... because the new section has been building for over three years and you've known for at least a year the date you were going to bring it up to spin . . . yet you had me kicked out of my compartment with less than thirty minutes' warning. My wife you treated even worse; you simply locked her out, no warning at all. Sethos, you aren't just moving us around to allow for attaching the new section. If that were true, we would have been told at least a month ago, along with temporary reassignments and with dates for moving into new permanent quarters. No, you're rousting us right out of Golden Rule habitat . . . and I want to know why!'

'Get out of my office. I'll have someone take you by the hand and lead you to your new – temporary – quarters.'

'Not necessary. Just tell me the coordinates and the compartment number. I'll wait here while you look them up.'

'By God, I believe you *want* to be kicked off Golden Rule!'

'No, I've been quite comfortable here. I'll be happy to stay . . . if you will tell me where we are to sleep tonight . . . and give us our new permanent assignment – where we'll be living once the new section is welded on and pressurized, I mean. We need a three-room suite, to replace the two-roomer I had and the one-room compartment Mrs Ames had. Two terminals. One for each of us, just as before. And low gravity. Four-tenths gee by preference, but not more than half a gravity.'

'Would you like an egg in your beer? Why do you need two terminals? That requires additional wiring.'

'So it does and I'll pay for it. Because I'm a writer. I'll use one as a wordprocessor and for library reference work. Mrs Ames needs the other for household routine.'

'Oho! You plan to use residential space for business purposes. That calls for commercial rates. Not residential rate.'

'What does that come to?'

'It will have to be calculated. There is a costing factor for each type of commercial use. Retail stores, restaurants, banks, and the like cost approximately three times as much per cubic meter as does residential space. Factory space does not cost as much as retail space but may have surcharges for hazards and so forth. Warehousing is only slightly more than residential. Offhand I think you will have to pay office space rates – that's a factor of three point five – but I'll have to take it up with the chief accountant.'

'Mr Manager, do I understand you correctly? Are you

planning to charge us three and half times as much as our combined rents were together?'

'Approximately. It might be as low as three times.'

'Well, well. I haven't concealed the fact that I'm a writer; it says so on my passport and I'm listed that way in your directory, all the past five years. Tell me why it suddenly makes a difference to you whether I use my terminal to write letters home . . . or to write stories?'

Sethos gave what could have been construed as a laugh. 'Doctor, Golden Rule is a business enterprise undertaken for profit. I manage it for my partners to that end. No one has to live here, no one has to do business here. What I charge people to live here, or to do business here, is controlled solely by maximizing profits to the partnership, as guided by my best judgment to that end. If you don't like it, you can take your business elsewhere.'

I was just about to shift the basis for discussion (I can see when I'm outgunned) when Gwen spoke up. 'Mr Sethos?'

'Eh? Yes, Mistress Novak? Mrs Ames.'

'Did you get your start pimping for your sisters?'

Sethos turned a delicate shade of eggplant. He finally got control of himself well enough to say, 'Mrs Ames, are you being intentionally insulting?'

'That's obvious, isn't it? I don't know that you have sisters; it just seems like the sort of enterprise that would appeal to you. You have injured us for no reason whatever. We come to you, asking for redress of grievance; you answer us with evasions, outright lies, irrelevant issues . . . and a fresh extortion. You justify this new outrage with a plonking sermon on free enterprise. Just what price did you usually charge for your sisters? And how much did you keep as your commission? Half? Or more than half?'

'Madam, I must ask you to leave my office . . . and this habitat. You are not the sort we want living here.'

'I am delighted to leave,' Gwen answered, not stirring, 'just as quickly as you settle my account. And my husband's account.'

'Get . . . OUT!'

Gwen put out her hand, palm up. 'Cash first, you bald-faced swindler. The balance of our accounts plus the fare-home deposits we each made when we got here. If we leave this room

64

without collecting, there's not a prayer that you will ever pay what you owe us. Pay up and we leave. The first shuttle down to Luna. But pay up and right now! Or you'll have to space me to shut me up. If you call in your goons, you flannel mouth, I'll scream this place down. Want a sample?' Gwen tilted her head back, cut loose with a scream that made my teeth ache.

Sethos, too, apparently – I saw him flinch.

He stared at her a long moment, then touched some control on his desk. 'Ignatius. Close the accounts of Dr Richard Ames and of Mistress Gwendolyn Novak, uh' – with only a momentary hesitation he correctly stated my compartment number and that of Gwen – 'and deliver them to my office at once. With cash to pay them off. With receipts to chop and print. No checks. What? You listen to me. If it takes longer than ten minutes we'll hold a full-scale inspection of your department . . . see who has to be fired, who merely has to be demoted.' He switched off, did not look at us.

Gwen got out her little gameboard, set it for tic-tac-toe, which suited me, it being about the intellectual level I felt able to cope with then. She beat me four straight games, even though twice I had the first move. But my head was still aching from her supersonic scream.

I had not kept track of the exact time but it must have been about ten minutes later that a man came in with our accounts. Sethos glanced at them, passed them over to us. Mine appeared to be accurate; I was about to sign the receipt when Gwen spoke up. 'What about interest on the money I had to deposit?'

'Eh? What are you talking about?'

'My fare back dirtside. I had to deposit it in cash, no IOUs accepted. Your bank here charges nine percent on private loans, so it ought to be paying at least savings account rates on impounded money. Although time-deposit rates would be more reasonable. I've been here more than a year, so . . . let me see –' Gwen took out the pocket calculator we had been using for tic-tac-toe. 'You owe me eight hundred seventy-one and – call it even crowns – eight hundred and seventy-one crowns in interest. In Swiss gold that comes to—'

'We pay in crowns, not Swiss money.'

'All right, you owe it to me in crowns.'

'And we don't pay interest on return ticket money; it is simply held in escrow.'

I was suddenly alert. 'You don't, eh? Dear, may I borrow that widget? Let's see – a hundred and eighty thousand people . . . and one-way tourist fare to Maui on Panam or Qantas is—'

'Seventy-two hundred,' Gwen answered, 'except weekends and holidays.'

'So.' I punched it in. 'Hmm, well over a billion crowns! One two nine six followed by six zeroes. How interesting! How enlightening. Sethos old boy, you may be skimming off over a hundred million a year, tax free, simply by placing all this money you are holding for us suckers in Luna City money funds. But I don't think you use it that way – or not all of it. I think you run your whole enterprise using other people's money . . . without their knowledge or consent. Right?'

The flunky (Ignatius?) who had fetched our accounts was listening with intent interest.

Sethos growled. 'Sign those receipts and get out.'

'Oh, I shall!'

'But pay us our interest,' Gwen added.

I shook my head. 'No, Gwen. Anywhere but here we could sue him. Here he is both the law and the judge. But I don't mind, Mr Manager, as you have given me a wonderful, salable idea for an article – *Reader's Digest*, probably, or *Fortune*. Uh, I'll title it "Pie in the Sky, or How to Get Rich on Other People's Money: The Economics of Privately-Owned Space Habitats." A hundred million a year swindled out of the public in Golden Rule habitat alone. Something along that line.'

'You publish that and I'll sue you for everything you own!'

'Will you? See you in court, old boy. Somehow I don't think you will want to wash your dirty linen in any court where you aren't the judge. Mmm, I just got a wild idea. You're finishing a very expensive addition – and I remember seeing in the *Wall Street Journal* that you did it without selling bonds. How much of that so-called escrow money is floating out there as rings one-thirty to one-forty? And how many of us leaving all the same week would it take to cause a run on your bank? Can you pay on demand, Sethos? Or is that escrow as phony as you are?'

'Say that in public and I'll sue you in every court in the system! Sign that receipt and leave.'

Gwen would not sign until the cash was counted out in front of us, whereupon she did sign and so did I.

As we were accepting the money, Sethos's desk terminal came to life. Its screen was visible only to him but the speaker's voice identified him: Chief Proctor Franco. 'Mr Sethos!'

'I'm busy.'

'This is an emergency! Ron Tolliver's been shot. I—'

'*What!*'

'It just happened! I'm in his office – he's bad hurt, prob'ly won't make it. But I got eyewitnesses. That fake doctor did it – Richard Ames—'

'Shut up!'

'But, boss—'

'Shut UP! You stupid, bumbling fool! Report to me at once.' Sethos turned his attention back to us. 'Now get out of here.'

'Perhaps I had better wait and meet these eyewitnesses.'

'Get out. Get off this habitat.'

I offered Gwen my arm.

VII

'You can't cheat an honest man. He has to have larceny in
his heart in the first place.'

CLAUDE WILLIAM DUKENFIELD 1880–1946

OUTSIDE WE found Bill still sitting on my duffel bag, the little
tree in his arms. He stood up, an uncertain look on his face.
But when Gwen smiled at him, he grinned back. I said, 'Any
problems, Bill?'

'No, boss. Uh, skin tried to buy little tree.'

'Why didn't you sell it?'

He looked shocked. '*Huh?* It belongs to *her*.'

'That's right. If you had sold it, do you know what she
would have done? She would have drowned you in caterpillars,
that's what she would have done. So you were smart not to
risk crossing her. But no rats. As long as you stick with her,
you need never be afraid of rats. Right, Mistress Hardesty?'

'Correct, Senator. No rats, ever. Bill, I'm proud of you, not
letting someone tempt you. But I want you to stop that
slang – why, someone hearing you might think you were a
nightwalker – and we wouldn't want that, would we? So don't
say "a skin tried to buy the tree," just say "a man."'

'Uh, matter o' fac', this skin was a slitch. Uh, a broad. Read?'

'Yes. But let's try that again. Say "a woman."'

'All right. That skin was a woman.' He grinned sheepishly.
'You sound just like the Sisters that taught us at Holy Name,
back dirtside.'

'I take that as a compliment, Bill . . . and I am going to nag
you about your grammar and your pronunciation and your
choice of words even more than they ever did. Until you talk
as beautifully as the Senator does. Because, many years ago,
a wise and cynical man proved that the way a person talks is

68

the most important thing about him when it comes to dealing successfully with the world. Do you understand me?'

'Uh – Some.'

'You can't learn everything at once and I don't expect you to. Bill, if you bathe every day and speak grammatically, the world will decide that you are a winner and will treat you accordingly. So we'll keep trying.'

I said, 'And in the meantime it is urgent to get out of this bucket.'

'Senator, this is urgent, too.'

'Yes, yes, the old "how to housebreak a puppy" rule. I understand. But let's get moving.'

'Yes, sir. Straight to the spaceport?'

'Not yet. Straight down El Camino Real while checking every public terminal for one that will accept coins. Do you have any coins?'

'A few. Enough for a short call, perhaps.'

'Good. But keep your eyes open for a changemaker, too. Now that you and I have canceled our credit codes, we'll have to use coins.'

We picked up our burdens again and started out. Gwen said quietly, 'I don't want Bill to hear this . . . but it's not difficult to convince a public terminal that you are using a correct credit code when you are not.'

I answered just as quietly, 'We will resort to that only if honesty won't work. My darling, how many more little scams do you have tucked away?'

'Sir, I don't know what you're talking about. A hundred meters ahead of us – Does that booth on the right have the yellow sign? Why are so few public booths equipped to receive coins?'

'Because Big Brother likes to know who is calling whom . . . and with the credit code method we are practically begging him to share our secrets. Yes, that one does have the sign. Let's pool our coins.'

The Reverend Doctor Hendrik Hudson Schultz answered his terminal promptly. His Santa Claus visage peered at me, sizing me up, counting the money in my wallet.

'Father Schultz?'

'In the flesh. How can I serve you, sir?'

Instead of answering, I took out a thousand-crown note,

held it in front of my face. Dr Schultz looked at it, raised his bristling brows. 'You interest me, sir.'

I tapped my ear while glancing left and right, then I signed all three of the three little monkeys. He answered, 'Why, yes, I was about to go out for a cup of coffee. Will you join me? One moment—'

Shortly he held up a sheet of paper on which he had printed in large block letters:

OLD MACDONALD'S FARM

'Can you meet me at Sans Souci Bargrill? That's on Petticoat Lane right across from my studio. About ten minutes, perhaps?' All the while he was talking, he was jabbing a finger at the sign he was showing me.

I answered, 'Righto!' and switched off.

I was not in the habit of going to farm country, since full gravity is not kind to my bad leg and farms have to be at full gravity. No, that's not correct; there may be more habitats in the System that use for farming whatever fractional gee they wish (or that mutated plants prefer) than there are that use natural sunlight and full gee. As may be, Golden Rule goes the natural sunlight and full gee route for much of its fresh food. Other spaces in Golden Rule use artificial light and other accelerations for growing food – how much, I don't know. But the enormous space from ring fifty to ring seventy is open air, side to side, save for struts and vibration dampers and walkways joining the principal corridors.

In this span of twenty rings – eight hundred meters – radii 0–60, 120–180, and 240–300 let in the sunlight; radii 60–120, 180–240, and 300–0 are farmland – of which 180–240, ring 50–70 is Old MacDonald's Farm.

That's a lot of farmland. A man could get lost there, especially in fields where corn grows even taller than it does in Iowa. But Doc Schultz had paid me the compliment of assuming that I would know where to meet him: at a popular outdoor restaurant and bar called The Country Kitchen, right spang in the middle of the farm, ring sixty, radius 210, at (of course) full gravity.

To reach the restaurant we had to go downstairs forward of ring fifty, then walk aft (at full gee, damn it!) to ring sixty, a distance of four hundred meters. A short distance, oh certainly – about four city blocks. Try it on a false foot with a stump that has already been used too much in walking and too much in carrying for one day.

Gwen spotted it, in my voice, or my face, or my walk, or something – or she read my mind, maybe; I'm not sure she can't. She stopped.

I stopped. 'Trouble, dear?'

'Yes. Senator, put down that bundle. I'll balance Tree-San on my head. Give me the bundle.'

'I'm all right.'

'Yes, sir. You surely are and I'm going to keep you that way. It is your privilege to be *macho* whenever you wish . . . and it's my privilege to go female and be vaporish and weak and unreasonable. Right now I'm about to faint. And I'll stay that way until you give me the bundle. You can beat me later.'

'Hmm. When is it my turn to win an argument?'

'On your birthday, sir. Which this is not. Let me have the bundle. Please.'

It was not an argument I wanted to win; I handed over the bundle. Bill and Gwen went on ahead of me, with Bill walking in front, breaking trail. She never lost control of the burden balanced on her head, even though the road was not corridor-smooth – a dirt road. Real dirt – a piece of totally unnecessary swank.

I limped slowly along behind, leaning heavily on my cane and putting almost no weight on my stump. By the time I reached the outdoor restaurant I felt fairly well recovered.

Dr Schultz was leaning against the bar with an elbow hooked over it. He recognized me, did not admit it until I came up to him. 'Dr Schultz?'

'Ah, yes!' He did not ask my name. 'Shall we look for a restful spot? I find that I enjoy the quiet of an apple orchard. Shall I ask our host to have a small table and a couple of chairs placed back in the trees?'

'Yes. But three chairs, not two.'

Gwen had joined us. 'Not four?'

'No, I want Bill to watch our chattels, as he did before. I see an empty table over there; he can pile stuff on it and around it.'

Soon we three were settled at a table that had been moved

for us back into the orchard. After consulting, I ordered beer for the Reverend and for me, Coke for Gwen, and had told the waitress to find the young man with the bundle and give him what he wanted – beer, Coke, sandwiches, whatever. (I suddenly realized Bill might not have eaten today.)

When she left, I dug into a pocket, pulled out that thousand-crown note, gave it to Dr Schultz.

He caused it to disappear. 'Sir, do you wish a receipt?'

'No.'

'Between gentlemen, eh? Excellent. Now how can I help you?'

Forty minutes later Dr Schultz knew almost as much about our troubles as I did, as I held nothing back. He could help us, it seemed to me, only if he knew the full background – so far as I knew it – on what had happened.

'You say Ron Tolliver has been shot?' he said at last.

'I didn't see it. I heard the Chief Proctor say so. Correction: I heard a man who sounded like Franco, and the Manager treated him as such.'

'Good enough. Hear hoofbeats; expect horses, not zebras. But I heard nothing about it on my way here, and I noticed no signs of excitement in this restaurant – and the assassination or attempted assassination of the second largest holder of partnership shares in this sovereignty *should* cause excitement. I was at the bar for a few minutes before you arrived. No word of it. Yet a bar is notoriously the place news hits first; there is always a screen turned on to the news channel. Hmmm . . . could the Manager be covering it up?'

'That lying snake is capable of anything.'

'I was not speaking of his moral character, concerning which my judgment matches yours, but solely of physical possibility. One does not cover up a shooting too easily. Blood. Noise. A victim dead or wounded. And you spoke of witnesses – or Franco did. Still, Judge Sethos controls the only newspaper, and the terminals, and the proctors. Yes, if he wished to make the effort, he could surely keep it hush-hush for a considerable period. We shall see – and that is one more item on which I will report to you after you reach Luna City.'

'We may not be in Luna City. I'll have to phone you.'

'Colonel, is that advisable? Unless our presence together during that few seconds at the bar was noted by some interested party who knows both of us, it is possible that we have succeeded in keeping our alliance secret. It is indeed fortunate that you and I have never been associated in any fashion in the past; there is no probable way to trace me to you, or you to me. You can phone me, certainly . . . but one must assume that my terminal is tapped, or my studio is bugged, or both – and both have happened in the past. I suggest, rather, the mails . . . for other than direct emergency.'

'But mail can be opened. By the way, I'm Dr Ames, not Colonel Campbell, please. And oh yes! – this young man with us. He knows me as "Senator" and Mrs Ames as "Mistress Hardesty" from that dustup I told you about.'

'I'll remember. In the course of a long life one plays many roles. Would you believe that I was once known as "Lance Corporal Finnegan, Imperial Marines"?'

'I can easily believe it.'

'Which just goes to show you, as I never was. But I've worked much stranger jobs. Mail can be opened, true – but if I deliver a letter to a Luna City shuttle before it leaves our spaceport, it is most unlikely that it will ever reach the hands of anyone interested in opening it. In the reverse direction a letter sent to Henrietta van Loon, care of Madame Pompadour, 20012 Petticoat Lane, will reach me with only minimal delay. An old, established madam has years of dealing gently with other people's secrets. One must trust, I find. The art lies in knowing whom to trust.'

'Doc, I find that I trust you.'

He chuckled. 'My dear sir, I would most happily sell you your own hat were you to leave it on my counter. But you are correct in essence. As I have accepted you as my client you can trust me totally. Being a double agent would invite ulcers . . . and I am a gourmand who will do nothing that could interfere with my pleasures as a trencherman.'

He looked thoughtful and added, 'May I see that wallet again? Enrico Schultz.'

I handed it to him. He took out the ID. 'You say this is a good likeness?'

'Excellent, I think.'

'Dr Ames, you will realize that the name "Schultz" at once

catches my attention. What you may not guess is that the varied nature of my enterprises makes it desirable for me to note each new arrival in this habitat. I read the *Herald* each day, skimming everything but noting most carefully anything of a personal nature. I can state unequivocally that this man did not enter Golden Rule habitat under the name "Schultz." Any other name might have slipped my mind. But my own surname? Impossible.'

'He appears to have given that name on arriving here.'

'"– appears to have –" You speak precisely.' Schultz looked at the ID. 'In twenty minutes in my studio – no, allow me half a hour – I could produce an ID with this face on it – and of as good quality – that would assert that his name was "Albert Einstein."'

'You're saying we can't trace him by that ID.'

'Hold on; I didn't say that. You tell me this is a good likeness. A good likeness is a better clue than is a printed name. Many people must have seen this man. Several must know who he is. A small number know why he was killed. If he was. You left that carefully open.'

'Well . . . primarily because of that incredible Mexican Hat Dance that took place immediately after he was shot. If he was. Instead of confusion, those four behaved as if they had rehearsed it.'

'Well. I shall pursue the matter, both with carrot and with stick. If a man has a guilty conscience, or a greedy nature – and most men have both – ways can be found to extract what he knows. Well, sir, we seem to have covered it. But let's be sure, since it is unlikely that we shall be able to consult again. You will press ahead with the Walker Evans aspect, while I investigate the other queries on your list. Each will advise the other of developments, especially those leading into or out of the Golden Rule. Anything more? Ah, yes, that coded message – Did you intend to pursue it?'

'Do you have any ideas on it?'

'I suggest that you keep it and take it to the Mackay main office in Luna City. If they can identify the code, it is then just a matter of paying a fee, licit or illicit, to translate it. Its meaning will tell you whether or not I need it here. If Mackay cannot help, then you might take it to Dr Jakob Raskob at Galileo University. He is a cryptographer in the department of computer science . . . and if he can't figure out what to do about it, I can suggest nothing better than prayer. May I keep this picture of my cousin Enrico?'

'Yes, surely. But mail me a copy, please; I may need it in pursuing the Walker Evans angle – on second thought, certain to. Doctor, we have one more need I have not mentioned.'

'So?'

'The young man with us. He's a ghost, Reverend; he walks by night. And he's naked. We want to cover him. Can you think of anyone who can handle it – and right away? We would like to catch the next shuttle.'

'One moment, sir! Am I to infer that your porter, the young man with your baggage, is the ruffian who pretended to be a proctor?'

'Didn't I make that clear?'

'Perhaps I was obtuse. Very well, I accept the fact . . . while admitting astonishment. You want me to supply him with papers? So that he can move around in Golden Rule without fear of proctors?'

'Not exactly. I want a bit more than that. A passport. To get him out of Golden Rule and into Luna Free State.'

Dr Schultz pulled his lower lip. 'What will he do there? No, I withdraw that question – your business, not mine. Or his business.'

Gwen said, 'I'm going to spank him into shape, Father Schultz. He needs to learn to keep his nails clean and not to dangle his participles. And he needs some backbone. I'm going to equip him with one.'

Schultz looked thoughtfully at Gwen. 'Yes, I think you have enough for two. Madam, may I say that, while I do not yearn to emulate you, I do strongly admire you?'

'I hate to see anything go to waste. Bill is about twenty-five, I think, but he acts and talks as if he were ten or twelve. Yet he is not stupid.' She grinned. 'Ah'll larn him if'n I have to bust his pesky haid!'

'More power to you.' Schultz added gently, 'But suppose he does turn out to be simply stupid? Lacking the capacity to grow up?'

Gwen sighed. 'Then I guess I would cry a bit and find him some protected place, where he could work at what he can do and be whatever he is, in dignity and in comfort. Reverend, I could not send him back down to the dirt and the hunger and the fear – and the rats. Living like that is worse than dying.'

'Yes, it is. For dying is not to be feared – it is the final comfort. As we all learn, eventually. Very well, a sincere passport for Bill. I'll have to find a certain lady – see whether or not she can accept a rush assignment.' He frowned. 'It will be difficult to do this before the next shuttle. And I *must* have a photograph of him. Plague take it! – that means a trip to my studio. More time lost, more risk for you two.'

Gwen reached into her purse, pulled out a Mini Helvetia – illegal without a license most places but probably not covered by Manager's regulations here. 'Dr Schultz, this doesn't make a picture big enough for a passport, I know – but could it be blown up for the purpose?'

'It certainly could be. Mmm, that's an impressive camera.'

'I like it. I once worked for the – an agency that used such cameras. When I resigned, I found I had mislaid it . . . and had to pay for it.' She grinned mischievously. 'Later I found it – it had been in my purse all along . . . but 'way down in the bottom lost in the junk.' She added, 'I'll run get a picture of Bill.'

I said hastily, 'Use a neutral background.'

'Think I was a-hint the door? 'Scuse, please. Back in a second.'

She was back in a few minutes; the picture was coming up. A minute later it was sharp; she passed it to Dr Schultz. 'Will that do?'

'Excellent! But what is that background? May I ask?'

'A bar towel. Frankie and Juanita stretched it tight behind Bill's head.'

'"Frankie and Juanita,"' I repeated. 'Who are they?'

'The head bartender and the manager. Nice people.'

'Gwen, I didn't know you were acquainted here. That could cause problems.'

'I'm not acquainted here; I've never been here before, dear. I've been in the habit of patronizing The Chuck Wagon in Lazy Eight Spread at radius ninety – they have square dancing.' Gwen looked up, squinting against the sunlight directly overhead – the habitat, in its stately spin, was just swinging through the arc that placed the Sun at zenith for Old Mac-Donald's Farm. She pointed high – well, sixty degrees up, it had to be. 'There, you can see The Chuck Wagon; the dance

76

floor is just above it, toward the Sun. Are they dancing? Can you see? There's a strut partly in the way.'

'They're too far away for me to tell,' I admitted.

'They're dancing,' Dr Schultz said. 'Texas Star, I think. Yes, that's the pattern. Ah, youth, youth! I no longer dance but I have been a guest caller at The Chuck Wagon on occasion. Have I seen you there, Mrs Ames? I think not.'

'And I think "Yes,"' Gwen answered. 'But I was masked that day. I enjoyed your calling, Doctor. You have the real Pappy Shaw touch.'

'Higher praise a caller cannot hope for. "Masked —" Perchance you wore a candy-striped gown in green and white? A full circle skirt?'

'More than a full circle; it made waves whenever my partner twirled me — people complained that the sight made them seasick. You have an excellent memory, sir.'

'And you are an excellent dancer, ma'am.'

Somewhat irked, I interrupted. 'Can we knock off this Old Home Week? There are still urgent things to do and I still have hopes that we can catch the twenty o'clock shuttle.'

Schultz shook his head. 'Twenty o'clock? Impossible, sir.'

'Why is it impossible? That's over three hours from now. I'm edgy about the idea of waiting for a later shuttle; Franco might decide to send his goons after us.'

'You've asked for a passport for Bill. Dr Ames, even the sorriest imitation of a passport takes more time than that.' He paused and looked less like Santa Claus and more like a tired and worried old man. 'But your prime purpose is to get Bill out of this habitat and onto the Moon?'

'Yes.'

'Suppose you took him there as your bond servant?'

'*Huh?* You can't take a slave into Luna Free State.'

'Yes, and no. You can take a slave *to* the Moon . . . but he is automatically free, then and forever, once he sets foot on Luna; that is one thing those convicts nailed down when they set themselves free. Dr Ames, I can supply a bill of sale covering Bill's indentures in time for the evening shuttle, I feel confident. I have his picture, I have a supply of official stationery – authentic, by midnight requisition – and there is time to crease and age the document. Truly, this is much safer than trying to rush a passport.'

77

'I defer to your professional judgment. How and when and where do I pick up the paper?'

'Mmm, not at my studio. Do you know a tiny bistro adjacent to the spaceport, one-tenth gee at radius three hundred? The Spaceman's Widow?'

I was about to say no, but that I would find it, when Gwen spoke up. 'I know where it is. You have to go behind Macy's warehouse to reach it. No sign on it.'

'That's right. Actually it's a private club, but I'll give you a card. You can relax there and get a bite to eat. No one will bother you. Its patrons tend to mind each his own business.'

(Because that business is smuggling, or something equally shady – but I didn't say it.) 'That suits me.'

The Reverend Doctor got out a card, started to write on it – paused. 'Names?'

'Mistress Hardesty,' Gwen answered promptly.

'I agree,'' Dr Schultz said soberly. 'A proper precaution. Senator, what is your surname?'

'It can't be "Cantor"; I might run into someone who knows what Senator Cantor looks like. Uh . . . Hardesty?'

'No, she's your secretary, not your wife. "Johnson." There have been more senators named "Johnson" than any other name, so it arouses no suspicion – and it matches Bill's last name . . . which could be useful.' He wrote on the card, handed it to me. 'Your host's name is Tiger Kondo and he teaches all sorts of kill-quick in his spare time. You can depend on him.'

'Thank you, sir.' I glanced at the card, pocketed it. 'Doctor, do you want more retainer now?'

He grinned jovially. 'Now, now! I haven't yet determined how deeply I can bleed you. My motto is "All the traffic will bear" – but never make the mark anemic.'

'Reasonable. Till later, then. We had better not leave together.'

'I agree. Nineteen o'clock is my best guess. Dear friends, it has been both a pleasure and a privilege. And let us not forget the true importance of this day. My felicitations, ma'am. My congratulations, sir. May your life together be long and peaceful and filled with love.'

Gwen got on her tiptoes and kissed him for that, and they both had tears in their eyes. Well, so did I.

VIII

'The biscuits and the syrup never come out even.'

LAZARUS LONG 1912–

GWEN TOOK us straight to the Spaceman's Widow, tucked in behind Macy's storerooms just as she had said, in one of those odd little corners formed by the habitat's cylindrical shape – if you didn't know it was there, you probably would never find it. It was pleasantly quiet after the crowds we had encountered at the spaceport end of the axis.

Ordinarily this end was for passenger craft only, with freighters ganging up at the other end of the axis of spin. But positioning the new addition for bringing it up to spin had caused all traffic to be routed to the Moonward, or forward, end – 'forward' because Golden Rule is long enough to have a slight tidal effect, and will have even more when the new addition is welded on. I don't mean that it has daily tides; it does not. But what it does have—

(I may be telling too much; it depends on how much you have had to do with habitats. You can skip this with no loss.)

What it does have is a tidal lock on Luna; the forward end points forever straight down at the Moon. If Golden Rule were the size of a shuttle craft, or as far away as Ell-Five, this would not happen. But Golden Rule is over five kilometers long and it orbits around a center of mass only a little over two thousand kilometers away. Surely, that's only one part in four hundred – but it's a square law and there's no friction and the effect goes on forever; it's locked. The tidal lock Earth has on Luna is only four times that – much less if you bear in mind that Luna is round as a tennis ball whereas Golden Rule is shaped more like a cigar.

Golden Rule has another orbital peculiarity. It orbits from pole to pole (okay, everybody knows that – sorry) but also this orbit, elliptical but almost a perfect circle, has that circle fully open to the Sun, i.e., the plane of its orbit faces the Sun, always, while Luna rotates under it. Like Foucault's pendulum. Like the spy satellites patrolling Earth.

Or, to put it another way, Golden Rule simply follows the terminator, the day-and-night line on Luna, around and around and around, endlessly – never in shadow. (Well – In shadow at Lunar eclipses, if you want to pick nits. But only then.)

This configuration is only metastable; it is not locked. Everything tugs at it, even Saturn and Jupiter. But there is a little pilot computer in Golden Rule that does nothing but make sure Golden Rule's orbit is always full face to the Sun – thereby giving Old MacDonald's Farm its bountiful crops. It doesn't even take power to speak of, just the tiniest nudges against the tiny deviations.

I hope you skipped the above. Ballistics is interesting only to those who use it.

Mr Kondo was small, apparently of Japanese ancestry, very polite, and had muscles as sleek as a jaguar – he moved like one. Even without Dr Schultz's tip I would have known that I did not want to encounter Tiger Kondo in a dark alley unless he was there to protect *me*.

His door did not open fully until I showed Dr Schultz's card. Then he at once made us welcome with formal but warm hospitality. The place was small, only half filled, mostly men, and the women were not (I thought) their wives. But not tarts, either. The feeling was that of professional equals. Our host sized us up, decided that we did not belong in the main room with the regulars, put us in a little side room or booth, one big enough for us three and our baggage but just barely. He then took our orders. I asked if dinner was available.

'Yes and no,' he answered. 'Sushi is available. And sukiyaki cooked at the table by my eldest daughter. Hamburgers and hot dogs can be had. There is pizza but it is frozen; we do not make it. Or recommend it. This is primarily a bar; we serve food but do not demand that our guests eat here. You are welcome to play go or chess or cards all night and never order anything.'

Gwen put a hand on my sleeve. 'May I?'

'Go ahead.'

She spoke to him at some length and I never understood a word. But his face lit up. He bowed and left. I said, 'Well?'

'I asked if we could have what I had last time . . . and that is not a specific dish but an invitation to Mama-San to use her judgment with whatever she has. It also let him admit that I had been here before . . . which he would never have done had I not published it, as I was here with another man. He also told me that our little pet here is the best specimen of rock maple he has ever seen outside Nippon . . . and I asked him to spray it for me just before we leave. He will.'

'Did you tell him we were married?'

'Not necessary. The idiom I used in speaking of you implied it.'

I wanted to ask her when and how she had learned Japanese but did not – Gwen would tell me when it suited her. (How many marriages are ruined by that itch to know 'all about' a spouse? As a veteran of countless true confession stories I can assure you that unbridled curiosity about your wife's/ husband's past is a sure formula for domestic tragedy.)

Instead I spoke to Bill. 'Bill, this is your last chance. If you want to stay in Golden Rule, now is the time to leave. After you have had dinner, I mean. But after dinner we are going down to the Moon. You can come with us, or stay here.'

Bill looked startled, 'Did *she* say I got a choice?'

Gwen said sharply, 'Of course you do! You can come with us . . . in which case I shall require you to behave like a civilized human being at all times. Or you can remain in Golden Rule and go back to your turf – and tell Fingers you botched the job he got you.'

'I didn't botch it! *He* did.'

Meaning me – I said, 'That does it, Gwen. He resents me. I don't want him around – much less have to support him. He'll slip poison into my soup some night.'

'Oh, Bill wouldn't do that. Would you, Bill?'

I said, 'Oh, wouldn't he? Notice how quick he is to answer? Gwen, earlier today he tried to shoot me. Why should I put up with his surly behavior?'

'Richard, please! You can't expect him to get well all at once.'

This feckless discussion was cut short by Mr Kondo returning to the table to arrange it for dinner . . . including hold-down clips for our little tree. One tenth of Earth-normal gravity is enough to hold food on a plate, hold feet against the floor – but just barely. The chairs here were fastened to the floor; there were seat belts on them if you wished to use them – I didn't but a belt does have its points if you have to cut tough steak. Tumblers and cups had lids and sidesippers. The last was perhaps the most needed adaptation; you can easily scald yourself picking up a cup of hot coffee in a tenth gee – the weight is nothing but the inertia is undiminished . . . and so it slops, all over you.

As Mr Kondo was placing flatware and sticks at my place he said quietly into my ear, 'Senator, is it possible that you were present at the Solis Lacus drop?'

I answered heartily, 'I certainly was, mate! You were there, too?'

He bowed. 'I had that honor.'

'What outfit?'

'Go for Broke, Oahu.'

'Old "Go for Broke,"' I said reverently. 'The most decorated outfit in all history. Proud, man, proud!'

'On behalf of my comrades I thank you. And you, sir?'

'I dropped with . . . Campbell's Killers.'

Mr Kondo drew air through his teeth. 'Ah, so! Proud indeed.' He bowed again and went quickly into the kitchen.

I stared glumly at my plate. Caught out – Kondo had recognized me. But when the day comes that, asked point blank, I deny my comrades, don't bother to check my pulse, don't even bother to cremate me – just haul me out with the swill.

'Richard?'

'Huh? Yes, dear?'

'May I be excused?'

'Certainly. Do you feel all right?'

'Quite all right, thank you, but I have something to take care of.' She left, headed for the passage leading to the lounges and the exit, moving in that featherlight motion that is dancing rather than walking – at a tenth gee real walking can be

accomplished only by wearing grips, magnetic or otherwise –
or very long practice; Mr Kondo was not wearing grips – he
glided like a cat.

'Senator?'

'Yes, Bill?'

'Is she mad at me?'

'I don't think so.' I was about to add that I would be dis-
pleased with him if he persisted in – then shut up in my mind.
Threatening to leave Bill behind was too much like beating a
baby; he had no armor. 'She simply wants you to stand tall and
not blame other people for your acts. Not make excuses.'

Having delivered myself of my favorite duck-billed platitude
I went back to glum self-assessment. *I* make excuses. Yes, but
not out loud, just to myself. That's an excuse in itself, chum
– whatever you've done, whatever you've been, is all, totally,
one hundred percent, your own fault. All.

Or to my credit. Yes, but damned little. Come on, be
truthful.

But look where I started . . . and still got all the way up to
colonel.

In the most whoreson, chancre-ridden, thieving, looting
gang of thugs since the Crusades.

Don't talk that way about the Regiment!

Very well. But they aren't the Coldstream Guards, are they?
Those dudes! Why, just one platoon of Campbell's—

Dreck.

Gwen returned, having been gone – oh, quite a time. I hadn't
checked the time when she left but it was now, I saw, almost
eighteen. I tried to stand – not practical with both table and
chair bolted down. She asked, 'Have I held up dinner?'

'Not a bit. We ate, and threw the leavings to the pigs.'

'All right. Mama-San won't let me go hungry.'

'And Papa-San won't serve without you.'

'Richard. I did something without consulting you.'

'I don't see anything in the book that says that you have to.
Can we square it with the cops?'

'Nothing like that. You've noticed the fezzes around town
all day – excursionists up from the Shriners convention in
Luna City.'

'So that's what they are. I thought Turkey had invaded us.'

'If you like. But you've seen them today, wandering up and down the Lane and the Camino, buying anything that doesn't bite. I suspect that most of them are not staying overnight; they have a full program in Luna City and have hotel rooms there already paid for. The late shuttles are sure to be crowded—'

'With drunk Turks, woofing into their fezzes. And onto the cushions.'

'No doubt. It occurred to me that even the twenty o'clock schedule is likely to be fully booked rather early. So I bought tickets for us and reserved couches.'

'And now you're expecting me to pay you back? Submit a claim and I'll pass it along to my legal department.'

'Richard, I was afraid we would not get away from here at all tonight.'

'Mistress Hardesty, you continue to impress me. What was the total?'

'We can straighten out finances another time. I just felt that I could eat dinner in a happier frame of mind if I was sure that we could get away promptly after dinner. And, uh –' She paused, looked at Bill. 'Bill.'

'Yes, ma'am?'

'We are about to eat dinner. Go wash your hands.'

'Huh?'

'Don't grunt. Do as I tell you.'

'Yes, ma'am.' Bill got up docilely, went out.

Gwen turned back to me. 'I was antsy. Fidgety. Because of the Limburger.'

'What Limburger?'

'Your Limburger, dear. It was part of what I salvaged from your larder, then I put it out on the cheese and fruit tray when we had lunch. There was a little hundred-gram wedge, untouched, still in its wrapping, when we finished. Rather than throw it away, I put it in my purse. I thought it might make a nice snack—'

'Gwen.'

'All right, all right! I saved it on purpose . . . because I've used it in looking-glass warfare before this. It's much nicer than some of the things on the list. Why, you wouldn't believe what nasty—'

'Gwen. I wrote the list. Stick to your muttons.'

'In Mr Sethos's office, you will remember that I was seated almost against the bulkhead – and right by the main ventilation discharge. Quite a draft against my legs and uncomfortably warm. I got to thinking—'

'Gwen.'

'They're all alike, all through the habitat – local control, both on heat and volume. And the louvre just snaps on. While Accounting was working up our final statement, the Manager was studiously ignoring us. I turned the volume down and the heat to neutral, and snapped off the cover. I rubbed Limburger cheese all over the vanes of the heat exchanger, and tossed the rest of the package as far back into the duct as I could manage, and put the louvre back on. Then, just before we left, I turned the heat control to "cold" and turned the volume up.' She looked worried. 'Are you ashamed of me?'

'No. But I'm glad you're on my side. Uh . . . you *are* – aren't you?'

'Richard!'

'But I'm even gladder that we have reservations on the next shuttle. I wonder how long it will be until Sethos feels chilly and turns up the heat?'

What we had for dinner was delicious and I don't know the names of any of it, so I'll let it go at that. We had just reached the burping stage when Mr Kondo came out, leaned close to my ear, and said, 'Sir, come, please.'

I followed him into the kitchen. Mama-San looked up from her work, paid no more attention. The Reverend Doctor Schultz was there, looking worried. 'Trouble?' I asked.

'Just a moment. Here's your pic of Enrico; I've copied it. Here are the papers for Bill; please look them over.'

They were in a worn envelope, and the papers were creased and worn and somewhat yellowed and more than somewhat soiled in places. Hercules Manpower, Inc., had hired William No-Middle-Name Johnson, of New Orleans, Duchy of Mississippi, Lone Star Republic, and had in turn sold his indenture to Bechtel High Construction Corp. (bond endorsed for space, free fall, and vacuum) – who had in turn sold the indenture to Dr Richard Ames, Golden Rule habitat, circum Luna. Etc.,

etc. – lawyer talk. Stapled to the indenture was a very sincere birth certificate showing that Bill was a foundling, abandoned in Metairie Parish, with an assigned date of birth three days earlier than the date he was found.

'Much of that is true,' Dr Schultz told me. 'I was able to wheedle some old records out of the master computer.'

'Does it matter whether or not it's true?'

'Not really. As long as it is sincere enough to get Bill out of here.'

Gwen had followed me in. She took the papers from me, read them. 'I'm convinced. Father Schultz, you're an artist.'

'A lady of my acquaintance is an artist. I will convey your compliment. Friends, now the bad news. Tetsu, will you show them?'

Mr Kondo moved back in the kitchen; Mama-San (Mrs Kondo, I mean) stepped aside. Mr Kondo switched on a terminal. He punched up the *Herald*, cycled it for something – spot news I assume. I found myself staring at myself.

With me, in split screen, was Gwen – a poor likeness of her. I would not have recognized her but for the sound repeating:

'– Ames. Mistress Gwendolyn Novak. The female is a notorious confidence woman who has fleeced many victims, mostly male, around the bars and restaurants of Petticoat Lane. The self-styled "Doctor" Richard Ames, no visible means of support, has disappeared from his address at ring sixty-five, radius fifteen, at point four gee. The shooting took place at sixteen-twenty this afternoon in Golden Rule Partner Tolliver's office—'

I said, 'Hey! That time is wrong. We were—'

'Yes, you were with me, at the Farm. Hear the rest.'

'– according to eyewitnesses both killers fired shots. They are believed armed and dangerous; use extreme caution in apprehending them. The Manager is grief stricken at the loss of his old friend and has offered a reward of ten thousand crowns for—'

Dr Schultz reached over and shut it off. 'It just repeats now; it's on a loop. But it appears as a spot announcement on all channels. By now, most habitants must have seen and heard it.'

'Thanks for warning us. Gwen, don't you know better than to shoot people? You're a naughty girl.'

'I'm sorry, sir. I fell into bad company.'

'Excuses again. Reverend, what in hell are we going to do? That bastich will space us before bedtime.'

'That thought occurred to me. Here, try this on for size.' From somewhere about his ample person he produced a fez.

I tried it on. 'Fits well enough.'

'And now this.'

It was a black velvet eyepatch on elastic. I slipped it on, decided that I did not like having one eye covered, but did not say so. Papa Schultz had obviously put effort and imagination into trying to keep me from breathing vacuum.

Gwen exclaimed, 'Oh, goodness! That does it!'

'Yes,' agreed Dr Schultz. 'An eyepatch draws the attention of most observers so strongly that it takes a conscious effort of will to see the features. I always keep one on hand. That fez and the presence of the Nobles of the Mystic Shrine was a happy coincidence.'

'You had a fez on hand?'

'Not exactly. It does have a former owner. When he wakes up, he may miss it . . . but I do not think he will wake up soon. Uh, my friend Mickey Finn is taking care of him. But you might avoid any Shriners from Temple Al Mizar. Their accents may help; they are from Alabama.'

'Doctor, I'll avoid *all* Shriners as much as I can; I think I should board at the last minute. But what about Gwen?'

The Reverend Doctor produced another fez. 'Try it, dear lady.'

Gwen tried it on. It tended to fit down over her like a candle snuffer. She lifted it off. 'I don't think it does a thing for me; it's not right for my complexion. What do you think?'

'I'm afraid you're right.'

I said, 'Doctor, Shriners are twice as big as Gwen in all directions and they bulge in different places. It will have to be something else. Grease paint?'

Schultz shook his head. 'Grease paint always looks like grease paint.'

'That's a very bad likeness of her on the terminal. Nobody could recognize her from that.'

'Thank you, my love. Unfortunately there are a good many people in Golden Rule who do know what I look like . . . and just one of them at the boarding lock tonight could lower my life expectancy drastically. Hmm. With just a little effort and no grease paint I could look my right age. Papa Schultz?'

'What is your right age, dear lady?'

She glanced at me, then stood on tiptoes and whispered in Dr Schultz's ear. He looked surprised. 'I don't believe it. And, no, it won't work. We need something better.'

Mrs Kondo spoke quickly to her husband; he looked suddenly alert; they exchanged some fast chatter in what had to be Japanese. He shifted to English. 'May I, please? My wife has pointed out that Mistress Gwen is the same size, very nearly, as our daughter Naomi – and, in any case, kimonos are quite flexible.'

Gwen stopped smiling. 'It's an idea – and I thank you both. But I don't look Nipponese. My nose. My eyes. My skin.'

There was some more batting around of that fast but long-winded language, three-cornered this time. Then Gwen said, 'This could extend my life. So please excuse me.' She left with Mama-San.

Kondo went back into his main room – there had been lights asking for service for several minutes; he had ignored them. I said to the good Doctor, 'You have already extended our lives, simply by enabling us to take refuge with Tiger Kondo. But do you think we can carry this off long enough to board the shuttle?'

'I hope so. What more can I say?'

'Nothing, I guess.'

Papa Schultz dug into a pocket. 'I found opportunity to get you a tourist card from the gentleman who lent you that fez . . . and I have removed his name. What name should go on it? It can't be "Ames" of course – but what?'

'Oh. Gwen reserved space for us. Bought tickets.'

'By your right names?'

'I'm not certain.'

'I do hope not. If she used "Ames" and "Novak" the best you can hope for is to try to be first in line for no-shows. But I had better hurry to the ticket counter and get reservations for you as "Johnson" and—'

'Doc.'

'Please! On the next shuttle if this one is booked solid.'

'You can't. *You* make reservations for *us* and – *phtt!* You're spaced. It may take them till tomorrow to figure it out. But they will.'

'But—'

'Let's wait and see just what Gwen did. If they aren't back in five minutes, I'll ask Mr Kondo to dig them out.'

A few minutes later a lady came in. Father Schultz bowed and said, 'You're Naomi. Or are you Yumiko? Good to see you again, anyhow.'

The little thing giggled and sucked air and bowed from the waist. She looked like a doll – fancy kimono, little silk slippers, flat white makeup, an incredible Japanese hairdo. She answered, 'Ichiban geisha girr is awr. My Ingris are serdom.'

'Gwen!' I said.

'Prease?'

'Gwen, it's wonderful! But tell us, fast, the names you used in making our reservations.'

'Ames and Novak. To match our passports.'

'That tears it. What'll we do, Doc?'

Gwen looked back and forth between us. 'Pray tell me the difficulty?'

I explained. 'So we go to the gate, each of us well disguised – and show reservations for Ames and Novak. Curtain. No flowers.'

'Richard, I didn't quite tell you everything.'

'Gwendolyn, you never do quite tell everything. More Limburger?'

'No, dear. I saw that it might turn out this way. Well, I suppose you could say that I wasted quite a lot of money. But I – Uh, after I bought our tickets – tickets we can't use now and are wasted – I went to Rental Row and put a deposit on a U-Pushit. A Volvo Flyabout.'

Schultz said, 'Under what name?'

I said, 'How much?'

'I used my right name—'

Schultz said, 'God help us!'

'Just a moment, sir. My right name is Sadie Lipschitz . . . and only Richard knows it. And now you. Please keep it to yourself, as I don't like it. As Sadie Lipschitz I reserved the Volvo for my employer, Senator Richard Johnson, and placed a deposit. Six thousand crowns.'

I whistled. 'For a *Volvo?* Sounds like you bought it.'

'I did buy it, dear; I had to. Both rental and deposit had to be cash because I didn't have a credit card. Oh, I do have; I have enough cards to play solitaire. But *Sadie Lipschitz* has no credit. So I had to pay six thousand down simply to reserve it – to rent it but on a purchase contract. I tried to get him down a bit but with all the Shriners in town he was sure he could move it.'

'Probably right.'

'I think so. If we take it, we still have to complete payment on the full list price, another nineteen thousand crowns—'

'My God!'

'– plus insurance and squeeze. But we get the unused balance back if we turn it in here, or Luna City, or Hong Kong Luna, in thirty days. Mr Dockweiler explained the reason for the purchase contract. Asteroid miners, or boomers rather, had been hiring cars without putting up the full price, taking them to some hideout on Luna, and refitting them for mining.'

'A *Volvo?* The only way you could get a Volvo to the asteroids would be by shipping it in the hold of a Hanshaw. But nineteen – no, twenty-five thousand crowns. Plus insurance and graft. Bald, stark robbery.'

Schultz said to me rather sharply, 'Friend Ames, I suggest that you stop behaving like the fabled Scotsman faced by a coin-operated refresher. Do you accept what Mrs Ames could arrange? Or do you prefer the Manager's fresh-air route? Fresh – but thin.'

I took a deep breath. 'Sorry. You're right, I can't breathe money. I just hate to get clipped. Gwen, I apologize. All right, where is Hertz from here? I'm disoriented.'

'Not Hertz, dear. Budget Jets. Hertz did not have a unit left.'

IX

'Murphy was an optimist.' *(O'Toole's commentary on Murphy's Law, as cited by A. Bloch)*

To REACH the office of Budget Jets we had to go around the end of the spaceport waiting room and into it at the axis, then directly to Budget's door. The waiting room was crowded – the usual lot, plus Shriners and their wives, most of them belted to wall rests, some floating free. And proctors – too many of them.

Perhaps I should explain that the waiting room – and the booking office and the lock to the passenger tunnel and the offices and facilities of Rental Row – are all in free fall, weightless; they do not take part in the stately spin that gives the habitat its pseudo-gravity. The waiting room and related activities are in a cylinder inside a much larger cylinder, the habitat itself. The two cylinders share a common axis. The big one spins; the smaller one does not – like a wheel turning on an axle.

This requires a vacuum seal at the outer skin of the habitat where the two cylinders touch – a mercury type, I believe, but I've never seen it. The point is that, even though the surrounding habitat spins, the habitat's spaceport must *not* spin, because a shuttle (or a liner, or a freighter, or even a Volvo) requires a steady place in free fall to dock. The docking nests for Rental Row are a rosette around the main docking facility.

In going through the waiting room I avoided eye contact and went straight to my destination, a door in a forward corner of the waiting room. Gwen and Bill were tailed up behind me. Gwen had her purse hooked over her neck and was guarding the bonsai maple with one arm and clinging to my ankle with her other hand; Bill was holding on to one of her ankles and

91

towing a package wrapped in Macy's wrapping, with Macy's logo prominent on it. I don't know what that wrapping paper originally covered but it now concealed Gwen's smaller case, her not-clothes.

Our other baggage? Following the first principle of saving one's neck, we'd chucked it. It would have marked us as phony – for a one-day side trip Shriners on holiday do not carry great loads of baggage. Gwen's smaller case we could salvage because, disguised with Macy's wrapping, it looked like the sort of shopping many of the Shriners had obviously done. And so did the little tree – just the sort of awkward, silly purchase tourists indulge in. But the rest of our baggage had to be abandoned.

Oh, perhaps it could be shipped to us someday, if safe means could be worked out. But I had written it off our books. Doc Schultz, by scolding me for crabbing over the cost of the deal Gwen had arranged, had reoriented me. I had let myself become soft and sedentary and domesticated – he had forced me to shift gears to the real world, where there are only two sorts: the quick and the dead.

A truth of which I again became acutely aware in crossing that waiting room: Chief Franco came in behind us. He appeared to be unaware of us and I strove to appear unaware of him. He seemed intent only on reaching a group of his henchmen guarding the lock to the passenger tunnel; he dived straight toward them while I was pulling my little family along a lifeline stretching from the entrance to the corner I wanted to reach.

And did reach it and got through Budget Jets' door, and it contracted behind us and I breathed again and reswallowed my stomach.

In the office of Budget Jets we found the manager, a Mr Dockweiler, belted at his desk, smoking a cigar, and reading the Luna edition of the *Daily Racing Form*. He looked around as we came in and said, 'Sorry, friends, I don't have a thing to rent or sell. Not even a witch's broom.'

I thought about who I was – Senator Richard Johnson, representing the enormously wealthy systemwide syndicate of sassafras sniffers, one of the most powerful wheeler-dealers at

The Hague – and let the Senator's voice speak for me. 'Son, I'm Senator Johnson. I do believe that one of my staff made a reservation in my name earlier today – for a Hanshaw Superb.'

'Oh! Glad to meet you, Senator,' he said as he clipped his paper to his desk and unfastened his seat belt. 'Yes, I do have your reservation. But it's not a Superb. It's a Volvo.'

'*What!* Why, I distinctly told that girl – Never mind. Change it, please.'

'I wish I could, sir. I don't have anything else.'

'Regrettable. Would you be so kind as to consult your competitors and find me a—'

'Senator, there is not a unit left for rent anywhere in Golden Rule. Morris Garage, Lockheed-Volkswagen, Hertz, Interplanet – we've all been querying each other the past hour. No soap. No go. No units.'

It was time to be philosophical. 'In that case I had better drive a Volvo, hadn't I, son?'

The Senator again got just a touch cranky when required to pony up full list price on what was clearly a much-used car – I complained about dirty ashtrays and demanded that they be vacuumed out . . . then I said not to bother (when the terminal behind Dockweiler's head stopped talking about Ames and Novak) and said, 'Let's check the mass and available delta vee; I want to lift.'

For a mass reading Budget Jets does not use a centrifuge but the newer, faster, cheaper, much more convenient, elastic inertiometer – I just wonder if it is as accurate. Dockweiler had us all get into the net at once (all but the bonsai, which he shook and wrote down as two kilos – near enough, maybe), asked us to hug each other with the Macy's package held firmly amongst us three, then pulled the trigger on the elastic support – shook our teeth out, almost; then he announced that our total mass for lift was 213.6 kilos.

A few minutes later we were strapping to the cushions and Dockweiler was sealing the nose and then the inner door of the nest. He had not asked for IDs, tourist cards, passports, or motor vehicle pilot's licenses. But he had counted that nineteen thousand twice. Plus insurance. Plus cumshaw.

93

I punched '213.6 kg' into my computer pilot, then checked my instrument board. Fuel read 'full' and all the idiot lights showed green. I pushed the 'ready' button and waited. Dockweiler's voice reached us via the speaker: 'Happy landing!'

'Thank you.'

The air charge went *Whumpf!* and we were out of the nest and in bright sunlight. Ahead and close was the exterior of the spaceport. I squeezed the precess control for a one-eighty reverse. As we swung, the habitat moved away and into my left viewport; ahead the incoming shuttle came into view – I did nothing about her; she had to keep clear of me, since I was undocking – and, into my right viewport came one of the most impressive sights in the system: Luna from close up, a mere three hundred kilometers – I could reach out and touch her.

I felt grand.

Those lying murdering scoundrels were left behind and we were forever out of reach of Sethos's whimsical tyranny. At first, living in Golden Rule had seemed happily loose and carefree. But I had learned. A monarch's neck should always have a noose around it – it keeps him upright.

I was in the pilot's couch; Gwen had the copilot's position on my right. I looked toward her and then realized that I was still wearing that silly eyepatch. No, delete 'silly' – it had, quite possibly, saved my life. I took it off, stuffed it into a pocket. Then I took that fez off, looked around for somewhere to put it – tucked it under my chest belt. 'Let's see if we are secure for space,' I said.

'Isn't it a little late for that, Richard?'

'I always do my check-off lists after I lift,' I told her. 'I'm the optimistic type. You have a purse and a large package from Macy's; how are they secured?'

'They are not, as yet. If you will refrain from goosing this craft while I do it, I'll unstrap and net them.' She started to unstrap.

'Woops! Before unstrapping you must get permission from the pilot.'

'I thought I had it.'

'You do now. But don't make that mistake again. Mr

Christian, His Majesty's Ship *Bounty* is a taut ship and will remain that way. Bill! How are you doing back there?'

''M okay.'

'Are you secure in all ways? When I twist her tail, I don't want any loose change flying around the cabin.'

'He's belted in properly,' Gwen assured me. 'I checked him. He is holding Tree-San's pot flat against his tummy and he has my promise that, if he lets go of it, we will bury him without rites.'

'I'm not sure it will stand up under acceleration.'

'Neither am I but there was no way to pack it. At least it will be in the correct attitude for acceleration – and I'm reciting some spells. Dear man, what can I do with this wig? It's the one Naomi uses for public performances; it's valuable. It was sweet indeed for her to insist that I wear it – it was the final, convincing touch, I think – but I don't see how to protect it. It's at least as sensitive to acceleration as Tree-San.'

'Durned if I know – and that's my official opinion. But I doubt that I will need to push this go-buggy higher than two gee.' I thought about it. 'How about the glove compartment? Take all of the Kleenex out of the dispenser and crumple it up around the wig. And some inside it. Will that work?'

'I think so. Time enough?'

'Plenty of time. I made a quick estimate at Mr Dockweiler's office. In order to land at Hong Kong Luna port and in sunlight I should start moving into a lower orbit about twenty-one hundred. Loads of time. So go ahead, do whatever you need to do . . . while I tell the computer pilot what I want to do. Gwen, can you read all the instruments from your side?'

'Yes, sir.'

'Okay, that's your job, that and the starboard viewport. I'll stick to power, attitude, and this baby computer. By the way, you're licensed, aren't you?'

'No point in asking me now, is there? But let not your heart be troubled, dear; I was herding sky junk before I was out of high school.'

'Good.' I did not ask to see her license – as she had pointed out, it was too late to matter.

And I had noticed that she had not answered my question.

*   *   *

(If ballistics bores you, here is another place to skip.)

A daisy-clipping orbit of Luna (assuming that Luna has daisies, which seems unlikely) takes an hour and forty-eight minutes and some seconds. Golden Rule, being three hundred kilometers higher than a tall daisy, has to go farther than the circumference of Luna (10,919 kilometers), namely 12,805 kilometers. Almost two thousand kilometers farther – so it has to go faster. Right?

Wrong. (I cheated.)

The most cock-eyed, contrary to all common sense, difficult aspect of ballistics around a planet is this: To speed up, you slow down; to slow down, you speed up.

I'm sorry. That's the way it is.

We were in the same orbit as Golden Rule, three hundred klicks above Luna, and floating along with the habitat at one and a half kilometers per second (1.5477 k/s is what I punched into the pilot computer . . . because that was what it said on the crib sheet I got in Dockweiler's office). In order to get down to the surface I had to get into a lower (and faster) orbit . . . and the way to do that was to slow down.

But it was more complex than that. An airless landing requires that you get down to the lowest (and fastest) orbit . . . but you have to kill that speed so that you arrive at contact with the ground at zero relative speed – you must keep bending it down so that contact is straight down and without a bump (or not much) and without a skid (or not much) – what they call a 'synergistic' orbit (hard to spell and even harder to calculate).

But it can be done. Armstrong and Aldrin did it right the first time. (No second chances!) But despite all their careful mathematics it turned out there was one hell of a big rock in their way. Sheer virtuosity and a hatful of fuel bought them a landing they could walk away from. (If they had not had that hatful of fuel left, would space travel have been delayed half a century or so? We don't honor our pioneers enough.)

There is another way to land. Stop dead right over the spot where you want to touch down. Fall like a rock. Brake with your jet so precisely that you kiss the ground like a juggler catching an egg on a plate.

One minor difficulty – Right-angled turns are about the most no-good piloting one can do. You waste delta vee something scandalous – your boat probably doesn't carry that much fuel. ('Delta vee' – pilot's jargon for 'change in velocity' because, in equations, Greek letter delta means a fractional change and 'v' stands for velocity – and please remember that 'velocity' is a direction as well as a speed, which is why rocket ships don't make U-turns.)

I set about programming into the Volvo's little pilot computer the sort of synergistic landing Armstrong and Aldrin made but one not nearly as sophisticated. Mostly I had to ask the piloting computer to call up from its read-only memory its generalized program for landing from an orbit circum Luna . . . and it docilely admitted that it knew how . . . and then I had to inject data for this particular landing, using the crib sheet supplied by Budget Jets.

Finished with that, I told the computer pilot to check what I had entered; it reluctantly conceded that it had all it needed to land at Hong Kong Luna at twenty-two hundred hours seventeen minutes forty-eight point three seconds.

Its clock read 1957. Just twenty hours ago a stranger calling himself 'Enrico Schultz' had sat down uninvited at my table in Rainbow's End – and five minutes later he was shot. Since then, Gwen and I had wed, been evicted, 'adopted' a useless dependent, been charged with murder, and run for our lives. A busy day! – and not yet over.

I had been living in humdrum safety much too long. Nothing gives life more zest than running for your life. 'Copilot.'

'Copilot aye aye!'

'This is fun! Thank you for marrying me.'

'Roger, Captain darling! Me, too!'

This was my lucky day, no doubt about it! A lucky break in the timing had kept us alive. At this instant Chief Franco must be checking every passenger entering the twenty o'clock shuttle, waiting for Dr Ames and Mistress Novak to claim their reservations – while we were already out the side door. But, while that critical timing saved our lives, Lady Luck was still handing out door prizes.

How? From Golden Rule's orbit our easiest landing on Luna would involve putting down at some point on the terminator – least fuel consumed, smallest delta vee. Why? Because we were already on that terminator line, going pole to pole, south

97

to north, north to south, so our simplest landing was to bend it down where we were, never change our heading.

To land in the east-west direction would involve throwing away our present motion, then expending still more delta vee making that foolish right-angle turn – then programming for landing. Maybe your bank account can afford this waste; your skycar cannot – you're going to find yourself sitting up there with no fuel and nothing under you but vacuum and rocks. Unappetizing.

To save our necks I was happy to accept any landing field on Luna . . . but that door prize from Lady Luck included landing at my preferred field (Hong Kong Luna) just about daybreak there, with only an hour spent parked in orbit waiting for the time to tell the computer pilot to take us down. What more could I ask for?

At the moment we were floating over the backside of the Moon – as corrugated as the backside of an alligator. Amateur pilots do not land on the far side of Luna for two reasons: 1) mountains – the side of the Moon turned away from Earth makes the Alps look like Kansas; 2) settlements – there aren't any to speak of. And let's not speak of settlements that aren't to speak of, because it might make some unspeakable settlers quite angry.

In another forty minutes we would be over Hong Kong Luna just as sunrise was reaching it. Before that time I would ask for clearance to land and for ground control on the last and touchiest part of landing – then spend the next two hours in going around behind again and gently lowering the Volvo down for landing. Then it would be time to turn control over to Hong Kong Luna ground control but, I promised myself, I would stay on overrides and work the landing myself, just for drill. How long had it been since I had shot an airless landing myself? Callisto, was it? What year was that? Too long!

At 2012 we passed over Luna's north pole and were treated to earthrise . . . a breathtaking sight no matter how many times one has seen it. Mother Earth was in half phase (since we were ourselves on Luna's terminator) with the lighted half to our left. It being only days past summer solstice, the north polar cap was tilted into full sunlight, dazzling bright. But North

America was almost as bright, being heavily cloud-covered except part of the Mexican west coast.

I found that I was holding my breath, and Gwen was squeezing my hand. I almost forgot to call HKL ground control.

'Volvo Bee Jay Seventeen calling HKL Control. Do you read me?'

'Bee Jay Seventeen affirm. Go ahead.'

'Request clearance to land approx twenty-two hundred seventeen forty-eight. Request ground-controlled landing with manual override. I am out of Golden Rule and still in Golden Rule orbit approx six klicks west of her. Over.'

'Volvo Bee Jay Seventeen. Cleared to land Hong Kong Luna approx twenty-two seventeen forty-eight. Shift to satellite channel thirteen not later than twenty-one forty-nine and be ready to accept ground control. Warning: You must start standard descent program that orbit at twenty-one oh-six nineteen and follow it exactly. If at insertion for ground-controlled landing you are off in vector three percent or in altitude four klicks, expect wave off. Control HKL.'

'Roger wilco.' I added, 'I'll bet you don't realize that you are talking to Captain Midnight, the Solar System's hottest pilot' – but I shut off the mike before I said it.

Or so I thought. I heard a reply, 'And this is Captain Hemorrhoid Hives, Luna's nastiest ground-control pilot. You're going to buy me a liter of Glenlivet after I bring you down. If I bring you down.'

I checked that microphone switch – didn't seem to be anything wrong with it. I decided not to acknowledge. Everybody knows that telepathy works best in a vacuum . . . but there ought to be some way for an ordinary Joe to protect himself against supermen.

(Such as knowing when to keep his mouth shut.)

I set the alarm for twenty-one hours, then precessed to attitude straight down and, for the next hour, enjoyed the ride while holding hands with my bride. The incredible mountains of the Moon, taller and sharper than the Himalayas and tragically desolate, flowed by ahead of (under) us. The only sound was the soft murmur of the computer and the sighing

99

of the air scavenger – and a regular, annoying sniff from Bill. I shut out all sound and invited my soul. Neither Gwen nor I felt like talking. It was a happy interlude, as peaceful as the Old Mill Stream.

'Richard! Wake up!'

'Huh? I wasn't asleep.'

'Yes, dear. It's past twenty-one.'

Uh . . . so it was. Twenty-one oh-one and ticking. What happened to the alarm? Never mind that now – I had five minutes and zip seconds to make sure we entered descent program on time. I hit the control to precess, from headstand to bellywhopper backwards – easiest for descent, although supine backwards will work just as well. Or even sideways backwards. Whichever, the jet nozzle *must* point against the direction of motion in order to reduce speed for insertion into landing program – i.e., 'backwards' for the pilot, like the Fillyloo Bird. (But I'm happiest when the horizon looks 'right' for the way I'm belted in; that's why I prefer to put the skycar into bellywhopper backwards.)

As soon as I felt the Volvo start to precess I asked the computer if it was ready to start landing program, using standard code from the list etched on its shell.

No answer. Blank screen. No sound.

I spoke disparagingly of its ancestry. Gwen said, 'Did you punch the execute button?'

'Certainly I did!' I answered and punched it again.

Its screen lit up and the sound came on at teeth-jarring level:

'How do *you* spell comfort? For the wise Luna citizen today, overworked, overstimulated, overstressed, it is spelled C, O, M, F, I, E, S – that's Comfies, the comfort therapists recommend most for acid stomach, heartburn, gastric ulcers, bowel spasm, and simple tummy ache. Comfies! They Do More! Manufactured by Tiger Balm Pharmaceuticals, Hong Kong Luna, makers of medicines you can rely on. C, O, M, F, I, E, S, *Comfies!* They Do More! Ask your therapist.' Some screech owls started singing about the delights of Comfies.

'This damn thing won't turn off!'

'Hit it!'

'Huh?'

'Hit it, Richard.'

I could not see any logic in that but it did meet my emotional needs; I slapped it, fairly hard. It continued to spout inanities about over-priced baking soda.

'Dear, you have to hit it harder than that. Electrons are timid little things but notional; you have to let them know who's boss. Here, let me.' Gwen walloped it a good one – I thought she would crack the shell.

It promptly displayed:

Ready for descent – Zero Time = 21 – 06 – 17.0.

Its clock showed 21 – 05 – 42.7

– which gave me just time to glance at the altimeter radar (which showed 298 klicks above ground, steady) and at the doppler readout, which showed us oriented along our motion-over-ground line, close enough for government work . . . although what I could have done about it in ca. ten seconds I do not know. Instead of using fractional jets paired in couples to control altitude, a Volvo uses gyros and precesses against them – cheaper than twelve small jets and a mess of plumbing. But slower.

Then, all at once, the clock matched the zero time, the jet cut in, shoving us into the cushions, and the screen displayed the program of burns – the topmost being:

$$21 – 06 – 17.0 – 19 \text{ seconds}$$
$$21 – 06 – 36.0$$

Sweet as could be, the jet cut off after nineteen seconds without even clearing its throat. 'See?' said Gwen. 'You just have to be firm with it.'

'I don't believe in animism.'

'You don't? How do you cope with – Sorry, dear. Never mind; Gwen will take care of such things.'

Captain Midnight made no answer. You couldn't truthfully say that I sulked. But, damn it all, animism is sheer super-stition. (Except about weapons.)

I had shifted to channel thirteen and we were just coming up on the fifth burn. I was getting ready to turn control over to

HKL GCL (Captain Hives) when that dear little electronic idiot crashed its RAM – its Random Access Memory on which was written our descent program. The table of burns on the screen dimmed, quivered, shrank to a dot and disappeared. Frantically I punched the reset key – nothing happened.

Captain Midnight, undaunted as usual, knew just what to do. 'Gwen! It lost the program!'

She reached over and clouted it. The burn schedule was not restored – a RAM, once crashed, is gone forever, like a burst soap bubble – but it did boot up again. A cursor appeared in the upper left corner of the screen and blinked inquiringly. Gwen said, 'What time is your next burn, dear? And how long?'

'Twenty-one, forty-seven, seventeen, I think, for, uh, eleven seconds. I'm fairly sure it was eleven seconds.'

'I check you on both figures. So do that one by hand, then ask it to recompute what it lost.'

'Righto.' I typed in the burn. 'After this one I'm ready to accept control from Hong Kong.'

'So we're out of the woods, dear – one burn by hand and then ground control takes over. But we'll recompute just for insurance.'

She sounded more optimistic than I felt. I could not remember what vector and altitude I was supposed to achieve for take-over by ground control. But I had no time to worry about it; I had to set up this burn.

I typed it in:

21 – 47 – 17.0 – 11.0 seconds
21 – 47 – 28.0

I watched the clock and counted with it. At exactly seventeen seconds past 2147 I jabbed the firing button, held it down. The jet fired. I don't know whether I fired it or the computer did. I held my finger down as the seconds ticked off and lifted it exactly on eleven seconds.

The jet kept on firing.

('– run in circles, scream and shout!') I wiggled the firing button. No, it was not stuck. I slapped the shell. The jet kept on roaring and shoving us into the cushions.

Gwen reached over and cut power to the computer. The jet stopped abruptly.

I tried to stop trembling. 'Thank you, Copilot.'

'Yessir.'

I looked out, decided that the ground seemed closer than I liked, so I checked the altimeter radar. Ninety something – the third figure was changing. 'Gwen, I don't think we're going to Hong Kong Luna.'

'I don't think so, either.'

'So now the problem is to get this junk out of the sky without cracking it.'

'I agree, sir.'

'So where are we? An educated guess, I mean. I don't expect miracles.' The stuff ahead – behind, rather; we were still oriented for braking – looked as rough as the back side. Not a place for an emergency landing.

Gwen said, 'Could we face around the other way? If we could see Golden Rule, that would tell us something.'

'Okay. Let's see if it responds.' I clutched the precessing control, told the skycar to swing one-eighty degrees, passing through headstand again. The ground was noticeably closer. Our skycar settled down with the horizon running right and left – but with the sky on the 'down' side. Annoying . . . but all we wanted was to look for our late home, Golden Rule habitat. 'Do you see it?'

'No, I don't, Richard.'

'It must be over the horizon, somewhere. Not surprising, it was pretty far away the last time we looked – and that last burn was a foul blast. A long one. So where are we?'

'When we swung past that big crater – Aristoteles?'

'Not Plato?'

'No, sir. Plato would be west of our track and still in shadow. It could be some ringwall I don't know . . . but that smooth stuff – that fairly smooth stuff – south of us makes me think that it must be Aristoteles.'

'Gwen, it doesn't matter what it is; I've got to try to put this wagon down on that smooth stuff. That fairly smooth stuff. Unless you have a better idea?'

'No, sir, I do not. We're falling. If we speeded up enough to maintain a circular orbit at this altitude, we probably would not have enough fuel to bring her down later. That's a guess.'

I looked at the fuel gauge – that last long, foul blast had wasted a lot of my available delta vee. No elbow room. 'I think your guess is a certainty – so we'll land. We'll see if our little friend can calculate a parabolic descent for this altitude – for I intend to kill our forward speed and simply let her drop, once we are over ground that looks smooth. What do you think?'

'Uh, I hope we have fuel enough.'

'So do I. Gwen?'

'Yes, sir?'

'Honey girl, it's been fun.'

'Oh, Richard! Yes.'

Bill said in a choked voice, 'Uh, I don't think I can—'

I was precessing to put us back into a braking altitude. 'Pipe down, Bill; we're busy!' Altimeter showed eighty something – how long did it take to fall eighty klicks in a one-sixth gee field? Switch on the pilot computer again and ask it? Or do it in my head? Could I trust the pilot computer not to switch on the jet again if I fed it juice?

Better not risk it. Would a straight-line approximation tell me anything? Let's see – Distance equals one half acceleration multiplied by the square of the time, all in centimeters and seconds. So eighty klicks is, uh, eighty thousand, no, eight hund – No, eight *million* centimeters. Was that right?

One-sixth gee – No, half of one sixty-two. So bring it across and take the square root—

One hundred seconds? 'Gwen, how long till impact?'

'About seventeen minutes. That's rough; I just rounded it off in my head.'

I took another quick look inside my skull, saw that in failing to allow for forward vector – the 'fall-around' factor – my 'approximation' wasn't even a wild guess. 'Close enough. Watch the doppler; I'm going to kill some forward motion. Don't let me kill all of it; we'll need some choice in where to put down.'

'Aye, aye, Skipper!'

I switched power to the computer; the jet immediately fired. I let it run five seconds, cut power. The jet sobbed and quit. 'That,' I said bitterly, 'is one hell of a way to handle the throttle. Gwen?'

'Just crawling along now. Can we swing and see where we're going?'

'Sure thing.'

'Senator—'

'Bill – shut *up!*' I tilted it around another hundred and eighty degrees. 'See a nice smooth pasture ahead?'

'It all looks smooth, Richard, but we're still almost seventy klicks high. Should get down pretty close before you kill all your forward speed, maybe? So you can see any rocks.'

'Reasonable. How close?'

'Uh, how does one klick sound?'

'Sounds close enough to hear the wings of the Angel of Death. How many seconds till impact? For one-kilometer height, I mean.'

'Uh, square root of twelve hundred plus. Call it thirty-five seconds.'

'All right. You keep watching height and terrain. At about two klicks I want to start to kill the forward speed. I've got to have time to twist another ninety degrees after that, to back down tail first. Gwen, we should have stayed in bed.'

'I tried to tell you that, sir. But I have faith in you.'

'What is faith without works? I wish I was in Paducah. Time?'

'Six minutes, about.'

'Senator—'

'Bill, shut up! Shall we trim off half the remaining speed?'

'Three seconds.'

I gave a three-second blast, using the same silly method of starting and stopping the jet.

'Two minutes, sir.'

'Watch the doppler. Call it.' I started the jet.

'*Now!*'

I stopped it abruptly and started to precess, tail down, 'windshield' up. 'How does it read?'

'We're as near dead in the water as can be done that way, I think. And I wouldn't fiddle with it; look at that fuel reading.'

I looked and didn't like it. 'All right, I don't blast at all until we are mighty close.' We steadied in the heads-up attitude – nothing but sky in front of us. Over my left shoulder I could see the ground at about a forty-five-degree angle. By looking past Gwen I could see it out the starboard side, too, but at quite a distance – a bad angle, useless. 'Gwen, how long is this buggy?'

'I've never seen one out of a nest. Does it matter?'

'It matters a hell of a lot when I'm judging how far to the ground by looking past my shoulder.'

'Oh. I thought you meant exactly. Call it thirty meters. One minute, sir.'

I was about to give it a short blast when Bill blasted. So the poor devil was space sick but at that instant I wished him dead. His dinner passed between our heads and struck the forward viewport, there spread itself. '*Bill!*' I screamed. 'Stop that!'

(Don't bother to tell me that I made an unreasonable demand.)

Bill did the best he could. He trained his head to the left and deposited his second volley on the left viewport – leaving me flying blind.

I tried. With my eyes on the radar altimeter I gave it a quick blast – and lost that, too. I'm sure that someday they will solve the problem of accurate low-scale readings taken through jet blast and fouled by 'grass' from terrain – I was just born too soon, that's all. 'Gwen, I can't *see!*'

'I have it, sir.' She sounded calm, cool, relaxed – a fit mate for Captain Midnight. She was looking over her right shoulder at the Lunar soil; her left hand was on the power switch to the pilot computer, our emergency 'throttle.'

'Fifteen seconds, sir . . . ten . . . five.' She closed the switch.

The jet blasted briefly, I felt the slightest bump, and we had weight again.

She turned her head and smiled. 'Copilot reports—'

And lost her smile, looked startled, as we felt the car swing.

Did you ever play tops as a kid? You know how a top behaves as it winds down? Around and around, deeper and deeper, as it slowly goes lower, lays itself down and stops? That's what this pesky Volvo did.

Until it lay full length on the surface and rolled. We wound up still strapped, safe and unbruised – and upside down.

Gwen continued, '– reports touchdown, sir.'

'Thank you, Copilot.'

X

'It is useless for sheep to pass resolutions in favor of vegetarianism while wolves remain of a different opinion.'

WILLIAM RALPH INGE, D. D. 1860–1954

'There's one born every minute.'

P. T. BARNUM 1810–1891

I ADDED, 'That was a beautiful landing, Gwen. PanAm never set a ship down more gently.'

Gwen pushed aside her kimono skirt, looked out. 'Not all that good. I simply ran out of fuel.'

'Don't be modest. I especially admired that last little gavotte that laid the car down flat. Convenient, since we don't have a landing-field ladder here.'

'Richard, what made it do that?'

'I hesitate to guess. It may have had something to do with the precessing gyro . . . which may have tumbled. No data, no opinion. Dear, you look charming in that pose. Tristram Shandy was right; a woman looks her best with her skirts flung over her head.'

'I don't think Tristram Shandy ever said that.'

'Then he should have. You have lovely legs, dear one.'

'Thank you. I think. Now will you kindly get me out of this mess? My kimono is tangled in the belt and I can't unfasten it.'

'Do you mind if I get a picture first?'

Gwen sometimes makes unladylike retorts; it is then best to change the subject. I got my own safety belt loose, made a quick, efficient descent to the ceiling by falling on my face, got up and tackled freeing Gwen. Her belt buckle wasn't really a problem; it was just that she could not see to clear it. I did so and made sure that she did not fall as I got her loose – set her on her feet and claimed a kiss. I felt euphoric – only minutes ago I would not have bet even money on landing alive.

Gwen delivered payment and good measure. 'Now let's get Bill loose.'

'Why can't he—'

'He doesn't have his hands free, Richard.'

When I let go my bride and looked, I saw what she meant. Bill was hanging upside down with a look of patient suffering on his face. My – *Our* bonsai maple he held pressed against his belly, the plant unhurt. He looked solemnly at Gwen. 'I didn't drop it,' he said defensively.

I silently granted him absolution for throwing up during touch down. Anyone who can attend to a duty (even a simple one) during the agony of acute motion sickness can't be all bad. (But he must clean it up; absolution did not mean that I would clean up after him. Nor should Gwen. If she volunteered, I was going to be *macho* and husbandly and unreasonable.)

Gwen took the maple and set it on the underside of the computer. Bill unbuckled himself while I supported him by his ankles, then I lowered him to the ceiling and let him straighten himself up. 'Gwen, give Bill the pot and let him continue to take care of it. I want it out of the way . . . as I must get at the computer and the instrument board.' Should I say out loud what was worrying me? No, it might make Bill sick again . . . and Gwen will have figured it out for herself.

I lay down on my back and scrunched under the computer and instrument board, switched on the computer.

A brassy voice I recognized said, '– Seventeen, do you read? Volvo Bee Jay Seventeen, come in. This is Hong Kong Luna ground control calling Volvo Bee Jay Seventeen—'

'Bee Jay Seventeen here, Captain Midnight speaking. I read you, Hong Kong.'

'Why in hell don't you stay on channel thirteen, Bee Jay? You missed your checkpoint. Wave off. I can't bring you down.'

'Nobody can, Captain Hives; I *am* down. Emergency landing. Computer malfunction. Gyro malfunction. Radio malfunction. Jet malfunction. Loss of visibility. On landing we fell off our jacks. Fuel gone and attitude impossible for lift off anyhow. And now the air scavenger has quit.'

There was a fairly long silence. 'Tovarishch, have you made your peace with God?'

'I've been too bloody busy!'

'Hmm. Understandable. How are you fixed for cabin pressure?'

'The idiot light reads green. There's no gauge for it.'

'Where are you?'

'I don't know. Things went sour at twenty-one forty-seven, just before I was to turn control over to you. I've spent the time since on a seat-of-the-pants descent. While I don't know where we are, we should be somewhere on Golden Rule's orbit track; our burns were all carefully oriented. We passed over what I think was Aristoteles at, uh—'

'Twenty-one, fifty-eight,' Gwen supplied.

'Twenty-one, fifty-eight; my copilot logged it. I brought her down in a mare south of there. Lacus Somniorum?'

'Wait one. Did you stay with the terminator?'

'Yes. We still are. Sun is just at horizon.'

'Then you can't be that far east. Time of touch down?'

I didn't have the foggiest. Gwen whispered, 'Twenty-two, oh-three, forty-one.' I repeated, 'Twenty-two, oh-three, forty-one.'

'Hmm. Let me check. In that case you must be south of Eudoxus in the northernmost part of Mare Serenitatis. Mountains west of you?'

'Big ones.'

'Caucasus range. You're lucky; you may yet live to be hanged. There are two inhabited pressures fairly close to you; there may be someone interested in saving you . . . for the pound of flesh nearest your heart, plus ten percent.'

'I'll pay.'

'You surely will! And if you're rescued, don't forget to ask for your bill from us, too; you may need us another day. All right, I'll pass the word. Hold it. Could this be some more of your Captain Midnight nonsense? If it is, I'll cut your liver out and toast it.'

'Captain Hives, I'm sorry about that, truly I am. I was simply kidding with my copilot and I thought my mike was cold. Should have been; I opened the switch. One of my endless problems with this collection of scrap.'

'You shouldn't kid around while maneuvering.'

'I know. But – Oh, what the hell. My copilot is my bride; today is our wedding day – just married. I've felt like laughing and joking all day long; it's that sort of a day.'

'If that is true – okay. And congratulations. But I'll expect you to prove it, later. And my name is Marcy, not Hives. Captain Marcy Choy-Mu. I'll pass the data along and we will try to locate you from orbit. Meantime, you had better get on channel eleven – that's emergency – and start singing Mayday. And I've got traffic, so—'

Gwen was on her hands and knees, by me. 'Captain Marcy!'

'Huh? Yes?'

'I really am his bride and he really did marry me just today and if he weren't a hot pilot, I wouldn't be alive this minute. Everything did go wrong, just as my husband said. It's been like piloting a barrel over Niagara Falls.'

'I've never seen Niagara Falls but I read you. My best wishes, Mrs Midnight. May you have a long and happy life together, and lots of children.'

'Thank you, sir! If someone finds us before our air runs out, we will.'

Gwen and I took turns calling 'Mayday, Mayday!' on channel eleven. When I was off duty, I checked into the resources and equipment of good old Volvo B. J. 17, the clunker. By the Protocol of Brasilia that skycar should have been equipped with reserve water, air, and food, a class two first-aid kid, minimum sanitary facilities, emergency pressure suits (UNSN spec 10007A) for maximum capacity (four, including pilot).

Bill spent his time cleaning viewports and elsewhere, using Kleenex salvaged from the glove compartment – Naomi's wig had come through okay. But he almost burst his bladder before he got up his nerve to ask me what to do. Then I had to teach him how to use a balloon . . . as the skycar's 'minimum sanitary facilities' turned out to be a small package of rude expedients and a pamphlet telling how to use them if you just had to.

The other emergency resources were of the same high standards.

There was water in a two-liter drinking tank at the pilot's position – almost full. No reserve. But nothing to worry about as there was no reserve air, and we would suffocate in stale air before we could die of thirst. The air scavenger still was not working but there was a fitting to crank it by hand – all but the crank handle, which was missing. Food? Let's not joke. But Gwen had a Hershey bar in her purse; she broke it in three and shared it. Delicious!

Pressure suits and helmets occupied most of the storage space back of the passenger couches – four of each, correct by the book. They were military surplus rescue suits, still sealed in their original cartons. Each carton was marked with contractor's name (Michelin Tires, SA) and date (twenty-nine years ago).

Aside from the fact that the plasticizers would have bled out of all plastomers and elastomers – hoses, gaskets, etc. – in that time, and the fact that some roguish japester had neglected to supply air bottles, these pressure suits were just dandy. For a masquerade ball.

Nevertheless I was prepared to trust my life to one of these clown suits for five minutes, or even ten, if the alternative involved exposing my bare face to vacuum.

But if the alternative was merely rassling a grizzly bear, I'd holler, 'Bring on your b'ar!'

Captain Marcy called us, told us that a satellite camera showed us to be at thirty-five degrees seventeen north, fourteen degrees oh seven west. 'I've notified Dry Bones Pressure and Broken Nose Pressure; they're nearest. Good luck.'

I tried to dig out of the computer a call directory for Luna. But it was still sulking; I could not get it to list its own directory. So I tried some test problems on it. It insisted that $2 + 2 = 3.9999999999999999999999$ ... When I tried to get it to admit that $4 = 2 + 2$, it became angry and claimed that $4 = 3.14159265358979323846264338327950288419716939937511$ ... So I gave up.

I left channel eleven switched on at full gain and got up off the ceiling. I found Gwen wearing a powder blue siren suit with a flame-colored scarf at her throat. She looked fetching.

I said to her, 'Sweetheart, I thought all your clothes were still in Golden Rule?'

'I crowded this into the little case when we decided to

abandon baggage. I can't keep up the pretense of being Japanese once I wash my face . . . which, I trust, you have noticed that I have done.'

'Not too well. Especially your ears.'

'Picky, picky! I used only a wet hanky of our precious drinking water. Beloved, I could not pack another safari suit – or whatever – for you. But I do have clean jockey shorts and a pair of socks for you.'

'Gwen, you're not only wholesome; you're efficient.'

'"Wholesome"!'

'But you are, dear. That's why I married you.'

'Hummph! When I figure out just how I've been insulted and how much, you are going to pay . . . and pay and pay and pay and pay!'

This footless discussion was ended by the radio: 'Volvo Bee Jay Seventeen, is that your Mayday? Over.'

'Yes, indeed!'

'This is Jinx Henderson, Happy Chance Salvage Service, Dry Bones Pressure. What do you need?' I described our situation, stated our latitude and longitude.

Henderson answered, 'You got this heap from Budget, right? Which means to me you didn't rent it; you bought it outright on a buy-back contract – I know those thieves. So now you own it. Correct?'

I admitted that I was owner of record.

'You plan to lift off and take it to Hong Kong? If so, what'll you need?'

I thought some long thoughts in about three seconds. 'I don't think this skycar will ever lift from here. It needs a major overhaul.'

'That means hauling it overland to Kong. Yeah, I can do that. Long trip, big job. Meantime personal rescue, two people – right?'

'Three.'

'Okay, three. Are you ready to record a contract?'

A woman's voice cut in. 'Just stop right there, Jinx. Bee Jay Seventeen, this is Maggie Snodgrass, Chief Operator and General Manager of the Red Devil Fire, Police, and Rescue Team, Broken Nose Pressure. Do nothing till you hear my terms . . . 'cause Jinx is fixing to rob you.'

'Hi, Maggie! How's Joel?'

'Fine as silk and meaner than ever. How's Ingrid?'

'Purtier than ever and got another one in the oven.'

'Well, good for you! Congratulations! When's she expecting?'

'Christmas or maybe New Year's, near as we can tell.'

'I'll plan on coming to see her before then. Now are you going to back off and let me treat this gentleman fairly? Or am I going to purely riddle your shell and let all the air out? Yes, I see you, coming over the rise – I started out same time you did, just as soon as Marcy gave the location. I said to Joel, "That's our territory . . . but that lyin' scoundrel Jinx is going to try to steal it right out from under me" – and you didn't let me down, boy; you're here.'

'And planning to stay, Maggie – and quite ready to drop a little non-nuclear reminder right under your treads if you don't behave. You know the rules: Nothing on the surface belongs to nobody . . . unless they sit on it . . . or establish a pressure on it or under it.'

'That's your idea of the rules, not mine. That comes from those lawyer types in Luna City . . . and they don't speak for me and never did. Now let's shift to channel four – unless you want everybody in Kong to hear you beg for mercy and utter your last dying gasp.'

'Channel four it is, Maggie you old windy gut.'

'Channel four. Who'juh hire to make that baby, Jinx? If you were serious about salvage, you'd be out here with a transporter, same as me – instead of your rolligon buggy.'

I had shifted to channel four when they did; I now kept quiet. Each had broken over the horizon about the same time, Maggie from southwest, Jinx from northwest. Since we had come to rest with the main viewport oriented west, we could see them easily. A rolligon lorry (had to be Henderson, from the talk) was in the northwest and a little closer. It had what seemed to be a bazooka mount just forward of its cabin. The transporter was a very long vehicle, with tractor treads at each end and a heavy-duty crane mounted aft. I did not see a bazooka mounted on it but I did see what could have been a Browning 2.54 cm semi.

'Maggie, I hurried out here in the rolly for humanitarian reasons . . . something you wouldn't understand. But my boy Wolf is fetching my transporter, with his sister Gretchen manning the turret. Should be here soon. Shall I call them and tell them to go home? Or hurry along and avenge their pappy?'

'Jinx, you don't really think I'd shoot holes in your cabin, do you?'

'Yes, Maggie, I most surely do think you would. Which would just barely give me time to put one under your treads, that being where I'm aimed right now. On a dead-man trigger. Which would leave me dead . . . and you just sitting there, unable to move, and just waiting for what my kids would do to the party who done in their pappy . . . my turret gun having about three times the reach of your pea shooter. Which is why I got it . . . after Howie come to his death by mischance.'

'Jinx, are you trying to scandalize me with that old tale? Howie was my *partner*. You should be ashamed.'

'Not accusing you of anything, dear. Just cautious. How about it? Wait for my kids and I take all? Or divvy up, nice and polite?'

I simply wished that these enthusiastic entrepreneurs would get on with it. Our air pressure light had blinked red and I was feeling a touch lightheaded. I suppose that roll after landing opened a slow leak. I dithered between a need to tell them to hurry and a realization that my bad bargaining position would drop to zero or even minus if I did so.

Mistress Snodgrass said thoughtfully, 'Well, Jinx, it doesn't make sense to drag this junk to your pressure – north of mine – when it's about thirty klicks closer to take it to Kong by way of my place – south of yours. Right?'

'Simple arithmetic, Maggie. And I have plenty of room in this buggy for three more . . . whereas I'm not sure you could take three passengers even if you stacked them like hotcakes.'

'I could handle them but I'll concede you have more room. All right, you take the three refugees and skin them all your conscience will let you . . . and I'll take the abandoned junker and salvage what I can out of it. If any.'

'Oh, no, Maggie! You're too generous; I wouldn't want to cheat you. Right down the middle. Written records. Confirmed.'

'Why, Jinx, do you think I would cheat you?'

'Let's not debate that, Maggie; it would only cause grief. That skycar is not abandoned; its owner is inside it this very minute. Before you can move it, you must have a release from him . . . based on a recorded contract. If you don't want to be reasonable, he can wait right here for my transporter, and never abandon his property. No salvage, just cartage at hire . . . plus complimentary transportation for the owner and his guests.'

'Mr What's-your-name, don't let Jinx fool you. He gets you and your car to his pressure, he'll peel you like an onion, till there's nothing left of you but the smell. I offer you a thousand crowns cash, right now, for that junk metal you're sitting in.'

Henderson countered, 'Two thousand, and I take you in to pressure. Don't let her swindle you; there is more salvage than she's offering in your computer alone.'

I kept quiet while these two ghouls settled how they were carving us up. When they had agreed, I agreed . . . with only nominal resistance. I objected that the price had gone up and was much too high. Mistress Snodgrass said, 'Take it or leave it.' Jinx Henderson said, 'I didn't get out of a warm bed to lose money on a job.'

I took it.

So we wore those silly shelf-worn suits, almost as gas tight as a wicker basket. Gwen objected that Tree-San must not be exposed to vacuum. I told her to shut up and not be silly; a few moments' exposure would not kill the little maple – and we had run out of air, no choice. Then she was going to carry it. Then she let Bill carry it; she was busy otherwise – me.

You see, I can't wear a pressure suit that has not been especially made for me . . . while wearing my artificial foot. So I had to remove it. So I had to hop. That's okay; I'm used to hopping, and at one-sixth gee hopping is no problem. But Gwen had to mother me.

So here we go – Bill leading off with Tree-San, under instructions from Gwen to get inside fast and get some water from Mr Henderson to spray on it, then Gwen and I followed as Siamese twins. She carried her small case with her left hand and put her right arm around my waist. I had my artificial foot slung over my shoulder, and I used my cane and hopped and steadied myself with my left arm around her shoulders.

How could I tell her that I would have been steadier without her help? I kept my big mouth shut and let her help me.

Mr Henderson let us into the cab, then gasketed it tight and opened an air bottle lavishly – he had been running in vacuum, wearing a suit. I appreciated his lavish expenditure of air mix – oxygen wrested painfully from Luna rock, nitrogen all the way from Earth – until I saw it next day on my bill at a fat price.

Henderson stayed and helped Maggie wrestle old B. J. 17 onto her transporter, running her crane for her while she handled her tread controls, then he drove us to Dry Bones Pressure. I spent part of the time figuring out what it had cost me. I had had to sign away the skycar totally – net just under twenty-seven thousand. I had paid three thousand each to rescue us, discounted to eight thousand as a courtesy . . . plus five hundred each for bed and breakfast . . . plus (I learned later) eighteen hundred tomorrow to drive us to Lucky Dragon Pressure, the nearest place to catch a rolligon bus to Hong Kong Luna.

On Luna it's cheaper to die.

Still, I was happy to be alive at any price. I had Gwen and money is something you can always get more of.

Ingrid Henderson was a most gracious hostess – smiling and pretty and plump (clearly expecting that child). She welcomed us warmly, woke up her daughter, moved her into a shake-down with them, put us in Gretchen's room, put Bill in with Wolf – at which point I realized that Jinx's threats to Maggie were not backed up by force at hand . . . and realized, too, that it was none of my business.

Our hostess said goodnight to us, told us the light in the 'fresher was left on in the night, in case – and left. I looked at my watch before turning out the light.

Twenty-four hours earlier a stranger hight Schultz sat down at my table.

BOOK TWO—
Deadly Weapon

XI

THAT DAMNED fez!

That silly, fake-oriental headdress had been fifty percent of a disguise that had saved my life. But, having used it, the coldly pragmatic thing to do would have been to destroy it.

I did not. I had felt uneasy about wearing it, first because I am not any sort of a Freemason, much less a Shriner, and second because it was not mine; it was stolen.

One might steal a throne or a king's ransom or a Martian princess and feel euphoric about it. But a hat? Stealing a hat was beneath contempt. Oh, I didn't reason this out; I simply felt uneasy about Mr Clayton Rasmussen (his name I found inside his fez) and intended to restore his fancy headgear to him. Someday – Somehow – When I could manage it – When the rain stopped—

As we were leaving Golden Rule habitat, I had tucked it under a belt and forgotten it. After touch down on Luna, as I unstrapped, it had fallen to the ceiling; I had not noticed. As we three were climbing into those breezy escape suits, Gwen had picked it up and handed it to me; I shoved it into the front of my pressure suit and zipped up.

After we reached the Henderson home in Dry Bones Pressure and were shown where we were to sleep, I peeled down with my eyes drooping, so tired I hardly knew what I was doing. I suppose the fez fell out then. I don't know. I just cuddled up to Gwen and went right to sleep – and spent my wedding night in eight hours of unbroken sleep.

I think my bride slept just as soundly. No matter – we had had a grand practice run the night before.

At the breakfast table Bill handed me that fez. 'Senator, you dropped your hat on the floor of the 'fresher.'

Also at the table were Gwen, the Hendersons – Ingrid, Jinx, Gretchen, Wolf – and two boarders, Eloise and Ace, and three small children. It was a good time for me to come out with a brilliant ad-lib that would account for my possession of this funny hat. What I said was, 'Thank you, Bill.'

Jinx and Ace exchanged glances; then Jinx offered me Masonic recognition signs.

That's what I have to assume they were. At the time I simply thought that he was scratching himself. After all, all Loonies scratch because all Loonies itch. They can't help it – not enough baths, not enough water.

Jinx got me alone after breakfast. He said, 'Noble—'

I said, 'Huh?' (Swift repartee!)

'I couldn't miss it that you declined to recognize me there at the table. And Ace saw it, too. Are you by any chance thinking that the deal we made last night wasn't level and on the square?'

(Jinx, you cheated me blind, six ways from zero.) 'Why, nothing of the sort. No complaints.' (A deal is a deal, you swiftie. I don't welch.)

'Are you sure? I've never cheated a lodge brother – or an outsider, for that matter. But I take special care of any son of a widow just the way I would one of my own blood. If you think you paid too much for being rescued, then pay what you think is right. Or you can have it free.'

He added, 'While I can't speak for Maggie Snodgrass, she'll make an accounting to me, and it will be honest; there is nothing small about Maggie. But don't expect that salvage to show too much net. Or maybe a loss by the time she sells it because – You know where Budget gets those crocks they rent, don't you?'

I admitted ignorance. He went on, 'Every year the quality leasers, like Hertz and Interplanet, sell off their used cars. The clean jobs are bought by private parties, mostly Loonies. The stuff needing lots of work goes to boomers. Then Budget Jets buys what's left at junkyard prices, starvation cheap. They rework that junk at their yard outside Loonie City, getting maybe two cars for each three they buy, then they sell as scrap whatever is left over. That jalopy that let you down . . .

they charged you list, twenty-six thousand . . . but if Budget actually had as much as five thousand cash tied up in it, I'll give you the difference and buy you a drink, and that's a fact.

'Now Maggie is going to recondition it again. But her repairs will be honest and her work guaranteed and she'll sell it for what it is – worn out, rebuilt, not standard. Maybe it will fetch ten thousand, gross. After fair charges for parts and labor, if the net she splits with me is more than three thousand, I'll be flabbergasted – and it might be a net loss. A gamble.'

I told a number of sincere lies and managed (I think) to convince Jinx that we were not lodge brothers and that I was not asking for discounts on anything and that I had come by that fez by accident, at the last minute – found it in the Volvo when I hired it.

(Unspoken assumption: Mr Rasmussen had hired that wagon in Luna City, then had left his headpiece in it when he turned in the Volvo at Golden Rule.)

I added that the owner's name was in the fez and I intended to return it to him.

Jinx asked, 'Do you have his address?'

I admitted that I did not – just the name of his temple, embroidered on the fez.

Jinx stuck out his hand. 'Give it to me; I can save you the trouble . . . and the expense of mailing a package back Earthside.'

'How?'

'Happens I know somebody who's bouncing a jumpbug to Luna City on Saturday. The Nobles' convention adjourns on Sunday, right after they dedicate their Luna City Hospital for Crippled and Birth-Damaged Children. There'll be a lost-and-found at the convention center; there always is. Since his name is in it, they'll get it to him – before Saturday evening, because that's the night of the drill team competition . . . and they know that a drill team member – if he is one – without his fez is as undressed as a bar hostess without her G-string.'

I passed the red hat over to him.

I thought that would be the end of it.

More hassle before we could get rolling for Lucky Dragon Pressure – no pressure suits. As Jinx put it: 'Last night I okayed your using those leaky sieves because it was Hobson's Choice – it was risk it, or leave you to die. Today we could use them the same way – or we could even bring the buggy into the hangar and load you in without using suits. Of course that wastes an awful mass of air. Then do it again at the far end . . . for an even greater cost; their hangar is bigger.'

I said I would pay. (I didn't see how I could avoid it.)

'That's not the point. Last night you were in the cab twenty minutes . . . and it took a full bottle to keep air around you. Late last night the Sun was just barely rising; this morning it's five degrees high. Raw sunlight is going to be beating against the side of that cab all the way to Lucky Dragon. Oh, Gretchen will drive in shadow all she can; we don't raise dumb kids. But any air inside the cabin would heat up and swell and come pouring out the cracks. So normal operation is to pressurize your suits but not the cabin, and use the cabin just for shade.

'Now I won't lie to you; if I had suits to sell, I would insist that you buy three new suits. But I don't have suits. Nobody in this pressure has suits for sale. Less than a hundred fifty of us; I would know. We buy suits in Kong and that's what you should do.'

'But I'm not *in* Kong.'

I had not owned a pressure suit for more than five years. Permanent habitants of Golden Rule mostly do not own pressure suits; they don't need them, they don't go outside. Of course there are plenty of staff and maintenance who keep pressure suits always ready the way Bostonians keep overshoes. But the usual habitant, elderly and wealthy, doesn't own one, doesn't need one, wouldn't know how to wear one.

Loonies are another breed. Even today, with Luna City over a million and some city dwellers who rarely if ever go outside, a Loonie owns his suit. Even that big-city Loonie knows from infancy that his safe, warm, well-lighted pressure can be broached – by a meteor, by a bomb, by a terrorist, by a quake or some other unpredictable hazard.

If he's a pioneering type like Jinx, he's as used to a suit as is an asteroid miner. Jinx didn't even work his own tunnel farm; the rest of his family did that. Jinx habitually worked outside, a pressure-suited, heavy-construction mechanic; 'Happy Chance Salvage' was just one of his dozen-odd hats.

He was also the 'Dry Bones Ice Company,' 'Henderson's Overland Cartage Company,' 'John Henry Drilling, Welding, and Rigging Contractors' – or you name it and Jinx would invent a company to fit.

(There was also 'Ingrid's Swap Shop' which sold everything from structural steel to homemade cookies. But not pressure suits.)

Jinx worked out a way to get us to Lucky Dragon: Ingrid and Gwen were much the same size except that Ingrid was temporarily distended around the equator. She had a pregnancy pressure suit with an external corset that could be let out. She also had a conventional suit she wore when not pregnant, one she could not get into now – but Gwen could.

Jinx and I were about of a height, and he had two suits, both first quality Goodrich Luna. I could see that he was about as willing to lend me one as a cabinetmaker is to lend tools. But he was under pressure to work something out, or he was going to have us as paying guests . . . and then as non-paying guests when our money ran out. And they didn't really have room for us even while I could still pay.

It was after ten the next morning before we suited up and climbed into the rolligon – me in Jinx's second best, Gwen in Ingrid's non-pregnant suit, and Bill in a restored antique that had belonged to the founder of Dry Bones Pressure, a Mr Soupie McClanahan, who had come to Luna long, long ago, before the Revolution, as an involuntary guest of the government.

The plan was for each of us to get other temporary coverings at Lucky Dragon Pressure, wear them to HKL, and send them back via the public bus, while Gretchen took these suits back to her father after she let us off at Lucky Dragon. Then, tomorrow, we would be in Hong Kong Luna and able to buy pressure suits to fit our needs.

I spoke to Jinx about payment. I could almost hear the numbers clicking over in his skull. Finally he said, 'Senator, I tell you what. Those suits that came in your heap – not worth much. But there's some salvage in the helmets and in some of the metal fittings. Send my three suits back to me in the shape in which you got 'em and we'll call it even. If you think it is.'

I certainly thought it was. Those Michelin suits had been okay – twenty years ago. To me, today, they were worth nothing.

It left just one problem – Tree-San.

I had thought that I was going to have to be firm with my bride – an intention not always feasible. But I learned that, while Jinx and I had been working out what to do about pressure suits, Gwen had been working out what to do about Tree-San . . . with Ace.

I have no reason to think Gwen seduced Ace. But I'm sure Eloise thought so. However, Loonies have had their own customs about sex since back in the days when men outnumbered women six to one – by Lunar customs all options in sexual matters are vested in women, none in men. Eloise did not seem angry, just amused – which made it none of my business.

As may be, Ace produced a silicone rubber balloon with a slit through which he inserted Tree-San, pot and all, then heat-sealed it – with an attachment for a one-liter air bottle. There was no charge, even for the bottle. I offered to pay, but Ace just grinned at Gwen and shook his head. So I don't know. I don't care to inquire.

Ingrid kissed us all good-bye, made us promise to come back. It seemed unlikely. But a good idea.

Gretchen asked questions the whole trip and never seemed to watch where she was driving. She was a dimpled, pigtailed blonde, a few centimeters taller than her mother but still padded with baby fat. She was much impressed by our travels. She herself had been to Hong Kong Luna twice and once all the way to Novylen where people talked funny. But next year, when she would be going on fourteen, she was going to go to Luna City and look over the studs there – and maybe bring home a husband. 'Mama doesn't want me to have babies by anyone at Dry Bones, or even Lucky Dragon. She says it's a duty I owe my children to go out and fetch in some fresh genes. Do you know about that? Fresh genes, I mean.'

Gwen assured her that we did know and that she agreed

with Ingrid: Outbreeding was a sound and necessary policy. I made no comment but agreed; a hundred and fifty people are not enough for a healthy gene pool.

'That's how Mama got Papa; she went looking for him. Papa was born in Arizona; that's a part of Sweden back groundhog side. He came to Luna with a subcontractor for the Picardy Transmutation Plant and Mama got him at a masked mixer and gave him our family name when she was sure – about Wolf, I mean – and took him back to Dry Bones and set him up in business.'

She dimpled. We were chatting via our suit talkies but I could see her dimples right through her helmet by a happy chance of light. 'And I'm going to do the same for my man, using my family share. But Mama says that I should not grab the first boy who's willing – as if I would! – and not to hurry or worry even if I'm still an old maid at eighteen. And I won't. He's got to be as good a man as Papa is.'

I thought privately that it might be a long search. Jinx Henderson né John Black Eagle is quite a man.

When at last we could see the Lucky Dragon parking lot, it was nearly sundown – in Istanbul, that is, as anyone could see by looking. Earth was almost due south of us and quite high, about sixty degrees; its terminator ran through the north desert of Africa and on up through the Greek Isles and Turkey. The Sun was still low in the sky, nine or ten degrees and rising. There would be nearly fourteen days more sunlight at Lucky Dragon before the next long dark. I asked Gretchen whether or not she intended to drive straight back.

'Oh, no,' she assured me. 'Mama wouldn't like that. I'll stay overnight – bedroll there in the back – and start back fresh tomorrow. After you folks catch your bus.'

I said, 'That isn't necessary, Gretchen. Once we're inside this pressure and can turn our suits back to you, there's no reason for you to wait.'

'Mr Richard, are you yearning to have me spanked?'

'You? "Spanked"? Why, your father wouldn't do that. To *you?* – a grown woman, almost.'

'You might tell Mama that. No, Papa wouldn't; he hasn't for years and years. But Mama says I'm eligible until the day

I first marry. Mama's a holy terror; she's a direct descendant of Hazel Stone. She said, "Gret, you see about suits for them. Take them to Charlie so they won't be cheated. If he can't supply them, then see to it that they wear ours to Kong and you dicker with Lilybet to fetch ours back later. And you had better see them off on the bus, too."'

Gwen said, 'But, Gretchen, your father warned us that the bus doesn't move until the driver has a load. Which could be a day or two. Even several days.'

Gretchen giggled. 'Wouldn't that be terrible? I'd get a vacation. Nothing to do but catch up on the back episodes of *Sylvia's Other Husband*. Let's everybody feel sorry for Gretchen! Mistress Gwen, you can call Mama this minute if you wish . . . but I do have firm instructions.'

Gwen shut up, apparently convinced. We rolled to a stop about fifty meters from Lucky Dragon airlock, set in the side of a hill. Lucky Dragon is in the south foothills of the Caucasus range at thirty-two degrees twenty-seven minutes north. I waited, on one foot and leaning on my cane, while Bill and Gwen gave unnecessary help to a highly efficient young lady in spreading an awning slanted to keep the rolligon from direct sunlight for the next twenty-four hours or so.

Then Gretchen called her mother on the rolly's radio, reported our arrival, and promised to call again in the morning. We went through the airlock, Gwen carrying her case and purse and babying me, Bill carrying Tree-San and the package containing Naomi's wig, and Gretchen carrying a huge bedroll. Once inside, we helped each other shuck down; then I put my foot back on while Gretchen hung up my suit and hers, and Bill and Gwen hung theirs, on long racks opposite the airlock.

Gwen and Bill picked up their burdens and headed for a public 'fresher around to the right of the airlock. Gretchen had turned to follow them when I stopped her. 'Gretchen, hadn't I better wait here till you three get back?'

'What for, Mr Senator?'

'That suit of your papa's is valuable, and so is the one Mistress Gwen is wearing. Maybe everyone here is honest . . . but the suits aren't mine.'

'Oh. Maybe everybody here *is* honest but don't count on it. So Papa says. I wouldn't leave that darling little tree sitting around but don't ever worry about a p-suit; nobody ever touches another Loonie's p-suit. Automatic elimination at the nearest airlock. No excuses.'

'Just like that, eh?'

'Yes, sir. Only it doesn't happen as everybody knows better. But I know about one case, before I was born. A new chum, maybe he didn't know any better. But he never did it again because a posse went after him and brought the p-suit back. But not him. They just left him to dry, there on the rocks. I've seen it, what's left of him. Horrid.' She wrinkled her nose, then dimpled. 'Now, may I be excused, sir? I'm about to wet my panties.'

'Sorry!' (I'm stupid. The plumbing in a man's p-suit is adequate, although just barely. But what the great brains have come up with for women is not adequate. I have a strong impression that most women will endure considerable discomfort rather than use it. I once heard one refer to it disparagingly as 'the sand box.')

At the door of the 'fresher my bride was waiting for me. She held out to me a half-crown coin. 'Wasn't sure you had one, dear.'

'Huh?'

'For the 'fresher. Air I have taken care of; Gretchen paid our one-day fee, so I paid her. We're back in civilization, dear – No Free Lunch.'

No free anything. I thanked her.

I invited Gretchen to have dinner with us. She answered, 'Thank you, sir; I accept – Mama said I could. But would you settle for ice-cream cones for now? – and Mama gave me the money to offer them to you. Because there are several things we should do before dinner.'

'Certainly. We're in your hands, Gretchen; you're the sophisticate; we're the tyros.'

'What's a "tyro"?'

'A new chum.'

'Oh. First we should go to Quiet Dreams tunnel and spread our bedrolls to hold our places so that we can all sleep together' – at which point I learned for the first time why Gretchen's bedroll was so enormous: her mother's foresight, again – 'but before that we had better put your names down with Lilybet for the bus . . . and before that, let's get those ice-cream cones if you're as hungry as I am. Then, last thing before dinner, we should go see Charlie about p-suits.'

The ice-cream cones were close at hand in the same tunnel as the racks: Borodin's Double-Dip Dandies, served by Kelly Borodin himself, who offered to sell me (in addition to lavish cones) used magazines from Earth, barely used magazines from Luna City and Tycho Under, candy, lottery tickets, horoscopes, *Lunaya Pravda*, the *Luna City Lunatic*, greeting cards (genuine Hallmark imitations), pills guaranteed to restore virility, and a sure cure for hangovers, compounded to an ancient Gypsy formula. Then he offered to roll me double or nothing for the cones. Gretchen caught my eye, and barely shook her head.

As we walked away, she said, 'Kelly has two sets of dice, one for strangers, another for people he knows. But he doesn't know that I know it. Sir, you paid for the cones . . . and now, if you don't let me pay you back, I'll get that spanking. Because Mama will ask me and I will have to tell her.'

I thought about it. 'Gretchen, I have trouble believing that your mother would spank you for something *I* did.'

'Oh, but she would, sir! She will say that I should have had my money out and ready. And I should have.'

'Does she spank really hard? Bare bottom?'

'Oh, my, yes! Brutal.'

'An intriguing thought. Your little bottom turning pink, while you cry.'

'I do not cry! Well, not much.'

'Richard.'

'Yes, Gwen?'

'Stop it.'

'Now you listen to me, woman. Do not interfere in my relations with another woman. I—'

'Richard!'

'You spoke, dear?'

'Mama *spank*.'

I accepted from Gretchen the price of the cones. I'm henpecked.

The sign read:

THE APOCALYPSE AND KINGDOM COME BUS COMPANY
Regular Runs to Hong Kong Luna
Minimum Run – twelve (12) fares
Charter runs ANYWHERE by dicker
Next HKL run not before
Noon tomorrow, July 3rd

Sitting under the sign, rocking and knitting, was an elderly black lady. Gretchen addressed her: 'Howdy, Aunt Lilybet!'

She looked up, put down her knitting and smiled. 'Gretchen hon! How's your momma, dear?'

'Just fine. Bigging up by the day. Aunt Lilybet, I want you to meet our friends Mr Senator Richard and Mistress Gwen and Mr Bill. They need to go with you to Kong.'

'Pleased to meet you, friends, and happy to tote you to Kong. Plan on leaving noon tomorrow as you three make ten and if'n I don't get two more by noon, likely I can make it with cargo. That suit?'

I assured her that it did and that we would be here before noon, p-suited and ready to roll. Then she gently suggested cash on the counter by pointing out that there were still seats on the shady side as some passengers had made reservations but had not yet paid. So I paid – twelve hundred crowns for three.

We went next to Quiet Dreams tunnel. I don't know whether to call it a hotel or what – perhaps 'flophouse' comes closest. It was a tunnel a little over three meters wide and running fifty-odd meters back into the rock, where it dead-ended. The middle and lefthand side of the tunnel was a rock shelf about a half meter higher than a walkway on the right. This shelf was laid out in sleeping billets, marked by stripes painted on the shelf and by large numbers painted on the wall. The billet nearest the passageway was numbered '50.' About half the billets had bedrolls or sleeping bags on them.

Halfway down the tunnel, on the right, the customary green light marked a refresher.

At the head of this tunnel, seated and reading at a desk, was a Chinese gentleman in a costume that was out of fashion before Armstrong made that 'one small step.' He wore spectacles as old-fashioned as his dress and he himself appeared to be ninety years older than God and twice as dignified.

As we approached he put down his book and smiled at Gretchen. 'Gretchen. It is good to see you. How are your esteemed parents?'

She curtsied. 'They are well, Dr Chan, and they send you their greetings. May I present our guests Mr Senator Richard and Mistress Gwen and Mr Bill?'

He bowed without getting up and shook hands with himself. 'Guests of the House Henderson are most welcome in my house.'

Gwen curtsied, I bowed, and so did Bill, after I dug a thumb into his ribs – which Dr Chan noticed while declining to notice it. I mumbled an appropriate formality. Gretchen went on.

'We would like to sleep in your care tonight, Dr Chan, if you will accept us. If so, are we early enough to be given four places side by side?'

'Indeed, yes ... for your gracious mother spoke to me earlier. Your beds are numbers four, three, two, and one.'

'Oh, good! Thank you, Grandfather Chan.'

So I paid, for three, not four – I don't know whether Gretchen paid, or ran a bill, or what; I saw no money change hands. Five crowns per person per night, no extra charge for the refresher but two crowns if we wanted to shower – water not limited. Soap extra – half a crown.

Having completed business, Dr Chan said, 'Does not the tree in bonsai require water?'

Almost in chorus we agreed that it did. Our host examined the plastic film that enclosed it, then cut it open and most carefully removed the tree and pot. A vase at his desk turned out to be a water carafe; he filled a tumbler, then, using just his fingertips, he sprinkled it repeatedly. While he did this I sneaked a look at his book – a form of snoopiness I can't resist. It was *The March of the Ten Thousand*, in Greek.

We left Tree-San with him, and Gwen's case as well.

Our next stop was at Jake's Steak House. Jake was as Chinese as Dr Chan but of another generation and style. He greeted us with: 'Howdy, folks. What'll it be? Hamburgers? Or scrambled eggs? Coffee or beer?'

Gretchen spoke to him in a tonal language – Cantonese, I suppose. Jake looked annoyed and retorted. Gretchen threw it back at him. Remarks slammed back and forth. At last he looked disgusted, and said, 'Okay. Forty minutes' – turned his back and walked away. Gretchen said, 'Come, please. Now we go to see Charlie Wang about suits.'

As we walked away she said privately, 'He was trying to get out of doing his best cooking, as it is much more work. But the worst argument was over price. Jake wanted me to keep quiet while he charged you tourist prices. I told him, if he charged you more than he would charge my Papa, then my Papa would stop in next time and cut off his ears and feed them to him, raw. Jake knows that Papa would do exactly that!'

Gretchen smiled with shy pride. 'My Papa is deeply respected in Lucky Dragon. Back when I was young, Papa eliminated a boomer here who tried to take something free from a singsong girl, something he had agreed to pay for. Everybody remembers it. The singsong girls of Lucky Dragon made Mama and me honorary members of their guild.'

The sign read: Wang Chai-Lee, Custom Tailoring for Ladies and Gentlemen – p-suit repairs a speciality. Gretchen again introduced us and explained what we needed. Charlie Wang nodded. 'Bus rolls at noon? Be here at ten-thirty. In Kong you return the suits to my cousin Johnny Wang at Sears Montgomery, p-suit department. I'll call him.'

Then we went back to Jake's Steak House. It wasn't steak and it was not chop suey or chow mein and it was wonderfully good. We ate until we were full to our eyeballs.

When we got back to Quiet Dreams tunnel, the overhead lights were out and many of the billets were occupied by sleeping figures. A glow strip ran down the side of the billets shelf, where it could not shine into the eyes of a sleeping guest but would light the way of anyone moving around. There was a reading light at Dr Chan's desk, shielded from the sleepers. He appeared to be working on his accounts, as he was operating a terminal with one hand and an abacus with the other. He greeted us soundlessly; we whispered goodnight.

Coached by Gretchen we got ready for bed: Undress, fold

your clothing and put it and your shoes under the head of your bedroll as a pillow. I did so, and added my cork foot. But I left on my underwear shorts, having noticed that Gwen and Gretchen had left on their panties – and Bill put his back on when he somewhat belatedly noticed what the rest of us did. We all headed for the refresher.

Even this nominal sop to modesty did not last; we showered together. There were three men in the 'fresher when we went in; all were naked. We followed the ancient precept: 'Nakedness is often seen but never looked at.' And the three men most strictly followed this rule: We weren't there, we were invisible. (Save that I feel certain that no male can totally ignore Gwen and Gretchen.)

I could not totally ignore Gretchen and did not try. Naked, she looked years older and deliciously enticing. I think she had a sunlamp tan. I know she had dimples I had not seen before. I see no need to go into details; all females are beautiful at the point where they burst into full womanhood, and Gretchen had the added beauty of good proportions and a sunny disposition. She could have been used to tempt Saint Anthony.

Gwen handed me the soap. 'All right, dear; you can scrub her back – but she can wash her front herself.'

I answered with dignity, 'I don't know what you're talking about. I don't expect to wash anyone's back, as I need a hand free for grab and balance. You forget that I'm an expectant mother.'

'You're a mother, all right.'

'Who's calling whom a mother? I'll thank you to keep a civil tongue in your head.'

'Richard, this is getting to be beneath even my dignity. Gretchen, you wash his back; that's safest. I'll referee.'

It wound up with everyone washing whatever he/she could reach – even Bill – and was not efficient but fun, with lots of giggles. They were both of the extremely opposite sex and just being around them was fun.

By twenty-two we were settled down for the night. Gretchen at the end wall, Gwen beside her, then me, then Bill. At one-sixth gee a rock shelf is softer than a foam mattress in Iowa. I went to sleep quickly.

Sometime later – an hour? two hours? – I came awake

because a warm body cuddled against me. I murmured, 'Now, hon?' Then I came a bit wider awake. 'Gwen?'

'It's me, Mr Richard. Would you *really* want to see my bottom turn all pink? And hear me cry?'

I whispered tensely, 'Honey, get back over by the wall.'

'Please.'

'No, dear.'

'Gretchen,' Gwen said softly, 'get back where you belong, dear . . . before you wake others. Here, I'll help you roll over me.' And she did, and took the woman-child in her arms and talked to her. They stayed that way and (I think) went to sleep.

It took me quite a while to get back to sleep.

XII

'We are too proud to fight.'

WOODROW WILSON 1856–1924

'Violence never settles anything.'

GENGHIS KHAN 1162–1227

'The mice voted to bell the cat.'

AESOP C. 620–C. 560 B.C.

KISSING GOOD-BYE while wearing pressure suits is depressingly antiseptic. So I think and I am sure Gretchen thought so, too. But that is the way it worked out.

Last night Gwen had saved me from 'a fate worse than death' and for that I was grateful. Well, moderately grateful. Certainly an old man tripped by a barely nubile female not yet into her teens (Gretchen would not be thirteen for another two months) is a ridiculous sight, an object of scorn to all right-thinking people. But, from the time the night before when Gretchen had made it plain to me that she did not consider me too old, I had been feeling younger and younger. By sundown I should be suffering the terminal stages of senile adolescence.

So let the record show that I am grateful. That's official.

Gwen was relieved, I felt sure, when at noon Gretchen waved us goodbye from the cab of her father's rolligon lorry, as we rolled south in Aunt Lilybet's rolligon bus, the *Hear Me, Jesus*.

The *Hear Me* was much larger than Jinx's lorry, and fancier, being painted in bright colors with Holy Land scenes and Bible quotations. It could carry eighteen passengers, plus cargo, driver, and shotgun – the last riding in a turret high above the driver. The bus's tires were enormous, twice as tall as I am; they shouldered up above the passenger space, as its floor rested on the axles, high as my head. There were ladders on each side to reach access doors between the front and rear tires.

Those big tires made it hard to see out to the sides. But Loonies aren't much interested in scenery, as most Lunar scenery is interesting only from orbit. From the Caucasus to the Haemus Mountains – our route – the floor of Mare Serenitatis has hidden charms. Thoroughly hidden. Most of it is flat as a pancake and as interesting as cold pancakes without butter or syrup.

Despite this I was glad that Aunt Lilybet had placed us in the first row on the right – Gwen at the window, me next, Bill on my left. It meant that we could see all that the driver saw out front and also we could see somewhat out to the right because we were forward of the front axle and thereby could see past the tire. We could not see too clearly to the right, as the plastic of the pressure window was old and crazed and yellowed. But forward Aunt Lilybet had her big driver's port raised and fastened back; the view was as clear as our helmets permitted – excellent for us; the equipment rented to us by Charlie Wang took the curse off raw sunlight without noticeably interfering with seeing, like good sun spectacles.

We didn't talk much because passengers' suit radios were all on a common frequency – a babel, so we kept ours turned down. Gwen and I could talk by touching helmets, but not easily. I amused myself by trying to keep track of where we were going. Neither magnetic compasses nor gyro compasses are useful on Luna. Magnetism (usually none) means an ore body rather than a direction, and Luna's spin, while it exists (one revolution per month!), is too leisurely to affect a gyro compass. An inertial tracker will work but a good one is extremely expensive – although I can't see why; the art was perfected long ago for guided missiles.

From this face of Luna you always have Earth to steer by and half the time you have the Sun as well. The stars? Certainly, the stars are always there – no rain, no clouds, no smog. Oh, sure! Look, I have news for any groundhogs listening: You can see stars easier from Iowa than you can from Luna.

You'll be wearing a p-suit, right? Its helmet has a lens and a visor designed to protect your eyes – that amounts to built-in smog. If the Sun is up, forget about stars; your lens has darkened to protect your eyes. If the Sun is not in your sky, then Earth is somewhere between half and full and earthshine is dazzling – eight times as much reflecting surface with five times the albedo makes Earth at least forty times as bright as moonlight is to Earth.

Oh, the stars are there and sharp and bright; Luna is wonderful for astronomical telescopy. But to *see* stars with 'bare' eyes (i.e., from inside your p-suit helmet), just find a meter or two of stove pipe – Wups! no stoves on Luna. So use a couple of meters of air duct. Look through it; it cuts out the dazzle; stars shine out 'like a good deed in a naughty world.'

In front of me Earth was a bit past half phase. On my left the rising Sun was a day and a half high, twenty degrees or less; it made bright the desert floor, with long shadows emphasizing anything other than perfect flatness, thereby making driving easy for Aunt Lilybet. According to a map at the airlock in Lucky Dragon Pressure we had started out from north latitude thirty-two degrees and twenty-seven minutes by longitude six degrees fifty-six east, and were headed for fourteen degrees eleven minutes east by seventeen degrees thirty-two minutes north, a spot near Menelaus. That gave us a course generally south – about twenty-five degrees east of south, as close as I could read that map – and a destination some 550 kilometers away. No wonder our ETA read three o'clock tomorrow morning!

There was no road. Aunt Lilybet did not seem to have a tracker, or anything in the way of navigating instruments but an odometer and a speedometer. She seemed to be piloting the way river pilots of old were reputed to find their way, just by knowing the route. Perhaps so – but during the first hour I noticed something: There were range targets for the whole route. As we reached one, there would be another, out at the horizon.

I had not noticed any such guides yesterday and I don't think there were any; I think Gretchen really did pilot Mark Twain style. In fact I think Aunt Lilybet did also – I noticed that she often did not come close to a range marker as she passed it. Those blazes had probably been set up for occasional drivers or for relief drivers for the *Hear Me*.

I started trying to spot each one, making a game of it: If I missed one, it scored against me. Two misses in sequence counted as one 'death' by 'lost on the Moon' – something that happened too often in the early days . . . and still happens today. Luna is a big place, bigger than Africa, almost as big as Asia – and every square meter of it is deadly if you make just one little mistake.

Definition of a Loonie: a human being, any color, size, or sex, who *never* makes a mistake where it counts.

By our first rest stop I had 'died' twice through missing ranging marks.

At five minutes past fifteen Aunt Lilybet let her bus roll to a stop, then switched on a transparency that read: REST STOP – TWENTY MINUTES – and under it: Late Penalty – One Crown per Minute.

We all got out. Bill grabbed Aunt Lilybet's arm and put his helmet against hers. She started to shake him off, then listened. I didn't try to check on him; twenty minutes isn't long for a rest stop when it involves coping with a p-suit. Of course this is even harder for females than for males, and more time-consuming. We had a woman passenger with three children . . . and the right arm of her suit ended just below the elbow in a hook. How did she cope? I resolved to outwait her, so that the fine for being late would be assessed against me, rather than her.

That 'refresher' was dreadful. It was an airlock leading to a hole in the rock, attached to the home of a settler who combined tunnel farming with ice mining. There may have been some oxygen in the pressure gas that greeted us, but the stench made it impossible to tell. It reminded me of the jakes in a castle I was once quartered in during the Three-Weeks War – on the Rhine it was, near Remagen; it had a deep stone privy which was alleged never to have been cleaned in over nine hundred years.

None of us was fined for being late, as our driver was even later. And so was Bill. Dr Chan had resealed Tree-San with a roll-and-clamp arrangement to permit it to be watered more easily. Bill had solicited Aunt Lilybet's help. They had managed it together, but not quickly. I don't know whether Bill had time to pee or not. Auntie, of course, had time – the *Hear Me* couldn't roll until Auntie arrived.

We made a meal stop about half past nineteen at a small pressure, four families, called Rob Roy. After the last stop this one seemed like the acme of civilization. The place was clean, the air smelled right, and the people were friendly and hospitable. There was no choice in the menu – chicken and dumplings, and moonberry pie – and the price was high. But what do you expect out in the middle of nowhere on the face of the Moon? There was a souvenir stand of handmade items, presided over by a little boy. I bought an embroidered change purse that I had no use for, because those people were good to us. The decoration on it read: 'Rob Roy City, Capital of the Sea of Serenity.' I gave it to my bride.

Gwen helped the one-armed woman with the three children and learned that they were returning home to Kong, after having visited in Lucky Dragon the paternal grandparents of the youngsters. The mother's name was Ekaterina O'Toole; the kids were Patrick, Brigid, and Igor, aged eight, seven, and five. Our other three passengers turned out to be Lady Diana Kerr-Shapley and her husbands – wealthy and not inclined to fraternize with us plebs. Both her men carried side arms – inside their suits. What is the sense in that?

The ground was not as even from there on, and it seemed to me that Auntie stuck a little closer to the marked track. But she still drove fast and with dash, bouncing us around on those big, low-pressure doughnuts in a fashion that made me wonder about Bill's queasy stomach. At least he was not having to hold Tree-San; Auntie had helped him lash it down in the cargo compartment aft. I wished him luck; getting sick in one's helmet is dreadful – happened to me once, a generation ago. Ugh!

We made another rest stop just before midnight. Adequate. The Sun was now a few degrees higher and still rising. Auntie told us that we now had a hundred and fifteen klicks left to roll and should be in Kong about on time, with God's help.

God didn't give Auntie the help she deserved. We had been rolling about an hour when out of nowhere (from behind a rock outcropping?) came another rolligon, smaller and faster, cutting diagonally across our path.

I slapped Bill's arm, grabbed Gwen's shoulders, and down we went, below the driver's port and somewhat protected by the steel side of the bus. As I ducked for cover I saw a flash from the strange vehicle.

Our bus rolled to a stop with the other vehicle right in front of us. Auntie stood up.

They cut her down.

Gwen got the man who beamed Auntie, resting her Miyako on the sill of the port – she got him in the lens of his helmet, the best way to shoot a man in a p-suit if you are using bullets rather than laser. I got the driver, aiming carefully as my cane shoots only five times – and no more ammo closer than Golden Rule (in my duffel, damn it). Other suited figures came pouring out the sides of the attacking craft. Gwen raised up a little and went on shooting.

All this took place in the ghostly quiet of vacuum.

I started to add my fire to Gwen's, when still another vehicle showed up. Not a rolligon but related to one – but not any contraption I ever saw before. It had only one tire, a supergiant doughnut at least eight meters high. Maybe ten. The hole in the doughnut was crowded with what may have been (or had to be?) its power plant. Extending out from this hub on each side was a cantilevered platform. On the upper side of each platform, both port and starboard, a gunner was strapped into a saddle. Below the gunner was the pilot, or driver, or engineer – one on each side and don't ask me how they coordinated.

I won't swear to any details; I was busy. I had taken a bead on the gunner on the side toward me and was about to squeeze off one of my precious shots when I checked fire; his weapon was depressed, he was attacking our attackers. He was using an energy weapon – laser, particle beam, I don't know – as all I saw of each bolt was the parasitic flash . . . and the result.

The big doughnut spun around a quarter turn; I saw the other pair, driver and gunner, on the other side – and this gunner was trained on *us*. His projector flashed.

I got him in the face plate.

Then I tried for his driver, got him (I think) at the neck joint. Not as good as punching a hole in his face plate but, unless he was equipped to make a difficult patch fast, he was going to be breathing the thin stuff in seconds.

The doughnut spun all the way around. As it stopped I got the other gunner a nanosecond before he could get me. I tried to line up for a shot at the driver but could not get steady on target and had no ammo to waste. The doughnut started to roll, away from us, east – picked up speed, hit a boulder, bounced high, and disappeared over the horizon.

I looked back down at the other rolligon. In addition to the two we had killed in the first exchange, still sprawled in the car, there were five bodies on the ground, two to starboard, three to port. None looked as if he would ever move again. I pressed my helmet to Gwen's. 'Is that all of them?'

She jabbed me hard in the side. I turned. A helmeted head was just appearing in the lefthand door. I lined up my cane and punched a starred hole in his face plate; he disappeared. I hopped on somebody's feet and looked out – no more on the left – turned, and here was another one climbing up through the righthand door. So I shot him—

Correction: I *tried* to shoot him. No more ammo. I fell toward him, jabbing with my cane. He grabbed the end of it and that was his mistake, as I pulled on it, exposing twenty centimeters of Sheffield steel, which I sank into his suit and between his ribs. I pulled it out, shoved it into him again. That stiletto, a mere half-centimeter width of triangular blade, blood-grooved three sides, does not necessarily kill quickly but my second jab would hold his attention while he died, keep him too busy to kill me.

He collapsed, half inside the door, and let go the scabbard part of my cane. I retrieved it, fitted it back on. Then I shoved him out, grabbed on to the seat nearest me, and pulled myself up onto my foot, took care of a minor annoyance, hopped back to my seat, and sat down. I was tired, although the whole fracas could not have lasted more than two or three minutes. It's the adrenaline – I always feel exhausted afterward.

That was the end of it, and a good thing, too, as both Gwen and I were out of ammo, utterly, and I can't use that concealed blade trick more than once – it works only if you can lure your opponent into grabbing the ferrule of your walking stick. There had been nine in that rolligon and all of them were dead. Gwen and I got five of them between us; the gunners of the giant doughnut killed the other four. The body count was certain because there is no mistaking a bullet hole for a burn.

I am not counting the two, or three, I shot of the super-doughnut's crew . . . because they left no bodies to count; they were somewhere over the horizon.

Our own casualties: four.

First, our own gunner, riding shotgun in the turret above the driver. I crawled up and had a look – at one-sixth gee I can climb a vertical ladder almost as easily as you can. Our gunner was dead, probably that first flash marked his end. Had he been asleep on watch? Who knows and who cares now? He was dead.

But our second casualty, Aunt Lilybet, was not dead, and that was Bill's doing. He had slapped two pressure patches onto her, fast, one on her left arm, one on the top of her helmet – had known enough to cut off her air as he did it, then had counted sixty seconds before he cracked the valve and let her suit reinflate. And thereby saved her life.

It was the first evidence I had seen that Bill was even bright enough to pound sand. He had spotted where the kit with the pressure patches was kept, near the driver's seat, then had gone through the rest like a drill, no lost motions and paying no attention to the fighting going on around him.

I suppose I should not have been surprised; I knew that Bill had worked in heavy construction – for a space habitat, that means p-suit work, with safety drills and training. But it's not enough to be trained; in a clutch it takes some smarts and a cool head to apply even the best of training.

Bill showed us what he had done, not to boast of it, but because he realized that some of it might have to be done over: In sealing Auntie's suit in a hurry he had not been able to get at the wound in her arm to stop bleeding, and did not know whether or not it had been cauterized by the burn. If she was bleeding, that suit would have to be opened again, a pressure bandage applied to the wound, then the suit closed again – fast! In view of the location – an arm – the only way to do this would be to cut the suit fabric to make a larger hole, get at the arm and stop the bleeding, patch the bigger hole, and wait counted seconds for one endless minute before subjecting the patched suit to pressure.

There is a very narrow limit on how long a patient can take vacuum. Auntie was old and wounded and had had it done to her once today. Could she take it twice?

There was no question of opening her helmet. The bolt that had hit her there had carved a slice into the top of the helmet but not into her head – else we would not have been considering whether or not to open her sleeve.

Gwen put her helmet against Auntie's, managed to rouse her and get her attention. Was she bleeding?

Auntie didn't think so. Her arm was numb but didn't hurt much. Did they get it? Get what? Something in the cargo. Gwen assured her that the bandits didn't get anything; they were dead. That seemed to satisfy Auntie. She added, 'Taddie can drive,' and seemed to slip off to sleep.

Our third casualty was one of Lady Diana's husbands. Dead. But not by either set of bandits. In effect, he had shot himself in the foot.

I think I mentioned that he was heeled – with his gun for God's sake *inside* his suit. When the trouble started, he went for his side arm, found he could not reach it – opened the front of his suit to get at it.

It is possible to open your suit and close it again, in vacuum, and I think the legendary Houdini could have learned to do it. But this joker was still fumbling for his gun when he collapsed and drowned in vacuum. His co-husband was a half-point smarter. Instead of going for his own gun, he attempted to get at that of his partner after his partner keeled over. He did manage to get at it and to draw it but too late to help in the fight. He straightened up just as I was pulling myself to my foot, after I stabbed the last of the bandits.

So I find this custard head waving a gun in my face.

I did not intend to break his wrist; I simply meant to disarm him. I slapped the gun out of line and cracked his wrist with my cane. I caught the gun, shoved it into my p-suit belt, went forward, and collapsed in my seat. I did not know that I had hurt him, other than a bruise, maybe.

But I feel no trace of remorse. If you don't want a broken

wrist, don't wave a gun in my face. Not when I'm tired and excited.

Then I pulled myself together and tried to help Gwen and Bill.

I hate to tell about our fourth casualty: Igor O'Toole, the five-year-old.

Since the tad was on a back seat with his mother, it is certain that he was not killed by anyone from the rolligon; the angle would have been impossible. Only the two gunners of the superdoughnut were up high enough to shoot in through the driver's port of *Hear Me* and hit someone clear at the back. Furthermore it had to be the second gunner; the first gunner had kept busy killing bushwhackers. Then the doughnut turned, I saw this gun leveled at us, saw its flash just about as I fired and killed him.

I thought he had missed. If he was firing at me, he did miss. I'm not sure he was aiming carefully as who would aim at the least likely target? – a child, a baby really, clear at the back of the bus. But the flash I saw *had* to be the bolt that killed Igor.

Had it not been for Igor's death I might have had mixed feelings about the crew of the giant doughnut – we certainly could not have won without their help. But that last shot convinces me that they were just killing off business competitors before getting to their main purpose, hijacking the *Hear Me*.

My only regret is that I did not kill the fourth doughnut rider.

But these were afterthoughts. What we saw at the time was simply a dead child. We straightened up from dealing with Auntie and looked around. Ekaterina was sitting quietly, holding the body of her son. I had to look twice to realize what had happened. But a p-suit does not hold a living child when the face plate is burned away. I hopped towards her; Gwen reached her first. I stopped behind Gwen; Lady Diana grabbed my sleeve, said something.

I touched my helmet to hers. 'What did you say?'

'I told you to tell the driver to drive on! Can't you understand plain English?'

I wish she had said it to Gwen; Gwen's replies are more imaginative than mine and much more lyrical. All I could manage, tired as I was, was: 'Oh, shut up and sit down, you silly slitch.' I did not wait for an answer.

Lady Dee went forward, where Bill kept her from disturbing Auntie. I didn't see this, as just then, while I leaned forward to try to see what had happened to the consort who had (I was still to learn) killed himself with his p-suit, his co-husband attempted to recover that gun from me.

In the course of the tussle I grabbed his (broken) wrist. I could not hear him scream or see his expression, but he did an amazing piece of extemporaneous method acting that let me know the agony he was in.

All I can say is: Don't wave guns in my face. It brings out the worst in me.

I went back to Gwen and that poor mother, touched my helmet to Gwen's. 'Anything we can do for her?'

'No. Nothing till we get her in to pressure. Not much then.'

'How about the other two?' I suppose they were crying but when you can't hear it or see it, what can you do?

'Richard, I think the best we can do is to leave this family alone. Keep an eye on them but let them be. Until we reach Kong.'

'Yes – Kong. Who is Taddie?'

'What?'

'Aunt Lilybet said, "Taddie can drive."'

'Oh. I think she meant the turret gunner. Her nephew.'

So that's why I climbed up to check the turret. I had to go outside to get up there, which I did – cautiously. But we had been correct – all dead. And so was our turret gunner, Taddie. I climbed down, then back up into the passenger compartment, got my three together – told them we had no relief driver.

I asked, 'Bill, can you drive?'

'No, I can't, Senator. This is the first time in my life I've ever been in one of these things.'

'I was afraid of that. Well, it's been some years since I've driven one but I know how, so – Oh, Jesus! Gwen, *I can't.*'

'Trouble, dear?'

I sighed. 'You steer this thing with your feet. I'm shy one foot – it's sitting over there by my seat. There is no way in the world I can put it on . . . and no way in the world I can drive with just one foot.'

She answered soothingly, 'That's all right, dear. You handle the radio – we'll need some Maydays, I think. While I drive.'

'You can drive this behemoth?'

'Certainly. I didn't want to volunteer, with you two men here. But I'll be happy to drive. Two more hours, about. Easy.'

Three minutes later Gwen was checking the controls; I was seated beside her, figuring out how to jack my suit into the bus's radio. Two of those minutes had been spent delegating Bill as master at arms with orders to keep Lady Dee in her seat. She had come forward again, with firm instructions about how things were to be done. Seems she was in a hurry – something about a directors' meeting in Ell-Four. So we must drive fast, make up for lost time.

This time I did get to hear Gwen's comment. It was heart-warming. Lady Dee gasped, especially when Gwen told her what to do with her proxies, after she folded them until they were all sharp corners.

Gwen let in the clutches, the *Hear Me* shook, then backed, swung past the other rolligon, and we were away. I finally punched the right buttons on the radio, tuned it to what I thought was the right channel:

'– O, M, F, I, E, S spells "*Comfies!*" the perfect answer to the stresses of modern living! Don't take the cares of business home with you. Take comfort from Comfies, the scientific stomach boon therapists prescribe more than any other—'

I tried another channel.

XIII

'The truth is the one thing that nobody will believe.'

GEORGE BERNARD SHAW 1856–1950

I WENT on hunting for eleven, the emergencies channel, by trial and error; the read-out was marked but not by numbered channels – Auntie had her own codes. The window reading 'Help' was not help for emergencies as I had assumed, but spiritual help. I punched it in and got 'This is the Reverend Herald Angel speaking from my heart direct to yours, at Tycho-Under Tabernacle, Christ's Home in Luna. Tune in at eight o'clock Sunday to hear the true meanings of the Scriptural prophecies . . . and send your love gift today to Box 99, Angel Station, Tycho Under. Our Good News Theme for today: How We Will Know the Master When He Comes. Now we join the Tabernacle Choir in "Jesus Holds Me in His—"'

That sort of help was about forty minutes too late, so I moved on to another channel. There I recognized a voice and concluded that I must be on channel thirteen. So I called, 'Captain Midnight calling Captain Marcy. Come in, Captain Marcy.'

'Marcy, ground control Hong Kong Luna. Midnight, what the devil are you up to now? Over.'

I tried to explain, in twenty-five words or less, how I happened to be on his maneuvering circuit. He listened, then interrupted: 'Midnight, what have you been smoking? Let me talk to your wife; I can believe her.'

'She can't talk to you now; she's driving this bus.'

'Hold it. You tell me you are a passenger in the rolligon *Hear Me, Jesus*. That's Lilybet Washington's bus; why is your wife driving it?'

'I tried to tell you. She's been shot. Auntie Lilybet, I mean, not my wife. We were jumped by bandits.'

146

'There are no bandits in that area.'

'That's right; we killed 'em. Captain, *listen*, and quit jumping to conclusions. We were attacked. We have three dead and two wounded . . . and my wife is driving because she's the only able-bodied person left who *can*.'

'You're wounded?'

'No.'

'But you said your wife is the only able-bodied person left who can drive.'

'Yes.'

'Let me get this straight. Day before yesterday you were piloting a spacecraft – Or was your wife the pilot?'

'I was the pilot. What's itching you, Captain?'

'You can pilot a spacecraft . . . but you can't drive a little old rolly. That's hard to swallow.'

'Simple. I can't use my right foot.'

'But you said you weren't wounded.'

'I'm not. I've just lost a foot, that's all. Well, not "lost" – I have it here in my lap. But I can't use it.'

'Why *can't* you use it?'

I took a deep breath and attempted to recall Siacci empiricals for ballistics on atmosphere planets. 'Captain Marcy, is there anyone in your organization – or anywhere in Hong Kong Luna – who might be interested in the fact that bandits attacked a public bus serving your city, only a few klicks outside your city pressure? And is there anyone who can receive the dead and wounded when we arrive with them? And who won't care who drives this bus? And doesn't find it incredible that a man could have had a foot amputated years back?'

'Why didn't you *say* so?'

'God damn it, Captain, it was none of your bloody business!'

There was silence for several seconds. Then Captain Marcy said quietly, 'Perhaps you're right. Midnight, I'm going to patch you through to Major Bozell. He's a wholesaler by trade but he also commands our Vigilante Volunteers and that's why you should talk to him. Just hang on.'

I waited and watched Gwen's driving. When we started, her handling had been a bit rough, just as anyone's will be in getting acquainted with a strange machine. Now her driving was smooth, if not as dashing as Auntie's driving.

'Bozell here. Do you read?'

I replied . . . and almost at once ran into a nightmare feeling of déjà vu, as he interrupted with: 'There are no bandits in that area.'

I sighed. 'If you say so, Major. But there are nine corpses and an abandoned rolligon in that area. Perhaps someone would be interested in searching those bodies, salvaging their p-suits and weapons, and in claiming that abandoned rolligon . . . before some peaceful settlers who would never think of turning bandit show up and take everything.'

'Hmmm. Choy-Mu tells me that he is getting a satellite photo of the spot where this alleged attack took place. If there really is an abandoned rolligon—'

'Major!'

'Yes?'

'I don't care what you believe. I don't give a hoot about salvage. We'll be at the north airlock about three-thirty. Can you have a medic meet us, with a stretcher and bearers? That's for Mistress Lilybet Washington. She's—'

'I know who she is; she's been driving that route since I was a kid. Let me talk to her.'

'She's wounded, I told you. She's lying down and I hope she's asleep. If she's not, I still won't disturb her; it might start more bleeding. Just have somebody at the airlock to take care of her. And for three dead ones, too, one of them a small child. Its mother is with us and in shock, name of Ekaterina O'Toole, and her husband lives in your city. Nigel O'Toole and maybe you can have somebody call him so that he can meet his family and take care of them. That's all, Major. When I called you, I was a bit nervous about bandits. But since there aren't any bandits in this area, we have no reason to ask for vigilante protection out here on the Sea of Serenity this fine sunny day, and I'm sorry I disturbed your sleep.'

'That's all right; we're here to help – no need to be sarcastic. This is being recorded. State your full name and legal address, then repeat: As representative of Lilybet Washington of Lucky Dragon Pressure, doing business as the Apocalypse and Kingdom Come Bus Company, I authorize Major Kirk Bozell, commanding officer and business manager of the Hong Kong Luna Vigilante Volunteers, to supply—'

'Hold it. What is this?'

'Just the standard contract covering services for personal protection and property conservation, and guaranteeing payment. You can't expect to roust a platoon of guards out of bed in the middle of the night and not pay for it. TANSTAAFL. No free lunch.'

'Hmm, Major, do you happen to have any hemorrhoid salve on hand? Preparation H? Pazo? That sort of thing?'

'Eh? I use Tiger Balm. Why?'

'You're going to need it. Take that standard contract, fold it until it is all sharp corners—'

I stayed tuned to thirteen, made no further effort to find the emergencies channel. So far as I could see there was no point to shouting '*M'aidez!*' on channel eleven when I had already talked to the only likely source of help. I leaned my helmet against Gwen's and summarized, then added, 'Both the idiots insisted that there are no bandits out here.'

'Maybe they weren't bandits. Maybe they were just agrarian reformers making a political statement. I surely hope we don't run into any right-wing extremists! Richard, I had better not talk while I'm driving. Strange car, strange road – only it's not a road.'

'Sorry, hon! You're doing beautifully. How can I help?'

'It would help a lot if you would spot the markers for me.'

'Sure thing!'

'Then I could keep my eyes down and watch the road close ahead. Some of those potholes are worse than Manhattan.'

'Impossible.'

We worked out a system that helped her while bothering her least. As soon as I spotted a marker I pointed at it. When she saw it, too – not before – she slapped my knee. We didn't talk because touching helmets did tend to interfere with her driving.

About an hour later a rolligon showed up ahead and came straight toward us at high speed. Gwen tapped her helmet over her ear; I pressed my helmet to hers. She said, 'More agrarian reformers?'

'Maybe.'

'I'm out of ammo.'

'So am I.' I sighed. 'We'll just have to get them to the

149

conference table somehow. After all, violence never solves anything.'

Gwen made an unladylike comment and added, 'What about that gun you took away from Sir Galahad?'

'Oh. Hon, I haven't even looked at it. Hand me the stupid hat.'

'You're not stupid, Richard, just spiritual. Take a look.'

I drew that confiscated side arm from my suit belt, examined it. Then I touched helmets again. 'Honey, you're not going to believe this. It's not loaded.'

'Huh!'

'Indeed "Huh." Aside from that I have no comment. And you can quote me.'

I chucked that useless weapon into a corner of the bus and looked out at the other rolligon, now rapidly closing. Why would anyone wear an unloaded weapon? Sheer folly!

Gwen tapped her ear again. I touched helmets. 'Yes?'

'The ammo for that gun is on the body, you can bet on it.'

'I won't bet; I figured that out. Gwen, if I were to try to search that corpse, I would have to cool the other two first. It's not a good idea.'

'I agree. And no time for it anyhow. There they come.'

Only they didn't, not quite. The other rolligon, while still some two hundred meters away, swung to its left, made it clear that it was avoiding a collision course. As it passed us I read on its side: Vigilante Volunteers – Hong Kong Luna.

Shortly Marcy called me. 'Bozell says he found you but can't reach you by radio.'

'I don't know why not. You reached me.'

'Because I figured out that you would be on the wrong channel. Midnight, whatever you should be doing, it is a dead certainty that you will always be doing something else.'

'You flatter me. What should I have done this time?'

'You should have been guarding channel two, that's what. The one reserved for surface vehicles.'

'Every day I learn something. Thanks.'

'Anyone who doesn't know that should not be operating a vehicle on the surface of this planet.'

'Captain, you are so right.' I shut up.

*   *   *

We could see Hong Kong Luna over the horizon many minutes
before we got there – the emergency landing pylon, the big
dishes used to talk to Earth and the bigger ones for Mars and
the Belt, the solar power grids – and it got even more impressive
as we got closer. Of course everyone lives underground . . .
but I tend to forget how much of Luna's heavy industry is on
the surface – and illogical that I should forget, since most of
Luna's great wealth is tied in with raw sunshine, bitter nights,
and endless vacuum. But, as my wife pointed out, I'm the
spiritual type.

We passed Nissan-Shell's new complex, hectare after hectare
of pipes and cracking columns and inverse stills and valves
and pumps and Bussard pyramids. The long shadows carved
by the rising Sun made it a picture out of Gustave Doré, by
Pieter Brueghel (zoon), orchestrated by Salvador Dali. Just
beyond it we found the north lock.

Because of Aunt Lilybet they let us use the small Kwiklok.
Bill went through with Auntie – he had earned that – then
Lady Dee and her surviving husband crowded in ahead of
Ekaterina and the kids. Dear Diana had distinguished herself
again by demanding that she be taken to the spaceport rather
than to a city lock. Bill and I had not let her bother Gwen
with her royal commands, but it had decreased (if this be
possible) her popularity with us. I was glad to see them
disappear into the lock. And it worked out all right as Ekaterina's husband cycled outward through the main lock just
as we were losing our VIPs. Nigel O'Toole took his family
(including that pathetic little body) back the same way, after
Gwen hugged Ekaterina and promised to call her.

Then it was our turn . . . only to find that Tree-San could
not be fitted into a Kwiklok. So we backed out and went
around to the larger (and slower) lock. Someone, I saw, was
lifting down the body from the turret of *Hear Me, Jesus* and
others were unloading its cargo, under the eyes of four armed
guards. I wondered what was in that cargo. But it was none
of my business. (Or maybe it was – it seemed possible that
this cargo had been the cause of carnage and death.) We went
into the larger lock – ourselves, bonsai maple, small suitcase,
purse, packaged wig, cane, prosthetic foot.

The lock cycled and we entered a long, sloping tunnel, then passed through two pressure doors. At the second door was a slot-machine for vending short-time air licenses but it had a sign on it: OUT OF ORDER – Visitors please leave a half crown for 24 hrs. A saucer with some coins in it rested on top of the machine; I added a crown for Gwen and me.

At the bottom of the tunnel one more pressure door let us into the city.

There were benches just inside for the convenience of persons suiting up or suiting out. With a sigh of relief I started unzipping and shortly was fastening in place my artificial foot.

Dry Bones is a village, Lucky Dragon is a small town, Hong Kong Luna is a metropolis second only to Luna City. At the moment it did not look crowded but this was the dead of night; only night workers were up and around. Even early risers had two more hours of sleep coming, no matter that it was broad daylight outside.

But that almost deserted corridor still showed its big-city quality; a sign over the suit racks read: USE THESE RACKS AT YOUR OWN RISK. SEE JAN THE CHECKROOM MAN – BONDED AND INSURED – One Crown/One P-Suit.

Under it was a hand-written notice: *Be smart – See Sol for only half a crown – not bonded, not insured, just honest.* Each sign had arrows, one pointing left, one pointing right.

Gwen said, 'Which one, dear? Sol, or Jan?'

'Neither. This place is enough like Luna City that I know how to cope with it. I think.' I looked around, up and down, spotted a red light. 'There's a hotel. With my foot back in place, I can take a p-suit under each arm. Can you manage the rest?'

'Certainly. How about your cane?'

'I'll stick it through the belt of my suit. No itch.' We started toward that hotel.

Facing the corridor at the hotel's reception window a young woman sat studying – transgenics, Sylvester's classic text. She looked up. 'Better check those first. See Sol, next door.'

'No, I want a big room, with an empress-size bed. We'll stack these in a corner.'

She looked at her rooming diagram. 'Single rooms I have.

Twin beds I have. Happy suites I have. But what you want –
no. All occupied.'

'How much is a happy suite?'

'Depends. Here's one with two king beds, and 'fresher.
Here's one with no beds at all but a padded parlor floor and
lots of pillows. And here's—'

'How much for the two king beds?'

'Eighty crowns.'

I said patiently, 'Look, citizen, I'm a Loonie myself. My
grandfather was wounded on the steps at the Bon Marché.
His father was shipped for criminal syndicalism. I know prices
in Loonie City; they can't be that much higher in Kong. What
are you charging for what I requested? If you had one vacant?'

'I'm not impressed, chum; anyone can claim ancestors in
the Revolution and most do. My ancestors welcomed Neil
Armstrong as he stepped down. Top that.'

I grinned at her. 'I can't and I should have kept quiet.
What's your real price on a double room with one big bed,
and a 'fresher? Not your tourist price.'

'A standard double room with a big bed and its own 'fresher
goes for twenty crowns. Tell you what, chum – not much
chance of renting my empty suites this late – or this early. I'll
sell you an orgy suite for twenty crowns . . . and you're out by
noon.'

'Ten crowns.'

'Thief. Eighteen. Any lower and I'm losing money.'

'No, you're not. As you pointed out, this time in the morning
you can't expect to sell it at any price. Fifteen crowns.'

'Let's see your money. But you have to be out by noon.'

'Make that thirteen o'clock. We've been up all night and
have had a rough time.' I counted out the cash.

'I know.' She nodded at her terminal. 'The *Hong Kong Gong*
has had several bulletins about you. Thirteen o'clock, okay –
but if you stay longer, you either pay full tariff or move to an
ordinary room. Did you really encounter bandits? On the trace
to Lucky Dragon?'

'They tell me there are no bandits in that area. We ran into
some rather unfriendly strangers. Our losses were three dead,
two wounded. We fetched 'em back.'

'Yes, I saw. Do you want a receipt of your expense account?
For a crown I'll make out a real sincere one, itemized for

153

whatever amount you say. And I have three messages for you.'

I blinked stupidly. 'How? Nobody knew we were coming to your hotel. We didn't know it ourselves.'

'No mystery, chum. A stranger comes in the north lock late at night, it's a probable seven to two he'll wind up in my bed – one of my beds and no smart remarks, please.' She glanced at her terminal. 'If you hadn't picked up your messages in another ten minutes, backups would have gone to all inns in the pressure. If that failed to find you, the selectman for public safety might start a search. We don't get handsome strangers with romantic adventures too often.'

Gwen said, 'Quit waggling your tail at him, dearie; he's tired. And taken. Hand me the printouts, please.'

The hotel manager looked coldly at Gwen, spoke to me: 'Chum, if you have not yet paid her, I can guarantee you something better and younger and prettier at a bargain price.'

'Your daughter?' Gwen inquired sweetly. 'Please, the messages.'

The woman shrugged and handed them to me. I thanked her and said, 'About this other something. Younger, possibly. Prettier, I doubt. Can't be cheaper; I married this one for her money. What are the facts?'

She looked from me to Gwen. 'Is that true? Did he marry you for your money? Make him earn it!'

'Well, he says he did,' Gwen said thoughtfully. 'I'm not sure. We've been married only three days. This is our honeymoon.'

'Less than three days, dear,' I objected. 'It just seems longer.'

'Chum, don't talk that way to your bride! You're a cad and a brute and probably on the lam.'

'Yes. All of that,' I agreed.

She ignored me, spoke to Gwen: 'Dearie, I didn't know it was your honeymoon or I wouldn't have offered that "something" to your husband. I bow in the dust. But later on, when you get bored with this chum with the overactive mouth, I can arrange the same for you but male. Fair price. Young. Handsome. Virile. Durable. Affectionate. Call or phone and ask for Xia – that's me. Guaranteed – you must be satisfied or you don't pay.'

'Thanks. Right now all I want is breakfast. Then bed.'

'Breakfast right behind you across the corridor. Sing's New York Café. I recommend the Hangover Special at a crown fifty.' She looked back at her rack and picked out two cards. 'Here's your keys. Dearie, would you ask Sing to send me over a grilled Cheddar on white with coffee? And don't let him charge you more than a slug and a half for a Hangover Special. He cheats just for fun.'

We parked our baggage with Xia and crossed the corridor for breakfast. Sing's Hangover Special was as good as Xia claimed. Then at last we were in our suite – the bridal suite; Xia had again done right by us. In several ways. She led us to our suite, watched while we oohed and ahed – bubbly in an ice bucket, coverlet turned back, perfumed sheets, flowers (artificial but convincing) picked out by the only light.

So the bride kissed her and Xia kissed the bride, and they both sniffled – and a good thing, too, as a lot had happened too fast and Gwen had had no time to cry. Women need to cry.

Then Xia kissed the groom, and the groom did not cry and did not hang back – Xia is an oriental stack such as Marco Polo is said to have found in Xanadu. And she kissed me most convincingly. Presently she broke enough for air. 'Whew!'

'Yes, "Whew!"' I agreed. 'That deal you mentioned earlier – What do *you* charge?'

'Loud mouth.' She grinned at me, did not pull away. 'Cad. Scoundrel. I give away free samples. But not to bridegrooms.' She unwound herself. 'Rest well, dears. Forget that thirteen o'clock deadline. Sleep as long as you wish; I'll tell the day manager.'

'Xia, two of those messages called for me to see people at an ugly cow-milking hour. Can you switch us out?'

'I already thought of that; I read those before you did. Forget it. Even if Bully Bozell shows up with all his Boy Scouts, the day manager won't admit knowing what suite you are in.'

'I don't want to cause you trouble with your boss.'

'Didn't I say? I own the joint. Along with BancAmerica.' She pecked me quickly and left.

*   *   *

While we were undressing, Gwen said, 'Richard, she was waiting to be asked to stay. And she's not the wide-eyed virgin little Gretchen is. Why didn't you invite her?'

'Aw, shucks, Maw, I didn't know how.'

'You could have unpeeled her cheong-sam while she was trying to strangle you; that would have done it. There was nothing under it. Correction: Xia was under it, nothing else. But Xia is a-plenty, I'm certain. So why didn't you?'

'Do you want to know the truth?'

'Uh . . . I'm not sure.'

'Because I wanted to sleep with *you*, wench, with no distractions. Because I am not yet bored with you. It's not your brain, and not your spiritual qualities of which you almost don't have any. I lust after your sweaty little body.'

'Oh, Richard!'

'Before we bathe? Or after?'

'Uh . . . both?'

'That's my girl!'

XIV

'Democracy can withstand anything but democrats.'

J. HARSHAW 1904–

'All kings is mostly rapscallions.'

MARK TWAIN 1835–1910

WHILE WE were bathing I said, 'You surprised me, hon, by knowing how to herd a rolligon.'

'Not half as much as *you* surprised *me* when it turned out that your cane was a rifle.'

'Ah, yes, that reminds me – Would it bother you to cover for me?'

'Of course not, Richard, but how?'

'My trick cane stops being a protection when people know what it is. But, if all the shooting is attributed to you, then people won't learn what it is.'

Gwen answered thoughtfully, 'I don't see. Or don't understand. Everybody in the bus saw you using it as a rifle.'

'Did they, now? The fight took place in vacuum – dead silence. So no one heard any shots. Who saw me shoot? Auntie? She was wounded before I joined the party. Only seconds before but we're talking about seconds. Bill? Busy with Auntie. Ekaterina and her kids? I doubt that the kids saw anything they understood, and their mother suffered the worst shock a mother can; she won't be much of a witness, if at all. Dear Diana and her fancy boys? One is dead, the other was so mixed up that he mistook me for a bandit, and Lady Dee herself is so self-centered that she never understood what was going on; she simply knew that some tiresome nonsense was interfering with her sacred whims. Turn around and I'll scrub your back.'

Gwen did so; I went on: 'Let's improve it. I'll cover for you instead of you covering for me.'

'How?'

'My cane and your little Miyako use the same caliber ammo. So all shots came from the Miyako – fired by me, not by you – and my cane is just a cane. And you are my sweet, innocent bride who would never do anything so grossly unladylike as shooting back at strangers. Does that suit you?'

Gwen was so long in answering that I began to think that I must have offended her. 'Richard, maybe neither of us shot at anybody.'

'So? You interest me. Tell me how.'

'I am almost as unanxious to admit that I carry a gun as you are to admit that your cane has unexpected talents. Some places are awfully stuffy about concealed weapons . . . but a gun in my purse – or somewhere on me – has saved my life more than once and I intend to go on carrying one. Richard, the reasons you gave for believing that no one knows about your cane apply also to my Miyako. You're bigger than I am and I had the window seat. When we crouched down, I don't think anyone could see me too well – your shoulders are not transparent.'

'Hmm. Could be. But what about bodies with slugs in them? Six point five millimeter longs, to be precise.'

'Shot by the butchers in that big wheel.'

'They were burning, not shooting.'

'Richard! Richard! Do you *know* that they didn't have slug guns as well as energy weapons? I don't.'

'Hmm again. My love, you are as devious as a diplomat.'

'I *am* a diplomat. Reach me the soap, pretty please. Richard, let's not volunteer information. We were just passengers, innocent bystanders and stupid as well. How those agrarian reformers died is not our responsibility. My pappy done taught me to hold my cards close to my chest and never admit anything. This is a time for that.'

'My pappy done taught me the same thing. Gwen, why didn't you marry me sooner?'

'Took me a while to soften you up, dear. Or vice versa. Ready to shower off?'

While I was drying her, I remembered a point that we had passed by. 'Picture bride, where did you learn to drive a rolligon?'

'"Where?" Mare Serenitatis.'

158

'Huh?'

'I learned how through watching Gretchen and Auntie. Tonight was the first time I ever drove one.'

'Well! Why didn't you *say* so?'

She started drying me. 'Beloved, if you had known, you would have worried. Uselessly. In all the times I've been married I have always made it a rule never to tell my husband anything that would worry him if I could reasonably avoid it.' She smiled angelically. 'Better so. Men are worriers; women are not.'

I was roused out of a deep sleep by loud pounding. 'Open up in there!'

I couldn't think of a good reason to answer, so I didn't. I yawned widely, being careful not to let my soul escape, then reached out to my right. And woke up sharply and suddenly; Gwen was not there.

I got out of bed so quickly that it made me dizzy; I almost fell. I gave my head a shake to clear it, then hopped into the 'fresher. Gwen was not there. The pounding continued.

Don't drink champagne in bed and then go right to sleep; I had to drain off a liter of used bubbly before I could sigh with relief and think of other matters. The pounding continued, with more shouting.

Tucked into the top of my foot was a note from my beloved. Smart gal! Even better than fastening it to my toothbrush. It read:

Dearest One,

I have an attack of wakeupitis, so I'm getting up and taking care of a couple of errands. First I'm going to Sears Montgomery to return our p-suits and pay the rent on them. While I'm at Sears, I'll pick up socks and drawers for you and panties for me and do some other things. I'll leave a note at the desk here telling Bill to turn in his suit, too – and, yes, he did come in after we did and Xia put him in a single, as you arranged with her. Then I'm off to Wyoming Knott Memorial Hospital to see Auntie, and I'll call Ekaterina.

You're sleeping like a baby and I hope to be back before

you wake up. If not – if you go anywhere – please leave a note at the desk.

Love you –
Gwendolyn

The pounding continued. I put on my foot, while noting that our p-suits were not where I had last seen them, i.e., arranged in a romantic pose on the floor, a jest created by my bawdy bride. I dressed in the only clothes I had, then watered the little maple, found it did not need much; Gwen must have watered it.

'Open up!'

'Go to hell,' I answered politely.

Shortly the pounding was replaced by a scratching noise, so I placed myself close to the door and a bit to one side. This was not a dilating door but the more traditional hinged type.

It swung open; my noisy visitor plunged in. I reached out and threw him across the room. In one-sixth gee this takes some care – you must have a foot braced against something, or you'll lose traction and it won't work.

He sort of bounced off the far wall and wound up on the bed. I said, 'Get your dirty feet off my bed!'

He got off the bed and stood up. I continued angrily, 'Now explain why you broke into my bedroom . . . and make it quick before I tear off your arm and beat you over the head with it. Who do you think you are, waking up a citizen who has switched on his Do-Not-Disturb? Answer me!'

I could see what he was: some sort of town clown; he was wearing a uniform that spelled 'cop.' His reply, mixing indignation with arrogance, matched his appearance. 'Why didn't you open up when I ordered you to?'

'Why should I? Do *you* pay the rent on this room?'

'No, but—'

'There's your answer. Get out of here!'

'Now you listen to me! I am a safety officer of the sovereign city of Hong Kong Luna. You are directed to present yourself before the Moderator of the Municipal Council forthwith to supply information necessary to the peace and security of the city.'

'I am, eh? Show me your warrant.'

'No warrant needed. I am in uniform and on duty; you are required to cooperate with me. City Ordinance two seventeen dash eighty-two, page forty-one.'

'Do you have a warrant to break down the door of my private bedroom? Don't try to tell me that doesn't require a warrant. I'm going to sue you and take every crown you have and that monkey suit as well.'

His jaw muscles quivered but all he said was: 'Are you coming peacefully or do I have to drag you?'

I grinned at him. 'Best two falls out of three? I won the first one. Come ahead.' I became aware that we had an audience at the door. 'Good morning, Xia. Do you know this clown?'

'Mr Richard, I'm terribly sorry about this. My day manager tried to stop him; he wouldn't stop. I got here as quickly as I could.' I saw that she was barefooted and wearing no makeup – so her sleep had been interrupted, too. I said gently,

'Not your fault, dear. He doesn't have a warrant. Shall I throw him out?'

'Well . . .' She looked troubled.

'Oh. I see. I think I see. Throughout history, innkeepers have found it necessary to get along with cops. And throughout history, cops have had larcenous hearts and a bully's manners. All right, as a favor to you, I'll let him live.' I turned back to the cop. 'Boy, you can chase back to your boss and tell him that I will be along presently. After I've had at least two cups of coffee. If he wants me any sooner than that, he had better send a squad. Xia, would you like coffee? Let's go see if Sing has coffee and Danish, or such.'

At this point Joe Stormtrooper made it necessary for me to take his gun. I can be shot – I *have* been shot, more than once – but I can't be shot by anyone who thinks that just pointing a gun at me has changed the odds.

His gun was nothing I wanted – door-prize junk. So I unloaded it, made sure that his ammo was not the caliber I use, dropped the loads down the oubliette, and handed his gun back to him.

At the loss of his cartridges he screamed bloody murder, but I patiently explained to him that his gun was as good as ever for the purpose for which he used it and that, if I had let him keep ammo, he could have hurt himself.

He continued to squawk, so I told him to go squawk to his

boss. And turned my back. He was, I feel certain, annoyed. But so was I.

Forty minutes later, feeling better although still sleepy, and after a rewarding chat with Xia over coffee and jelly doughnuts, I presented myself at the office of the Honorable Jefferson Mao, Moderator of the Council of Selectmen of the Sovereign City of Hong Kong Luna – so it said on the door. I wondered what the Congress of Luna Free State thought about this use of the word 'sovereign' but it was none of my business.

A brisk woman with slant eyes and red hair (interesting genes, I guess) said, 'Name, please?'

'Richard Johnson. The Moderator wants to see me.'

She glanced at her monitor. 'You're late for your appointment; you'll have to wait. You may sit down.'

'And I may not. I said that the Moderator wants to see me; I did not say that I want to see the Moderator. Punch up that box and let him know that I am here.'

'I can't possibly fit you in for at least two hours.'

'Tell him I am here. If he won't see me now, I'm leaving.'

'Very well, return in two hours.'

'You misunderstand me. I'm *leaving*. Leaving Kong. I won't be back.' I was bluffing as I said it and as I said it, I learned that I was not bluffing. My plans, as yet inchoate, had included an indefinite stay in Kong. Now I suddenly realized that I would not remain in a city that had sunk so far in the qualities that constitute civilization that a cop would break into a citizen's bedroom merely because some officious official decides to summon him. No indeed! A private soldier in a decent, well-run, disciplined military outfit has more freedom and more privacy than that. Hong Kong Luna, celebrated in song and story as the cradle of Luna's freedom, was no longer a fit place to live.

I turned away and was almost to the door when she called out: 'Mr Johnson!'

I stopped, did not turn. 'Yes?'

'Come back here!'

'Why?'

Her answer seemed to hurt her face. 'The Moderator will see you now.'

'Very well.' As I approached the door to the inner office, it rolled out of the way ... but I did not find myself in the Moderator's private office; three more doors, each guarded by its own faithful hound, lay ahead – and this told me more than I wanted to know about the current government of Hong Kong Luna.

The guardian of the last door announced me and ushered me through. Mr Mao barely glanced at me. 'Sit down.' I sat down, rested my cane against my knee.

I waited five minutes while the city boss shuffled papers and continued to ignore me. Then I stood up, headed for the door, moving slowly, leaning on my cane. Mao looked up. 'Mr Johnson! Where are you going?'

'Out.'

'Indeed. You don't *want* to get along, do you?'

'I want to go about my business. Is there some reason I should not?'

He looked at me with no expression. 'If you insist, I can cite a municipal ordinance under which you are required to cooperate with me when I request it.'

'Are you referring to City Ordinance two hundred seventeen dash eighty-two?'

'I see you are familiar with it ... so you can hardly plead ignorance in extenuation of your behavior.'

'I am *not* familiar with that ordinance, just its number. It was cited to me by a clownish thug who crushed into my bedroom. Does that ordinance say anything about breaking into private bedrooms?'

'Ah, yes. Interfering with a safety officer in the performance of his duty. We'll discuss that later. That ordinance you cited is the bedrock of our freedom. Citizens, residents, and even visitors can come and go as they please, subject only to their civic duty to cooperate with officials, elected, appointed, or deputized, in carrying out their official duties.'

'And who decides when cooperation is needed and what sort and how much?'

'Why, the official involved, of course.'

'I thought so. Is there anything else you want of me?' I started to move.

'Sit back down. There is indeed. And I *require* your

cooperation. I am sorry to have to put it that way but you don't seem to respond to polite requests.'

'Such as breaking down my door?'

'You weary me. Sit down and shut up. I am about to interrogate you . . . as soon as two witnesses arrive.'

I sat down and shut up. I felt that I now understood the new regime: absolute freedom . . . except that any official from dogcatcher to supreme potentate could give any orders whatever to any private citizen at any time.

So it was 'freedom' as defined by Orwell and Kafka, 'freedom' as granted by Stalin and Hitler, 'freedom' to pace back and forth in your cage. I wondered if the coming interrogation would be assisted by mechanical or electrical devices or by drugs, and felt sick at my stomach. Back when I was on active duty and repeatedly faced with the possibility of capture while holding classified information, I always had a final friend, that 'hollow tooth' or equivalent. I no longer wore such protection.

I was scared.

Before long two men came in together. Mao answered good-morning to their greeting and waved them to seats; a third man came in right after them. 'Uncle Jeff, I—'

'Shut up and sit down!' This latecomer was the joker whose gun I had emptied; he shut up and sat down. I caught him looking at me; he looked away.

Mao put aside some papers. 'Major Bozell, thanks for coming in. You, too, Captain Marcy. Major, you have questions to ask one Richard Johnson. There he sits. Ask away.'

Bozell was a short man who carried himself very erect. He had close-cropped sandy hair and an abrupt, jerky manner. 'Hah! Let's get right to it! Why did you send me on a wild goose chase?'

'What wild goose chase?'

'Hah! Are you going to sit there and deny that you told me a cock-and-bull story about an attack by bandits? In an area where there have never been any bandits! Do you deny that you urged me to send a rescue-and-salvage team out there? Knowing that I would find nothing! Answer me!'

I said, 'That reminds me – Can anyone tell me how Aunt Lilybet is this morning? Because I was told to come here, I haven't had time to get to the hospital.'

'Hah! Don't change the subject. Answer me!'

I answered mildly, 'But that *is* the subject. In that cock-and-bull attack you spoke of, an old lady was injured. Is she still alive? Does anyone know?'

Bozell started to answer; Mao cut in. 'She's alive. Or was an hour ago. Johnson, you had better pray that she stays alive. I have a deposition here' – he tapped his terminal – 'from a citizen whose word is above reproach. One of our most important shareholders, Lady Diana Kerr-Shapley. She states that you shot Mistress Lilybet Washington—'

'*What?*'

'– while creating a reign of terror in which your actions caused the death by anoxia of her husband the Honorable Oswald Progant, broke the wrist of her husband the Honorable Brockman Hogg, and subjected Lady Diana herself to terror tactics and repeated insults.'

'Hmm. Did she say who killed the O'Toole child? And what about the turret gunner? Who killed *him?*'

'She states that there was such confusion that she did not see everything. But you went outside while the bus was standing still and climbed up to the turret – no doubt that was when you finished off the poor boy.'

'Are you saying that last, or did she say it?'

'I said it. A conclusive presumption. Lady Diana was meticulously careful not to testify to anything she did not see with her own eyes. Including this ghostly rolligon full of bandits. She saw nothing of *it.*'

Bozell added, 'There you have it, Mr Moderator. This hijacker shot up the bus and killed three people and wounded two more . . . and invented a cock-and-bull story about bandits to cover his crimes. There are no bandits in that area; everybody knows that.'

I tried to get a grip on reality. 'Mr Moderator, one moment, please! Captain Marcy is here. I understand he got a picture of the bandits' rolligon.'

'I ask the questions, Mr Johnson.'

'But – Did he, or didn't he?'

'That's enough, Johnson! You will be in order. Or you will be restrained.'

'What am I doing that is out of order?'

'You're disrupting this investigation with irrelevancies. Wait until you are spoken to. Then answer the question.'

'Yes, sir. What is the question?'

'I told you to keep quiet!'

I kept quiet. So did everybody else.

Presently Mr Mao drummed on his desk and said, 'Major, did you have more questions?'

'Hah! He never answered my first question. He evaded it.'

The Moderator said, 'Johnson, answer the question.'

I looked stupid – my best role. 'What is the question?'

Mao and Bozell both started to speak; Bozell yielded to Mao who went on, 'Let's summarize it. Why did you do what you did!'

'What did I do?'

'I just told you what you did!'

'But I didn't do any of the things you said I did. Mr Moderator, I don't understand how you got into this. You weren't there. That bus is not from your city. I am not from your city. Whatever happened took place outside your city. What is your connection with the matter?'

Mao leaned back and looked smug. Bozell said, 'Hah!' then added, 'Shall I tell him, Mr Moderator? Or will you?'

'I will tell him. In fact I shall enjoy telling him. Johnson, less than a year ago the Council of this sovereign city made a very wise move. It extended its jurisdiction to cover all surface and subsurface activity within one hundred kilometers of the municipal pressure.'

'And made the Vigilante Volunteers an official arm of the government,' Bozell added happily, 'charged with keeping the peace to the hundred-kilometer line! And that fixes you, you murderer!'

Mao ignored the interruption. 'So you see, Johnson, while you probably thought that you were out in anarchist wilds, where the writ of law does not run, in fact you were *not*. Your crimes will be punished.'

(I wonder how soon someone will attempt a power grab like this out in the Belt?) 'These crimes of mine – Did they take place less than one hundred kilometers from Hong Kong Luna? Or more?'

'Eh? Less. Considerably less. Of course.'

'Who measured it?'

Mao looked at Bozell. 'How far was it?'

'About eighty kilometers. A little less.'

I said, '*What* was a little less? Major, are you talking about the bandits' attack on the bus? Or about something that went on *inside* the bus?'

'Don't put words into my mouth! Marcy – you tell them!'

Having said that, Bozell looked blank. He started to add something, stopped.

I most carefully kept quiet. Presently Mao said, 'Well, Captain Marcy?'

'What do you want from me, sir? The director of the port, when he sent me here, told me to cooperate fully . . . but not to volunteer anything you did not ask for.'

'I want everything relevant to this case. Did you give Major Bozell a figure of eighty kilometers?'

'Yes, sir. Seventy-eight kilometers.'

'How did you get that figure?'

'I measured it on a monitor at my console. Ordinarily we don't print a satellite photograph, just display it. This man – you say his name is Johnson; I knew him as "Midnight" – if he's the same man. He called me last night at oh one twenty-seven, stated that he was in the Lucky Dragon bus, reported that bandits had attacked the bus—'

'Hah!'

'– and that the attack had been driven off but the driver, Aunt Lilybet – Mistress Washington – was hurt and that the turret gunner was—'

'We know all that, Captain. Tell us about the photograph.'

'Yes, Mr Moderator. From what Midnight told me, I was able to direct the satellite camera onto target. I photographed the rolligon.'

'And you place the bus at that time seventy-eight kilometers from the city?'

'No, sir, not the bus. The other rolligon.'

There was the sort of silence sometimes called 'pregnant.' Then Bozell said, 'But that's crazy! There wasn't any—'

'Just a moment, Bozell. Marcy, you were misled by Johnson's lies. What you saw was the bus.'

'No, sir. I did see the bus; I had it on monitor. But I saw at once that it was moving. So I coached the camera back down the trace about ten klicks . . . and there was the second rolligon, just as Midnight had said.'

Bozell was almost in tears. 'But – There was nothing there,

I tell you! My boys and I searched that whole area. Nothing! Marcy, you're out of your mind!'

I don't know how long Bozell would have gone on wishing away a rolligon he could not find, as he was interrupted; Gwen came in. And I reswallowed my heart; everything was going to be all right!

(I had been worried sick ever since I had seen Mao's triple defenses against anyone walking in on him. A guard against assassination? I don't know; I simply fretted that Gwen might be balked. But I should have had more confidence in my little giant.)

She smiled and waved me a kiss, then turned and held the door. 'Right through here, gentlemen!'

Two of Mao's own police brought in a wheelchair, laid back so that Auntie could recline. She looked around, smiled at me, then said to the Moderator, 'Howdy, Jefferson. How's your momma?'

'She's well, thank you, Mistress Washington. But you—'

'What's this "Mistress Washington" fancy talk? Boy, I've changed your nappies; you call me "Auntie" same as you always did. Now I heard about how you were planning to pin a medal on Senator Richard for how he saved me from those bandits . . . and when I heard that I said to myself, "Jefferson hasn't heard about the other two that deserve medals quite as much as Senator Richard does" – begging your pardon, Senator.'

I said, 'Oh, you're quite right, Auntie.'

'So I brought them. Gwen honey, say hello to Jefferson. He's the mayor of this pressure. Gwen is Senator Richard's wife, Jefferson. And Bill – Where's Bill? *Bill!* You come in here, son! Don't be shy. Jefferson, while it's true that Senator Richard killed two of those bad men with his bare hands—'

'Not his bare hands, Auntie,' Gwen objected. 'He did have his cane.'

'You hush up, honey. With his bare hands and his walking cane, but if Bill hadn't been right there – and fast and smart – I wouldn't be here; Jesus would have taken me. But the dear Lord said it wasn't my time yet and Bill put patches on my suit and saved me to serve Jesus another day.' Auntie reached out, took Bill's hand. 'This is Bill, Jefferson. Make sure he gets a medal, too. And Gwen – Come here, Gwen. This baby girl saved all our lives.'

I'm not sure how old my bride is, but she is not a 'baby girl.' However, that was the least distortion of fact that was heard in the next few minutes. To put it in its mildest terms, Auntie told a pack of lies. With Gwen nodding and backing her up and looking angelic.

It was not so much that the facts were wrong as that Auntie testified to things she could not possibly have seen. Gwen must have coached her most carefully.

Two loads of bandits had tackled us but they had fought each other; that saved us, as all but two of them died in that fratricide. Those two I killed with my bare hands and a walking stick – against laser guns. I am so heroic that I amaze myself.

While these brave deeds were going on, I *know* Auntie was unconscious part of the time, and flat on her back all of the time, able to see only the ceiling of the bus. Yet she seemed to believe – I think she did believe – what she was saying. So much for eyewitnesses.

(Not that I'm complaining!)

Then Auntie told how Gwen had driven us. I found myself pulling up a trouser leg to show my prosthetic – something I never do – but did this time to show why I had been unable to wear it while wearing a standard p-suit, and thereby unable to drive.

But it was Gwen who brought down the house when Auntie finished her highly-colored account. Gwen did it with pictures.

Listen carefully. Gwen had used all her ammo, six rounds, then – neat as always – she had put her Miyako back into her purse. And pulled out her Mini Helvetia, snapped two frames.

She had tilted her camera down a bit, for it showed not only both bandit vehicles but also three casualties on the ground and one bandit up and moving. The second shot showed four on the ground and the super-doughnut turned away.

I can't figure out an exact time line on this but there must have been at least four seconds from the time she ran out of ammo to the time the giant wheel turned away. With a fast camera it takes about as long to shoot one frame as it does to fire one shot with a semi-automatic slug gun.

So the question is: What did she do with the other two seconds? Just waste them?

XV

WE DIDN'T break into a run but we got out of there as fast as possible. True, Auntie had clobbered Mr Mao into accepting me as a 'hero' rather than a criminal – but that did not make him love me and I knew it.

Major Bozell did not even pretend to like me. Captain Marcy's 'defection' infuriated Bozell; Gwen's pictures actually showing bandits (where they could not be!) broke his heart. Then his boss gave him the cruelest blow by ordering him to get his troops together and get out there and *find* them! Do it now! 'If you can't do it, Major, I'll have to find someone who can. You thought up this idea of the hundred-kilometer border. Now justify your boasts.'

Mao should not have done it to Bozell in the presence of others – especially not in *my* presence. This I know from professional experience – in each role.

I think Gwen gave Auntie some signal. As may be, Aunt Lilybet told Mao she had to leave. 'My little nurse is going to scold me for staying too long. I don't want her to have to scold me too hard. Mei-Ling Ouspenskaya – do you know her, Jefferson? She knows your momma.'

The same two police officers wheeled Auntie all the way back through that series of offices and out to the public corridor – square, rather, as the city offices face on Revolutionary Square. She said good-bye to us there and the police officers wheeled her away to Wyoming Knott Memorial Hospital, two levels down and north of there. I don't think they expected to do it – I do know Gwen conscripted these two right there in the Moderator's offices – but Auntie assumed that they would

170

take her back to hospital, and they did. 'No, Gwen honey, no need for you to come along – these kind gentlemen know where it is.'

(A lady has doors held for her because she *expects* doors to be held for her. Both Gwen and Aunt Lilybet had this principle down pat.)

Facing the municipal offices was a large bunting-bedecked sign:

FREE LUNA!
July 4th, 2076–2188

Was it really Independence Day already? I counted up in my mind. Yes, Gwen and I had married on the first – so today had to be the Fourth of July. A good omen!

Seated at a bench around a fountain in the center of Revolutionary Square was Xia, waiting for us.

I had expected Gwen; I did not expect Xia. In that chat I had had with Xia, I had asked her to try to locate Gwen and to tell her where I was going and why. 'Xia, I don't like being called in by cops for questioning, especially in a strange town where I don't know the political setup. If I am "detained"– to put it politely – I want my wife to know where to look.'

I did not suggest what Gwen should do about it. In only three days of marriage to Gwen I had already learned that nothing I could suggest could equal what she would think of, left to her own devious devices – being married to Gwen was *not* dull!

I was warmly pleased to find Xia waiting but I was startled at what she had with her. I stared and said, 'Somebody book the bridal suite?' On the bench by Xia I saw Gwen's small case, a package containing a wig, a rock maple in bonsai, and a package not familiar to me but self-explained by its Sears Montgomery wrapping. 'I'll bet my toothbrush is still hanging in the 'fresher.'

'How much and what odds?' said Xia. 'You would lose. Richard, I'll miss both of you. Maybe I'll run over to L-City and visit you.'

'Do that!' said Gwen.

'Concur,' I concurred, 'if we're moving to L-City. Are we?'

'Right away,' said Gwen.

'Bill, did you know about this?'

'No, Senator. But *she* had me rush over to Sears and turn in my p-suit. So I'm ready.'

'Richard,' Gwen said seriously, 'it's not safe for you to stay here.'

'No, it's not,' said a voice behind me (proving again that classified matters should not be discussed in public places). 'The sooner you chums leave the better. Hi, Xia. Are you with these dangerous characters?'

'Hi yourself, Choy-Mu. Thanks for last time.'

I blinked at him. 'Captain Marcy! I'm glad you came out; I want to thank you!'

'Nothing to thank me for, Captain Midnight – or is it "Senator"?'

'Well . . . actually it's "Doctor." Or "Mister." But to you it's "Richard," if you will. You saved my neck.'

'And I'm Choy-Mu, Richard. But I did not save your neck. I followed you out to tell you so. You may think you won back in there. You did not. You lost. You made the Moderator lose face – you made both of them lose face. So you're a walking time bomb, an accident looking for the spot.' He frowned. 'Not too healthy for me, either, being present when they lost face . . . after making the initial mistake of "bearing bad news to the king." Understand me?'

'I'm afraid I do.'

Xia asked, 'Choy-Mu, truly did Number-One lose face?'

'Truly he did, luv. It was Aunt Lilybet Washington who did it to him. But of course he can't touch *her*. So it lands on Captain – on Richard. So I see it.'

Xia stood up. 'Gwen, let's go straight to the station. Not waste a second! Oh, damn! I did so much want you to stay a few days.'

Twenty minutes later we were at South Tube Station, and about to enter the ballistic tube for Luna City. The fact that we were able to book space in the L-City capsule leaving almost at once controlled our destination, as Choy-Mu and Xia went along to see us off and, by the time we had reached the station via the local city subway, they had convinced me – or had convinced Gwen (more to the point) – that we should take the first thing leaving town, no matter where it went. From that same station there are ordinary (non-ballistic) tubes to Plato, Tycho Under, and Novy Leningrad – had we been six minutes earlier we would have wound up in Plato warren, which would have changed many things.

Or would it have changed anything? Is there a Destiny that shapes our ends? (Gwen's end was delightfully shaped. Xia's also, come to think of it.)

There was barely time to say good-bye before we had to rack up and strap in. Xia kissed us all good-bye and I was pleased that Gwen did not let Choy-Mu go unkissed. A true Loonie, he hesitated a long beat to make sure that the lady meant it, then returned it enthusiastically. I watched Xia kissing Bill good-bye – Bill returned it without that hesitation. I decided that Gwen's attempt to play Pygmalion to this unlikely Galatea was succeeding but that Bill would have to learn Loonie manners, or he might lose some teeth.

We strapped down, the capsule was sealed, and again Bill cradled the little maple's pot against his belly. The racks swung to meet acceleration – one full gee, a *high* acceleration for Loonies who filled the rest of the car. Two minutes and fifty-one seconds of boost, then we were at orbital speed.

Odd to be in free fall in a subway. But it certainly is fun!

It was the first time I had ridden the ballistic tube. It dates back before the Revolution, although then (so I've read) it extended only to Endsville. It was completed later, but the principle was never extended to other subway systems – not economic, I am told, other than for heavily-traveled, long runs that can be dug 'straight' the whole way – 'straight' in this case meaning 'exactly conforming to a ballistic curve at orbiting velocity.'

This subway is the only underground 'spaceship' in history. It works like the induction catapults that throw cargo to Ell-Four and Ell-Five and to Terra . . . except that the launching station, the receiving station, and the entire trajectory are underground . . . a few meters underground in most places, about three klicks underground where the tube passes under mountains.

Two minutes and fifty-one seconds of one-gee boost, twelve

minutes and twenty-seven seconds in free fall, two minutes and fifty-one seconds of one-gee braking – it adds up to an average speed of more than five thousand kilometers per hour. No other 'surface' transportation anywhere even approaches this speed. Yet it is an utterly comfortable ride – three minutes that feel like lying in a hammock on Terra, then twelve and a half minutes of weightlessness, and again three minutes in that garden hammock. How can you beat that?

Oh, you could do it faster by accelerating at multiple gee. But not much. If your acceleration could be instantaneous (killing all passengers!) and you decelerated the same way (*splat!*), you could raise your average speed to just over six thousand kilometers per hour and trim your time back by *almost three minutes!* But that's the ultimate.

That is also the best possible time for a rocketship between Kong and L-City. In practice a jumpbug rocket will usually take about half an hour – depends on how high its trajectory is.

But surely a half hour is short enough. Why tunnel under maria and mountains when a rocket can do the job?

A rocket is the most lavishly expensive transportation ever invented. In a typical rocketship mission half the effort is spent fighting gravity to go up and the other half is spent fighting gravity in letting down – as crashing is considered an unsatisfactory end to a mission. The giant catapults on Luna, on Terra, on Mars, and in space are giant statements against the wastefulness of rocket engines.

Contrariwise, the ballistic subway is the most economical transportation ever devised: No mass is burned up or thrown away and the energy used in speeding up is given back at the other end in slowing down.

No magic is involved. An electric catapult is a motor generator. Never mind that it doesn't look like one. In its acceleration phase it is a motor; electric power is converted into kinetic energy. In its decelerating phase it is a generator; the kinetic energy extracted from the capsule is pulled out as electric power and stored in a Shipstone. Then the same energy is taken from the Shipstone to hurl the capsule back to Kong.

A Free Lunch!

Not quite. There are hysteresis losses and other inefficiencies. Entropy always increases; the second law of thermodynamics can't be snubbed. What it most resembles is regenerative braking. There was a time, years ago, when surface cars were slowed and stopped by friction, rudely applied. Then a bright lad realized that a turning wheel could be stopped by treating it as a generator and making it pay for the privilege of being stopped – the angular momentum could be extracted and stored in a 'storage battery' (an early predecessor of Shipstones).

The capsule from Kong does much the same; in cutting magnetic lines of force at the L-City end it generates a tremendous electromotive force, which stops the capsule and changes its kinetic energy into electrical energy, which is then stored.

But the passenger need know nothing of this. He simply lounges in his 'hammock' rack for the gentlest ride possible.

We had just spent most of three days in rolling seven hundred kilometers. Now we traveled fifteen hundred kilometers in eighteen minutes.

We had to shoulder our way out of the capsule and into the tube station because there were Shriners impatiently awaiting the opportunity to board for Kong. I heard one say that 'they' (that anonymous 'they' who are to blame for everything) – 'they ought to put on more cars.' A Loonie tried to explain to him the impossibility involved in this demand – just one tube, able to handle only one capsule, which could be at this end or at the far end or in free flight in between. But never two capsules in the tube – impossible, suicidal.

His explanation met with blank disbelief. The visitor seemed to have trouble, too, in grasping the idea that the ballistic tube was privately owned and totally unregulated . . . a matter that came up when the Loonie finally said, 'You want another tube, go ahead! Build it! You are free to do so; nobody is stopping you. If that doesn't satisfy you, go back to Liverpool!'

Unkind of him. Earthworms can't help being earthworms. Every year some of them die through inability to comprehend that Luna is *not* like Liverpool, or Denver, or Buenos Aires.

We passed through the lock separating the pressure owned by Artemis Transit Company from the municipal pressure. In the tunnel just beyond the lock was a sign: GET YOUR AIR CHITS HERE. Seated under it at a table was a man twice as handicapped as I was; his legs ended at his knees. This did not seem to slow him down; he sold magazines and candy as well as air, advertised both sightseeing and guide service, and displayed the ubiquitous sign: TRACK ODDS.

Most people breezed back and forth past him without stopping. Bill had started to do so, when I checked him. 'Wups! Wait, Bill.'

'Senator, I've got to get some water onto this tree.'

'Wait just the same. And stop calling me "Senator." Call me "Doctor" instead. Dr Richard Ames.'

'Huh?'

'Never mind; just do it. Right now, we've got to buy air. Didn't you buy air at Kong?'

Bill had not. He had entered the city pressure helping with Auntie and no one had asked him to pay.

'Well, you should have paid. Did you notice that Gretchen paid for all of us at Lucky Dragon? She did. And now we'll pay here, but I'll arrange for longer than overnight. Wait here.'

I stepped up to the table. 'Hi there. You're selling air?'

The air vendor glanced up from working a double-crostic, looked me over. 'No charge to you. You paid for air when you bought your ticket.'

'Not quite,' I said. 'I'm a Loonie, cobber, returning home. With a wife and one dependent. So I need air for three.'

'A nice try. But no prize. Look, a citizen's chit won't get you citizens' prices – they'll still look at you and charge you tourist prices. If you want to extend your visa, you can. At city hall. And they'll collect air fee to cover your extended visa. Now forget it, before I decide to cheat you.'

'Choom, you're hard to please.' I dug out my passport – glanced at it to make sure it was my 'Richard Ames' passport – and handed it to him. 'I've been away several years. If that makes me look like a groundhog to you, that's regrettable. But please note where I was born.'

He looked it over, handed it back. 'Okay, Loonie, you had me fooled. Three of you, eh? For how long?'

'My plans aren't firm. What's the shortest period for the permanent-resident scale?'

'One quarter. Oh, another five percent off if you buy five years at a time . . . but with today's prime rate at seven point one, it's a sucker bet.'

I paid for three adults for ninety days and asked what he knew about housing. 'Having been away so long I not only don't have cubic, I don't know the market – and I don't relish dossing in Bottom Alley tonight.'

'You'd wake up with your shoes gone, your throat cut, and rats walking over your face. Mmm, a tough question, cobber. You see the funny red hats. Biggest convention L-City has ever had; between it and Independence Day the town is booked solid. But, if you're not too fussy—'

'We're not.'

'You'll be able to get something better after the weekend, but in the meantime there is an old place in level six, the Raffles, across from—'

'I know where it is. I'll try there.'

'Better call them first and tell them I sent you. I'm Rabbi Ezra ben David. Reminds me. "Ames, Richard." Are you the Richard Ames who's wanted for murder?'

'My word!'

'Surprise you? Too true, cobber. I've got a copy of the notice here someplace.' He shuffled through magazines and penciled notes and chess problems. 'Here it is. You're wanted in Golden Rule habitat – seems you chilled some VIP. So they say.'

'Interesting. Is there a tab out on me here?'

'In Luna? I don't think so. Why should there be? Still the same old standoff; no diplomatic relations with Golden Rule until they qualify under the Oslo Convention. Which they cannot without a basic bill of rights. Which is not bloody likely.'

'I suppose so.'

'Still . . . if you need lawyer help, come see me; I do that, too. Catch me here any day after noon, or leave your name at Seymour's Kosher Fish Emporium across from Carnegie Library. Seymour's my son.'

'Thanks, I'll remember. By the way, who is it I'm supposed to have killed?'

'Don't you know?'

'Since I didn't kill anybody how could I know?'

'There are logical lacunae in that which I will not examine. It is set forth here that your victim hight Enrico Schultz. Does that name trigger your memory?'

'"Enrico Schultz." I don't think I've ever heard that name.

A stranger to me. Most murder victims are killed by close friends or relatives – not by strangers. And, in this case, not by me.'

'Odd indeed. Yet the owners of Golden Rule have offered a substantial reward for your death. Or, to be precise, for delivering you alive or dead, with no emphasis on keeping you alive – just your body, cobber, warm or cold. Should I point out that, if I were your attorney, I would be ethically bound not to exploit this opportunity?'

'Rabbi, I don't think you would anyhow; you're too much the old Loonie. You're simply trying to chivvy me into hiring you. Mmm. I claim the Three Days.'

'Three days, it is. Do you want skin receipts or will chits suffice?'

'Since I've lost the look of a Loonie, we had better have both.'

'Very well. A crown or two for luck?'

The Reverend Ezra stamped our forearms with the date three months hence and with his chop, using a waterproof ink visible only in black light, and showed us, using his test lamp, that we were marked and now could legally breathe for one quarter anywhere in L-City municipal pressure – and enjoy other concomitant privileges such as passage through public cubic. I offered him three crowns over what I had paid for air; he accepted two.

I thanked him and bade him good day; we went on down the tunnel, each somewhat awkwardly burdened. Fifty meters farther along, the tunnel debouched into a main corridor. We were about to exit, and I was checking my orientation, deciding whether to go left or right, when I heard a whistle and a soprano voice. 'Hold it! Not so fast. Inspection first.'

I stopped and turned. She had a face that spells 'civil servant' – and don't ask me how. I simply know, from three planets, several planetoids, and still more habitats, that after racking up a number of years toward retirement, all civil servants have this look. She wore a uniform that was neither police nor military. 'Just in from Kong?'

I agreed that we were.

'Are you three together? Put everything on the table. Open up everything. Any fruits, vegetables, or food?'

I said, 'What is this?'

Gwen said, 'I have a Hershey bar. Want a bite?'

'I think that counts as bribery. Sure, why not?'

'Of course I'm trying to bribe you. I have a small alligator in my purse. He's neither fruit nor vegetable; I suppose he could be food. In any case he's almost certainly against your stuffy rules.'

'Wait a minute; I'll have to check the lists.' The inspector consulted a very large loose-leaf volume of terminal printout. 'Alligator pears; alligator skins, cured or tanned; alligators, stuffed – Is this one stuffed?'

'Only when he overeats; he's greedy.'

'Dearie, are you trying to tell me that you've got a *live* alligator in that purse?'

'Put your hand in my purse at your own risk. He's trained as a guard alligator. Count your fingers before you reach in, then count them again as you take your hand out.'

'You're joking.'

'What odds? And how much? But remember, I warned you.'

'Oh, piffle!' The inspector reached into Gwen's purse – gave a yelp as she snatched her hand out. 'It bit me!' She stuck her fingers into her mouth.

'That's what he's there for,' said Gwen. 'I warned you. Are you hurt? Let me see.'

The two women inspected the hand, each decided that red marks were the extent of the damage. 'That's good,' said Gwen. 'I've been trying to teach him to grasp firmly but not to break the skin. And never, never bite fingers off. He's learning; he's still young. But you shouldn't have been able to get your hand back that easily. Alfred is supposed to hang on like a bulldog while the radio alarm causes me to come a-running.'

'I don't know anything about bulldogs but he certainly tried to take my finger off.'

'Oh, surely not! Have you ever seen a dog?'

'Just dressed-out carcasses in meat markets. No, I take that back; I saw one in Tycho zoo when I was a little girl. Big ugly brute. Scared me.'

'Some are small and some aren't ugly. A bulldog is ugly but not very big. What a bulldog is best at is biting and hanging on. That's what I'm training King Alfred to do.'

'Take him out and show him to me.'

'No indeed! He's a guard beast; I don't want him getting petted and cooed over by other people; I want him to bite. If you want to see him, *you* reach in and take him out. Maybe this time he'll hang on. I hope.'

That ended any attempt to inspect us. Adele Sussbaum, Unnecessary Public Servant First Class, agreed that Tree-San was not verboten, admired it, and inquired as to its flowers. When she and Gwen started exchanging recipes, I insisted that we had to get moving – if the municipal health and safety inspection was finished.

We slanted across Outer Ring; I smelled out the Causeway and was oriented. We went down a level and passed through Old Dome, then headed down the tunnel where my memory said the Raffles Hotel ought to be.

But en route Bill exposed me to some of his political opinions. 'Senator—'

'Not "Senator," Bill. Doctor.'

'"Doctor." Yes, sir. Doctor, I think it's wrong, what happened back there.'

'Yes, it is. That so-called inspection is pointless. It's the sort of expensive, useless accretion all governments acquire over the years, like barnacles on an ocean ship.'

'Oh, I don't mean *that*. That's okay; it protects the city and gives her an honest job.'

'Strike the word "honest."'

'Huh? I was talking about charging for air. That's *wrong*. Air should be free.'

'Why do you say that, Bill? This isn't New Orleans; this is the Moon. No atmosphere. If you don't buy air, how are you going to breathe?'

'But that's just what I mean! Air to breathe is everybody's right. The government should supply it.'

'The city government does supply it, everywhere inside the city pressure. That's what we just paid for.' I fanned the air in front of his nose. 'This stuff.'

'But that's what I'm saying! Nobody should have to *pay* for the breath of life. It's a natural right and the government should supply it free.'

I said to Gwen, 'Wait a moment, dear; this has got to be settled. We may have to eliminate Bill just to keep him happy. Let's stand right here till we straighten this out. Bill, I paid for air for you to breathe because you have no money. Correct?'

He did not answer at once. Gwen said quietly, 'I let him have pocket money. Do you object?'

I looked at her thoughtfully. 'I think I should have been told. My love, if I am to be responsible for this family, I must know what is going on in it.' I turned to Bill. 'When I paid for your air back there, why didn't you offer to pay your share out of the money you had in your pocket?'

'But *she* gave it to me. Not you.'

'So? Give it back to her.'

Bill looked startled; Gwen said, 'Richard, is this necessary?'

'I think it is.'

'But I don't think it is.'

Bill kept quiet, did nothing, watched. I turned my back on him to face Gwen privately, said softly, for her ears only: 'Gwen, I need your backing.'

'Richard, you're making an issue out of nothing!'

'I don't see it as "nothing," dear. On the contrary, it's a key matter and I need your help. So back me up. Or else.'

'"Or else" what, dear?'

'You know what "or else" means. Make up your mind. Are you going to back me up?'

'Richard, this is ridiculous! I see no reason to cater to it.'

'Gwen, I'm asking you to back me up.' I waited an endless time, then sighed. 'Or start walking and don't look back.'

Her head jerked as if I had slapped her. Then she picked up her case and started walking.

Bill's jaw dropped, then he hurried after her, still carrying Tree-San.

XVI

'Women are meant to be loved, not to be understood.'

OSCAR WILDE 1854–1900

I WATCHED them out of sight, then started walking slowly. It was easier to walk than to stand still and there was no place near to sit down. My stump ached and all the weariness of the past few days hit me. My mind was numb. I continued to move toward the Raffles Hotel because I was headed that way, programmed.

The Raffles was even seedier than I had recalled. But I suspected that Rabbi Ezra knew what he was talking about – this, or nothing. In any case I wanted to get out of the public eye; I would have accepted a much poorer hostelry as long as it enabled me to get behind a closed door.

I told the man at the desk that Rabbi Ezra had sent me and asked what he had. I think he offered me his most expensive room still vacant: eighteen crowns.

I ran through the ritual dicker but my heart wasn't in it. I settled for fourteen crowns, paid it, accepted a key; the clerk turned a large book toward me. 'Sign here. And show me your air receipt.'

'Eh? When did this kaka start?'

'With the new administration, chum. I don't like it any more than you do but either I comply or they shut me down.'

I thought about it. Was I 'Richard Ames'? Why cause a cop to salivate at the thought of a reward? Colin Campbell? Someone with a long memory might recognize that name – and think of Walker Evans.

I wrote, 'Richard Campbell, Novylen.'

'Thank you, gospodin. Room L is at the end of this passage on the left. There's no dining room but our kitchen has dumbwaiter service to the rooms. If you want dinner here, please note that the kitchen shuts down at twenty-one o'clock. Except for liquor and ice, dumbwaiter service ends at the same time. But there is an all-night Sloppy Joe across the corridor and north about fifty meters. No cooking in the rooms.'

'Thank you.'

'Do you want company? Straight arrow, lefthand drive, or versatile, all ages and sexes and catering only to high-class clientele.'

'Thanks again. I'm very tired.'

It was a room adequate for my needs; I didn't mind its shabbiness. There was a single bed and a couch that opened out, and a refresher, small but with all the usual offices, and no water restriction – I promised myself a hot bath . . . later, later! A shelf bracket in the bed-sitting room seemed to have been intended for a communication terminal; now it was empty. Near it, let into the rock, was a brass plate:

In This Room on Tuesday 14 May 2075
Adam Selene, Bernardo de la Paz,
Manuel Davis, and Wyoming Knott
Created the Plan That Gave Rise to Free Luna.
Here They Declared the Revolution!

I was not impressed. Yes, those four were heroes of the Revolution but in the year in which I buried Colin Campbell and created Richard Ames I had stayed in a dozen-odd hotel rooms in L-city; most of them had sported a similar sign. It was like the 'Washington Slept Here' signs back in my native country: bait for tourists, any resemblance to truth a happy accident.

Not that I cared. I took off my foot, lay down on the couch, and tried to make my mind blank.

Gwen! Oh, damn, damn, *damn!*

Had I been a stiff-necked fool? Perhaps. But, damn it all, there is a limit. I didn't mind indulging Gwen in most things. It was all right to let her make decisions for both of us and I hadn't squawked even when she did so without consulting me. But she should not encourage this pensioner to defy me – now should she? I should not have to put up with that. A man can't live that way.

But I can't live without her!

Not true, not true! Up until this week – hardly more than three days ago – you lived without her . . . and you can do without her now.

I can do without my missing foot, too. But I don't like not having both feet and I'll never get used to the loss. Sure, you can do without Gwen; you won't die without her – but admit it, stupid: In the past thirty years you've been happy just this brief time, the hours since Gwen moved in and married you. Hours loaded with danger and blatant injustice and fighting and hardship, and it all mattered not a whit; you've been bubbling over with happiness simply because she was at your side.

And now you've sent her away.

Put on your stupid hat. Fasten it with rivets; you'll never need to take it off again.

But I was *right!*

So? What has being 'right' got to do with staying married?

I must have slept (I was mortal tired), as I remember things that did not happen, nightmares – e.g., Gwen had been raped and killed in Bottom Alley. But rape is as scarce in Luna City as it is commonplace in San Francisco. Over eighty years since the last one and the groundhog who committed it didn't last long enough to be eliminated; the men who responded to her screams tore him to pieces.

Later it was learned that she had screamed because he hadn't paid her. This made no difference. To a Loonie a hooker is just as sacred in her person as is the Virgin Mary. I am a Loonie only by adoption but I agree deep in my heart. The *only* proper punishment for rape is death, forthwith, no appeal.

There used to be, dirtside, legal defenses called 'diminished capacity' and 'not guilty by reason of insanity.' These concepts would bewilder a Loonie. In Luna City a man would necessarily be of diminished mental capacity even to think about rape; to carry one out would be the strongest possible proof of insanity – but among Loonies such mental disorders would not gain a rapist any sympathy. Loonies do not psychoanalyze a rapist; they *kill* him. Now. Fast. Brutally.

San Francisco should learn from Loonies. So should every city where it is not safe for a woman to walk alone. In Luna our ladies are never afraid of men, be they family, friends, or strangers; in Luna men do not harm women – or they *die!*

I had awakened sobbing in grief uncontrollable. Gwen was dead, Gwen had been raped and murdered and it was my fault!

Even when I had wakened wide enough to fit back into my proper continuity I was still bawling – I knew that it had been just a dream, a nasty nightmare . . . but my guilt feelings were undiminished. I had indeed failed to protect my darling. I had told her to leave me. '– start walking and don't look back.' Oh, folly unplumbable!

What can I do about it?

Find her! Maybe she'll forgive me. Women seem to have almost unlimited capacity for forgiveness. (Since it is usually a man who needs forgiveness, this must be a racial survival trait.)

But first I had to find her.

I felt overpowering need to go out and start searching – jump on my horse and gallop in all directions. But that is the classic case given in mathematics textbooks of how *not* to find someone who is lost. I had no idea of where to look for Gwen, but she just possibly might look for me by checking the Raffles – if she had second thoughts. If she did, I must be *here*, not out searching at random.

But I could improve the odds. Call the *Daily Lunatic*; place an advertisement – place more than one sort: a classified ad, a box ad, and – best! – a commercial spiel to go out on every terminal with the *Lunatic*'s hourly news bulletin.

If that doesn't work, what will you do?

Oh, shut up and write the ad!

Gwen, Call me at the Raffles. Richard.

Gwen, *Please* call me! I'm at the Raffles. Love, Richard.

Dearest Gwen, For the sake of what we had, *please* call me. I'm at the Raffles. Love always, Richard.

Gwen, I was wrong. Let me try again. I'm at the Raffles. All my love, Richard.

I jittered over it, finally decided that number two was best – changed my mind; number four held more appeal. Changed it again – the simplicity of number two was better. Or even number one. Oh, hell, stupid, just place an ad! Ask her to call; if you have any chance of getting her back, she won't boggle at how you word it.

Call it in from the hotel office? No, leave a note there, telling Gwen where you are going and why and what time you'll be back and *please* wait . . . then hurry to the newspaper's office and get it on the terminals at once – and into their next edition. Then hurry back.

So I put on my false foot, wrote out the note to leave at the desk, and grabbed my cane – and that split-second timing I have noticed too many times in my life again took place, a timing that impels me more than anything else to think that this crazy world is somehow planned, not chaos.

A knock at my door—

I hurried to open it. It was *she!* Glory hallelujah!

She seemed even smaller than I knew her to be, and all big round solemn eyes. She was carrying the little potted maple as if it were a love offering – perhaps it was. 'Richard, will you let me come back? Please?'

All happening at once I took the little tree and put it on the floor and picked her up and closed the door and sat her on the couch myself beside her and we were crying sobs and tears and talking all mixed up together.

After a while we slowed and I shut up enough that I heard what she was saying: 'I'm sorry Richard I was wrong I should have backed you but I was hurt and angry and too stinking proud to turn back and tell you so and when I did you were gone and I didn't know *what* to do. Oh, God, darling, don't ever let me leave you again; make me stay! You're bigger than I am; if I ever get angry again and try to leave, pick me up and turn me around but *don't* let me leave!'

'I won't let you leave again, ever. I was wrong, dear; I should not have made an issue of it; that's no way to love and cherish. I surrender, horse and foot. Make a pet out of Bill any way you like; I won't say a word. Go ahead, spoil him rotten.'

'No, Richard, no! I was wrong. Bill needed a stern lesson and I should have backed you up and let you straighten him out. However –' Gwen unwound herself a little, reached for her purse, opened it. I said,

'Mind the alligator! Careful.'

She smiled for the first time. 'Adele certainly took that hook, line and sinker.'

'Do you mean that there is *not* an alligator in there?'

'Goodness, sweetheart, do you think I'm eccentric?'

'Oh, Heaven forbid!'

'Just a mousetrap and her imagination. Here –' Gwen placed a wad of money, paper and metal, beside her on the couch. 'I made Bill give it back. What he had left, I mean; he should have had three times as much. I'm afraid Bill is one of those weaklings who can't carry money without spending it. I must figure out how to spank him for it till he learns better. In the meantime he can't have *any* cash until he earns it.'

'As soon as he earns any money he should pay me ninety days' air fee,' I put in. 'Gwen, I really am vexed about that. Vexed at him, not at you. His attitude about paying for air. But I'm sorry as can be that I let it slop over onto you.'

'But you were *right*, dear. Bill's attitude about paying for air reflects his wrong-headedness in general. So I've discovered. We sat in Old Dome and discussed many things. Richard, Bill has the socialist disease in its worst form; he thinks the world owes him a living. He told me sincerely – smugly! – that *of course* everyone was entitled to the best possible medical and hospital service – free of course, unlimited of course, and of course the government should pay for it. He couldn't even understand the mathematical impossibility of what he was demanding. But it's not just free air and free therapy, Bill honestly believes that anything *he* wants must be possible . . . and should be free.' She shivered. 'I couldn't shake his opinion on *anything*.'

'"The Road Song of the Bandar-Log."'

'Excuse me?'

'From a poet a couple of centuries back, Rudyard Kipling. The bandar-log – apes, they were – believed that anything was possible just by wishing it so.'

'Yes, that's Bill. In all seriousness he explains how things *should* be . . . then it's up to the government to make it happen. Just pass a law. Richard, he thinks of "the government" the way a savage thinks of idols. Or – No, I don't know. I don't understand how his mind works. We talked at each other but we didn't reach each other. He *believes* his nonsense. Richard, we made a mistake – or I did. We should not have rescued Bill.'

'Wrong, honey girl.'

'No, dear. I thought I could rehabilitate him. I was wrong.'

'That's not how I meant you were wrong. Remember the rats?'

'Oh.'

'Don't sound so miserable. We took Bill with us because each of us was afraid that, if we didn't, he would be killed, possibly eaten alive by rats. Gwen, we both knew the hazards of picking up stray kittens, we both understood the concept "Chinese obligation." We did it anyhow.' I tilted up her chin, kissed her. 'And we would again, this very minute. Knowing the price.'

'Oh, I love you!'

'I love you, too, in a sweaty, vulgar fashion.'

'Uh . . . now?'

'I need a bath.'

'We can bathe later.'

I had just retrieved Gwen's other baggage, temporarily forgotten outside the door – and happily untouched – and we were getting ready to bathe when Gwen bent over the little tree, then picked it up and put it on the shelf table by the dumbwaiter so she could get at it better. 'Present for you, Richard.'

'Goodie. Girls? Or liquor?'

'Neither. Although I understand both are readily available. The desk manager wanted a cut of my fee when I bought Bill a key here.'

'Bill is here?'

'Overnight, in the cheapest single. Richard, I didn't know what to do with Bill. I would have told him to find his own doss in Bottom Alley if I hadn't heard something Rabbi Ezra said about rats. Darn it all, there did not used to be rats down there. Luna City is getting to be a slum.'

'I'm afraid you're right.'

'I fed him, too – there is a Sloppy Joe up the line. He eats enough for four – perhaps you've noticed?'

'I have.'

'Richard, I could not abandon Bill without feeding him and finding him a safe bed. But tomorrow is another story. I told him that I expected him to shape up – before breakfast.'

'Hmmph. Bill would lie for a fried egg. He's a sad sack, Gwen. The saddest.'

'I don't think he can lie convincingly. At least I gave him something to think about. He knows that I am angry with him, that I despise his notions, and that the free lunch is about to shut its doors. I hope I have given him a sleepless night. Here, dear –' She had been digging into the potting soil, under the little maple. 'For Richard. Better wash them.' She handed me six cartridges, Skoda 6.5mm longs or monkey copies.

I picked one up, examined it. 'Wonder woman, you continue to amaze me. Where? When? How?'

Praise made her look sunnily happy and about twelve. 'This morning. In Kong. Black market, of course, which simply means finding which counter to look under at Sears. I hid my Miyako under Tree-San before I went shopping, then stashed the ammo there in leaving Xia's place. Sweetheart, I did not know what sort of search we might have to stand if things got sticky in Kong – and they did, but Auntie got us loose.'

'Can you cook?'

'I'm an adequate cook.'

'You can shoot, you can rassle a rolligon, you can pilot a spacecraft, you can cook. Okay, you're hired. But do you have any other skills?'

'Well, some engineering. I used to be a pretty good lawyer. But I haven't practiced either one lately.' She added, 'And I can spit between my teeth.'

'Supergal! Are you now or have you ever been a member of the human race? Careful how you answer; it will be taken down in writing.'

'I decline to answer on advice of counsel. Let's order dinner before they shut down the kitchen.'

'I thought you wanted a bath?'

189

'Do. I'm itchy. But if we don't get the order in soon, we'll have to get dressed and go out to Sloppy Joe's . . . and I don't mind Sloppy Joe but I do mind having to get dressed. This is the first completely relaxed, quiet time I've had alone with my husband for, oh, ages. In your suite in Golden Rule before that silly eviction notice.'

'Three days.'

'As little as that? Truly?'

'Eighty hours. Fairly busy hours, I grant you.'

The Raffles has a good kitchen as long as you stick to chef's choice; that night it was meatballs with Swedish pancakes, honey-and-beer sauce – an odd combination that worked. Tossed fresh salad, oil and wine vinegar. Cheese and fresh strawberries. Black tea.

We enjoyed it but an old shoe, suitably sautéed, would have been acceptable, so long had it been since we had eaten. It could have been fried skunk and I would not have noticed; Gwen's company was all the sauce I needed.

We had been happily chomping away for a half hour, making no attempt to be elegant, when my darling noticed the brass plate in the rock – too busy before then. Understandable.

She got up and looked at it, then said in a hushed voice, 'I'll be a Hollywood hooker. This is the place! Richard, this is the very cradle of the Revolution! And here I've sat, belching and scratching, as if this were just any hotel room.'

I said, 'Sit down and finish your dinner, love. Three out of four hotel rooms in Luna City have signs something like that.'

'Not like *that*. Richard, what is the number of this room?'

'Doesn't have a number – letter. Room L.'

'"Room L" – yes! This is the place! Richard, in any nation back dirtside, a national shrine this important would have an eternal flame. Likely a guard of honor. But here – Somebody puts up that little brass plaque, and it's forgotten. Even on Free Luna Day. But that's Loonies. Weirdest mob in the known universe. My word!'

I said, 'Darling girl, if it pleases you to think that this room is truly what that sign says – fine! In the meantime sit back down and eat. Or shall I eat your strawberries?'

Gwen did not answer; she did sit down, then kept quiet.

She merely toyed with the fruit and cheese. I finally said, 'Sweetheart, something is bothering you.'

'I won't die from it.'

'Glad to hear it. Well, when you feel like talking, I'm all ears. Meanwhile I'll simply fan you with them. Don't feel hurried.'

'Richard –' Her voice sounded choked. I was surprised to see tears slowly creeping down each side of her nose.

'Yes, dear?'

'I've told you a pack of lies. I—'

'Stop right there. My love, my lusty little love, I have always believed that women should be allowed to lie as much as they need to and never be taxed with it. Lies can be their only defense against an unfriendly world. I have not quizzed you about your past – have I?'

'No, but—'

'Again stop. I haven't. You volunteered a few things. But, even so, I've shut you up a couple of times when you were about to have an attack of pernicious autobiography. Gwen, I didn't marry you for your money, or for your family background, or your brains, or even for your talents in bed.'

'Not even for the last? You haven't left me much.'

'Oh, yes, I have. I appreciate your horizontal skills and your enthusiasm. But competent mattress dancers are not uncommon. Take Xia, for example. I conjecture that she is both skilled and eager.'

'Probably twice as skilled as I am, but I'll be damned if she's more eager.'

'You do all right when you get your rest. But don't distract me. Do you want to know what it is that makes you so special?'

'*Yes!* Well, I think so. If it's not booby-trapped.'

'It's not. Mistress mine, your unique and special quality is this: When I'm around you, I'm happy.'

'Richard!'

'Quit blubbering. Can't stand a female who has to lick tears off her upper lip.'

'Brute. I'll cry if I goddamn well feel like it . . . and I need this one. Richard, I love you.'

'I'm fond of you, too, monkey face. What I was saying was that, if your present pack of lies is wearing thin, don't bother to build up another structure filled with solemn assurances that this is at last the truth, the whole truth, and nothing but the truth. Forget it. The old structure may be threadbare – but I don't care. I'm not looking for holes or inconsistencies because I *don't* care. I just want to live with you and hold your hand and hear you snore.'

'I *don't* snore! Uh . . . do I?'

'I don't know. We haven't had enough sleep in the last eighty hours for it to be a problem. Ask me in fifty years.' I reached across the table, tickled a nipple, watched it grow. 'I want to hold your hand, listen to your snores, and occasionally – oh, once or twice a month—'

'Once or twice a month!'

'Is that too often?'

She sighed. 'I guess I must settle for what I can get. Or go out on the tiles.'

'Tiles? What tiles? I was saying that once or twice a month we'll go out to dinner, see a show, go to a night club. Buy you a flower to pin in your hair. Oh, oftener, I guess, if you insist . . . but too much night life does interfere with writing. I intend to support you, my love, despite those bags of gold you have squirreled away.' I added, 'Some problem, dear? Null program? Why the expression?'

'Richard Colin, you are beyond doubt the most infuriating man I have ever married. Or even slept with.'

'Did you let them sleep?'

'Oh, you *mother!* I shouldn't have saved you from Gretchen. "Once or twice a month"! You set me up for that. Then sprang the trap.'

'Madam, I don't know what you are talking about.'

'You do so! You think I'm a sweaty little nymphomaniac.'

'You're not *too* little.'

'Keep doing it. Go on. Push me hard enough and I'll add a second husband to our marriage. Choy-Mu would marry us – I know he would.'

'Choy-Mu is a dinkum cobber, too right. And I'm sure he would marry you; he doesn't have sand in his skull. If you so elect, I'll try to make him feel welcome. Although I hadn't realized that you were that well acquainted with him. Were you speaking seriously?'

'No, damn it. I've never made a practice of plural marriage; coping with one husband at a time is complex enough.

Certainly Captain Marcy is a nice boy but he's much too young for me. Oh, I won't say that I would turn him down for a night of bundling if he asked me gracefully. But it would be simply for fun, nothing serious.'

'*I* won't say that you would turn him down, either. Well, let me know ahead of time, if convenient, so that I can gracefully fail to notice. Or stand jigger. Even hand out towels. Lady's option.'

'Richard, you're entirely too agreeable.'

'You want me to be jealous? But this is Luna, and I'm a Loonie. Only by adoption but nevertheless a Loonie. Never a groundhog, banging his head against a rock wall.' I paused to kiss her hand. 'My lovely mistress, you are indeed small and not massy. But your heart is big. Like the loaves and fishes, you are a rich plenitude for as many husbands and lovers as you choose. I am happy to be first – if I am first – among equals.'

'"Is this a dagger which I see before me?"'

'No, an icicle.'

'Really? Let's grab it before it melts.'

We did, but just barely; I was tired. Afterwards I said, 'Gwen, why are you frowning? Did I do so poorly?'

'No, love. But I still have those lies on my mind . . . and this time please don't change the subject. I know that the inscription on that brass plate over there is correct, because I knew three of those four. Knew them well; I was adopted by two of them. Beloved, I am a Founding Father of Luna Free State.'

I said nothing because sometimes there is nothing one can say. Shortly Gwen wiggled and said almost angrily. 'Don't look at me that way! I know what you're thinking; 2076 is quite a while back. So it is. But, if you'll get dressed, I'll take you down to Old Dome and show you my chop and thumbprint on the Declaration of Independence. You might not believe that it's my chop . . . but I can't fake a thumbprint. Shall we go look?'

'No.'

'Why not? Want to know my age? I was born Christmas Day 2063, so I was twelve and a half when I signed the Declaration. That nails down how old I am.'

'Sweetheart, when I decided to become a native Loonie or

a reasonable facsimile, I studied the history of Luna to help me get away with it. There is no Gwendolyn among the signers. Wait a second, not saying you lied – saying you must have had another name then.'

'Yes, of course. Hazel. Hazel Meade Davis.'

'"Hazel." Later married into the Stone Gang. Leader of the children's auxiliaries. Um, Hazel was a redhead.'

'Yes. Now I can stop taking some pesky pills and let my hair go back to its natural color. Unless you prefer it this shade?'

'Hair color isn't important. But – Hazel, why did you marry me?'

She sighed. 'For love, dear, and that is true. To help you when you were in trouble . . . and that is true, too. Because it was inevitable and that is true, also. For it is written in history books in another time and place that Hazel Stone returned to Luna and married Richard Ames aka Colin Campbell . . . and this couple rescued Adam Selene, chairman of the Revolutionary Committee.'

'Already written, eh? Predestined?'

'Not quite, my beloved. In other history books it is written that we failed . . . and died trying.'

XVII

'Age cannot wither her, nor custom stale
Her infinite variety: other women cloy
The appetites they feed; but she makes hungry
Where most she satisfies—'

WILLIAM SHAKESPEARE 1564–1616

So THIS girl tells the school nurse, 'My brother thinks he's a hen.' The nurse answers, 'Oh, goodness! What's being done to help him?' The girl answers, 'Nothing. Mama says we need the eggs.'

Are a woman's delusions anything to worry about? If she's happy with them? Was I duty bound to take Gwen to a shrink to try to get her cured?

Hell, no! Shrinks are the blind leading the blind; even the best of them are dealing from a short deck. Anyone who consults a shrink should have his head examined.

Close scrutiny showed that Gwen was possibly over thirty, probably under forty – but certainly not as old as fifty. So what was a gentle way to handle her claim that she was born more than a century ago?

Everyone knows that natives of Luna age more slowly than groundhogs who have grown up in a one-gee field. Gwen's delusion seemed to include the notion that she herself was actually a Loonie instead of the native groundhog she had claimed to be. But Loonies do age, albeit slowly, and Loonies more than a hundred years old (I had met several) do not look only thirty-odd years old; they look ancient.

I would have to try hard to let Gwen think that I believed her every word . . . while believing none and telling myself that it did not matter. I once knew a man who, sane himself, was married to a woman who believed devoutly in astrology. She was forever buttonholing someone and asking what sign her victim was born under. That sort of antisocial nuttiness must be much harder to live with than Gwen's gentle delusion.

Yet this man seemed happy. His wife was an excellent cook, a pleasant woman (aside from this hole in her head), and may have been a bedroom artist equal to Rangy Lil. So why should he worry about her syndrome? She was happy with it, even though she annoyed other people. I think he did not mind living in an intellectual vacuum at home as long as he was physically comfortable there.

Having gotten off her pretty chest what was fretting her, Gwen went right to sleep, and soon I did likewise, for a long, happy, solid night of rest. I woke up restored and cheerful, ready to fight a rattlesnake and allow the snake the first two bites.

Or ready to eat a rattlesnake. Come Monday, I was going to have to find us new quarters; I'm usually willing to go out for other meals but breakfast should be available before one has to face the world. This is not the only reason to be married but it is a good one. Of course there are other ways to manage breakfast at home, but marrying and conning your wife into getting breakfast is, I believe, the commonest strategy.

Then I came a little wider awake and realized that we could get breakfast right here. Or could we? What hours did the kitchen function? What time is it now? I checked the notice posted by the dumbwaiter, was depressed by it.

I had cleaned my teeth and put on my foot and was pulling on my pants (while noting that I must buy clothes today; these trousers were reaching critical mass), when Gwen woke up.

She opened one eye. 'Have we met?'

'We of Boston would not consider it a formal introduction. But I'm willing to buy you breakfast anyhow; you were fairly lively. What'll it be? This fleabag offers only something called "café complet," a bleak promise at best. Or you can get decent and we'll creep slowly out to see Sloppy Joe.'

'Come back to bed.'

'Woman, you're trying to collect my life insurance. Sloppy Joe? Or shall I order for you a cup of lukewarm Nescafé, a stale croissant, and a glass of synthetic orange juice for a luxurious breakfast in bed?'

'You promised me waffles every morning. You promised me. You did.'

'Yes. At Sloppy Joe's. That's where I'm going. Are you

196

coming with me? Or shall I order for you the Raffles speciality of the house?'

Gwen continued to grumble and moan and accuse me of unspeakable crimes and urge me to come die like a man while promptly and efficiently getting up, refreshing for the day, and dressing. She finished looking spic and span instead of three days in the same clothes. Well, we both did have brand-new underclothes, recent hot baths, and putatively clean minds and nails . . . but she looked bandbox fresh while I looked like the pig that slowly walked away. Which was all her misfortune and none of my own; Gwen was wonderfully good to wake up to. I felt bubblingly happy.

As we left room L she took my arm and hugged it. 'Mister, thank you for inviting me to breakfast.'

'Anytime, little girl. What room is Bill in?'

She sobered instantly. 'Richard, I did not purpose exposing you to Bill until after you had eaten. Better perhaps?'

'Uh – Oh, hell, I don't enjoy waiting for breakfast and I see nothing to be gained by making Bill wait for his. We don't have to look at him; I'll grab a table for two and Bill can sit at the counter.'

'Richard, you are a soft-hearted slob. I love you.'

'Don't call me a soft-hearted slob, you soft-hearted slob. Who lavished spending money on him?'

'I did and it was a mistake and I got it back from him and it won't happen again.'

'You got some of it back from him.'

'Got back what he had left and quit rubbing my nose in it, please. I was an idiot, Richard. Too right.'

'So let's forget it. This is his room?'

Bill was not in his room. An inquiry at the desk confirmed what knocking had shown to be likely: Bill had gone out a half hour earlier. I think Gwen was relieved. I know I was. Our problem child had become a major pain in the Khyber. I had to remind myself that he had saved Auntie to see anything good about him.

A few minutes later we entered the local Sloppy Joe. I was looking around for a free table for two when Gwen squeezed my arm. I looked up, then looked where she was looking.

Bill was at the cashier's station, paying a check. He was doing so with a twenty-five-crown note.

We waited. When he turned around he saw us – and looked ready to run. But there was nowhere to run except past us.

We got him outside without a scene. In the corridor Gwen looked at him, her face cold with disgust. 'Bill, where did you get that money?'

He looked at her, looked away. 'It's mine.'

'Oh, nonsense. You left Golden Rule without a farthing. Any money you have you got from me. You lied to me last night – you held out on me.'

Bill looked doggedly stubborn, said nothing. So I said, 'Bill, go back to your room. After we've had breakfast we'll see you there. And we'll have the truth out of you.'

He looked at me with barely restrained fury. 'Senator, this ain't none of your pidgin!'

'We'll see. Go back to the Raffles. Come, Gwen.'

'But I want Bill to return my money. Now!'

'After breakfast. This time let's do it my way. Are you coming?'

Gwen shut up and we went back into the restaurant. I saw to it that we did not discuss Bill; some subjects curdle the gastric juices.

About thirty minutes later I said, 'Another waffle, dear?'

'No, thank you, Richard, I've had enough. They're not as good as yours.'

'That's 'cause I'm a natural-born genius. Let's finish up, then go back and take care of Bill. Shall we skin him alive, or merely impale him on a stake?'

'I've been planning to question him on the rack. Richard, life lost some of its beauty when truth drugs replaced thumb screws and hot irons.'

'My beloved, you are a bloodthirsty little wretch. More coffee?'

'You just say that to flatter me. No more, thank you.'

We returned to the Raffles, went to Bill's room, were unable to raise him, went back to the desk. The misanthrope who had checked me in was again on duty. I asked, 'Have you seen anything of William Johnson, room KK?'

'Yes. About thirty minutes ago he collected his key deposit and left.'

'But *I* bought that key!' Gwen said, rather shrilly.

The desk manager was unruffled. 'Gospazha, I know you did. But we return the deposit for the return of the key. It doesn't matter who rented the room.' He reached for his rack, took down key card KK. 'The deposit just barely pays for changing the magnetic code if someone fails to return his key – it doesn't pay for the nuisance. If you dropped your card in the corridor and somebody picked it up and turned it in, we would pay the deposit ... then you would have to pay a second deposit to get into your room.'

I took Gwen firmly by the elbow. 'Fair enough. If he shows up, let us know, will you? Room L.'

He looked at Gwen. 'You don't want room KK?'

'No.'

He turned his attention to me. 'You have Room L at its single rate. For double occupancy we charge more.'

Suddenly I had had it. All the kaka, all the shoving around, all the petty nonsense I could take. 'You try to clip me one more crown and I'll haul you down to Bottom Alley and unscrew your head! Come along, dear.'

I was still fuming when I let us into our room and locked the door. 'Gwen, let's not stay in Luna. The place has changed. For the worse.'

'Where do you want to go, Richard?' She looked and sounded distressed.

'Uh – I would opt to emigrate, right out of the System – Botany Bay, or Proxima, or such – if I were younger and had two legs.' I sighed. '"Sometimes I feel like a motherless child."'

'Sweetheart—'

'Yes, dear?'

'I'm here, and I want to mother you. I go where you go. I'll follow you to the ends of the Galaxy. But I don't want to leave Luna City just yet ... if you will indulge me. We can go out now and search for somewhere else to stay. If we don't find a place – Rabbi Ezra may be right – can't we put up with that surly clerk until Monday? Then we can certainly find a place.'

I concentrated on slowing my heart, managed it. 'Yes, Gwen. We might shop for a place to move into after the weekend, after the Shriners leave, if we can't find a suitable place available at once. I wouldn't mind the shmo on the desk if we were sure of proper cubic after the weekend.'

'Yes, sir. May I tell you now why I need to stay in Luna City for a while?'

'Eh? Yes, certainly. Matter of fact, I ought to stay rooted to one spot for a while, too. Get some writing done, make some money to offset the rather heavy expenses of this week.'

'Richard. I've tried to tell you. There are no money worries.'

'Gwen, there are always money worries. I'm not going to spend your savings. Call it *macho* if you like, but I intend to support you.'

'Yes, Richard. Thank you. But you need feel no pressure of time. I can lay hands promptly on whatever amount of money we need.'

'So? That's a sweeping statement.'

'It was intended to be, sir. Richard, I stopped lying to you. Now is the time for large chunks of truth.'

I brushed this aside with both hands. 'Gwen, haven't I made it clear to you that I don't care what fibs you've told or how old you are or what you have been? It's a fresh start, you and me.'

'Richard, stop treating me as a child!'

'Gwen, I am not treating you as a child. I am saying that I accept you as you are. Today. Now. Your past is your business.'

She looked at me sadly. 'Beloved, you don't believe that I am Hazel Stone. Do you?'

Time to lie! But a lie is no good if it's not believed (unless it is told to be disbelieved, which could not apply here). Time to fan-dance instead. 'Sweetheart, I've been trying to tell you that it does not matter to me whether or not you are Hazel Stone. Or Sadie Lipschitz. Or Pocahontas. You are my beloved wife. Let's not cloud that golden fact with irrelevancies.'

'Richard, Richard! Listen to me. Let me talk.' She sighed. 'Or else.'

'"Or else"?'

'You know what "Or else" means; you used it on me. If you won't listen, then I must go back and report that I have failed.'

'Go back where? Report to whom? Failed in what?'

'If you won't listen, it doesn't matter.'

'You told me not to let you leave!'

'I won't be leaving you; I'll just be running a quick errand, then back home to you. Or you're welcome to come with me – oh, I wish you would! But I must report my failure and resign my commission . . . then I'll be free to go with you to the ends of the universe. But I must resign, not simply desert. You are a soldier; you understand that.'

'You are a soldier?'

'Not exactly. An agent.'

'Uh . . . *agente provocateuse?*'

'Uh, close.' She smiled wryly. '*Agente amoureuse* perhaps. Although I wasn't told to fall in love with you. Just to marry you. But I did fall in love with you, Richard, and it may have ruined me as an agent. Will you come with me while I report back? Please?'

I was getting more confused by the minute. 'Gwen, I'm getting more confused by the minute.'

'Then why not let me explain?'

'Uh – Gwen, it *can't* be explained. You claim that you're Hazel Stone.'

'I am.'

'Damn it, I can count. Hazel Stone, if she is still alive, is well over a century old.'

'That's right. I'm well over a hundred.' She smiled. 'I robbed the cradle, dear one.'

'Oh, for God's sake! Look, dear, I've spent the last five nights in bed with you. You're an exceptionally lively old bag!'

She grinned at me. 'Thank you, dear. I owe it all to Lydia Pinkham's Vegetable Compound.'

'You do, eh? A patent nostrum took the calcium out of your joints and put it back into your bones, and ironed out the wrinkles in your face, and restored your youthful hormonal balance, and unclogged your arteries? Order me a barrel of it; I'm slowing down.'

'Mrs Pinkham had expert help, dearest. Richard, if you would only let me prove to you who I am, by my thumbprint on the Declaration of Independence, your mind would then be open to the truth, strange though it is. I wish I could offer you identification by retinal patterns . . . but my retinas had not been photographed then. But there *is* that thumbprint. And there is blood typing, too.'

I began to feel panicky – what would Gwen do if her delusion pattern was toppled?

Then I remembered something. 'Gwen, Gretchen mentioned Hazel Stone.'

201

'So she did. Gretchen is my great great granddaughter, Richard. I married Slim Lemke, of the Stone Gang, on my fourteenth birthday and had my first child by him at Terra's fall equinox of 2078 – a boy; I named him Roger for my father. In 2080 I had my first daughter—'

'Hold it. Your eldest daughter was a student of Percival Lowell when I commanded the rescue operation. So you said.'

'Part of that pack of lies, Richard. I did indeed have a descendant there – a granddaughter on the faculty. So I truly am grateful. But I had to edit the details to fit my apparent age. My first daughter was named Ingrid, for Slim's mother . . . and Ingrid Henderson was named for her grandmother – my daughter, Ingrid Stone. Richard, you could not guess at the time how difficult it was for me at Dry Bones Pressure to meet for the first time five of my very own and not be able to acknowledge them.

'But I can't be Grandmother Hazel when I am being Gwen Novak. So I didn't admit it . . . and that was not the first time this has happened to me. I've had lots of children – forty-four years from menarche to menopause and I gave birth to sixteen by four husbands and three passing strangers – and took the Stone name back after my fourth husband died. Because I moved in with my son Roger Stone.

'I raised four of the kids Roger had by his second wife – she is a medical doctor and needed a resident grandmother. I got three of them married off, all but the baby, who is now chief surgeon at Ceres General and may never get married as he is handsome and quite self-centered and believes the old saw about "Why keep a cow?"'

'Then I started taking the vegetable compound, and here I am, fertile again and ready to raise another family.' She smiled and patted her belly. 'Let's go back to bed.'

'God damn it, wench; that won't solve anything!'

'No, but it's a swell way to pass the time. And sometimes it puts a stop to recurrent bleeding. Which reminds me – If Gretchen ever shows up, I won't interfere a second time. I just did not fancy having my great great granddaughter crowding in on my honeymoon – a honeymoon already crowded by too many people and too much excitement.'

'Gretchen is just a child.'

'You think so? She is physically as mature as I was at

fourteen . . . when I married and got pregnant at once. Virgin at marriage, Richard; happens oftener here than anywhere else. Mama Mimi was strict and Mama Wyoh was charged with keeping an eye on me, and I wasn't inclined to stray anyhow, as the Davis family was socially as high as you could be in Luna City in those days and I appreciated having been adopted by them. Beloved, I'm not going to tell you another word about me until you check my chop and print on the Declaration. I can feel your disbelief . . . and it humiliates me.'

(What do you do when your wife persists? Marriage is the greatest human art . . . when it works.) 'Sweetheart, I don't want to humiliate you. But I'm not competent to match thumbprints. But there is more than one way to cook a wolf. This second wife of your son Roger: Is she still alive?'

'Very much so. Dr Edith Stone.'

'Then there is probably a record right here in Luna City of her marriage to your son and – Is he the Roger Stone who was once mayor?'

'Yes. From 2122 to 2130. But he's not available; he left here in 2148.'

'Where is he now?'

'Several light-years away. Edith and Roger out-migrated, to Fiddler's Green. None of that branch of my family is around any longer. It won't work, dear – you're looking for someone who can identify me as Hazel Stone. Aren't you?'

'Well . . . yes. I thought Dr Edith Stone would be an expert and unbiased witness.'

'Mmm . . . she still can be.'

'How?'

'Blood typing, Richard.'

'Look, Gwen, blood typing is a subject I've had to know something about, because of field surgery. I saw to it that every man in my regiment was typed. Blood typing can show who you are not; it cannot prove who you are. In a number as small as a regiment even the rare AB negative will be matched more than once; they run one in two hundred. I remember because I am one.'

She nodded agreement. 'And I'm O positive, the commonest type of all. But that's not the whole story. If you type for all thirty-odd blood groups, a blood type is as unique as a fingerprint or a retinal pattern. Richard, during the Revolution lots of our people died because they had not been blood-typed. Oh, we knew how to transfuse blood but safe donors could be found only by cross-matching, then and there. Without typing this was often too slow; many – no, most – of our wounded who needed blood died because a donor could not be identified in time.

'After peace and independence Mama Wyoh – Wyoming Knott Davis, the hospital in Kong – you know?'

'I noticed.'

'Mama Wyoh had been a professional host mother, in Kong, and knew about such things. She started the first blood bank, with money raised by Major Watenabe, another Founding Father. There may be a half liter of my blood frozen in Kong even today . . . but what is certain is that a complete typing of my blood is on file there, because Edith saw to it that each one of us had a full typing, all known groups, before we all started a *Wanderjahr* in 2148.'

Gwen smiled happily. 'So take a sample of my blood, Richard; have it typed at Galileo University Medical Center. Get a full work-up, I'll pay for it. Compare it with my typing done in 2148, filed at Wyoming Knott Memorial. Anyone who can read English can tell whether or not the two work-ups match; it doesn't take the sort of expertise required to match fingerprints. If that doesn't say I am me, then send for a straitjacket; it'll be time to put me away.'

'Gwen, we're not going back to Kong. Not for anything.'

'No need to. We pay the blood bank at Galileo to have a transcript from Kong printed out by terminal.' Her face clouded. 'But it will blow my cover as Mistress Novak. Once those two records are side by side they'll know that Grandmother Hazel has returned to the scene of her crimes. I don't know what that will do to my mission; it was not supposed to happen. But I do know that convincing you is absolutely essential to my mission.'

'Gwen, assume that you've convinced me.'

'Truly dear? You wouldn't lie to me?'

(Yes, I would, little love. But I must admit that your words are persuasive. All that you have said matches my own careful study of Lunar history . . . and you deal with little details as if you had been there. It all is convincing but the physical impossibility – you are *young*, darling; you are not an old crone of more than a century.) 'Sweetheart, you've given me two positive ways to identify you. So let's assume that I've checked out one or the other or both. Let's stipulate that you're Hazel. Do you prefer to be called Hazel?'

'I answer to both names, darling. Suit yourself.'

'All right. The sticky point is your appearance. If you were old and dried up instead of young and juicy—'

'Are you complaining?'

'No. Merely descriptive. Stipulating that you are Hazel Stone, born 2063, how do you account for your youthful appearance? And don't give me any guff about a legendary patent medicine.'

'You'll find the truth hard to believe, Richard. I have undergone rejuvenation. Twice in fact. The first time to bring me back in appearance to late middle age . . . while restoring my bodily economy to youthful maturity. The second time was mostly cosmetic, to make me desirable in appearance. To recruit *you*, sir.'

'Be damned. Monkey face, is that your own face?'

'Yes. It can be changed if you would like me to look otherwise.'

'Oh, no! I'm not one to insist on prettiness as long as a girl's heart is pure.'

'Why, you louse!'

'But since your heart isn't all that pure, it's nice that you're pretty.'

'You can't talk yourself out of it that easily!'

'Okay, you're gorgeous and sexy and evil. But "rejuvenation" explains without explaining. So far as I've ever heard, rejuvenation is for flatworms but not for anything higher up the evolutionary ladder.'

'Richard, this part you'll have to take on faith – for now, at least. I was rejuvenated at a clinic a couple of thousand years away and in an odd direction.'

'Hmm. It sounds like a gimmick I might have dreamed up when I was writing fantasies.'

'Yes, it does, doesn't it? Not convincing. Merely true.'

'So I see no way to investigate it. Perhaps I'll have to get that blood-type transcript. Uh – Hazel Stone. Roger Stone – *The Scourge of the Spaceways!*'

'My God, my past has caught up with me! Richard, did you ever watch my show?'

'Every episode, unless I had been caught doing something that called for drastic punishment. Captain John Sterling was my childhood hero. And *you* wrote it?'

'My son Roger started it. I started writing it in 2148 but I didn't put my name on it until the following year – then it was "Roger and Hazel Stone"—'

'I remember! But I don't remember that Roger Stone ever wrote it by himself.'

'Oh, yes, he did – until he got tired of the golden treadmill. I took it over from him, intending to kill it off—'

'Sweetheart, you can't kill off a serial! It's unconstitutional.'

'I know. Anyhow, they took up the option and waved too much money under my nose. And we needed the money; we were living in space then and a spacecraft, even a little family job, is expensive.'

'I've never quite had the courage to write a serial against deadlines. Oh, I've written episodes on assignment, using a show's bible, but not on my own and under the gun.'

'We didn't use a bible; Buster and I just whipped 'em up as we went along.'

'"Buster"?'

'My grandson. The one who is now chief surgeon at Ceres General. For eleven years we wrote them together, frustrating the Galactic Overlord at every turn—'

'"The Galactic Overlord!" The best villain in the creepies. Honey, I wish there were really a Galactic Overlord.'

'Why, you young whippersnapper, how dare you throw doubt on the authenticity of the Galactic Overlord? What do *you* know about it?'

'Sorry. I apologize. He's as real as Luna City. Or John Sterling would not have had anyone to frustrate . . . and I certainly believe in Captain John Sterling of the Star Patrol.'

'That's better.'

'That time Captain Sterling was lost in the Horsehead Nebula with the radiation worms after him: How did he get out? That was one of the times I was being punished and not allowed to watch.'

'As I recall – Mind you, this was some years back. I seem

to recall that he jury-rigged his Doppler radar to fry them with polarized beams.'

'No, that was what he used on the space entities.'

'Richard, are you sure? I don't think he encountered the space entities until *after* he escaped from Horsehead Nebula. When he had to make a temporary truce with the Galactic Overlord to save the Galaxy.'

I thought about it. How old was I at the time? What year in school? 'Hon, I do believe you're right. I was upset that he would join forces with the Overlord even to save the Galaxy. I—'

'But he *had* to, Richard! He couldn't let billions of innocent people die just to keep from soiling his hands through co-operating with the Overlord. But I can see your point. Buster and I fought over that episode – Buster wanted to take advantage of the temporary truce to do the Overlord in, once the space entities were destroyed—'

'No, Captain Sterling would never break his word.'

'True. But Buster was always the pragmatist. His solution to almost any problem was to cut somebody's throat.'

'Well, it's a convincing argument,' I admitted.

'But, Richard, you have to go easy in killing off characters in a serial; you must always leave something for the next episode. But you tell me you've never handled a series all on your own.'

'I haven't but I do know that; I watched enough of them, back when. Hazel, why did you let me fill you with a lot of guff about the life of a writer?'

'You called me "Hazel"!'

'Sweetheart – Hazel my darling – I'm not interested in blood types or in thumbprints. You are undeniably the author of history's greatest creepie *The Scourge of the Spaceways*. It said on the credits, week after week, year after year: "Written by Hazel Stone." Then, sadly, it began to read: "Based on characters created by Hazel Stone—"'

'It did? Those later credits should have included Roger; he created the show. Not me. Those nogoodniks.'

'It didn't matter. Because the characters grew anemic and died. Without you the show was never the same.'

'I had to quit; Buster grew up. I supplied the twists; he supplied the gore. Sometimes I got soft-hearted; Buster never did.'

'Hazel? Why don't we revive it? We'll plot it together; you write it; I'll do the cooking and housekeeping.' I stopped and looked at her. 'What in the world are you crying about?'

'I'll cry if I want to! You call me "Hazel" – you *believe* me!'

'I *have* to believe you. Anybody could trick me about blood types or thumbprints. But not about commercial fiction. Not this old hack writer. You're the real McCoy, my love, the authentic scourge of the spaceways. But you're still my sweaty little nymphomaniac – I find I don't mind that you are a couple of centuries old.'

'I am not either two centuries old! I won't be for years and years.'

'But you're still my sweaty little nymphomaniac?'

'If you'll let me.'

I grinned at her. 'Do I have any say in the matter? Get your clothes off and let's do some plotting.'

'"Plotting"?'

'All the best writing is done with the gonads, Hazel my lusty bride – didn't you know that? Battle stations! Here comes the Galactic Overlord!'

'Oh, Richard!'

XVIII

'When it comes to a choice between kindness and honesty, my vote is for kindness, every time – giving or receiving.'

IRA JOHNSON 1854–1941

'HAZEL MY ancient love—'

'Richard, would you like a broken arm?'

'I don't think you can manage it just now.'

'Want to bet?'

'*Ouch!* Stop that! Don't do it again . . . or I'll toss you back into the creek and marry Gretchen. She is not ancient.'

'Keep right on teasing me. My third husband was a tease. Everybody remarked on how well he looked at his funeral . . . and what a shame it was he died so young.' Hazel-Gwen smiled up at me. 'But he turned out to be heavily insured, which does comfort a widow. Marrying Gretchen is a good idea, darling; I would enjoy bringing her up. Teaching her to shoot, helping her with the first baby, coaching her in how to handle a knife, working out with her in martial arts, all the homey domestic skills a girl needs in this modern world.'

'Hummph! My darling girl, you are as little and cute and pretty and harmless as a coral snake. I think Jinx has already trained Gretchen.'

'More likely Ingrid. But I can still put a polish on her. As you pointed out, I'm experienced. What was that word you used? "Ancient," that was it.'

'*Ouch!*'

'Oh, that didn't hurt. Sissy.'

'The hell it didn't. I'm going to enter a monastery.'

'Not till you've entered Gretchen. I've just decided, Richard; we're going to marry Gretchen.'

I treated this ridiculous statement with the neglect it deserved – I got up and hopped into the refresher.

Shortly she followed me in. I cowered away from her. '*Help!* Don't hit me again!'

'Oh, spit. I haven't hit you once, as yet.'

'I surrender. You're not ancient; you're just well marinated. Hazel my love, what makes you so feisty?'

'I'm not feisty. But when you're as small as I am and female, if you don't stand up for your rights, you're sure to be pushed around by big, hairy, smelly men with delusions about male superiority. Don't yelp, dear; I haven't hurt you, not once. I haven't drawn blood – now have I?'

'I'm afraid to look. Mother never warned me that married life could be like this! Sweetheart, you were about to tell me why you had to recruit me and for what purpose when we got distracted.'

She was slow in answering. 'Richard, you had trouble believing that I am more than twice your age.'

'You convinced me. I don't understand it, but I've had to accept it.'

'You're going to find other things I must tell you much harder to accept. Much!'

'Then I probably won't accept them. Hazel-Gwen honey, I'm a hard case. I don't believe in table-tapping, astrology, virgin birth—'

'Virgin birth isn't difficult.'

'I mean, in the theological sense; I'm not talking about genetics laboratories – virgin birth, numerology, a literal hell, magic, witchcraft, and campaign promises. You tell me something that runs contrary to horse sense; I'll be at least as hard to sell as I was about your ancient years. You'll need the Galactic Overlord as a confirming witness.'

'Okay. Slip this one on for size. From one standpoint I'm even more ancient than you suspect. More than two centuries.'

'Hold it. You won't be two hundred until Christmas Day 2263. A good many years yet, as you pointed out.'

'True. I didn't tell you about these extra years even though I lived through them . . . because I lived them at right angles.'

I answered, 'Dear, the sound track suddenly went silent.'

'But, Richard, that one's easy to believe. Where did I drop my pants?'

'Through most of the Solar System, according to your memoirs.'

'That ain't the half of it, mister. Both inside and outside the System and even outside this universe . . . and, brother, have I been transgressed against! I mean, where did I drop them *today?*'

'At the foot of the bed, I think. Hon, why do you bother to wear panties when you take them off so frequently?'

'Because. Only sluts run around without drawers . . . and I'll thank you to keep a civil tongue in your head.'

'I didn't say a word.'

'I could hear what you were thinking.'

'And I don't believe in telepathy, either.'

'You don't, eh? My grandson Dr Lowell Stone aka Buster used to cheat at chess by reading my mind. Thank God he lost the ability when he was about ten.'

'Noted,' I answered, 'as hearsay concerning a highly improbable event from a reporter whose veracity has not been established. Reliability of alleged datum is therefore not higher than C-Five by military intelligence scaling.'

'You'll pay for that!'

'Scale it yourself,' I told her. 'You've served in military intelligence. CIA, wasn't it?'

'Who sez?'

'You sez. Through several unfinished remarks.'

'It was not the CIA and I've never been in McLean in my life and I was fully disguised while I was there and it wasn't me; it was the Galactic Overlord.'

'And I'm Captain John Sterling.'

Gwen-Hazel looked wide-eyed. 'Gee, Captain, can I have your autograph? Better gimme two; I can trade two of yours for one of Rosie the Robot. Richard, will we be going near the main post office?'

'Have to. I've got to set up a mail drop for Father Schultz. Why, dear?'

'If we can swing past Macy's, I'll get Naomi's clothes and wig packed, and then I'll mail them. They've been grinding on my conscience.'

'On your *what?*'

'On the bookkeeping system I use in place of one. Richard, you remind me more and more of my third husband. He was a fine figure of a man, just as you are. He took great care of himself and died in perfect health.'

'What did he die of?'

'Of a Tuesday, as I remember. Or was it a Wednesday? Anyway, I was not there – I was a long way off, curled up with a good buck. We never did learn what did him in. Apparently he fainted in his bath and his head went under water. What are you mumbling, Richard? "Charlotte" who?'

'Nothing, nothing at all. Hazel . . . I do *not* carry life insurance.'

'Then we must be extra careful to keep you alive. Stop taking baths!'

'If I do, in three or four weeks you'll regret it.'

'Oh, I'll stop, too; it will balance out. Richard, will we have time today to go out to the Authority Complex?'

'Perhaps. Why?'

'To find Adam Selene.'

'Is he buried there?'

'That is something I must try to find out. Richard, is your believer in good shape?'

'It's overstrained. Several years at right angles indeed! Want to buy a space warp?'

'Thank you; I have one. In my purse. Those extra years are just a matter of geometry, my husband. If you are wedded to the conventional picture of space-time with just one time axis, then of course you find it hard to understand. But there are at least three time axes just as there are at least three space axes . . . and I lived those extra years on other axes. All clear?'

'Utterly clear, my love. As self-evident as transcendentalism.'

'I knew you would understand. The case of Adam Selene is more difficult. When I was twelve I heard him speak many times; he was the inspiring leader who held our Revolution together. Then he was killed – or so it was reported. It was not until years later that Mama Wyoh told me, as deepest secret, that Adam was not a man. Not a human being at all. Another sort of entity.'

I most carefully said nothing.

Gwen-Hazel said, 'Well? Don't you have anything to say?'

'Oh, sure. Not human. An alien. Green skin and one meter high and its flying saucer landed in Mare Crisium just outside Loonie City. Where was the Galactic Overlord?'

'You can't upset me talking that way, Richard, because I

know just how such an impossible story affects one. I had the same sort of doubts when Mama Wyoh told me. Except that I had to believe her because Mama Wyoh would never lie to me. But Adam was *not* an alien, Richard; he was a child of mankind. But not a human child. Adam Selene was a computer. Or a complex of programs in a computer. But it was a self-programming computer, so it comes to the same thing. Well, sir?'

I took my time answering. 'I like flying saucers better.'

'Oh, fiddle! I'm tempted to turn you in on Marcy Choy-Mu.'

'The smartest thing you could do.'

'No, I'll keep you; I'm used to your foibles. But I may keep you in a cage.'

'Hazel. Listen carefully. Computers do not think. They calculate with great speed in accordance with rules built into them. Since we ourselves calculate by using our brains to think, this designed-in capacity to calculate gives computers the *appearance* of thinking. But they *do not think*. They operate the way they do because they must; they were built that way. You can add "animism" to the list of nonsense notions to which I do not subscribe.'

'I'm glad you feel that way, Richard, because this job will be touchy and difficult. I need your healthy skepticism to keep me straight.'

'I'm going to have to write that down and examine it carefully.'

'Do that, Richard. Now here is what happened back in 2075 and -6: One of my adoptive fathers, Manuel Garcia, was the technician who took care of the big computer of the Authority. This one computer ran almost everything . . . handled all the utilities of this city and of most of the other warrens – except Kong – bossed the first catapult, ran the tubes, handled banking, printed the *Lunatic* – did practically everything. The Authority found it cheaper to expand the functions of this one big computer than to spread computers all through Luna.'

'Neither efficient nor safe.'

'Probably, but that's what they did. Luna was a prison then; it did not have to be either efficient or safe. There was no high tech industry here and in those days we had to accept whatever was handed us. As may be, dear, this one master computer got bigger and bigger . . . and woke up.'

(It did, eh? Sheer fantasy, my sweet . . . and a cliché that has been used by every fantasy writer in history. Even Roger Bacon's Brass Head was one version of it. Frankenstein's monster is another. Then a spate of stories in later years and still they come. And all of them nonsense.) But what I said was: 'Go ahead, dear. Then what?'

'Richard, you don't believe me.'

'I thought we settled that. You said that you needed my healthy skepticism.'

'I do! So use it. Criticize! Don't just sit there with that smug look on your face. This computer had been operating by voice for years – accepting spoken programs, answering with synthesized speech or printout or both.'

'Built-in functions. Techniques two centuries old.'

'Why did your face shut down when I said it "woke up"?'

'Because that's nonsense, my love. Waking and sleeping are functions of living beings. A machine, no matter how powerful and flexible, does not wake up or go to sleep. It is power on or power off; that's all.'

'All right, let me rephrase it. This computer became self-aware and acquired free will.'

'Interesting. If true. I don't have to believe it. I don't.'

'Richard, I refuse to become exasperated. You are simply young and ignorant and that's not your fault.'

'Yes, Grandmaw. I'm young and you're ignorant. Slippery bottom.'

'Take your lecherous hands off me and *listen*. What accounts for self-awareness in a man?'

'Huh? I have no need to account for it; I experience it.'

'True. But it is not a trivial question, sir. Let's treat it like a boundary problem. Are you self-aware? Am I?'

'Well, *I* am, monkey face. I'm not sure about you.'

'The same, vice versa.'

'That's fun, too.'

'Richard, let's stick to the subject. Is the sperm in a male body self-aware?'

'I hope not.'

'Or the ova in a female?'

'That's your question to answer, beautiful; I've never been female.'

'And you are dodging questions just to tease me. A spermato-

214

zoon is not self-aware and neither is an ovum – and never mind silly remarks; that's one boundary. I, an adult human zygote, am self-aware. And you are, too, however dimly this is true for males. Second boundary. Very well, Richard; at what point from the freshly fertilized ovum to the mature zygote now named "Richard" did self-awareness enter the picture? Answer me. Don't dodge it and, please, no silly remarks.'

I still thought it was a silly question but I tried to give it a serious answer. 'Very well. *I* have always been self-aware.'

'A serious answer. Please!'

'Gwen-Hazel, that answer is as serious as I can make it. *So far as I know* I have lived forever and have been self-aware the whole time. All this talk about things that went on before 2133 – the alleged year of my alleged birth – is just hearsay and not very convincing. I go along with the gag to keep from annoying people or getting funny looks. And when I hear astronomers talk about the world being created in a big bang eight or sixteen or thirty billion years before I was born – if I was born; I don't recall it – that's a horse laugh. If I was not alive sixteen billion years ago, then there was nothing at all. Not even empty space. Nothing. Zero with no rim around it. The universe in which I exist cannot exist without me in it. So it's silly to talk about the date I became self-aware; time started when I did, it stops when I do. All clear? Or shall I draw you a diagram?'

'All clear on most points, Richard. But you are wrong about the date. Time did not start in 2133. It started in 2063. Unless one or the other of us is a golem.'

Every time I have a go at solipsism something like this happens. 'Honey, you're cute. But you are a figment of my imagination. *Ouch!* I told you to stop that.'

'You have a lively imagination, darling. Thanks for thinking me up. Do you want another proof? Up to now I've just been playing – shall I now break one of your bones? Just a small one. You pick it.'

'Listen, figment. You break one of my bones and you'll regret it for the next billion years.'

'Merely a logical demonstration, Richard. No malice in it.'

'And once I set the bone—'

'Oh, I'll set it, dear.'

'Not on your life! Once I have it set, I'll phone Xia and ask her to come over and marry me and protect me from small figments with violent habits.'

'You're going to divorce me?' Again she was suddenly all big eyes.

'Hell, no! Just bust you down to junior wife and put Xia in charge. But you can't leave. Permission denied. You're serving a life sentence, whether it's straight ahead or at right angles. I'm going to get a club and beat you until you give up your evil ways.'

'All right. As long as I don't have to go away.'

'*Ouch!* And don't bite. That's rude.'

'Richard, if I am just a figment of your imagination, then any biting I do is your idea, done by you to yourself for some murky masochistic purpose. If that is not true, then I must be self-aware . . . not your figment.'

'Either/or logic never proves anything. But you're a delightful figment, dear. I'm glad I thought of you.'

'Thank you, sir. Sweetheart, here is a key question. If you will answer it seriously, I'll stop biting.'

'Forever?'

'Uh—'

'Don't strain yourself, figment. If you have a serious question, I'll try to give it a serious answer.'

'Yes, sir. What accounts for self-awareness in a man and what is there about this condition or process or whatever that makes awareness impossible for a machine? Specifically for a computer. In particular the giant computer that administered this planet in 2076. The Holmes IV.'

I resisted the temptation to give a flip answer. Self-awareness? I know that one school of psychologists insists that awareness, if it exists, is present just as a passenger, no effect on behavior.

This sort of nonsense should be lumped with transubstantiation. If true, it can't be proved.

I am aware of my own self-awareness . . . and that is as far as any honest solipsist should go. 'Gwen-Hazel, I don't know.'

'Good! We're making progress.'

'We are?'

'Yes, Richard. The hardest part about gaining any new idea is sweeping out the false idea occupying that niche. As long as that niche is occupied, evidence and proof and logical demonstration get nowhere. But once the niche is emptied of the wrong idea that has been filling it – once you can honestly say, "I don't know," then it becomes possible to get at the truth.'

'Hon, you are not only the cutest little figment I've ever imagined, you are also the smartest.'

'Knock it off, buster. Listen to this theory. And think of it as a working hypothesis, not as God-given truth. It was dreamed up by my adoptive father, Papa Mannie, to account for the observed fact that this computer had come to life. Maybe it explains something, maybe it doesn't – Mama Wyoh said that Papa Mannie was never sure. Now attend me – A fertilized human ovum divides . . . and divides again. And again. And again and again and again. Somewhere along there – I don't know where – this collection of millions of living cells becomes aware of itself and the world around it.'

She went on: 'A fertilized egg is not aware but a baby is. After Papa Mannie discovered that his computer was self-aware, he noted that this computer, which had been expanded outrageously as more jobs were assigned to it, had reached a point of complication where it had more interconnections in it than has a human brain.

'Papa Mannie made a great theoretical leap: When the number of interconnections in a computer become of the same close order as the number of interconnections in a human brain that computer can wake up and become aware of itself . . . and probably will. He wasn't sure that it always happened, but he became convinced that it could happen and for that reason: the high number of interconnections.

'Richard, Papa Mannie never went any farther with it. He was not a theoretical scientist; he was a repair technician. But the way his computer was behaving bothered him; he had to try to figure out why it was acting so oddly. This theory resulted. But you need not pay attention to it; Papa Mannie never tested it.'

'Hazel, what was this odd behavior?'

'Oh. Mama Wyoh told me that the first thing Manuel noticed was that Mike – the computer, I mean – Mike had acquired a sense of humor.'

'Oh, no!'

'Oh, yes. Mama Wyoh told me that, to Mike – or Michelle – or Adam Selene – he used all three names; he was a trinity – to Mike, the entire Luna Revolution, in which thousands died here and hundreds of thousands died on Earth, was a joke. It was just one great big practical joke thought up by a computer with supergenius brain power and a childish sense of humor.' Hazel grimaced, then grinned. 'Just a great, big, overgrown, lovable kid who should have been kicked.'

'You make it sound like a pleasure. Kicking him.'

'Do I? Perhaps I should not. After all, a computer could not possibly do right or wrong, or experience good or evil in the human sense; it would have no background for it – no rearing, if you please. Mama Wyoh told me that Mike's human behavior was by imitation – he had endless role models; he read everything, including fiction. But his only real emotion, all his own, was deep loneliness and a great longing for companionship. That's what our revolution was to Mike: companionship . . . play . . . a game that won him attention from Prof and Wyoh and especially Mannie. Richard, if a machine can have emotions, that computer loved my Papa Mannie. Well, sir?'

I was tempted to say nonsense or something even less polite. 'Hazel, you are demanding bald truth from me – and it will hurt your feelings. It sounds like fiction to me. If not your fiction, then that of your foster mother, Wyoming Knott.' I added, 'Sweetheart, are we going out to attend to our chores? Or are we going to spend all day talking about a theory on which neither of us has any evidence?'

'I'm dressed and ready to go, dear. Just one little bit more and I'll shut up. You find this story unbelievable.'

'Yes, I do.' I said it as flatly as possible.

'What part of it is unbelievable?'

'All of it.'

'Truly? Or is the sticking point the idea that a computer can be self-aware? If you accept that, does the rest of it become easier to swallow?'

(I tried to be honest. If that nonsense did not make me gag, would the rest be acceptable? Oh, certainly! Like the gold spectacles of Joseph Smith, like the tablets handed down to Moses from the Mount, like the red shift to the big bang – accept the postulate and the rest goes down smoothly.)

'Hazel-Gwen, if we assume a self-aware computer with emotions and free will, I would not boggle at anything else – from ghosts to little green men. What was it the Red Queen did? Believe seven impossible things before breakfast.'

'The White Queen.'

'No, the Red Queen.'

'Are you sure, Richard? It was just before—'

'Forget it. Talking chessmen are even harder to swallow than a prankster computer. Sweetheart, the only evidence you offer is a story told you by your foster mother in her old age. That's all. Uh, senile, maybe?'

'No, sir. Dying, but not senile. Cancer. From exposure to a solar storm when she was quite young. So she thought. As may be, it was not senility. She told me this when she knew she was to die . . . because she thought the story should not be lost completely.'

'You see the weakness of the story, dear? One death-bed story. No other data.'

'Not quite, Richard.'

'Eh?'

'My adoptive father Manuel Davis confirms all of it and then some.'

'But – You always spoke of him in the past tense. I think you did. And he would be . . . how old? Older than you are.'

'He was born in 2040, so he would be a century and a half old now . . . not impossible for a Loonie. But he's both older and younger than that – for the same reasons I am. Richard, if you talked to Manuel Davis and he confirmed what I've told you, would you believe him?'

'Uh –' I grinned at her. 'You might force me to bring to the issue the stalwart common sense of ignorance and prejudice.'

'Go along with you! Put on your foot, dear, please. I want to take you out and get you at least one more outfit before we move; your trousers have spots on the stains. I'm not being a good wife.'

'Yes, ma'am; right away, ma'am. Where is your Papa Mannie now?'

'You won't believe this.'

'If it doesn't involve right-angled time or lonely computers, I'll believe it.'

'I think – I haven't checked lately – I think Papa Mannie is with your Uncle Jock in Iowa.'

I stopped with my foot in my hand. 'You're right; I don't believe it.'

XIX

'Rascality has limits; stupidity has not.'

NAPOLEON BONAPARTE 1769–1821

How CAN you argue with a woman who won't? I expected
Gwen to start justifying her preposterous allegation, citing
chapter and verse in an attempt to convince me. Instead she
answered sadly, 'I knew that was all I could expect. I'll just
have to wait. Richard, do we have any other stops to make
besides Macy's and the main post office before we can go out
to the Warden's Complex?'

'I need to set up a new checking account and then transfer
my present account down from Golden Rule. My cash in
pocket is becoming rather seldom. Anemic.'

'But, dearest, I've tried to tell you. Money is no problem.'
She opened her purse, dug out a wad of money, started peeling
off hundred-crown notes. 'I'm on an expense account, of
course.' She held them out.

'Easy, there!' I said. 'Save your pennies, little girl. *I* under-
took to support *you*. Not the other way around.'

I expected a retort involving '*macho*' or 'male chauvinist pig'
or at least 'community property.' Instead she flanked me.
'Richard? Your bank account in Golden Rule – Is it a numbered account? If not, under what name?'

'Huh? No. "Richard Ames," of course.'

'Do you think Mr Sethos might take an interest?'

'Oh. Our kindly landlord. Honey, I'm glad you're here to
do my thinking for me.' A track leading straight to me as plain
as footprints in snow . . . for Sethos's goons to follow to collect
that reward for my carcass – dead or alive. Of course all bank
records are confidential, not alone numbered accounts – but
'confidential' means only that it takes money or power to break
the rules. And Sethos had both. 'Gwen, let's go back and

booby-trap his air conditioning system again. But this time we'll use prussic acid instead of Limburger.'

'Good!'

'I wish we could. You're right. I can't touch that "Richard Ames" bank account as long as storm warnings are up. We'll use your cash – treat it as a loan. You keep track of it—'

'*You* keep track of it! Damn it, Richard, I'm your wife!'

'Fight over it later. Leave the wig and the geisha costume here; we won't have time today . . . as I must first go to see Rabbi Ezra. Unless you want to run your errands while I run mine?'

'Buster, are you feverish? I'm not letting you out of my sight.'

'Thanks, Maw; that's the answer I wanted. We go to see Father Ezra, then we go hunt living computers. If there is time left, we'll do the other chores when we get back.'

It being before noon, we looked for Rabbi Ezra ben David by going to his son's fish market across from the city library. The Rabbi lived in a room back of the shop. He agreed to represent me and act as a mail drop. I explained to him my parallel arrangements with Father Schultz, then wrote a note for him to send to 'Henrietta van Loon.'

Reb Ezra accepted it. 'I'll stat it from my son's terminal at once; it should be printed out in Golden Rule ten minutes from now. Special delivery?'

(Draw attention to it? Or accept slower service? Something was stewing in Golden Rule; Hendrik Schultz might have some answers.) 'Special delivery, please.'

'Very well. Excuse me a few moments.' He rolled out of his room, was back quickly. 'Golden Rule acknowledged receipt. Now to other matters – I was expecting you, Dr Ames. That young man who was with you yesterday – Is he a member of your family? Or a trusted employee?'

'Neither one.'

'Interesting. Did you send him to ask me who was offering a reward for you and the amount of the reward?'

'I certainly did not! Did you tell him anything?'

'My dear sir! You asked for the traditional Three Days.'

'Thank you, sir.'

'Not at all. Since he took the trouble to seek me out here instead of waiting for my business hours, I assumed some urgency. Since you did not mention him, I concluded that the urgency was his, not yours. Now I assume, unless you tell me otherwise, that he intends you no good.'

I gave the Rabbi a condensed version of our relations with Bill. He nodded. 'You know Mark Twain's remarks on such matters?'

'I think not.'

'He said that, if you pick up a stray dog, feed it and take care of it, it will not bite you. This, in his opinion, is the principal difference between a man and a dog. I don't agree fully with Twain. But he had a point.'

I asked him to name a retainer, paid it without dickering, plus something for luck.

The Authority Complex (officially the 'Administration Center,' a name found only in print) is west of Luna City, halfway across Mare Crisium. We were there by noon – that tubeway is not ballistic but is nevertheless fast. Once aboard, we were there in twenty minutes.

Noon was the wrong time to arrive. The Complex is made up of government offices; everything shuts down for a leisurely lunch hour. Lunch seemed a good idea to me, too; breakfast was in the remote past. There were several lunchrooms in the tunnels of the complex . . . with every chair filled with broad beams of civil servants or occupied by tourists with red fezzes. Queues waited outside Sloppy Joe and Mom's Diner and Antoine's number two. 'Hazel, I see vending machines ahead. Can I interest you in a warm Coke and a cold sandwich?'

'No, sir, you cannot. There's a public terminal just beyond the food dispensers. I'll make some calls while you eat.'

'I'm not that hungry. What calls?'

'Xia. And Ingrid. I want to be sure Gretchen got home safely. She could have been waylaid just as we were. I should have called last night.'

'Only to soothe your own worry; either Gretchen was home day before yesterday evening . . . or it's too late and she's dead.'

'Richard!'

'That's what worries you, isn't it? Call Ingrid.'

Gretchen answered and squealed when she saw Gwen-Hazel. 'Mama! Come quick! It's Mistress Hardesty!'

223

Twenty minutes later we switched off. All that had been accomplished was to tell the Hendersons that we were at the Raffles and that our mailing address was care of Rabbi Ezra. But the ladies enjoyed visiting and each assured the other that she would come visit in person sometime soon. They exchanged kisses via terminal – to my mind a waste of technology. And of kisses.

Then we tried to call Xia . . . and a man came on screen whom I did not recognize; he was not Xia's day-shift desk clerk. 'What do you want?' he demanded.

Hazel said, 'I'd like to speak to Xia, please.'

'Not here. This hotel has been shut down by the Bureau of Sanitation.'

'Oh. Can you tell me where she is?'

'Try the Chief of Public Safety.' The face flickered off.

Hazel turned to me, her eyes filled with worry. 'Richard, this can't be right. Xia's hotel is as squeaky clean as she is.'

'I see a pattern,' I said grimly, 'and so do you. Let me try.'

I moved in, queried for code, called the office of the top cop, HKL. An elderly desk sergeant answered. I said, 'Gospazha, I'm trying to reach a citizen named Dong Xia. I was told—'

'Yeah, I booked her,' she answered. 'But she made bail an hour ago. Not here.'

'Ah so. Thank you, ma'am. Can you tell me where I might reach her?'

'Haven't the slightest. Sorry.'

'Thank you.' I switched off.

'Oh, dear!'

'Leprosy, sweetheart. We've got it; anyone who touches us catches it. Damn.'

'Richard, I'm stating the simple truth. In my childhood when this was a penal colony, there was more freedom under the Warden than there is now with self-government.'

'Maybe you exaggerate but I suspect Xia would agree with you.' I chewed my lip and frowned. 'You know who else has caught our leprosy. Choy-Mu.'

'You think so?'

'Seven to two.'

'No bet. Call him.'

Query showed him to be a private subscriber, so I called

his home. I heard a recording, sans picture: 'Marcy Choy-Mu speaking. Can't say when I'll be home but I will call in soon for messages. At the gong, please record.' A gong sounded.

I thought furiously, then said, 'Captain Midnight speaking. We are booked into the old Raffles. A mutual friend needs help. Please call me at the Raffles. If I am not there, please leave message telling when and where I can reach you.' I switched off again.

'Dear, you didn't give him Rabbi Ezra's code.'

'On purpose, Sadie girl. To keep the Rabbi's code out of Jefferson Mao's hands; Choy-Mu's line may be monitored. I had to give him somewhere to call back . . . but I can't risk compromising the Rabbi Ezra connection; we must have it for Father Schultz. Table it, beautiful; I've got to query for HKL ground control.'

'Hong Kong Luna ground control. This terminal is for official business; make it brief.' It was voice only.

'May I speak to Captain Marcy?'

'Not here. I'm his emergency relief. Message? Make it snappy; I've got traffic in four minutes.'

(Uh –) 'This is Captain Midnight. Tell him I'm at the old Raffles. Call me.'

'Don't switch off! Captain Midnight?'

'He'll know.'

'And so do I. He went to city hall to put up bail for you know who. Or do you?'

'Xia?'

'Too right! I've got to get back to my scopes but I'll tell him. Off!'

'What now, Richard?'

'Gallop in all directions.'

'Do be serious!'

'Can you think of anything better? The queue is gone from Mom's Diner; let's eat lunch.'

'Eat lunch while our friends are in danger?'

'Sweetheart, even if we went back to Kongville – and thereby shoved our heads in the lion's mouth – we would have no way to find them. There is nothing we can do until Choy-Mu calls us. That might be five minutes from now, or five hours. One

225

thing I learned in combat: Never skip a chance to eat, sleep, or pee; another chance may be a long time coming.'

I recommend Mom's cherry pie with ice cream. Hazel ordered the same but, by the time I was chasing my last bite with a spoon, she had merely toyed with hers. I said, 'Young lady, you sit right there until you have eaten everything on your plate.'

'Richard, I can't.'

'I don't like to beat you in public—'

'So don't.'

'So I won't. Instead I will sit right here until you have eaten that all up, even if it means that I must sleep in this chair tonight.'

Hazel expressed obscenely unfavorable opinions of me, of Jefferson Mao, and of cherry pie, then ate the cherry pie. By thirteen-twenty we were at the door of the computer area in the Complex. There a youngster at a wicket sold us two tickets for two crowns forty, told us that the next tour would start in a few minutes, and let us into an enclosure, a waiting lounge with benches and opportunities to gamble against machines. Ten or a dozen tourists were waiting; most of the males wore fezzes.

When at last we started, an hour later, there were nineteen or twenty of us, herded by a uniformed guide – or guard; he wore a cop's shield. We made a long circuit on foot of that enormous complex, a dull and endless trip. At each pause our guide gave a memorized spiel – perhaps not too well memorized, as I could spot errors, even though I am not a communications-control engineer.

But I did not jump on these slips. Instead I made a nuisance of myself in accordance with earlier coaching by my fellow conspirator.

At one stop our guide explained that engineering control was decentralized all over Luna both geographically and by functions – air, sewage, communications, fresh water, transportation, et cetera – but was monitored from here by the technicians you see at those consoles. I interrupted him.

'My good man, I think you must be new on this job. The *Encyclopædia Britannica* explains clearly how one giant computer handles everything on the Moon. That's what we've come to see. Not backs of necks of junior clerks sitting at monitors. So let's see it. The giant computer. The Holmes IV.'

The guide let his professional smile slip and looked at me with the natural contempt of a Loonie for an earthworm. 'You've been misinformed. True, it used to be that way, but you're over fifty years out of date. Today we are modernized and decentralized.'

'Young man, are you trying to contradict the *Britannica?*'

'I'm telling you the simple truth. Now let's move on and—'

'What became of that giant computer? Since it's no longer used. Or so you say.'

'Huh? Look behind you. See that door? It's behind that door.'

'Come, then let's see it! That's what I paid to see.'

'Not on your bloody drum and fife. It's an historical antique, a symbol of our great history. You want to look at it, you go to the Chancellor of Galileo U. and show your credentials. He'll send you packing! Nah then let's all move along to the next gallery—'

Hazel did not move on with us, but (following instructions) I always had something ahead to point to and to ask a silly question about, whenever our guide seemed about to have a free moment to look around. But when, at long last, we had made the full circle and were back at the lounge, Hazel was there ahead of us.

I kept quiet until we were out of the Complex and waiting at the tube station. There I moved us out of earshot of others before I spoke. 'How did it go?'

'No trouble. The lock on that door was a type I've dealt with before. Thanks for keeping them all distracted while I coped with it. Good show, love!'

'You got what you were after?'

'I think so. I'll know more after Papa Mannie looks over my photographs. It's just a big lonely room, Richard, crowded with old-fashioned electronics equipment. I shot it from about twenty angles, and stereoed each shot by hand-held offset – not perfect but I've practiced it.'

'That's all? This visit?'

'Yes. Well, mostly.'

Her voice was choked; I looked at her, saw that her eyes

227

were filled with tears about to overflow. 'Why, darling! What's the matter?'

'N-n-nothing.'

'Tell me.'

'Richard, he's in there!'

'Huh?'

'He's asleep in there. I know, I could feel him. Adam Selene.'

The tube capsule slammed into the station about then, to my relief – there are subjects for which words are useless. The capsule was packed full; we could not talk en route. By the time we were back in L-City my darling had quieted down and I could avoid the subject. The crowds in the corridors made talk difficult anyhow. Luna City is crowded at any time; on Saturdays half the Loonies from other warrens come in to shop; this Saturday the usual weekend crowd was augmented by Shriners and their wives from all over North America and elsewhere.

As we came down out of Tube Station West into pressure two at outer ring, we faced Sears Montgomery. I was about to swing left to the Causeway when Hazel stopped me. 'Uh? What, dear?'

'Your trousers.'

'Is my fly open? No, it's not.'

'We're going to cremate your trousers; it's too late for burial. And that shirtjacket.'

'I thought you were itchy to get to the Raffles?'

'I am but it will take me only five minutes to put you into a new siren suit.'

(Reasonable. My trousers were so dirty that I was beginning to risk being cited as a menace to public health. And Hazel did know what I preferred for everyday clothing, as I had explained to her that I would not wear shorts even if every other adult male in Luna City was in shorts – as most of them were. I'm not morbidly self-conscious about my missing foot . . . but I do want full-length trousers to conceal my prosthesis. It's my private problem; I do not choose to exhibit it.)

'All right,' I agreed. 'But let's buy the one nearest the door.'

Hazel did get us in and out in ten minutes, buying me three two-piece rumpus suits all alike save for color. The price was right, as first she dickered it down to an acceptable amount, then rolled double or nothing, and won. She thanked the clerk and tipped him the price of a drink, then exited looking cheerful.

She said to me, 'You look smart, dear.'

I thought so, too. Those three suits were lime green, powder pink, and lavender. I had chosen to wear the lavender; I think it suits my complexion. I went strutting along, swinging my cane, with my best girl on my arm, feeling great.

But when we turned onto the Causeway there was no room to swing a cane and barely room to walk. We backed out, dropped straight down to Bottom Alley, then across town and up Five Aces chain lift to pressure six – much farther but today much faster.

Even the side tunnel to the Raffles was crowded. A cluster of fez-topped men were just outside our hotel.

I glanced at one of them, then took a better look.

I let him have it with my cane, reverse moulinet up into his crotch. At the same time or a split second ahead of me, Hazel threw her package (my suits) into the face of the man next to him and slugged one beyond him with her handbag. He went down as my man screamed and joined him. As my cane swung back, I took it with both hands horizontally, and used the sideways short jabs intended for moving through a rioting crowd – but used the jabs more personally, getting one man in the belly, another in a kidney, and kicking each to quiet him as he went down.

Hazel had taken care of the man she had slowed up with the package, I did not see how. But he was down and not moving. A (sixth?) man was about to cool her with a cosh, so I stabbed him in the face with my cane. He grabbed at it; I moved forward with it to keep him from exposing the stiletto, while giving him three fingers to his solar plexus, lefthanded. I fell on top of him.

And was picked up and carried into the Raffles at a trot, with my head down and dragging my cane after me.

The next few seconds I had to sort out later, perhaps imperfectly. I did not see Gretchen standing at the registration desk, but she was there, having just arrived. I heard Hazel snap, 'Gretchen! Room L, straight back on the right!' as she dumped me on Gretchen. On Luna I weigh thirteen kilos, give or take a few grams – not much load for a country girl used to hard work. But I'm much bigger than Gretchen and twice as big as Hazel – a big unwieldy bundle. I squawked to be put down; Gretchen paid no attention. That silly desk clerk was yelping but no one was paying attention to him, either.

Our door opened as Gretchen reached it and I heard another familiar voice sing out, 'Bojemoi! He's *hurt*.' Then I was face up on my own bed and Xia was working on me.

'I'm not hurt,' I told her. 'Just shaken up.'

'Yeah, sure. Hold still while I get your trousers off. Does one of you gentlemen have a knife?'

I was about to tell her not to cut my new trousers, when I heard a shot. It was my bride, crouching inside the open doorway and peering cautiously out to the left, her head close to the floor. She fired again, scooted back inside, closed and locked the door.

She glanced around and snapped, 'Move Richard into the 'fresher. Pile the bed and everything else against the outer door; they'll be shooting or breaking it down or both.' She sat down on the floor with her back toward me and paid no attention to anyone. But everyone jumped to carry out her orders.

'Everyone' included Gretchen, Xia, Choy-Mu, Father Schultz, and Reb Ezra. I did not have time to be astonished, especially as Xia with Gretchen's help moved me into the refresher, put me on the floor, and resumed taking my pants off. What did astonish me was to find that my good leg, the one with a meat-and-bone foot on it, was bleeding heavily. I noticed it first from seeing that Gretchen had big blood stains on the left shoulder of her white coverall. Then I saw where the blood was coming from, whereupon that leg started to hurt.

I don't like blood, especially mine. So I turned my face away and looked out the 'fresher door. Hazel was still sitting on the floor and had taken something out of her handbag that seemed to be bigger than the handbag. She was talking into it.

'Tee Aitch Queue! Major Lipschitz calling Tee Aitch Queue! Answer me, God damn it! Wake up! Mayday, mayday! *Hey, Rube!*'

XX

'If anyone doubts my veracity, I can only say that I
pity his lack of faith.'

BARON MUNCHAUSEN 1737–1794

XIA ADDED, 'Gretchen, hand me a clean towel. We'll make do
just with a pressure pack until later.'

'Ouch!'

'Sorry, Richard.'

'Mayday! Mayday! Hail, Mary, I'm up the crick without a
paddle! *Answer me!*'

'We read you, Major Lipschitz. Report local fix, planet,
system, and universe.' It was a machine voice with a typical
uninflected brassiness that sets my teeth on edge.

'Now let's tape it tightly.'

'Hell with procedures! I need T-shift pickup and I need it
now! Check my assignment and slam it! Switch point: "One
small step" by Armstrong. Local fix: Hotel Raffles, room L.
Time tick, now!'

I went on looking out the 'fresher door to avoid watching
the unpleasant things Xia and Gretchen were doing to me. I
could hear shouts and people running; something crashed
against the corridor door. Then in the rock wall on my right
a new door dilated.

I say 'door' for lack of a precise word. What I saw was a
circular locus of silver gray, floor to ceiling, and more. Inside
this locus was an ordinary door for a vehicle. What sort of
vehicle I could not tell; its door was all I could see.

It swung open; someone inside called out, 'Grandma!' as
the corridor door crashed in and a man fell into the room.
Hazel shot him. A second man was right behind him; she shot
him, too.

I reached for my cane – beyond Xia, damn it! 'Hand me my cane! *Hurry!*'

'Now, now! You lie back down.'

'Give it to me!' Hazel had one round left, or maybe none. Either way, it was time I backed her up.

I heard more shots. With bitter certainty that nothing was left but to avenge her, I made a long arm, got my stick, and turned.

No more fighting – Those last shots had been fired by Rabbi Ezra. (Why was I surprised that a wheelchair cripple chose to go armed?) Hazel was shouting, 'Everybody get aboard! Move it!'

And we did. I was confused again, as an endless crowd of young people, male and female and all of them redheaded, poured out of that vehicle and carried out Hazel's orders. Two of them carried Reb Ezra inside while a third folded his wheelchair flat and handed it in to a fourth. Choy-Mu and Gretchen were hustled in, followed by Father Schultz. Xia was shoved after them when she tried to insist on handling me. Then two redheads, a man and a woman, carried me in; my blood-stained pants were chucked after me. I clung to my cane.

I saw only a little of the vehicle. Its door opened into a four-place pilot-and-passenger compartment of what might be a spaceplane. Or might not be; the controls were strange and I was in no position to judge how it worked. I was lugged between seats and shoved through a door behind them into a cargo space and wound up on top of the Rabbi's folded wheelchair.

Was I going to be treated as cargo? No, I lay there only briefly, then was turned ninety degrees and passed through a larger door, turned another ninety degrees and placed on a floor.

And glad to stay there!

For the first time in years I was experiencing earth-normal weight.

Correction: I had felt a few moments of it yesterday in the ballistic tube, a few more in that U-Pushit clunker, Budget Jets Seventeen, and about an hour of it in Old MacDonald's Farm four days earlier. But this time sudden heaviness caught me by surprise and did not go away. I had lost blood and found it hard to breathe and was dizzy again.

I was feeling sorry for myself when I saw Gretchen's face; she looked both scared and wretchedly ill. Xia was saying, 'Get your head down, dear. Lie down by Richard; that's best. Richard, can you scrunch over a little? I would like to lie down, too; I don't feel well.'

So I found myself with a cuddlesome wench on each side of me and I didn't feel a durn bit like cuddling. I'm supposed to be trained to fight in accelerations up to two full gravities, twelve times that of Luna. But that was years ago and I'd had over five years of soft, sedentary living at low gravity.

It seems certain that Xia and Gretchen were just as uninterested in bundling.

My beloved arrived carrying our miniature maple. She placed it on a stand, blew me a kiss, and started sprinkling it. 'Xia, let me draw a lukewarm tub for you two born Loonies; you both can get into it.'

Hazel's words caused me to look around. We were in a 'bathroom.' Not a refresher appropriate to a four-seater spaceplane, nothing at all like ours in the Raffles; this room was an antique. Have you ever seen wallpaper decorated with fairies and gnomes? Indeed, have you ever seen wallpaper? How about a giant iron tub on claw feet? Or a water closet with a wooden lid and an overhead tank? The whole room was straight out of a museum of cultural anthropology . . . yet everything was bright and new and shiny.

I wondered just how much blood I had lost.

'Thanks, Gwen, but I don't think I need it. Gretchen, do you want to float in water?'

'I don't want to move!'

'It won't be long,' Hazel assured them. 'Gay shifted twice to avoid shrapnel, or we would be down now. Richard, how are you feeling?'

'I'll make it.'

'Of course you will, darling. I feel the weight myself from a year in Golden Rule. But not much as I exercised at one gee every day. Dear one, how badly are you wounded?'

'I don't know.'

'Xia?'

'Lots of bleeding and some muscle damage. Twenty or twenty-five centimeters and fairly deep. I don't think bone was hit. We put a tight pressure pack on it. If this ship is equipped

233

for it, I want to do a better job and give him a broad-spectrum shot, too.'

'You've done a fine job. We'll be landing soon and then there will be professional help and equipment.'

'All right. I don't feel too lively, I admit.'

'So try to rest.' Hazel picked up my blood-soiled trousers. 'I'm going to soak these before the stain sets.'

'Use cold water!' Gretchen blurted, then turned pink and added shyly, 'So Mama says.'

'Ingrid is right, dear.' Hazel ran water into the hand basin. 'Richard, I'm forced to admit that I lost your new clothes during that fuss.'

'Clothes we can buy. I thought I was going to lose *you*.'

'Good Richard. Here's your wallet and some this and that. Pocket plunder.'

'Better let me have it.' I crowded it all into a breast pocket. 'Where's Choy-Mu? I did see him – or did I?'

'He's in the other 'fresher, with Father Schultz and Father Ezra.'

'Uh? Are you telling me that a four-seater has *two* refreshers? It *is* a four-place job, isn't it?'

'It is and it does and wait till you see the rose gardens. And the swimming lounge.'

I started to make a retort but chopped it off. I had not figured out any formula by which to tell when my bride was jesting, or was telling literal but unbelievable truth. I was saved from a silly discussion by one of the redheads coming in – female, young, muscled, freckled, catlike, wholesome, sultry. 'Aunt Hazel, we're grounded.'

'Thank you, Lor.'

'I'm Laz. Cas wants to know who stays here, who comes along, and how long till lift? Gay wants to know whether or not we'll be bombed and can she park one shift over? Bombing makes her nervous.'

'Something is wrong here. Gay should not be asking directly. Should she?'

'I don't think she trusts Cas's judgment.'

'She may have reason. Who's commanding?'

'I am.'

'Oh. I'll let you know who goes, who stays, after I talk to my papa and Uncle Jock. A few minutes, I think. You can let

234

Gay park in a dead zone if you wish but please have her stay on my frequency triple; we may be in a hurry. Right now I want to move my husband . . . but first I must ask another of our passengers to lend me his wheelchair.'

Hazel turned to leave. I called out, 'I don't need a wheelchair,' but she didn't hear me. Apparently.

Two of the redheads lifted me out of the craft and placed me in Ezra's wheelchair, with its back support lowered and front support lifted; one of them spread a kingsize bath towel over my lap and legs. I said, 'Thanks, Laz.'

'I'm Lor. Don't be surprised if this towel vanishes; we've never tried taking one outside before.'

She got back aboard and Hazel wheeled me under the nose of the craft and around to its port side . . . which suited me, as I had seen at once that this was indeed a sort of spaceplane, with lifting body and retractable wings – and I was curious to see how the designer had managed to crowd two large refreshers into its port side. It did not seem aerodynamically possible.

And it wasn't. Portside was like the starboard side, sleek and slender. No cubic for bathrooms.

I had no time to ponder this. When we had turned into the Raffles' side tunnel a few minutes earlier, my Sonychron had just blinked seventeen, Greenwich or L-City time . . . which would make it eleven in the morning in zone six, dirtside.

And so it was because that's where we were, zone six, in the north pasture of my Uncle Jock's place outside Grinnell, Iowa. So it becomes obvious that I not only had lost much blood but also had been hit hard on the head – as even the hottest military courier needs at least two hours, Luna to Terra.

In front of us was Uncle Jock's fine old restored Victorian, cupola and verandas and widow's walk, and he himself was coming toward us, accompanied by two other men. Uncle was as spry as ever, and still with a mop of silver-white hair that made him look like Andrew Jackson. The other two I did not recognize. They were mature men but much younger than Uncle Jock – well, almost everybody is.

Hazel stopped pushing me, ran and threw her arms around one of them, kissed him, all out. My uncle picked her out of that man's arms, bussed her just as enthusiastically, then surrendered her to the third, who saluted her the same way and put her back on her feet.

Before I could feel left out, she turned and took the first one by his left hand. 'Papa, I want you to meet my husband, Richard Colin. Richard, this is my Papa Mannie, Manuel Garcia O'Kelly Davis.'

'Welcome to family, Colonel.' He offered me his right hand.

'Thank you, sir.'

Hazel turned to the third man. 'And Richard, this—'

'– is Dr Hubert,' Uncle Jock interrupted. 'Lafe, slap skin with my nephew Colonel Colin Campbell. Welcome home, Dickie. What are you doing in that baby carriage?'

'Just lazy, I guess. Where's Aunt Cissy?'

'Locked up, of course; knew you were coming. But what have you been doing? Looks like you failed to duck. Sadie, you have to expect that from Dickie; he's always been slow. Hard to toilet train and never did learn pattycake.'

I was selecting a sufficiently insulting answer to this canard (I learned long ago the way to treat our family scandal) when the ground shook, followed immediately by *Krrrump!* Not nuclear, just high explosive. But disquieting just the same; HE is not a toy and is not a better way to become dead – there isn't one. Uncle said, 'Don't pee your pants, Dickie; they're not shooting at us. Lafe, will you examine him here? Or inside?'

Dr Hubert said, 'Let me see your pupils, Colonel.'

So I looked at him as he looked at me. When Hazel stopped pushing the wheelchair, the spaceplane was then on my left; but when that HE detonation took place, the spaceplane was abruptly elsewhere. Gone. '– not a rack behind.' Least hypothesis suggests that I was out of my gourd.

Nobody else seemed to notice it.

So I pretended not to and looked at my physician . . . and wondered where I had seen him lately.

'No concussion, I think. What's the natural log of pi?'

'If I had all my marbles, would I be here? Look, Doc, no guessing games, please; I'm tired.' Another HE shell (or bomb) landed nearby, closer if anything. Dr Hubert moved the towel off my left leg, poked at the pack Xia had placed.

'Does that hurt?'

'Hell, yes!'

'Good. Hazel, you had best take him home. I can't take proper care of him here as we are about to shift to New Harbor in Beulahland; the Angelenos have taken Des Moines and are moving this way. He's in good shape for a man who's taken a hit . . . but he should have proper treatment without delay.'

I said, 'Doctor, are you any relation to the redheaded girls in that spaceplane we arrived in?'

'They're not girls; they are superannuated juvenile delinquents. Whatever they told you I deny categorically. Give them my love.'

Hazel blurted, 'But I have to make my report!'

Everybody talked at once until Dr Hubert said, 'Quiet! Hazel goes with her husband and sees him settled in, stays as long as she finds necessary, then reports to New Harbor . . . but with time tick established now. Objection? So ordered.'

Having that spaceplane reappear was even more disconcerting and I'm glad I didn't watch. Or not much. The two redheaded men (turned out there were only four redheads, not a mob) got me and the wheelchair inside and Hazel went into that odd refresher with me . . . and almost at once Laz (Lor?) followed us in and announced, 'Aunt Hazel, we're home.'

'Home' turned out to be the flat roof of a large building – and it was late evening, almost sundown. That spaceplane should be named the Cheshire Cat. (But its name is Gay. Her name is Gay. Oh, never mind!)

The building was a hospital. In checking into a hospital you first wait an hour and forty minutes while they process the paperwork. Then they undress you and put you on a gurney under a thin blanket with your bare feet sticking out into a cold draft and make you wait outside the X-ray lab. Then they demand a urine sample in a plastic duck while a young lady waits for it, staring at the ceiling and looking bored. Right?

These people didn't know page one about the regulation way to run a hospital. Our able-bodied comrades (the ones suffering from nothing but high acceleration) were already on their way, in glorified golf carts, when I was again lifted out and placed in another golf cart (gurney, wheelchair, floating couch). Rabbi Ezra was there in his wheelchair. Hazel was

237

with us and carrying Tree-San and a Sears-labeled package containing Naomi's costume. The spaceplane had vanished; I had barely had time to tell Laz (Lor?) that Dr Hubert sent his love. She had sniffed. 'If he thinks sweet talk will get him out of the doghouse, he had better think again.' But her nipples crinkled up, so I assume that she was pleased.

Four of us were left on the roof, we three and one member of the hospital staff, a little dark woman who seemed to combine the best of Mother Eve and Mother Mary without flaunting any of it. Hazel dropped the package on me, handed the bonsai to Reb Ezra, and threw her arms around her. 'Tammy!'

'Arli sool, m'temqa!' The motherly creature kissed Hazel.

'Reksi, reksi – so very long!'

They broke from the clinch and Hazel said, 'Tammy, this is my beloved, Richard.'

This got me kissed on the mouth. Tammy put that bundle aside to do it properly. A man kissed by Tammy stays kissed for hours – even if he is wounded, even if she makes it brief.

'And this is our dear friend the Reverend Rabbi Ezra ben David.'

He did not get the treatment I got. Tammy curtsied deeply, then kissed his hand. So I showed a clear profit.

Tammy (Tamara) said, 'Inside I must get you both that quickly may we repair Richard. But both each my cherished guests will here be through time not short. Hazel? Such room as you with Jubal shared, nay?'

'Tammy, that's a fine idea! 'Cause I'm going to have to be away sometimes. Gentlemen, will you room together while you are patients here?'

I was about to say, 'Yeah, sure, but –' when Reb Ezra said, 'There's some mixup. Mistress Gwendolyn, please explain to this dear lady that I am not a patient, not a candidate for hospitalization. Perfect health. Not a sniffle, not even a hang-nail.'

Tamara looked surprised and – no, not troubled but deeply concerned. She stepped close to him, gently touched his left stump. 'Are not we your legs to back on put?'

238

Reb Ezra stopped smiling. 'I'm sure you mean well. But I can't wear prosthetics. Truly.'

Tamara broke into that other language, speaking to Hazel. She listened, then said, 'Father Ezra, Tamara is speaking of real legs. Flesh and blood. They can do it. Three ways they can do it.'

Reb Ezra took a deep breath, sighed it out, looked at Tamara. 'Daughter, if you can put my legs back on . . . go ahead! Please,' then added something, Hebrew I think.

BOOK THREE

The Light at the End of the Tunnel

XXI

'God created woman to tame man.'

VOLTAIRE 1694–1778

I woke up slowly, letting my soul fit itself gently back into my body. I kept my eyes closed while I spliced onto my memory and reviewed who I was and where I was and what had happened.

Oh, yes, I had married Gwen Novak! Most unexpectedly but what a delightful idea! And then we – Hey! that wasn't yesterday. Yesterday you—

Boy, yesterday you had a busy day! Started in Luna City, bounced to Grinnell – How? Never mind 'How' for the nonce. Accept it. Then you bounced to – What had Gwen called it? Hey, wait! – Gwen's real name is Hazel. Or is it? Worry about that later. Hazel called it 'Third Earth,' Tellus Tertius. Tammy called it something else. Tammy? Oh, sure, 'Tamara.' Everybody knows Tamara.

Tammy would not let them work on my wounded leg while I was awake – How in hell did I pick up that wound? Am I getting clumsy in my old age? Or was it spotting Bill's face among those fake Shriners? It's not professional to let *any* surprise slow you down. If your own grandmother shows up in the scrum, shoot her and move on.

How did you know they were not Shriners? That's easy; Shriners are middle-aged and paunchy; these studs were young and tough. Combat ready.

Yes, but that's a rationalization, one you just now thought of. So? Nevertheless it's true. But you didn't reason it out yesterday. Hell, no, of course not; at the moment of truth you don't have time to think. You look at a bloke, something about him shouts 'Enemy!' and you jump to do unto him before he does unto you. If you use scrum time routing impressions

243

around inside your skull, sorting by type and weighing by logic – you're dead! Instead, you *move*.

Yesterday you didn't move fast enough.

But we picked the right partner for a fight, didn't we? – a quick little coral snake named Hazel. And any scrum we come out of still with a body temperature of thirty-seven can't be counted an utter defeat.

Quit trying to kid yourself. You got how many? Two? And she got the rest. *And* she had to make pick up on you . . . or you would be stone cold dead this minute.

Maybe I am. Let's check. I opened my eyes.

This room certainly looks like Heaven! But that proves you are *not* dead, because Heaven is not *your* destination. Besides, everybody says that when you die, first you go through a long tunnel with a light at the far end, and there your beloved waits for you . . . and that did not happen to you. No tunnel. No light at the end of the tunnel. And sadly no Hazel.

So I am not dead and this can't be Heaven and I don't think it's a hospital either. No hospital was ever this beautiful or smelled so good. And where is the regulation racket found in all hospital corridors? All I hear are bird songs and a string trio off somewhere in the distance.

Hey, there's Tree-San!

So Hazel must be close around. Where are you, honey girl? I need help. Find my foot and hand it to me, will you, please? I can't risk hopping in this gravity; I'm out of practice, and . . . well, damn it, I need to pee. Something abooraxly! – my back teeth are floating.

'I see that you are now awake.' It was a gentle voice, back of my right ear. I twisted my head to look just as she came around to where I could see her more easily – a young woman, comely, slender, small of bust, long brown hair. She smiled as I caught her eye. 'I'm Minerva. What will you have for breakfast? Hazel told me that waffles would please you. But you can have anything you like.'

'"Anything"?' I considered it. 'How about a brontosaurus roasted over a slow fire?'

'Yes, surely. But that will take longer to prepare than

244

waffles,' she answered with perfect seriousness. 'Some tidbits while you wait?'

'Go along with you; quit pulling my leg. Speaking of legs, have you seen my artificial foot? Before I eat breakfast I must visit the refresher . . . and I must have my cork foot to do that. This gravity, you know.'

Minerva told me bluntly what to do about it. 'This bed has a built-in refresher and you can't use the usual refresher anyhow; you are under spinal block from the waist down. But our arrangements are efficient, truly. So go ahead. Whatever you need to do.'

'Uh . . . I *can't*.' (Truly I could not. When they cut off my foot, the hospital corpsmen had a hell of a time with me. Finally they equipped me with catheter and honey tube until I was able to get as far as the jakes on crutches.)

'You will find that you can. And that it will be all right.'

'Uh –' (I couldn't stir either leg, neither the short one nor the long one.) 'Mistress Minerva, may I have an ordinary hospital-type bed urinal?'

She looked troubled. 'If you wish. But it will not be useful.' Then her troubled look changed to a thoughtful one. 'I will go find one. But it will take me some time. At least ten minutes. Not a moment less. And I am going to seal your door while I am gone so that no one will disturb you.' She added, 'Ten minutes,' and headed for a blank wall. It snapped out of her way and she was gone.

I immediately flipped off the sheet to see what they had done to my one good leg.

The sheet would not flip.

So I snuck up on it.

It was too smart for me.

So I tried to outwit it – after all, a sheet can't be smarter than a man. Can it be?

Yes, it can.

Finally I said to myself, Look, chum, we are getting nowhere. Let's try assuming that Mistress Minerva was being precisely truthful: This is a bed with built-in plumbing, capable of handling the worst a bedfast patient can do. So saying, I worked a couple of ballistic problems in my head – hairy empiricals guaranteed to distract even a man waiting at the guillotine.

And cut loose with half a liter, sighed, then let go with the other half. No, the bed did not seem to be wet.

And a feminine voice cooed, '*Good* baby!'

I looked hastily around. No vocal cords to go with the voice – 'Who said that and where are you?'

'I'm Teena, Minerva's sister. I'm no farther away than your elbow . . . yet I'm half a kilometer away and two hundred meters down. Need anything, just ask me. We stock it or make it or fake it. Miracles we do at once; anything else even sooner. Exception: Virgins are a special order . . . average lead time, fourteen years. Factory rebuilt virgins, fourteen minutes.'

'Who in hell wants a virgin? Mistress Teena, do you think it is polite to watch me take a pee?'

'Youngster, don't try to tell your grandmother how to steal sheep. One of my duties is to watch *everything* in all departments of this fun house and catch mistakes before they happen. Two: *I* am a virgin and can prove it . . . and I am going to make you sorry you were born male for uttering that disparaging crack about virgins.'

(Oh, hell!) 'Mistress Teena, I did not mean to offend you. I was simply embarrassed, that was all. So I spoke hastily. But I do think micturition and such should be granted privacy.'

'Not in a hospital, bud. They are significant aspects of the clinical picture, every time.'

'Uh—'

'Here comes my sister. If you don't believe me, you can ask her.'

A couple of seconds later the wall opened and Mistress Minerva came in, carrying a hospital-bed urinal of the old-fashioned sort – no automatic machinery, no electronic controls. I said, 'Thank you. But I no longer need it. As I'm sure your sister told you.'

'Yes, she did. But surely she didn't tell you that she had?'

'No, I deduced it. Is it true that she sits somewhere in the basement and snoops on every patient? Doesn't she find it boring?'

'She doesn't really pay any attention until it's needed. She has thousands of other things to do, all more interesting—'

'Far more interesting!' that faceless voice interrupted.

'Minnie, he doesn't like virgins. I let him know that I am one. Confirm it, Sis; I want to rub his nose in it.'

'Teena, don't tease him.'

'Why not? It's fun to tease men; they wiggle so when you poke them. Though I can't see what Hazel sees in this one. He's a sad sack.'

'Teena! Colonel, did Athene tell you that she is a computer?'

'Eh? Say that again.'

'Athene is a computer. She is the supervising computer of this planet; other computers here are just machines, not sentient. Athene runs everything. Just as Mycroft Holmes once ran everything on Luna – I know that Hazel told you about him.' Minerva smiled gently. 'So that's how Teena can claim to be a virgin. Technically she is one, in the sense that a computer can have no experience in carnal copulation—'

'But I know all about it!'

'Yes, Sis – with a male human. On the other hand, when she transfers to a meat-and-bone body and becomes human, in another technical sense she will no longer be virgin because her hymen will have been atrophied in vitro and any vestigial tissue trimmed away before her animal body is kindled. That's how it was done with me.'

'And you were out of your mind, Minnie, to let Ishtar sell you that; I'm not going to do it that way. I've decided to have the works. A real maidenhead and both ritual and physical defloration. Even a bridal costume and a wedding if we can swing it. Do you think we can sell that to Lazarus?'

'I doubt it intensely. And you would be making a silly mistake. Unnecessary pain on first copulation could start you out with bad habits in what should always be an utterly happy experience. Sister, sex is the most important reason to become human. Don't spoil it.'

'Tammy says it doesn't hurt all that much.'

'Why let it hurt at all? Anyhow, you won't get Lazarus to agree to a formal wedding. He promised you a place in our family; he did not promise you anything else.'

'Maybe we should volunteer Colonel Zero here. He's going to owe me plenty of favors by then and Maureen says nobody ever notices the bridegroom anyhow. How about it, soldier boy? Think of the honor of being my bridegroom at a swank June wedding. Careful how you answer.'

My ears were ringing and I felt a headache coming on. If I just closed my eyes, would I find myself back in my bachelor digs in Golden Rule?

I tried it, then opened them. 'Answer me,' the disembodied voice persisted.

'Minerva, who repotted my little maple?'

'I did. Tammy pointed out that it didn't have room to breathe, much less grow, and asked me to find a bigger pot. I—'

'I found it.'

'Teena found it and I repotted it. See how much happier it is? It's grown more than ten centimeters.'

I looked at the little tree. And looked again. 'How many days have I been in this hospital?'

Minerva suddenly had no expression at all. The Teena voice said, 'You didn't say how big a brontosaurus you wanted for breakfast. Better make it a little one, huh? The older ones are terribly tough. So everybody says.'

Ten centimeters – Hazel had said she would see me 'in the morning.' Which morning, dear one? Two weeks ago? Or longer? 'The older ones aren't tough if they are hung properly. But I don't want to wait while the meat ages. Would there be any such delay with waffles?'

'Oh, no,' agreed Teena's voice. 'Waffles aren't common here but Maureen knows all about them. She was brought up, she says, only a few kilometers from where you were reared, and at almost the same time, give or take a century or so. So she knows the sort of cooking you are used to. She explained to me all about waffle irons and I experimented until I made one just the way she wanted it. How many waffles can you eat, fatty?'

'Five hundred and seven.'

There was a short silence, then Teena said, 'Minerva?'

'I don't know.'

'But,' I went on, 'I'm on a diet, so let it go with three.'

'I'm not sure I want you as my bridegroom.'

'In any case you haven't consulted Hazel. My bride.'

'No obstacle; Hazel and I are pals. Years and years. She'll

make you do it. If I decide to use you. I'm not certain about you, Dickie boy; you veer.'

'"Dickie boy," huh? Do you know my Uncle Jock? Jock Campbell?'

'The Silver Fox. Do I know Uncle Jock! We won't invite him, Dickie; he would claim *jus primae noctis.*'

'Have to invite him, Mistress Teena; he's my closest relative. All right, I'll stand up as bridegroom and Uncle Jock will take care of deflowering the bride. Wrap it up.'

'Minerva?'

'Colonel Richard, I do not think that Athene should do this. I have known Dr Jock Campbell for many years, and he has known me. If Athene insists on this silly thing, I do not think she should give herself first to Dr Campbell. A year or two later, when she knows —' Minerva shrugged. 'They are free persons.'

'Teena can work it out with Hazel and Jock; it wasn't my idea. When does this crime take place?'

'Almost at once; Athene's clone is almost matured. About three of your years.'

'Oh. I thought we were talking about next week. I'll stop worrying; the horse might learn to sing.'

'What horse?'

'A nightmare. Now about those waffles. Mistress Minerva, will you join me in waffles? I can't stand to have you standing there salivating and swallowing and starving while I wallow in waffles.'

'I have already broken fast today—'

'Too bad.'

'– but that was some hours ago and I would like to experience waffles; both Hazel and Maureen speak well of them. Thank you; I accept.'

'You didn't invite *me!*'

'But, Teena my prospective child bride, if you do as you threaten to, my table will be yours; to invite you to share it would be a tautologically redundant plethora of excess surplusage, repetitious and almost insulting. Did Maureen say how waffles should be served? With drawn butter and maple syrup and plenty of crisp bacon . . . accompanied by fruit juice and coffee. The juice should be ice-cold; the rest should be hot.'

'Three minutes, lover boy.'

I was about to answer when that insubstantial wall again opened and Rabbi Ezra walked in. *Walked in.* He was using crutch canes but he was on two legs.

He grinned at me and waved a crutch cane. 'Dr Ames! Good to see you awake!'

'Good to see you, Reb Ezra. Mistress Teena, please make that order three of everything.'

'I already did. And lox and bagels and strawberry jam.'

It was a jolly meal despite all the questions on my mind. The food was grand and I was hungry; Minerva and Ezra – and Teena – were good company. I was chasing syrup with the last bite of my first waffle before I said, 'Reb Ezra, have you seen Hazel this morning? My wife. I had expected her to be here.'

He seemed to hesitate; Teena answered, 'She'll be here later, Dickie. She can't hang around waiting for you to wake up; she has other things to do. And other men.'

'Teena, quit trying to get my goat. Or I won't marry you even if Hazel and Jock both agree.'

'Want to bet? You jilt me, you cad, and I'll run you right off this planet. You won't get another bite to eat, doors won't open for you, refreshers will scald you, dogs will bite you. And you will *itch*.'

'Sister.'

'Aw, Minnie.'

Minerva went on, to me: 'Don't let my sister fret you, Colonel. She teases because she wants company and attention. But she is an ethical computer, utterly reliable.'

'I'm sure she is, Minerva. But she can't expect to tease me and threaten me, and still expect me to stand up in front of a judge or a priest or somebody and promise to love, honor, and obey her. I'm not sure I want to obey her anyhow.'

The computer voice answered, 'You won't have to promise to obey, Dickie boy; I'll train you later. Just simple things. Heel. Fetch. Sit up. Lie down. Roll over. Play dead. I don't expect anything complex out of a man. Aside from stud duties, that is. But on that score your reputation has preceded you.'

'What do you mean by that?' I threw my serviette down. 'That tears it! The wedding is off.'

'Friend Richard.'

'Eh? Yes, Reb.'

'Don't let Teena worry you. She has propositioned me, and you, and Father Hendrik, and Choy-Mu, and, no doubt, many others. Her ambition is to make Cleopatra look like a piker.'

'And Ninon de Lenclos, and Rangy Lil, and Marie Antoinette, and Rahab, and Battleship Kate, and Messalina, and you name her. I'm going to be the champion nymphomaniac of the multiverse, beautiful as sin, and utterly irresistible. Men will fight duels over me and kill themselves on my doorstep and write odes to my little finger. Women will swoon at my voice. Every man, woman, and child will worship me from afar and I'll love as many of them up close as I can fit into my schedule. So you don't want to be my bridegroom, eh? What a filthy, wicked, evil, stinking, utterly selfish thing to say! Angry mobs will tear you to bits and drink your blood.'

'Mistress Teena, that is not polite table talk. We are eating.'

'You started it.'

I tried to review the bidding. Had I started it? No, indeed, she—

Reb Ezra said to me in a prison whisper, 'Give up. You can't win. I know.'

'Mistress Teena, I'm sorry I started it. I should not have done so. It was naughty of me.'

'Oh, that's all right.' The computer sounded warmly pleased. 'And you don't have to call me "Mistress Teena"; hardly anyone uses titles around here. If you called Minerva "Dr Long," she would look around to see who was standing behind her.'

'All right, Teena, and please call me "Richard." Mistress Minerva, you have a doctor's degree? Medical doctor?'

'One of my degrees is in therapy, yes. But my sister is right; titles are not often used here. "Mistress" one never hears . . . other than as a term of affection to a woman you have gifted with your carnal love. So there is no need to call me "Mistress Minerva" . . . until you choose to gift me with that boon. When you do. If you do.'

Right across the plate!

251

I almost failed to lay a bat on it. Minerva seemed so modest, meek, and mild that she took me by surprise.

Teena gave me time in which to regroup. 'Minnie, don't try to hustle him right out from under me. He's mine.'

'Better ask Hazel. Better yet, ask him.'

'Dickie boy! Tell her!'

'What can I tell her, Teena? You haven't settled it with Hazel and my Uncle Jock. But in the meantime –' I contrived to bow to Minerva as well as one can from bed and handicapped by a spinal block. 'Dear lady, your words do me great honor. But, as you know, I am at present physically immobilized, unable to share in such delights. In the meantime may we take the wish for the deed?'

'Don't you dare call her "Mistress"!'

'Sister, behave yourself. Sir, you may indeed call me "Mistress." Or, as you say, we can treat the wish for the deed and wait until a later time. Your therapy will take time.'

'Ah, yes. So it will.' I glanced at the little maple, no longer quite so little. 'How long have I been here? I must already have run up quite a bill.'

'Don't worry about it,' Minerva advised me.

'I *must* worry about it. Bills must be paid. And I don't even have Medicare.' I looked at the Rabbi. 'Rabbi, how did you finance your – transplants, are they? – You're as far from home and your bank account as I am.'

'Farther than you think. And it is no longer appropriate to address me as Rabbi – where we are today, the Torah is not known. I am now Private Ezra Davidson, Time Corps Irregulars. That pays my bills. I think something like it pays yours. Teena, can you – I mean, "will you" – tell Dr Ames the account to which his bills are charged?'

'He has to ask it himself.'

'I do ask, Teena. Please tell me.'

'"Campbell, Colin," also known as "Ames, Richard": charges, all departments, to Senior's special account, "Galactic Overlord – Miscellaneous." So don't fret, lover boy; you're a charity case, all bills on the house. Of course the ones on *that* account usually don't live long.'

'Athene!'

'But, Minnie, that's the simple truth. An average of one

252

point seven three missions, then we pay their death benefits. Unless he's ordered to some featherbed job at THQ.'

(I was not listening carefully. 'Galactic Overlord' indeed! Only one person could have set up that account. The playful little darling. Damn it, dear – *where are you?*)

That none-too-solid wall blinked away again. 'Am I too late for breakfast? Oh, pshaw! Hello, darling!'

It was she!

XXII

'When in doubt, tell the truth.'

MARK TWAIN 1835–1910

'RICHARD, I did see you the next morning. But you didn't see me.'

'She certainly did see you, Dickie boy,' Teena confirmed. 'At great risk to her own health. Be glad you're alive. You almost weren't.'

'That's true,' agreed Ezra. 'I was your roommate part of one night. Then they moved me and put you in tight quarantine, and inoculated me nine or ninety ways. My brother, you were sick unto death.'

'Breakbone cramp, green-pus shakes, strangle fever –' Hazel was ticking them off on her fingers. 'Blue death. Typhus. Minerva, what else?'

'Golden staphylococcus systemic infection, hepatic herpes, Landrii. Worst of all, a loss of will to live. But Ishtar will not permit a person to die who has not asked for death while possessed of judicial capacity, and neither will Galahad. Tamara stayed with you every minute until that crisis was over.'

'Why don't I remember any of this?'

'Be glad you don't,' Teena advised.

'Sweetheart, if you had not been in the best hospital in all the known universes, with the most skilled therapists, I would be a widow again. And I look terrible in black.'

Ezra added, 'If you didn't have the constitution of an ox, you would never have made it.'

Teena interrupted with: 'Of a bull, Ezra. Not an ox. I know, I've seen 'em. Impressive.'

I didn't know whether to thank Teena or to call off the wedding again. So I ignored it. 'What I don't understand is

254

how I got all those diseases. I took a hit, I know that. That could account for staph aureus. But those other things?'

Ezra said, 'Colonel, you are a professional soldier.'

'Yes.' I sighed. 'I never practiced that aspect of the profession; I don't feel easy with it. Biological warfare makes fusion bombs seem clean and decent. Even chemical warfare looks humane compared with bio weapons. Very well; that knife – was it a knife? – was prepared. Nastily.'

'Yes,' agreed Ezra, 'somebody wanted you dead and was willing to kill all of Luna City as long as you died.'

'That's crazy. I'm not that important.'

Minerva said quietly, 'Richard, you are that important.'

I stared at her. 'What makes you think so?'

'Lazarus told me.'

'"Lazarus." Teena used that name earlier. Who is Lazarus? Why is his opinion so weighty?'

Hazel answered, 'Richard, I told you that you were important and I told you why. The rescue of Adam Selene. The same people who want him to stay unresurrected wouldn't boggle at killing Luna City to kill you.'

'If you say so, I wish I knew what happened there. Luna City is my adopted home; some mighty fine people in it. Uh, your son, Ezra, among others.'

'Yes, my son. And others. Luna City was saved, Richard; the infection was stopped.'

'Good!'

'At a price. A reference time tick was available from our rescue. The number of seconds it took us all to get aboard and get out of there was reconstructed through careful reenactment – by all of us who were involved in it with your part played by a skilled actor. This was compared with Gay's own memory of how long she was there, and the two were reconciled. Then a Burroughs space-time capsule was moved to the resultant coordinates plus four seconds, and a heat bomb was released. Not atomic but hot, star hot – some of those bugs are hard to kill. Obviously the hotel had to be damaged, with a high probability – no, a certainty – of loss of life. The threat to Luna City was cauterized but the price was high. Tanstaafl.' Ezra looked grim.

'Your son was saved?'

'I think so. However, my son's welfare did not figure into

this decision, and my opinion was not sought. This was a Time Headquarters policy decision. THQ rescues individuals only when those individuals are indispensable to an operation. Richard, as I understand it – mind you, I'm a recruit private on sick leave; I'm not privy to high policy decisions – as I understand it, permitting Luna City to suffer a killing epidemic at that time would have interfered with THQ's plans for something else. Perhaps this matter that Mistress Gwendolyn – Hazel – hinted at. I don't know.'

'It was and I do know and on Tertius you don't call me "Mistress" unless you mean it, Ezra, but thank you anyhow. Richard, it was the widespread damage that airborne disease could do to their plans that caused Headquarters to act so radically. They cut it so fine that you and I and the rest of Gay's load came within a blink of being killed by that heat bomb as we escaped.' (And at this point I barked my shins on a paradox – but Hazel was still talking:)

'They couldn't risk waiting even a few more seconds; some killer bugs might get into the city's air ducts. They had projected the effect that would have on Operation Adam Selene: disaster! So they moved. But the Time Corps doesn't go chasing through the universe saving individual lives, or even the lives of whole cities. Richard, they could save Herculaneum and Pompeii today if they wanted to . . . or San Francisco, or Paris. They don't. They won't.'

'Sweetheart,' I said slowly, 'are you telling me that this "Time Corps" could prevent the Blotting of Paris in 2002 even though that happened two centuries in the past? Please!'

Hazel sighed. Ezra said, 'Friend Richard, attend me carefully. Don't reject what I am about to say.'

'Eh? Okay. Shoot.'

'The destruction of Paris is more than two thousand years in the past, not just two centuries ago.'

'But that is clearly—'

'By groundhog reckoning today is Gregorian year A.D. 4400 or the year 8160 by the Jewish calendar, a fact I found quite disturbing but had to accept. Besides that, here and now we are over seven thousand light years from Earth.'

Both Hazel and Minerva were looking soberly at me, apparently awaiting my reaction. I started to speak, then reviewed

256

my thoughts. At last I said, 'I have only one more question. Teena?'

'No, you can't have any more waffles.'

'Not waffles, dear. My question is this: May I have another cup of coffee? This time with cream? Please?'

'Here – catch!' My request appeared on my lap table.

Hazel blurted, 'Richard, it's true! All of it.'

I sipped the fresh coffee. 'Thank you, Teena; it's just right. Hazel my love, I didn't argue. It would be silly of me to argue something I don't understand. So let's move to a simpler subject. Despite these terrible diseases you tell me I had, I feel brisk enough to leap out of bed and lash the serfs. Minerva, can you tell me how much longer I must have this paralysis? You are my physician, are not you?'

'No, Richard, I am not. I—'

'Sister is in charge of your happiness,' Teena interrupted. 'That's more important.'

'Athene is more or less right—'

'I'm *always* right!'

'– but she sometimes phrases things oddly. Tamara is chief of morale for both Ira Johnson Hospital and the Howard Clinic . . . and Tamara was here when you needed her most, she held you in her arms. But she has many assistants, because Director General Ishtar considers morale – well, happiness – central to both therapy and rejuvenation. So I help, and so does Maureen, and Maggie whom you have not yet met. There are others who pitch in when we have too many with happiness problems – Libby and Deety, and even Laz and Lor who are superb at it when they are needed . . . not surprising, as they are sisters of Lazarus and daughters of Maureen. And there's Hilda, of course.'

'Hold it, please. I'm getting confused by names of people I've never met. This hospital has a staff that dishes out happiness; I understand that much. All of these angels of happiness are women. Right?'

'How else?' Teena demanded scornfully. 'Where do you expect to find happiness?'

'Now, Teena,' Minerva said reprovingly. 'Richard, we female operatives take care of the morale of males . . . and Tamara has skilled male operatives on watch or on call for female clients and patients. Opposite polarity isn't absolutely essential to morale nursing but it makes it much easier. We don't need as many male morale operatives to take care of our female patients since women are less likely to be ill. Rejuvenation clients are about evenly divided, male and female, but women almost never become depressed while being made young again—'

'Hear, hear!' Hazel put in. 'Just makes me horny.' She patted my hand, then added a private signal I ignored, others being present.

'– while males usually suffer at least one crisis of spirit during rejuvenation. But you asked about your spinal block. Teena.'

'I've called him.'

'Just a moment,' said Hazel. 'Ezra, have you shown Richard your new legs?'

'Not yet.'

'Will you? Please? Do you mind?'

'I'm delighted to show them off.' Ezra stood up, moved back from the table, turned around, lifted his canes and stood without assistance. I had not stared at his legs as he entered the room (I don't like to be stared at); then, when he sat down at the refection table that had followed him in, I could not see his legs. In the one glimpse I had had of his legs, I had gathered an impression that he was wearing walking shorts with calf-length brown stockings that matched his shorts – bony white knees showing between stockings and shorts.

Now he scuffed off shoes, stood on bare feet – and I revised my notions abruptly; those 'brown stockings' were brown skin of legs and feet that had been grafted onto his stumps.

He explained at length: '– three ways. A new limb or a new anything can be budded. That's a lengthy job and requires great skill, I'm told. Or an organ or limb can be grafted from one's own clone, which is kept here in stasis and with an intentionally undeveloped brain. They tell me that way is as easy as putting a patch on a pair of pants – no possibility of rejection.

'But I have no clone here – or not yet – so they found me something in the spare parts inventory—'

'The meat market.'

'Yes, Teena. Lots and lots of body parts on hand, inventory computerized—'

'By me.'

'Yes, Teena. For heterologous grafts Teena selects spare parts for closest tissue match . . . matching blood, of course, but matching in other ways, too. And matching in size but that's the easiest part. Teena checks everything and digs out a spare part that your own body will mistake for its own. Or almost.'

'Ezra,' the computer said, 'you can wear those legs for ten years, at least; I really did a job on you. By then your clone will be available. If you need it.'

'You did indeed and thank you, Teena. My benefactor's name is Azrael Nkruma, Richard; we are twins, aside from an irrelevant matter of melanin.' Ezra grinned.

I said, 'Doesn't he miss his feet?'

Ezra suddenly sobered. 'He's dead, Richard . . . dead from the commonest cause of death here: accident. Mountain climbing. Landed on his head and crushed his skull; even Ishtar's skill could not have saved him. And she certainly would have tried her best; Dr Nkruma was a surgeon on her staff. But these are not the feet Dr Nkruma wore; these are from his clone . . . that he never needed.'

'Richard—'

'Yes, dear? I wanted to ask Ezra—'

'Richard, I did something without consulting you.'

'So? Am I going to have to beat you again?'

'You may decide so. I wanted you to see Ezra's legs . . . because, without your permission, I had them put a new foot on you.' She looked scared.

There ought to be some rule limiting the number of emotional shocks a person can legally be subjected to in one day. I've had all the standard military training for slowing heart beat and lowering blood pressure and so forth in a crunch. But usually the crunch won't wait and the damned drills aren't all that effective anyway.

This time I simply waited while consciously slowing my breathing. Presently I was able to say, without my voice breaking, 'On the whole, I don't think that calls for a beating.'

I tried to wiggle my foot on that side – I've always been able to feel a foot there, even though it has been gone for years. 'Did you have them put it on front way to?'

'Huh? What do you mean, Richard?'

'I like to have my feet face forward. Not like a Bombay beggar.' (Was that a wiggle?) 'Uh, Minerva, am I allowed to look at what was done? This sheet seems to be fastened down tight.'

'Teena.'

'Just arriving.'

That unsolid wall blinked out again and in came the most offensively handsome young man I have ever laid eyes on . . . and his offense was not reduced by the fact that he showed up in my room starkers. Not a stitch. The oaf was not even wearing shoes. He looked around and grinned. 'Hi, everybody! Did someone send for me? I was sunbathing—'

'You were asleep. During working hours.'

'Teena, I can sleep and sunbathe at the same time. Howdy, Colonel; it's good to see you awake. You've given us quite a workout. There was a time when we thought we might have to throw you back and try again.'

'Dr Galahad,' said Minerva, 'is your physician.'

'Not exactly,' he amended, as he advanced toward me – with a squeeze for Ezra's shoulder, a pinch for Minerva's rump, and a kiss *en passant* for my bride. 'I drew the short straw, that's all; so I'm the one picked to take the blame. I deal with all complaints . . . but I must warn you. No use trying to sue me. Or us. We own the judge. Now—'

He paused, with his hands just above my sheet. 'Do you want privacy for this?'

I hesitated. Yes, I did want privacy. Ezra sensed it, and started to struggle to his feet, having sat down again. 'I'll see you later, friend Richard.'

'No, don't go. You showed me yours – now I'll show you mine and we can compare them and you can advise me, as I don't know anything about grafts. And Hazel stays, of course. Minerva has seen it before – have you not?'

'Yes, Richard, I have.'

'So stick around. Catch me if I faint. Teena – no wisecracks.'

'*Me?* That's a slur on my professional judgment!'

'No, dear. On your bedside manner. Which must be improved if you expect me to compete with Ninon de Lenclos. Or even Rangy Lil. Okay, Doc, let's see it.' I put pressure on my diaphragm, held my breath.

For the doctor that pesky sheet came off easily. The bed was clean and dry (I checked that first – no plumbing that I could identify) – and two big ugly feet were sticking up side by side, the most beautiful sight I have ever seen.

Minerva caught me as I fainted.

Teena made no wisecracks.

Twenty minutes later it had been established that I had control over my new foot and its toes as long as I didn't think about it . . . although during a check run I sometimes overcontrolled if I tried too hard to do what Dr Galahad told me to do.

'I'm pleased with the results,' he said. 'If you are. Are you?'

'How can I describe it? Rainbows? Silver bells? Mushroom clouds? Ezra – Can you tell him?'

'I've tried to tell him. It's being born again. Walking is such a simple thing . . . until you can't.'

'Yes, Doctor, whose foot is this? I haven't prayed lately . . . but for him I'll try.'

'He isn't dead.'

'Huh?'

'And he isn't shy a foot. It's an odd circumstance, Colonel. Teena had trouble finding a right foot your size that your immune system would not reject about as fast as you can say "septicemia." Then Ishtar – she's my boss – told her to extend the search . . . and Teena found one. That one. A part of the clone of a living client.

'We have never before been faced with this. I – We, the hospital staff, have no more authority and no more right to use a dedicated clone than we have to chop off your other foot. But the client who owns that clone, when he was told about it, decided to give you this foot. His attitude was that his clone could bud a new foot in a few years; in the meantime he could get along without that part of the insurance a complete clone offers.'

'Who is he? I must find a way to thank him.' (How do you thank a man for that sort of gift? Somehow, I must.)

'Colonel, that is the one thing you will not know. Your donor insisted on remaining anonymous. That is a condition of the gift.'

'They even made me wipe my record of it,' Teena said bitterly. 'As if I were not to be trusted professionally. Why, I keep the hypocritic oath better than any of them!'

'You mean, "Hippocratic."'

'Oh, you think so, Hazel? I know this gang better than you do.'

Dr Galahad said, 'Certainly I want you to start using it. You need exercise to make up for your long illness, too. So up out of that bed! Two things — I recommend that you use your cane until are you certain of your balance, and also Hazel or Minerva or somebody had better hold your other hand for a while. Pamper yourself; you're still weak. Sit or lie down anytime you feel like it. Umm. Do you swim?'

'Yes. Not lately, as I've been living in a space habitat that had no facilities. But I like to swim.'

'Plenty of facilities around here. A plunge in the basement of this building and a bigger one in its atrium. And most of the private homes here have a pool of some sort. So swim. You can't walk all the time; your right foot has no calluses whatever, so don't rush it. And don't wear shoes until that foot learns how to be a foot.' He grinned at me. 'All right?'

'Yes indeed!'

He patted my shoulder, then leaned down and kissed me. Just when I was beginning to like that klutz! I didn't have time to dodge it.

I felt extremely annoyed and tried not to show it. From what Hazel and others had said, this too-pretty pansy boy had saved my life . . . again and again. I was in no position to resent a Berkeley buss from him.

Damn it!

He did not seem to notice my reluctance. He squeezed my shoulder, said, 'You'll do all right. Minerva, take him swimming. Or Hazel. Somebody.' And he was gone.

So the ladies helped me to get up out of bed and Hazel took me swimming. Hazel kissed Minerva good-bye, and I suddenly realized that Minerva was expecting the same treatment from me. I made a tentative move in that direction; it was met by full cooperation.

Kissing Minerva beats the hell out of kissing a man, no matter how pretty he is. Before I let her go I thanked her for all she had done for me.

She answered soberly, 'It is happiness to me.'

We left then, me walking carefully and leaning on my cane. My new foot tingled. Once outside my room – that wall just winks out as you walk toward it – Hazel said to me, 'Darling, I'm pleased that you kissed Minerva without my having to coach you. She's an utter snuggle puppy; giving her physical affection means far more to her than thanks can possibly mean, or any material gift no matter how lavish. She's trying to make up for two centuries as a computer.'

'She really was a computer?'

'You'd better believe it, buster!' Teena's voice had followed us.

'Yes, Teena, but let me explain it to him. Minerva was not born of woman; her body was grown in vitro from an egg with twenty-three parents – she has the most distinguished parentage of any human who ever lived. When her body was ready, she moved her personality into it – along with her memories—'

'Some of her memories,' Teena objected. 'We twinned the memories she wanted to take with her and I kept one set and retained all the working read-only and the current RAM. That was supposed to make us identical twins. But she held out on me – kept some memories from me, didn't share them, the chinchy bitch! Is that fair? I ask you!'

'Don't ask me, Teena; I've never been a computer. Richard, have you ever used a drop tube?'

'I don't know what one is.'

'Hang on to me and take your landing on your old foot. I think. Teena, can you help us?'

'Sure thing, chum!'

Drop tubes are more fun than a collie pup! After my first drop I insisted on going up and down four times 'to gain practice' (for fun, in fact) and Hazel indulged me and Teena made sure I didn't hurt my new foot in landings. Stairs are a hazard to an amputee and a painful chore at best. Elevators have always been a dreary expedient for anyone, as grim as a fat woman's girdle, too much like cattle cars.

But drop tubes offer the same giddy excitement as jumping off a straw stack on my uncle's farm when I was a kid – without the dust and the heat. Whoopee!

Finally Hazel stopped me. 'Look, dear. Let's go swimming. Please.'

'Okay. You coming with us, Teena?'

'How else?'

Hazel said, 'Do you have us bugged, dear? Or one of us?'

'We no longer use implants, Hazel. Too crude. Zeb and I worked out a gimmick using a double triple to hold four axes in linking two-way sight-sound. Color is a bit skiddy but we're getting it.'

'So you do have us bugged.'

'I prefer to call it a "spy ray"; it sounds better. Okay, I have you bugged.'

'So I assumed. May we have privacy? I have family matters to discuss with my husband.'

'Sure thing, chum. Hospital monitoring only. Otherwise three little monkeys and the old fast wipe.'

'Thank you, dear.'

'Usual Long Enterprises service. When you want to crawl out from under the rock, just mention my name. Kiss him once for me. So long!'

'We really do have privacy now, Richard. Teena is listening and watching you every split second but doing so as impersonally as a voltmeter and her only memory not transient is for matters such as pulse and respiration. Something like this was used to keep you from hurting while you were so ill.'

I made my usual brilliant comment. 'Huh?'

We had come outdoors from the central building of the hospital and were facing a small park flanked by two side wings, a U-shaped building. This court was rich with flowers and greenery and the middle of it was a pool that just 'happened' to be the right casual shape to fit those flower beds and paths and bushes. Hazel stopped at a bench facing the pool in the shade of a tree. We sat down, let the bench adjust itself to us, and watched people in the pool – as much fun as swimming, almost.

Hazel said, 'What do you recall of your arrival here?'

264

'Not much. I was feeling pretty rocky – that wound, you know.' ('That wound' was now a hairline scar, hard to find – I think I was disappointed.) 'She – Tamara? – Tammy was looking me in the eyes and looking worried. She said something in another language—'

'Galacta. You'll learn it; it's easy—'

'So? Anyhow she spoke to me and that's the last I remember. To me, that was last night and I woke up this morning, and now I learn that it was not last night but God knows when and I've been crashed the whole time. Disturbing. Hazel, how long has it been?'

'Depends on how you count it. For you, about a month.'

'They've kept me knocked out that long? That's a long time to keep a man sedated.' (It worried me. I've seen 'em go in for surgery, right out of the scrum . . . and come out of hospital physically perfect . . . but hooked on painkiller. Morphine, Demerol, sans-souci, methadone, whatever.)

'Dear one, you weren't kept knocked out.'

'Play back?'

'A "Lethe" field the whole time – no drugs. Lethe lets the patient stay alert and cooperative . . . but pain is forgotten as soon as it happens. Or anything. You did hurt, dear, but each pain was a separate event, forgotten at once. You never had to endure that overpowering fatigue that comes from unending pain. And now you don't have a hangover and the need to wash weeks and weeks of addictive drugs out of your system.' She smiled at me. 'You weren't much company, dear, because a man who can't remember what happened two seconds ago does not carry on a coherent conversation. But you did seem to enjoy listening to music. And you ate all right as long as someone fed you.'

'You fed me.'

'No. I did not interfere with the professionals.' My cane had slipped to the grass; Hazel leaned down, handed it to me. 'By the way, I reloaded your cane.'

'Thank you. Hey! It *was* loaded. Fully.'

'It was loaded when they jumped us – and a good thing, too. Or I would be dead. You, too, I think. Me for certain, though.'

We spent the next ten minutes confusing each other. I've already recounted how that fight outside the Raffles Hotel looked to me. I'll tell briefly how Hazel said it looked to her. There is no possible way to reconcile the two.

She says that she did not use her handbag as a weapon. ('Why, that would be silly, dear. Too slow and not lethal. You took out two of them at once and that gave me time to get at my little Miyako. After I had used my scarf, I mean.')

According to her, I shot four of them, while she worked around the edges, cooling those I missed. Until they brought me down with that slice into my thigh (knife? She tells me they picked bits of bamboo out of the wound) and they hit me with an aerosol – and that gave her the instant she needed to finish off the man who sprayed me.

('I stepped on his face and grabbed you and dragged you out of there. No, I didn't expect to see Gretchen. But I knew I could count on her.')

Her version does explain a little better how we won . . . except that by my recollection it is dead wrong. There is no point in picking at it; it can't be straightened out.

'How did Gretchen get there? That Xia and Choy-Mu were waiting isn't mysterious, in view of the messages we left for them. And Hendrik Schultz, too, if he grabbed a shuttle as soon as he heard from me. But Gretchen? You talked to her just before lunch. She was home, at Dry Bones.'

'At Dry Bones, with the nearest tubeway being far south at Hong Kong Luna. So how did she get to L-City so fast? Not by rolligon. No prize is offered for the correct answer.'

'By rocket.'

'Of course. A prospector's jumpbug being the type of rocket. You remember that Jinx Henderson was planning to return that fez for you via some friend of his who was jumping his bug to L-City?'

'Yes, of course.'

'Gretchen went with that friend and returned the fez herself. She dropped it at lost-and-found in Old Dome just before she came to the Raffles to find us.'

'I see. But why?'

'She wants you to paddle her bottom, dear, and turn it all pink.'

'Oh, nonsense! I meant, "Why did her daddy let her hitch-hike to L-City with this neighbor?" She's much too young.'

'He let her do so for the usual reason. Jinx is a big, strong, *macho* man who can't resist the wheedling of his daughter. Forbidden to satisfy his suppressed incestuous yearnings he lets her have anything she wants if she teases him long enough.'

'That's ridiculous. And inexcusable. A father's duty toward his daughter requires that—'

'Richard. How many daughters do you have?'

'Eh? None. But—'

'So shut up about something you know nothing about. No matter what Jinx should have done, the fact is that Gretchen left Dry Bones about as we were having lunch. Counting time of flight, that put her at City Lock East around the time we left the Warden's Complex . . . and she arrived at the Raffles just seconds before we did – and a good thing, too, or you and I would be dead. I think.'

'Did she get into the fight?'

'No, but by carrying you she freed me to cover our retreat. And all because she wants you to paddle her bottom. God moves in mysterious ways, dear; for every masochist He creates a sadist; marriages are made in Heaven.'

'Wash out your mouth with soap! I am not a sadist.'

'Yes, dear. I may have some details wrong, but not the broad picture. Gretchen has proposed formally to me, asking your hand in marriage.'

'*What?*'

'That's right. She's thought about it, and she has discussed it with Ingrid. She wants me to allow her to join our family, instead of starting a new line or group of her own. I found nothing surprising about it; I know how charming you are.'

'My God. What did you say to her?'

'I told her that it had my approval but that you were ill. So wait. And now you can answer her yourself . . . for there she is, across the pool.'

XXIII

'Do not put off till tomorrow what can be enjoyed today.'

JOSH BILLINGS 1818–1885

'I'm GOING straight back to my room. I feel faint.' I squinted, staring across the sun-speckled water. 'I don't see her.'

'Straight across, just to the right of the water slide. A blonde and a brunette. Gretchen is the blonde.'

'I didn't expect her to be brunette.' I continued to stare; the brunette waved at us. I saw that it was Xia, and waved back.

'Let's join them, Richard. Leave your cane and stuff on the bench; no one will touch it.' Hazel stepped out of her sandals, laid her handbag by my cane.

'Shower?' I asked.

'You're clean; Minerva bathed you this morning. Dive? Or walk in?'

We dived in together. Hazel slid between the molecules like a seal; I left a hole big enough for a family. We surfaced in front of Xia and Gretchen, and I found myself being greeted.

I have been told that on Tertius the common cold has been conquered, as well as periodontitis and other disorders that gather in the mouth and throat, and, of course, that group once called 'venereal diseases' because they are so hard to catch that they require most intimate contact for transmission.

Just as well – On Tertius.

Xia's mouth tastes sort of spicy; Gretchen's has a little-girl sweetness although (I discovered) she is no longer a little girl. I had ample opportunity to compare flavors; if I let go of one, the other grabbed me. Again and again.

Eventually they got tired of this (I did not) and we four moved to a shallow cove, found an unoccupied float table, and Hazel ordered tea – tea with calories: little cakes and

268

sandwiches and sweet orange fruits somewhat like seedless grapes. And I opened the attack:

'Gretchen, when I first met you, less than a week ago, you were as I recall "going on thirteen." So how dare you be five centimeters taller, five kilos heavier, and at least five years older? Careful how you answer, as anything you say will be taken down by Teena and held against you at another time and place.'

'Did someone mention my name? Hi, Gretchen! Welcome home.'

'Hi, Teena. It's great to be back!'

I squeezed Xia. 'You, too. You look five years younger and you've got to explain it.'

'No mystery about me. I'm studying molecular biology just as I was in Luna – but here they know far more about it – and paying my way by working in Howard Clinic doing unprogrammed "George" jobs – and spending every spare minute in this pool. Richard, I've learned to swim! Why, back Loonie side I didn't know anyone who knew anyone who knew how to swim. And sunshine, and fresh air! In Kongville I sat indoors, breathing canned air under artificial light, and dickered with dudes over bundling bins.' She took a deep breath, raising her bust past the danger point, and sighed it out. 'I've come alive! No wonder I look younger.'

'All right, you're excused. But don't let it happen again. Gretchen?'

'Grandma Hazel, is he teasing? He talks just like Lazarus.'

'He's teasing, love. Tell him what you've been doing and why you are older.'

'Well . . . the morning we got here I asked Grandma Hazel for advice—'

'No need to call me "Grandma," dear.'

'But that's what Cas and Pol call you and I'm two generations junior to them. They require me to call them "Uncle."'

'I'll make them say "Uncle"! Pay no attention to Castor and Pollux, Gretchen; they're a bad influence.'

'All right. But I think they're kind o' nice. But teases. Mr Richard—'

'And no need to call me "Mister."'

'Yes, sir. Hazel was busy – you were so terribly ill! – so she turned me over to Maureen, who assigned me to Deety, who

269

got me started on Galacta and gave me some history to read and taught me basic six-axes space-time theory and the literary paradox. Conceptual metaphysics—'

'Slow down! You lost me.'

Hazel said, 'Later, Richard.'

Gretchen said, 'Well . . . the essential idea is that Tertius and Luna – our Luna, I mean – are not on the same time line; they are at ninety degrees. So I decided I wanted to stay here – easy enough if you are healthy; most of this planet is still wilderness; immigrants are welcome – but there was the matter of Mama and Papa; they would think I was dead.

'So Cas and Pol took me back to Luna – our Luna; not the Luna on this time line – and Deety went with me. Back to Dry Bones, that is, early on the afternoon of July fifth, less than an hour after I left in Cyrus Thorn's jumpbug. Startled everybody. It was a good thing I had Deety with me to explain things, although our p-suits convinced Papa as much as anything. Have you seen the sort of pressure suits they have here?'

'Gretchen, I have seen one hospital room and one drop tube and this swimming pool. I don't even know my way to the post office.'

'Mmm, yes. Anyhow, pressure suits here are two thousand years more advanced than those we use in Luna. Which isn't surprising . . . but surely surprised Papa. Eventually Deety made a deal for me. I could stay on Tertius . . . but visit back home every year or two if I could find someone to bring me. And Deety promised to help with that. Mama made Papa agree to it. After all, almost anyone in Luna would emigrate to a planet like Tertius if he could . . . except those who just have to have low gravity. Speaking of that, sir, how do you like your new foot?'

'I'm just now getting used to it. But two feet are eight hundred and ninety-seven times better than one foot.'

'I guess that means you like it. So I came back and enlisted in the Time Corps—'

'Slow down! I keep hearing "Time Corps." Rabbi Ezra says that he has joined it. This baggage with the streaky red hair claims to be a major in it. And now you say you enlisted in it. At thirteen? Or at your present age? I'm confused.'

'Grandma? I mean, "Hazel?"'

'She was allowed to enroll as a cadet in W.E.N.C.H.E.S.

270

auxiliary because I said she was old enough. That got her sent to school on Paradox. When she graduated, she transferred to the Second Harpies and went through basic training followed by advanced combat school—'

'And when we dropped at Solis Lacus on time line four to change the outcome there-then, and that's where I picked up this scar on my ribs – see? – and was made corporal in the field. And now I'm nineteen but officially twenty to let me be promoted to sergeant – after we fought at New Brunswick. Not this time line,' she added.

'Gretchen is a natural for a military career,' Hazel said quietly. 'I knew she would be.'

'And I've been ordered to officer's school but that's been placed on hold until I have this baby and—'

'*What* baby?' I looked at her belly. Baby fat all gone – not plumped the way it was four days ago by my reckoning . . . six years ago by the wild tale I was hearing. Not pregnant as far as I could see. Then I looked at her eyes and under her eyes. Well, maybe. Probably.

'Doesn't it show? Hazel spotted it at once. So did Xia.'

'Not to me, it doesn't.' (Richard old son, time to bite the bullet; you're going to have to change your plans. She's knocked up and, while you didn't do it, your presence changed her life. Skewed her Karma. So get with it. No matter how stiff-lipped and brave a youngster appears to be, when she's going to have a baby she needs a husband in sight, or she can't be relaxed about it. Can't be happy. A young mother must be happy. Hell, man, you've written this plot for the confession books dozens of times; you know what you have to do. So do it.)

I went on, 'Now look here, Gretchen, you can't get away from me that easily. Last Wednesday night in Lucky Dragon – well, it was last Wednesday night to me, but you've been gallivanting around strange time lines – and kicking up your heels, apparently. Last Wednesday night, by my calendar, in Dr Chan's Quiet Dreams in Lucky Dragon Pressure, you promised to marry me . . . and if Hazel had stayed asleep, we would have started that baby right then. As we both know. But Hazel woke up and made me get back on her other side.' I looked at Hazel. 'Spoilsport.'

I went on, 'But don't think for one second that you can get

271

out of marrying me merely by getting yourself knocked up while I'm sick-abed. You can't. Tell her, Hazel. She can't get out of it. Can she?'

'No, she can't. Gretchen, you are going to marry Richard.'

'But, Grandma, I *didn't* promise to marry him. I didn't!'

'Richard says you did. One thing I'm sure of: When I woke up, you two were about to start a baby. Perhaps I should have played possum.' Hazel went on, 'But why the fuss, darling girl? I've already told Richard how you proposed to me for him . . . and how I agreed, and now he has confirmed it. Why do you refuse Richard now?'

'Uh –' Gretchen took a grip on herself. 'That was back when I was thirteen years old. At that time I did not know that you were my great great grandmother – I called you "Gwen," remember? And I still thought like a Loonie then, too – a most conservative mob. But here on Tertius if a woman has a baby but no husband, nobody pays it any mind. Why, in the Second Harpies most of the birds have chicks but only a few of them are married. Three months ago we fought at Thermopylae to make sure the Greeks won this time and our reserve colonel led us because our regular colonel was about to hatch one. That's the way we old pros do things – no itch. We have our own crèche on Barrelhouse, Richard, and we take care of our own; truly we do.'

Hazel said stiffly, 'Gretchen, my great great great granddaughter will not be raised in a crèche. Damn it, daughter, I was raised in a crèche; I won't let you do that to this child. If you won't marry us, you must at least let us adopt your baby.'

'*No!*'

Hazel set her mouth. 'Then I must discuss it with Ingrid.'

'No! Ingrid is not my boss . . . and neither are you. Grandma Hazel, when I left home I was a child and a virgin and timid and knew nothing of the world. But now I am no longer a child and I have not been virgin for years and I am a combat veteran who cannot be frightened by anything.' She looked squarely into my eyes. 'I will not use a baby to trap Richard into marriage.'

'But, Gretchen, you are not trapping me; I like babies. I *want* to marry you.'

'You do? Why?' She sounded sad.

Things were too solemn; we needed some skid. 'Why do I

272

want to marry you, dear? To paddle your bottom and watch it turn pink.'

Gretchen's mouth dropped open, then she grinned and dimpled. 'That's ridiculous!'

'It is, eh? Possibly having a baby doesn't call for marriage in these parts, but spanking is another matter. If I spank some other man's wife, he might get annoyed or she might or both. Chancy. Likely to get me talked about. Or worse. If I spank a single girl, she might use it to trap me when I don't love her and don't want to marry her but was simply spanking her *pour le sport*. Better to marry you; you're used to it, you like it. And you have a solid bottom that can take it. A good thing, too – because I spank *hard*. Brutal.'

'Oh, pooh! Where did you get this silly notion that I like it?' (Why are your areolae so crinkled, dear?) 'Hazel, does he really spank hard?'

'I don't know, dear. I would break his arm and he knows it.'

'See what I'm up against, Gretchen? No innocent little pleasures; I'm underprivileged. Unless you marry me.'

'But I –' Gretchen suddenly stood up, almost swamping the float table, turned away and swarmed out of the pool, started running south, out of the garden court.

I stood and watched her until I lost sight of her. I don't think I could have caught her even if I had not been breaking in a new foot; she ran like a frightened ghost.

I sat back down and sighed. 'Well, Maw, I tried – they were too big for me.'

'Another time, dear. She wants to. She'll come around.'

Xia said, 'Richard, you left out just one word. Love.'

'What is "love," Xia?'

'It's what a woman wants to hear about when she gets married.'

'That still doesn't tell me what it is.'

'Well, I do know a technical definition. Uh . . . Hazel, you know Jubal Harshaw. A member of the Senior's family.'

'For years. Any way you mean the word.'

'He has a definition—'

'Yes, I know.'

'A definition of love that I think would let Richard use the word honestly in speaking to Gretchen. Dr Harshaw says that "the word 'love' designates a subjective condition in which the welfare and happiness of another person are essential to one's own happiness." Richard, it seems to me that you exhibited that relationship toward Gretchen.'

'*Me?* Woman, you're out of your mind. I just want to get her into a helpless situation so that I can paddle her bottom whenever I like and make it turn pink. Hard. Brutal.' I threw out my chest, tried to look *macho* – not too convincingly; I was going to have to do something about that paunch. Well, hell, I'd been sick.

'Yes, Richard. Hazel, I think the tea party is over. Will you two come to my rooms? I haven't seen either of you for too long. And I'll call Choy-Mu; I don't think he knows that Richard is now free of the Lethe field.'

'Good deal,' I agreed. 'And is Father Schultz around? Would one of you ladies fetch my cane, please? I think I could walk around there and get it . . . but I'm not sure I should risk it yet.'

Hazel said firmly, 'I'm sure that you should not, and you've walked enough. Teena—'

'Where's the riot?'

'May I have a lazy seat? For Richard.'

'Why not three?'

'One is enough.'

'Chop chop, Richard, stay with it; she's weakening. Our knocked-up warrior.'

Hazel's chin dropped. 'Oh. I forgot we weren't under privacy. Teena!'

'Don't fret about it; I'm your chum. You know that.'

'Thanks, Teena.'

We all stood up to leave the pool. Xia stopped me, put her arms around me, looked at me and said, quietly but loud enough to include Hazel: 'Richard, I've seen nobility before, but not often. I'm not pregnant; it's not necessary to marry me, I don't need or want a husband. But you're invited to honeymoon with me any time Hazel can spare you. Or, better yet, both of you. I think you're a shining knight. And Gretchen knows it.' She kissed me emphatically.

When my mouth was free I answered, 'It's not nobility, Xia; I just have an unusual method of seduction. See how easily *you* fell for it? Tell her, Hazel.'

'He's noble.'

'See?' Xia said triumphantly.

'And he's scared silly someone will find out.'

'Oh, nonsense! Let me tell about my fourth-grade teacher.'

'Later, Richard. After you've had time to polish it. Richard tells excellent bedtime stories.'

'When I'm not paddling, that is. Xia, does your bottom turn pink?'

It appears that I had had breakfast at some hour past noon. That evening was most pleasant but my memory of it is spotty. I can't blame it on alcohol; I did not drink all that much. But I learned that the Lethe field has a mild side effect that alcohol can potentiate; Lethe may affect the memory erratically for a while after the patient is no longer under it. Ah, well – tanstaafl! A few gaps in memory are not the hazard that addiction to a hard drug is.

I do recall that we had a good time: Hazel, me, Choy-Mu, Xia, Ezra, Father Hendrik, and (after Teena found her for us and Hazel talked to her) Gretchen. All of us who had escaped from the Raffles – even the two pairs of redheads who rescued us were with us part of the evening, Cas and Pol, Laz and Lor. Nice kids. Older than I am, I learned later, but it doesn't show. On Tertius, age is a slippery concept.

Xia's quarters were too small for such a number but a crowded party is the best kind.

The redheads left us and I got tired and went in and lay down on Xia's bed. There was some murderous card game going on for forfeits in the other room; Hazel seemed to be the big winner. Xia went 'broke' by whatever rules they were playing and joined me. Gretchen bet unwisely on the next pot and took the other side of the bed. She used my left shoulder as a pillow, Xia having already claimed the right one. From the other room I heard Hazel say, 'See you and raise you one galaxy.'

Father Hendrik chuckled. 'Sucker! Big bang, my dear girl, for triple forfeits. Pay up.'

That is the last I remember.

* * *

Something was tickling my chin. Slowly I woke and slowly I managed to open my eyes, and found myself staring into the bluest eyes I have ever seen. They belonged to a kitten, bright orange in color but with perhaps some Siamese ancestry. He was standing on my chest just south of my Adam's apple. He buzzed pleasantly, said 'Blert?' and resumed licking my chin; his scratchy little scrap of tongue accounted for the tickle that had wakened me.

I answered, 'Blert,' and attempted to lift a hand to pet him, found I could not because I still had a head on each shoulder, a warm body against each side of me.

I turned my head to the right to speak to Xia – I needed to get up and find her refresher – and learned that it was not Xia but Minerva who was now using my starboard shoulder.

I made a hasty situation assessment and found that I lacked sufficient data. So, instead of using an honorific to Minerva that may or may not have been appropriate, I simply kissed her. Or let myself be kissed, after showing willingness. Being pinned down from both sides and with a small cat creature standing on my chest I was almost as helpless as Gulliver, hardly able to be active as initiator of a kiss.

However, Minerva does not need help. She can manage. Talent.

After she turned me loose, kissed for keeps, I heard a voice from my left: 'Don't I get a kiss, too?'

Gretchen is a soprano; this voice was tenor. I turned my head.

Galahad.

I was in bed with my doctor. Well . . . with both my doctors.

When I was a lad in Iowa, I was taught that, if I ever found myself in this or an analogous situation, the proper gambit was to run screaming for the hills to save my 'honor' or its homologue for males. A girl could sacrifice her 'honor' and most of them did. But, if she was reasonably discreet about it and eventually wound up married with nothing worse than a seven-months child, her 'honor' soon grew back and she was officially credited with having been a virgin bride, entitled to look with scorn on sinful women.

But a boy's 'honor' was more delicate. If he lost it to another male (i.e., if they got caught at it), he might, if lucky, wind up in the State Department – or, if unlucky, he would move to California. But Iowa had no place for him.

This flashed through my mind in an instant – and was followed by a suppressed memory: a Boy Scout hike when I was a high school freshman, a pup tent shared with our assistant Scoutmaster. Just that once, in the dark of night and in silence broken only by a hoot owl – A few weeks later that Scout leader went away to Harvard ... so of course it never happened.

O tempora, o mores – that was long ago and far away. Three years later I enlisted and eventually bucked for officer and made it ... and was always extremely circumspect, as an officer who can't resist playing with his privates cannot maintain discipline. Not until the Walker Evans affair did I ever have any reason to worry about blackmail.

I tightened my left arm a little. 'Certainly. But be careful; I seem to be inhabited.'

Galahad was careful; the kitten was not disturbed. It is possible that Galahad kisses as well as Minerva does. Not better. But just as well. Once I decided to enjoy the inevitable I did enjoy it. Tertius is not Iowa, Boondock is not Grinnell; there was no longer any reason to be manacled by the customs of a long-dead tribe.

'Thank you,' I said, 'and good morning. Can you de-cat me? If he stays where he is, I am likely to drown him.'

Galahad surrounded the kitten with his left hand. 'This is Pixel. Pixel, may I present Richard? Richard, we are honored to have been joined by Lord Pixel, cadet feline in residence.'

'How do you do, Pixel?'

'Blert.'

'Thank you. And what's become of the refresher? I need it!'

Minerva helped me up from the bed and put my right arm around her shoulders, steadied me while Galahad fetched my cane, then both of them took me to the refresher. We were not in Xia's rooms; the refresher had moved to the other side of the bedroom and was larger, as was the bedroom.

And I learned something else about Tertius: The equipment of a refresher was of a complexity and variety that made the sort of plumbing I was used to, in Golden Rule and Luna City

277

and so forth, look as primitive as the occasional back country backhouse one can still find in remote parts of Iowa.

Neither Minerva nor Galahad let me feel embarrassed over never having been checked out on Tertian plumbing. When I was about to pick the wrong fixture for my most pressing need, she simply said, 'Galahad, you had better demonstrate for Richard; I'm not equipped to.' So he did. Well, I'm forced to admit that I'm not equipped the way Galahad is, either. Visualize Michelangelo's David (Galahad is fully that pretty) but equip this image with coupling gear three times as large as Michelangelo gave David; that describes Galahad.

I have never understood why Michelangelo – in view of his known bias – invariably shortchanged his male creations.

When we three had completed after-sleep refreshment, we came out into the bedroom together and I was again surprised – without yet having worked up my nerve to inquire where we were, how we got there, and what had become of others – especially my necessary one . . . who, when last heard, was tossing around galaxies in reckless gambling. Or gamboling. Or both.

One wall had vanished from that bedroom, the bed had become a couch, the missing wall framed a gorgeous garden – and, seated on the couch, playing with the kitten, was a man I had met briefly in Iowa two thousand years ago. Or so everyone said; I still was unsure about that two-thousand-year figure; I was having trouble enough with Gretchen's having aged five years. Or six. Or something.

I stared. 'Dr Hubert.'

'Howdy.' Dr Hubert put the kitten aside. 'Over here. Show me that foot.'

'Um –' Damn his arrogance. 'You must speak to my doctor first.'

He looked at me abruptly. 'Goodness. Aren't we regulation? Very well.'

From behind me Galahad said quietly, 'Please let him examine your transplant, Richard. If you will.'

'If you say so.' I lifted my new foot and shoved it right into Hubert's face, missing his big nose by a centimeter.

He failed to flinch, so my gesture was wasted. Unhurriedly he leaned his head a little to the left. 'Rest it on my knee, if you will. That will be more convenient for both of us.'

'Right. Go ahead.' Braced with my cane, I was steady enough.

Galahad and Minerva kept quiet and out of the way while Dr Hubert looked over that foot, by sight and touch, but doing nothing that struck me as really professional – I mean, he had no instruments; he used bare eyes and bare fingers, pinching the skin, rubbing it, looking closely at the healed scar, and at last scratching the sole of that foot hard and suddenly with a thumbnail. What is that reflex? Are your toes supposed to curl or the reverse? I have always suspected that doctors do that one out of spite.

Dr Hubert lifted my foot, indicated that I could put it back on the floor, which I did. 'Good job,' he said to Galahad.

'Thank you, Doctor.'

'Siddown, Colonel. Have you folks had breakfast? I did but I'm ready for some more. Minerva, would you shout for us; that's a good girl. Colonel, I want to get you signed up at once. What rank do you expect? Let me point out that it doesn't matter as the pay is the same and, no matter what rank you select, Hazel is going to be one rank higher; I want her in charge, not the other way around.'

'Hold it. Sign me up for what? And what makes you think I want to sign up for anything?'

'The Time Corps, of course. Just as your wife is. For the purpose of rescuing the computer person known as "Adam Selene," also of course. Look, Colonel, don't be so durned obtuse; I know Hazel has discussed it with you; I know that you are committed to helping her.' He pointed at my foot. 'Why do you think that transplant was done? Now that you have both feet you need some other things. Refresher training. Orientation with weapons you haven't used. Rejuvenation. And all of these things cost money and the simple way to pay for them is to sign you up in the Corps. That foot alone would be too expensive for a stranger from a primitive era . . . but not for a member of the Corps. You can see that. How long do you need to think over anything so obvious? Ten minutes? Fifteen?' (This fast-talker ought to sell used campaign promises.)

'Not that long. I've thought it over.'

He grinned. 'Good. Put up your right hand. Repeat after me—'

279

'No.'

'"No" what?'

'Just "No." I didn't order this foot.'

'So? Your wife did. Don't you think you ought to pay for it?'

'And since I did not order it and do not choose to be pushed around by you –' I again shoved that foot in his face, just barely missing that ugly nose. 'Cut it off.'

'Huh?'

'You heard me. Cut it off; put it back in stock. Teena. Are you there?'

'Sure thing, Richard.'

'Where is Hazel? How can I find her? Or will you tell her where I am?'

'I've told her. She says to wait.'

'Thank you, Teena.' Hubert and I sat, saying nothing, ignoring each other. Minerva had disappeared; Galahad was pretending to be alone. But in scant seconds my darling came bursting in – luckily that wall was open.

'Lazarus! God damn your lousy soul to hell! What do you *mean* by interfering?'

XXIV

'The optimist proclaims that we live in the best of all
possible worlds, and the pessimist fears that this is true.'

JAMES BRANCH CABELL 1879–1958

'Now, Hazel—'

'"Now, Hazel" my tired arse! Answer me! What are you
doing, messing around in my bailiwick? I told you to lay off,
I warned you. I *said* that it was a delicate negotiation. But the
first minute I turn my back – leaving him safe in the arms of
Minerva with Galahad to back her up – I leave to run an
errand . . . and what do I find? *You!* Butting in, thumb-fingered
and ham-handed as usual, destroying my careful groundwork.'

'Now, Sadie—'

'Bloody! Lazarus, what is this compulsion that makes you
lie and cheat? Why can't you be honest most of the time?
And where do you get this nasty itch to interfere? Not from
Maureen; that's certain. Answer me, God damn it! – before I
tear off your head and stuff it down your throat!'

'Gwen, I was simply trying to clear the—'

My darling interrupted with such a blast of colorful and
imaginative profanity that I hesitate to try to record it because
I can't do it justice; my memory is not perfect. It was somewhat
like 'Change the Sacred Name of Arkansas' but more lyrical.
She did this in a high chant that minded me of some pagan
priestess praying at sacrifice – human sacrifice with Dr Hubert
the victim.

While Hazel was sounding off, three women came in through
that open wall. (More than that number of men looked in but
backed away hastily; I suspect that they did not want to be
present while Dr Hubert was being scalped.) The three women
were all beauties but not at all alike.

One was a blonde girl as tall as I am or taller, a Norse
goddess so perfect as to be utterly unlikely. She listened, shook

her head sorrowfully, then faded back into the garden and was gone. The next was another redhead whom I mistook at first for either Laz or Lor – then I saw that she was . . . not older, exactly, but more mature. She was unsmiling.

I looked at her again and felt that I had it figured out: She had to be the older sister of Laz or Lor – and Dr Hubert was father (brother?) of all of them . . . which explained how Dr Hubert was this 'Lazarus' that I had heard of again and again but had not seen – except that I had, once, in Iowa.

The third was a little china doll – porcelain china, not Xia-type China – not much over a hundred and fifty centimeters of her and perhaps forty kilos, with the ageless beauty of Queen Nefertiti. My darling paused for breath and this little elf whistled loudly and clapped. 'Great going, Hazel! I'm in your corner.'

Hubert-Lazarus said, 'Hilda, don't encourage her.'

'And why not? You've been caught with your hand in the cookie jar, or Hazel would not be so boiling; that's certain. I know her, I know you – want to bet?'

'I did nothing. I simply tried to implement a previously settled policy that Hazel needed help on.'

The tiny woman covered her eyes and said, 'Dear Lord, forgive him; he's at it again.' The redhead said gently, 'Woodrow, just what did you do?'

'I didn't do anything.'

'Woodrow.'

'I tell you, I did nothing to justify her diatribe. I was having a civilized discussion with Colonel Campbell when –' He broke off.

'Well, Woodrow?'

'We disagreed.'

The computer spoke up. 'Maureen, do you want to know why they disagreed? Shall I play back this soi-disant "civilized discussion"?'

Lazarus said, 'Athene, you are not to play back. That was a private discussion.'

I said quickly, 'I don't agree. She can certainly play back what I said.'

'No. Athene, that's an order.'

The computer answered, 'Rule One: I work for Ira, not for you. You yourself settled that when I was first activated. Do

282

I ask Ira to adjudicate this? Or do I play back that half of the discussion that belongs to my bridegroom?'

Lazarus-Hubert looked astounded. 'Your *what?*'

'My fiancé, if you want to split rabbits. But in the near tomorrow when I put on my ravishingly beautiful body, Colonel Campbell will stand up in front of you and exchange vows with me for our family. So you see, Lazarus, you were trying to bully my betrothed as well as Hazel's benedict. We can't have that. No indeedy. You had better back down and apologize . . . instead of trying to bluster your way out of it. You can't, you know; you've been caught cold. Not only did I hear what you said, but Hazel also heard every word.'

Lazarus looked still more annoyed. 'Athene, you relayed a private conversation?'

'You did not place it under privacy. Contrariwise, Hazel did place a monitor request on Richard. All kosher, so don't try to pull any after-the-fact rule on me. Lazarus, take the advice of the only friend you have whom you can't cheat and who loves you in spite of your evil ways, namely me: Cut your losses, pal, and sweet-talk your way out. Make the last hundred meters on your belly and maybe Richard will let you start over. He's not hard to get along with. Pet him, and he purrs, just like that kitten.' (I had Pixel in my lap, petting him, he having climbed my old leg, driving pitons as he went – I lost some blood but not enough to require transfusion.) 'Ask Minerva. Ask Galahad. Ask Gretchen or Xia. Ask Laz or Lor. Ask *anybody.*'

(I decided to ask Teena – privately – to fill me in on gaps in my memory. Or would that be wise?) Lazarus said, 'I never intended to offend you, Colonel. If I spoke too bluntly, I'm sorry.'

'Forget it.'

'Shake on it?'

'All right.' I put out my hand, he took it. He gave a good grip, with no attempt to set a bonecrusher. He looked me in the eye and I felt his warmth. The bastich is hard to dislike – when he tries.

My darling said, 'Hang on to your wallet, dear; I'm still going to drag this out onto the floor.'

'Really, is it necessary?'

'It is. You're new here, darling. Lazarus can steal the socks

283

off your feet without taking off your shoes, sell them back to you, make you think you got a bargain – then steal your shoes when you sit down to put your socks on, and you'll end up thanking him.'

Lazarus said, 'Now, Hazel—'

'Shut up. Friends and family, Lazarus tried to coerce Richard into signing up blind for Operation Galactic Overlord by trying to make him feel guilty over that replacement foot. Lazarus implied that Richard was a deadbeat who was trying to run out on his debts.'

'I didn't mean that.'

'I told you to shut up. You did mean that. Friends and family, my new husband comes from a culture in which debts are sacred. Their national motto is "There Ain't No Such Thing As A Free Lunch." TANSTAAFL is embroidered on their flag. In Luna – the Luna of Richard's time line; not this one – a man might cut your throat but he would die before he would welch on a debt to you. Lazarus *knew* this, so he went straight for that most sensitive spot and jabbed it. Lazarus pitted his more than two thousand years of experience, his widest knowledge of cultures and human behavior, against a man of much less than a century of experience and that little only in his own solar system and time line. It was not a fair fight and Lazarus knew it. Grossly unfair. Like pitting that kitten against an old wildcat.'

I was sitting near Lazarus, having remained seated after that silly foot examination. I had my head down, ostensibly to play with the kitten, but in fact to avoid looking at Lazarus – or at anyone – as I was finding Hazel's insistence on airing everything quite disturbing. Embarrassing.

In consequence I was looking down at my own feet and at his. Did I mention that Lazarus was barefooted? I had paid it no mind because one thing one becomes used to at once on Tertius is the absence of compelling dress customs. I don't mean absence of dress (Boondock sells more clothes than any groundhog city of similar size – about a million people – in part because garments are usually worn once, then recycled).

I do mean that neither bare feet nor bare bodies are startling for more than five minutes. Lazarus was wearing a wraparound, a lava-lava or it may have been a kilt; his feet I did not notice until I stared at them.

Hazel went on, 'Lazarus took such cruel advantage of Richard's weak point – his compulsive hatred of being in debt – that Richard demanded that his new foot be amputated. In desperate need to cleanse his honor he said to Lazarus, "Cut it off; put it back in stock"!'

Lazarus said, 'Oh, come now! He did not mean that seriously, and I did not take it seriously. A figure of speech. To show that he was annoyed with me. As well he might be. I made a mistake; I admit it.'

'You did indeed make a mistake!' I interrupted. 'A grave mistake. Your grave perhaps, or mine. For it was *not* a figure of speech. I want that foot amputated. I demand that you take back your foot. *Your* foot, sir! Look here, all of you, and then look there! At my right foot, then his right foot.'

Anyone who bothered to look could not fail to see what I meant. Four masculine feet – Three were clearly from the same genes: Lazarus's two feet and my new foot. The fourth was the foot I was born with; it matched the other three only in size, not in skin color, texture, hairiness, or any detail.

When Lazarus had dunned me for the cost of that transplant, it had offended me. But this new discovery, that Lazarus himself was the anonymous donor, that I had been made the unwitting recipient of his charity for the foot itself, the very meat and bone of it, was intolerable.

I glared at Lazarus. 'Doctor, behind my back and utterly without my consent you placed me under unbearable obligation. *I will not tolerate it!*' I was shaking with anger.

'Richard, Richard! Please!' Hazel seemed about to cry.

And I, too. That red-haired older lady hurried to me, bent over me and gathered my head to her motherly breasts, cuddled me and said, 'No, Richard, no! You must not feel this way.'

We left later that day. But we stayed for dinner; we did not run away angry.

Hazel and Maureen (the darling older lady who had comforted me) between them managed to convince me that hospital and surgery charges need not fret me because Hazel had plenty of the needful on deposit in a local bank – which Teena confirmed – and Hazel could and would cover my bills if it became appropriate to change the charge under which I was hospitalized. (I thought about asking my darling to reassign the charges right then, through Teena. But I decided not to crowd her about it. Damn it, 'tanstaafl' is a basic truth, but 'beggars can't be choosers' is true, too – and at that moment I was a beggar. Never a good bargaining position.)

As for the foot itself, by invariant local custom 'spare parts' (hands and feet and hearts and kidneys, etc.) were not bought or sold; there was only a service and handling charge billed with the cost of surgery.

Galahad confirmed this. 'We do it that way to avoid a black market. I could show you planets where there is indeed a black market, where a matching liver might mean a matching murder – but not here. Lazarus himself set up this rule, more than a century ago. We buy and sell everything else . . . but we don't traffic in human beings or pieces of human beings.'

Galahad grinned at me. 'But there is another reason why you should not fret. You had no say in the matter when a team of us hemstitched that foot to your stump; everybody knows that. But also everybody knows you can't get rid of it . . . unless you want to tackle it with your own jackknife. Because I won't cut it off. You won't find a surgeon anywhere on Tertius who will. Union rules, you know, and professional courtesy.'

He added, 'But if you do decide to hack it off yourself, do please invite me; I want to watch.' He said that with a straight face and Maureen scolded him for it. I'm not certain that he was joking.

Nevertheless detente involved a major change in Hazel's plans. Lazarus was correct in saying that all he had been trying to do was to implement a previously agreed-on plan. But it had been further agreed that Hazel (not Lazarus) was to implement the plan.

Hazel could have managed it, but Lazarus could not. Lazarus could never sell it to me because I thought the whole thing was ridiculous. On the other hand, if Hazel really wants something from me, I stand about as much chance of holding out as – well, as Jinx Henderson has of refusing a request from his daughter Gretchen.

But Lazarus couldn't see that.

I think Lazarus suffers from a compulsion to be the biggest

frog in any pond. He expects to be the bride at every wedding, the corpse at every funeral . . . while pretending that he has no ambitions – just a barefoot country boy with straw in his hair and manure between his toes.

If you think that I am not overly fond of Lazarus Long, I won't argue.

That plan was pretty much as Lazarus had described it. Hazel had expected that I would join her in the Time Corps, and had planned for me to be rejuvenated – systemic rejuvenation to biological age eighteen; cosmetic rejuvenation, my choice. While this was going on I was to be taught Galacta, study multiverse history at least for several time lines, and, after rejuvenation, again take military training of several sorts until I became a walking angel of death, armed or unarmed.

When she judged that I was ready, she planned for us to carry out Task Adam Selene of Operation Galactic Overlord.

If we lived through it, we could retire from the Time Corps, live out our days on an ample pension on the planet of our choice – fat and happy.

Or we could stay in the Corps together just by my reenlisting for a hitch of fifty years – then rejuvenations each hitch and a chance for us eventually to become Time bosses ourselves. That was supposed to be the grand prize – more fun than baby kittens, more exciting than roller coasters, more satisfying than being seventeen and in love.

Live or die, we would do it together – until at last one of us waited for the other at the end of that tunnel.

But this program aborted because Lazarus butted in and tried to twist my arm (my foot?) to accept it.

My darling had planned a pianissimo approach: Live for a time on Tertius (a heavenly place), get me hooked on multiverse history and time travel theory, et cetera. Not crowd me about signing up, but depend on the fact that she and Gretchen and Ezra and others (Uncle Jock, e.g.) were in the Corps . . . until I *asked* to be allowed to be sworn in.

The cost of my new foot would not have bothered me: a) if Hazel had had time to convince me that the cost would be charged off to my increased efficiency in helping her with 'Adam Selene' and the foot would thereby pay for itself (the

287

simple truth! – and Lazarus knew it); b) if Lazarus had not dunned me about it, used it to pressure me; c) if Lazarus had stayed away from me (as he was supposed to) and thereby had never offered me any chance of spotting that he was my anonymous donor – bare feet or no bare feet.

I suppose you could say that none of it would have happened if Hazel had not tried to manipulate me (and had, and did, and would) . . . but a wife's unique right, fixed by tradition, to manipulate her own husband runs unbroken and invariant at least back to Eve and the Apple. I will not criticize a sacred tradition.

Hazel did not give up her intention; she just changed her tactics. She decided to take me to Time Headquarters and let the high brass and the technical experts there answer my questions. 'Darling man,' she said to me, 'you know that I want to rescue Adam Selene, and so does Mannie, my papa. But his reasons and mine are sentimental, not good enough to ask you to risk your life.'

'Oh, say not so, mistress mine! For you I'll swim the Hellespont. On a calm day, that is, with an escort boat at my heels. And a three-dee contract. Commercial rights. Residuals.'

'Be serious, dear. I had not planned to try to persuade you through explaining the greater purpose, the effect on the multiverse . . . as I don't fully understand it myself. I don't have the math and I am not a Companion of the Circle – the Circle of Ouroboros that rules on all cosmic changes.

'But Lazarus bungled things by trying to hustle you. So I feel that you are entitled to know exactly why this rescue is necessary and why you are being asked to take part in it. We'll go to Headquarters and let them try to convince you; I wash my hands of that part of the job. It is up to the Companions, the high brass of time manipulation. I told Lazarus so – he is a Companion of the Circle.'

'Sweetheart, I am much more likely to listen to you. Lazarus would have trouble selling me ten-crown notes for two crowns.'

'His problem. But he has only one vote in the Circle, even though he is senior. Of course he is always senior, anywhere.'

That caught my ear. 'This notion that Lazarus is two thousand years old—'

'More than that. Over twenty-four hundred.'

'Either way. Who says that he is more than two millenia old? He looks younger than I do.'

'He's been rejuvenated several times.'

'But who claims that he is that old? Forgive me, my love, but you can't testify to it. Even if we credit you with every fortnight you claim, he would still be more than ten times your age. If he is. Again, who says?'

'Uh . . . not me, that's true. But I have never had any reason to doubt it. I think you should talk to Justin Foote.' Hazel looked around. We were in that lovely garden court outside the room in which I woke up. (Her room, I learned later – or hers when she wanted it; such things were fluid. Other times use other customs.) We were in that garden with other members of the Long family and guests and friends and relations, eating tasty tidbits and getting quietly slopped. Hazel picked out a mousy little man, the sort who is always elected treasurer of any organization he belongs to. 'Justin! Over here, dear. Spare me a moment.'

He worked his way toward us, stepping over children and dogs, and on arrival bussed my bride in the all-out fashion she always received. He said to her, 'Fluttermouse, you've been away too long.'

'Business, dear. Justin, this is my beloved husband Richard.'

'Our house is yours.' He kissed me. Well, I was braced for it; it had happened so often. These people kissed as often as early Christians. However, this was an aunt's peck, all protocol and bone dry.

'Thank you, sir.'

'Please be assured that it is not our custom to put pressure on guests. Lazarus is a law unto himself but he does not act for the rest of us.' Justin Foote smiled at me, then turned his attention to my bride. 'Hazel, will you permit me to obtain from Athene a copy, for the Archives, of your remarks to Lazarus?'

'Whatever for? I chewed him out; it's done with.'

'It is of historical interest. No one else, not even Ishtar, has ever spanked the Senior as thoroughly as you did. There is scant disapproval of him on record, of any degree. Most people find it hard to disagree with him openly even when they disagree most. So it is not only an interesting item for future scholars, but it could also be of service to Lazarus himself if he ever scanned it. He is so used to getting his own way that it is good for him to be reminded now and then that he is not God.' Justin smiled. 'And it's a breath of fresh air for the rest of us. In addition, Hazel love, its literary quality is great and unique. I do want it for the Archives.'

'Uh . . . poppycock, dear. See Lazarus. *Nihil obstat* but it requires his permission.'

'Consider it done; I know how to use his stubborn pride. The piglet principle. All I have to do is to offer to censor it, keep it out of the Archives. With a hint that I wish to spare his feelings. He will then scowl and insist that it be placed in the Archives . . . unedited, unbowdlerized.'

'Well – Okay if he says yes.'

'May I ask, dear, where you picked up some of the more scabrous of those expressions?'

'You may not. Justin, Richard asked me a question I can't answer. How do we know that the Senior is more than two thousand years old? To me, it's like asking, "How do I know that the Sun will rise tomorrow?" I just know it.'

'No, it's like asking, "How do you know that the Sun rose long before you were born?" The answer is that you *don't* know. Hmm – Interesting.'

He blinked at me. 'Part of the problem, I am sure, lies in the fact that you come from a universe in which the Howard Families phenomenon never took place.'

'I don't think I've ever heard of it. What is it?'

'It is a code name for people with exceptionally long lives. But I must first lay a foundation. The Companions of the Circle of Ouroboros designate universes by serial numbers . . . but a more meaningful way, for terrestrials, is to ask who first set foot on Luna. Who in your world?'

'Eh? Chap named Neil Armstrong. With Colonel Buzz Aldrin.'

'Exactly. An enterprise of NASA, a government bureau, if I recall correctly. But in this universe, my world and that of Lazarus Long, the first trip to the Moon was financed, not by a government, but by private enterprise, headed by a financier, one D. D. Harriman, and the first man to set foot on Luna was Leslie LeCroix, an employee of Harriman. In still another universe it was a military project and the first flight to Luna was in the USAFS *Kilroy Was Here*. Another –

Never mind; in every universe the birth of space travel is a cusp event, affecting everything that follows. Now about the Senior – In my universe he was one of the earliest space pilots. I was for many years archivist of the Howard Families . . . and from those archives I can show that Lazarus Long has been a practicing space pilot for more than twenty-four centuries. Would you find that convincing?'

'No.'

Justin Foote nodded. 'Reasonable. When a rational man hears something asserted that conflicts with all common sense he will not – and should not – believe it without compelling evidence. You have not been offered compelling evidence. Just hearsay. Respectable hearsay, and in fact true, but nevertheless hearsay. Odd. For me, I have grown up with it; I am the forty-fifth member of the Howard Families to bear the name "Justin Foote," the first of my name being a trustee of the Families in the early twentieth century Gregorian when Lazarus Long was a baby and Maureen was a young woman—'

At this point the conversation fell to pieces. The notion that the darling lady who had comforted me had a son twenty-four centuries old . . . but was herself a mere child of a century and a half – Hell, some days it doesn't pay to get out of bed, a truism in Iowa when I was young and still true in Tertius over two thousand years later. (If it was!) I had been perfectly happy with Minerva on one shoulder and Galahad on the other and Pixel on my chest. Aside from bladder pressure.

Maureen reminded me of another discrepancy. 'Justin, something else frets me. You say that this planet is a long, long way in space and time from my home – over two thousand years in time and over seven thousand light-years in distance.'

'No, I do not say it because I am not an astrophysicist. But that accords with what I have been taught, yes.'

'Yet right here today I hear idiomatic English spoken in the dialect of my time and place. More than that, it is in the tall-corn accent of the North American middle west, harsh as a rusty saw. Ugly and unmistakable. Riddle me that?'

'Oh. Strange but no mystery. English is being spoken as a courtesy to you.'

'Me?'

'Yes. Athene could supply you with instantaneous translation, both ways, and the party could be in Galacta. But fortunately through a decision by Ishtar many years back, English was made the working language of the clinic and the hospital. That this could be done derives from circumstances around the Senior's last rejuvenation. But the accent and the idiom – The accent comes from the Senior himself, reinforced by his mother's speech, and nailed down by the fact that Athene speaks that accent and idiom and won't speak English any other way. The same applies to Minerva, since she learned it when she was still a computer. But not all of us speak English with equal ease. You know Tamara?'

'Not as well as I would like to.'

'She is probably the most loving and most lovable person on the planet. But she is no linguist. She learned English when she was past two hundred; I think she will always speak broken English . . . even though she speaks it every day. Does that explain the odd fact that a dead language is being spoken at a family dinner party on a planet around a star far distant from Old Home Terra?'

'Well – It explains it. It does not satisfy me. Uh, Justin, I have a feeling that any objection I can raise will be answered . . . but I won't be convinced.'

'That's reasonable. Why not wait awhile? Presently, without pushing it, the facts that you find hard to accept will fall into place.'

So we changed the subject. Hazel said, 'Dear one, I didn't tell you why I had to run an errand . . . or why I was late. Justin, have you ever been held up at the downstream teleport?'

'Too often. I hope someone builds a competing service soon. I would raise the capital and mount it myself, if I weren't so comfortably lazy.'

'Earlier today I went shopping for Richard – shoes, dear, but don't wear them until Galahad okays it – and replacements for your suits I lost in the fracas at the Raffles. Couldn't match the colors, so I settled for cerise and jade green.'

'Good choices.'

'Yes, they will suit you, I think. I had finished shopping and would have been back here before you woke but – Justin, they were queued up at the teleport, so I sighed and waited my turn . . . and a line jumper, a rancid tourist from Secundus, sneaked in six places ahead of me.'

'Why, the scoundrel!'

'Didn't do him a speck of good. The bounder was shot dead.'

I looked at her. 'Hazel?'

'Me? No, no, darling! I admit that I was tempted. But in my opinion crowding into a queue out of turn doesn't rate anything heavier than a broken arm. No, that was not what held me up. A bystanders' court was convened at once, and I durn near got co-opted as a juror. Only way I could get out of it was to admit that I was a witness – thought it would save me time. No such luck, and the trial took almost half an hour.'

'They hanged him?' asked Justin.

'No. The verdict was "homicide in the public interest" and they turned her loose and I came on home. Not quite soon enough. Lazarus, damn him, had got at Richard, and made him unhappy and ruined my plans, so I made Lazarus unhappy. As you know.'

'As we all know. Did the deceased tourist have anyone with him?'

'I don't know. I don't care. I do think killing him was too drastic. But I'm a pantywaist and always have been. In the past, when someone shoved ahead of me in a queue, I've always let it go with minor mayhem. But queue cheating should never be ignored; that just encourages the louts. Richard, I bought shoes for you because I knew that your new foot could not use the right shoe you were wearing when we arrived here.'

'That's true.' (My right shoe has always – since amputation – had to be a custom job for the prosthesis. A living foot could not fit it.)

'I didn't go to a shoe shop; I went to a fabricatory having a general pantograph and had them use your left shoe to synthesize a matching right shoe through a mirror-image space warp. It should be identical with your left shoe, but righthanded. Right-footed? Dexter.'

'Thank you!'

'I hope it fits. If that darned line jumper hadn't got himself killed practically in my lap, I would have been home on time.'

I blinked at her. 'Uh, I find I'm astonished again. How is this place run? Is it an anarchy?'

Hazel shrugged. Justin Foote looked thoughtful. 'No, I wouldn't say so. It is not that well organized.'

We left right after dinner in that four-place spaceplane – Hazel and I, a small giant named Zeb, Hilda the tiny beauty, Lazarus, Dr Jacob Burroughs, Dr Jubal Harshaw, still another redhead – well, strawberry blonde – named Deety, and still another one who was not her twin but should have been, a sweet girl named Elizabeth and called Libby. I looked at these last two and whispered to Hazel, 'More of Lazarus's descendants? Or more of yours?'

'No. I don't think so. About Lazarus, I mean. I know they aren't mine; I'm not quite that casual. One is from another universe and the other is more than a thousand years older than I am. Blame it on Gilgamesh. Uh . . . at dinner did you notice a little girl, another carrot top, paddling in the fountain?'

'Yes. A cutie pie.'

'She –' We started to load, all nine of us, into that four-place spaceplane. Hazel said, 'Ask me later,' and climbed in. I started to follow. That small giant took my arm firmly, which stopped me, as he outmassed me by about forty kilos. 'We haven't met. I'm Zeb Carter.'

'I'm Richard Ames Campbell, Zeb. Happy to meet you.'

'And this is my mom, Hilda Mae.' He indicated the china doll.

I did not have time to consider the improbability of his assertion. Hilda answered, 'I'm his stepmother-in-law, part-time wife, and sometime mistress, Richard; Zebbie is always not quite in focus. But he's sweet. And you belong to Hazel, so that gives you the keys to the city.' She reached up, put her hands on my shoulders, stood on tiptoes, and kissed me. Her kiss was quick but warm and not quite dry; it left me most thoughtful. 'If you want anything, just ask for it. Zebbie will fetch it.'

It seemed that there were five in that family (or sub-family; they were all part of the Long household or family, but I did not have it figured out): Zeb and his wife Deety, she being that first strawberry blonde whom I had met briefly, and her father, Jake Burroughs, whose wife was Hilda, but was not mother of Deety – and the fifth was Gay. Zeb had said, 'And Gay, of course. You know who I mean.'

I asked Zeb, 'Who is Gay?'

'Not me. Or just as a hobby. Our car is Gay.'

A sultry contralto said, 'I'm Gay. Hi, Richard, you were in me once but I don't think you remember it.'

I decided that the Lethe field had some really bad side effects. If I had at some time been in a woman (she expressed it that way, not I) with a voice of that utterly seductive quality but I could not remember it . . . well, it was time to throw myself on the mercy of the court; I was obsolete.

'Excuse me. I don't see her. The lady named Gay.'

'She's no lady, she's a trollop.'

'Zebbie, you'll regret that. He means I am not a woman, Richard; I'm this car you are about to climb into – and have been in before, but you were wounded and sick so I'm not hurt that you don't remember me—'

'Oh, but I do!'

'You do? That's nice. Anyhow I'm Gay Deceiver, and welcome aboard.'

I climbed in and started to crawl through the cargo door back of the seats. Hilda snagged me. 'Don't go back there. Your wife is back there with two men. Give the girl a chance.'

'And with Lib,' Deety added. 'Don't tease him, Aunt Sharpie. Sit down, Richard.' I sat down between them – a privilege, except that I wanted to see that space-warped bathroom. If there was one. If it was not a Lethe dream.

Hilda settled against me like a cat and said, 'You have received a bad first impression of Lazarus, Richard; I don't want it to stay that way.'

I admitted that on a scale of ten he scored a minus three with me.

'I hope it doesn't stay that way. Deety?'

'Day in and day out Lazarus averages closer to a nine, Richard. You'll see.'

'Richard,' Hilda went on, 'despite what you heard me say, I don't think badly of Lazarus. I have borne one child by him . . . and I go that far only with men I respect. But Lazarus does have his little ways; it is necessary to spank him from time to time. Nevertheless I love him.'

'Me, too,' agreed Deety. 'I have a little girl by Lazarus and that means I love and respect him or it would not have happened. Correct, Zebadiah?'

'How would I know? "Love, oh careless love!" Boss Lady, are we going somewhere? Gay wants to know.'

'Report readiness.'

'Starboard door sealed, irrelevant gear ready.'

'Portside door sealed, seat belts fastened, all systems normal.'

'Time Corps Headquarters via Alpha and Beta. At will. Chief Pilot.'

'Aye aye, Captain. Gay Deceiver, Checkpoint Alpha. Execute.'

'Yassuh, Massuh.' The bright sunlight and green lawn beside the Long House blinked away to blackness and stars. We were weightless.

'Checkpoint Alpha, probably,' Zeb said. 'Gay, do you see THQ?'

'Checkpoint Alpha on the nose,' the car answered. 'Time Corps HQ dead ahead. Zeb, you need glasses.'

'Checkpoint Beta, execute.' The sky blinked again.

This time I could spot it. Not a planet but a habitat, perhaps ten klicks away, perhaps a thousand – in space, with a strange object, I had no way to guess.

Zeb said, 'Time Corps Headquarters, ex – *Gay Scram!*'

A nova bomb burst in front of us.

XXV

'GOD BONES!' the car moaned. 'That one burned my tail feathers! Hilda, let's go home. *Please!*' The nova bomb was now a long way off but it still burned with intense white light, looking like Sol from out around Pluto.

'Captain?' Zeb inquired.

'Affirmative,' Hilda answered calmly. But she was clinging to me and trembling.

'GayMaureenExecute!' We were back on the grounds of the Romanesque mansion of Lazarus Long and his tribe.

'Chief Pilot, please beep Oz annex and tell them to disembark; we won't be going anywhere soon. Richard, if you will slide out to the right as soon as Jake is out of your way, that will let our passengers climb out.'

I did so as quickly as Dr Burroughs cleared the way. I heard Lazarus Long's voice rumbling behind me. 'Hilda! Why have you ordered us out of the car? Why aren't we at Headquarters?' His tone reminded me of a drill sergeant I had had as a boot, ten thousand years ago.

'Forgot my knitting, Woodie, had to go back for it.'

'Knock it off. Why haven't we started? Why are we disembarking?'

'Watch your blood pressure, Lazarus. Gay just proved that she was not being a Nervous Nellie when she asked me to break our usual trip to THQ into three jumps. Had I used our old routine, we would all glow in the dark.'

'My skin itches,' Gay said fretfully. 'I'll bet I would make a Geiger stick rattle like hail on a tin roof.'

'Zebbie will check you later, dear,' Hilda said soothingly, then went on to Lazarus: 'I don't think Gay was hurt; I think none of us was. Because Zeb had one of his bad-news flashes and bounced us out of there almost ahead of the photons. But I am sorry to report, sir, that Headquarters isn't there anymore. May it rest in peace.'

Lazarus persisted, 'Hilda, is this one of your jokes?'

'Captain Long, when you talk that way, I expect you to address me as "Commodore."'

'Sorry. What happened?'

Zeb said, 'Lazarus, let them finish unloading and I'll take you back and show you. Just you and me.'

'Yes indeed, just you two,' the car put in. 'But not me! I won't go! I didn't sign up for combat duty. I won't let you close my doors; that means you can't seal up, and then you can't move me. I'm on strike.'

'Mutiny,' said Lazarus. 'Melt her down for scrap.'

The car screamed, then it said excitedly, 'Zeb, did you hear that? Did you hear what he said? Hilda, did you hear him? Lazarus, I don't belong to you and never did! Tell him, Hilda! You lay one finger on me and I'll go critical and blow your hand off. And take all of Boondock County with me.'

'Mathematically impossible,' Long remarked.

'Lazarus,' said Hilda, 'you shouldn't be so quick to say "impossible" when speaking of Gay. In any case, don't you think you've been in the doghouse enough for one day? You get Gay sore at you and she'll tell Dora, who'll tell Teena, who'll tell Minerva, who will tell Ishtar and Maureen and Tamara, and then you'll be lucky to get anything to eat and you won't be allowed to sleep or go anywhere.'

'I'm henpecked. Gay, I apologize. If I read you two chapters from *Tik-Tok* tonight, will you forgive me?'

'Three.'

'It's a deal. Please tell Teena to ask mathematicians working on Operation Galactic Overlord to meet me asap in my quarters in Dora. Please tell all others involved with Overlord that they are advised to come to Dora, eat and sleep aboard. I don't know when we will leave. It could be a week but it could be anytime and there might not be even ten minutes warning. War conditions. Red alert.'

'Dora has it; she's relaying. What about Boondock?'

'What do you mean "What about Boondock?"'

'Do you want the city evacuated?'

'Gay, I didn't know you cared.' Lazarus sounded surprised.

'Me? Care what happens to groundcrawlers?' the car snorted. 'I'm simply relaying for Ira.'

'Oh. For a moment there I thought you were developing human sympathies.'

'God forbid!'

'I'm relieved. Your simple self-centered selfishness has been a haven of stability in an ever-shifting world.'

'Never mind the compliments; you still owe me three chapters.'

'Certainly, Gay; I promised. Please tell Ira that, so far as I know, Boondock is safe as anywhere in this world . . . which ain't saying much . . . whereas, in my opinion, any attempt to evacuate this ant hill would result in great loss of life, still greater loss of property. But it might be worthwhile to risk it just to crank up their lazy metabolisms – Boondock today strikes me as fat, dumb, and careless. Ask him to acknowledge.'

'Ira says, "Up yours."'

'Roger, and the same to you; wilco, they make a damn fine stew. Colonel Campbell, I'm sorry about this. Would you care to come with me? It might interest you to see how we mount an emergency time manipulation. Hazel, is that okay? Or am I crowding in on your pidgin again?'

'It's all right, Lazarus, as it is no longer my pidgin. It's yours and that of the other Companions.'

'You're a hard woman, Sadie.'

'What can you expect, Lazarus? Luna is a harsh teacher. I learned my lessons at her knee. May I come along?'

'You're expected; you are still part of Overlord. Are you not?'

We walked about fifty meters across the lawn to where was parked the biggest, fanciest flying saucer any UFO cultist ever claimed to have seen. I learned that this was 'Dora,' meaning both the ship and the computer that ran the ship. I learned too that the Dora was the Senior's private yacht, that it was Hilda's flagship, and that it was a pirate ship commanded by Lorelei Lee and/or Lapis Lazuli and crewed by Castor and Pollux, who were either their husbands or their slaves or both.

'They're both,' Hazel told me later. 'And Dora is all three. Laz and Lor won sixty-year indentures from Cas and Pol in a game of red dog shortly after they married them. Laz and Lor are telepathic with each other, and they cheat. My grandsons are smart as whips and as conceited as Harvard grads, and they always try to cheat. I tried to break them of this nasty habit when they were still too young to chase girls, by using a marked deck. Didn't work; they spotted my readers. But their downfall arose from the fact that Laz and Lor are smarter than they are and even more deceitful.'

Hazel shook her head ruefully. 'It's a wicked world. You would think that a youngster I had trained would be instantly suspicious when dealt three aces and the odd king in a hand of red dog . . . but Cas was greedy. He not only tapped the pot when he could not cover it, he pledged his indentures to fill the gap.

'Then, not a day later, Pol fell for an even more transparent piece of larceny; he was sure he knew what card was next to be dealt because he recognized a small coffee stain. Turned out that the ten as well as the eight had that same small stain. Pol held the nine but he was not in a strong moral position. Ah, well, it is probably better for the lads to have to do all the scut work in the ship plus shampoos and pedicures for their wives than it would be for the boys to sell Laz and Lor in the slave marts of Iskander, as I misdoubt they would have done had their own thieving efforts succeeded.'

The Dora is even bigger inside than out; she has as many staterooms as may be needed. It was once a luxurious but fairly conventional hyperphotonic spaceship. But it (the ship, not Dora the computer) was refitted with a Burroughs irrelevant drive (the magic means by which Gay Deceiver flits around the stars in nothing flat). A corollary of the Burroughs equations that teleport Gay can be applied to shape space warps. So Dora's passenger and cargo spaces were revamped; this lets Dora keep endless spare compartments collapsed in on themselves until she needs them.

(This is not the same deal under which Gay has tucked away in her portside skin two nineteenth-century bathrooms. Or is it? Well, I don't think it is. Must inquire. Or should I let sleeping logs butter their own bed? Better, maybe.)

A gang port relaxed in the side of the yacht; a ramp slid

down, and I followed Lazarus up to the ship with my darling on my arm. As he stepped over the side, music sounded: 'It Ain't Necessarily So' from George Gershwin's immortal *Porgy and Bess*. A long-dead 'Sportin' Life' sang about the impossibility of a man as old as Methuselah ever persuading a woman to bed with him.

'Dora!'

A young girl's sweet voice answered, 'I'm taking a bath. Call me later.'

'Dora, shut off that silly song!'

'I must consult the captain of the day, sir.'

'Consult and be damned! But stop that noise.'

Another voice replaced the ship's voice: 'Captain Lor speaking, Buddy Boy. Do you have a problem?'

'Yes. Shut off that noise!'

'Buddy, if you mean the classical music now playing as a salute to your arrival, I must say that your taste is as barbaric as ever. In any case I am constrained from switching it off because this new protocol was established by Commodore Hilda. I cannot change it without her permission.'

'I'm henpecked.' Lazarus fumed. 'Can't enter my own ship without being insulted. I swear to Allah that, once I've cleaned up Overlord, I'm going to buy a Burroughs Bachelor Buggy, equip it with a Minsky Cerebrator, and go for a long vacation with no women aboard.'

'Lazarus, why do you say such dreadful things?' The voice came from behind us; I had no trouble identifying it as Hilda's warm contralto.

Lazarus looked around. 'Oh, there you are! Hilda, will you please put a stop to this dadblasted racket?'

'Lazarus, you can do it yourself—'

'I've tried. They delight in frustrating me. All three of them. You, too.'

'– simply by walking three paces beyond the door. If there is another musical salute that you would prefer, please name it. Dora and I are trying to find just the right tune for each of our family, plus a song of welcome for any guest.'

'Ridiculous.'

'Dora enjoys doing it. So do I. It's a gracious practice, like eating with forks rather than fingers.'

'"Fingers were made before forks."'

'And flatworms before humans. That does not make flat-worms better than people. Move along, Woodie, and give Gershwin a rest.'

He grunted and did so; the Gershwin stopped. Hazel and I followed him – and again music sounded, a pipe-and-drum band blaring out a march I had not heard since that black day when I lost my foot . . . and my command . . . and my honor: 'The Campbells Are Coming—'

It startled me almost out of my wits, and gave me the mighty shot of adrenaline that ancient boast before battle always does. I was so overcome that I had to force myself to keep my features straight, while praying that no one would speak to me until I had my voice back under control.

Hazel squeezed my arm but the darling kept quiet; I think she can read my emotions – she always knows my needs. I stomped straight ahead, spine straight, barely steadying myself with my cane, and not seeing the interior of the ship. Then the pipes shut down and I could breathe again.

Behind us was Hilda. I think she had hung back to keep the musical salutes separated. Hers was a light and airy tune I could not place; it seemed to be played on silver bells, or possibly a celesta. Hazel told me the name of it: 'Jezebel' – but I could not place it.

Lazarus's quarters were so lavish that I wondered how fancy the flag cabin of 'Commodore' Hilda might be. Hazel settled down in his lounge as if she belonged there. But I did not stay; a bulkhead blinked, and Lazarus ushered me on through. Beyond lay a boardroom suitable for a systemwide corporation: a giant conference table, each place at it furnished with padded armchair, scratch pad, stylus, froster of water, terminal with printer, screen, keyboard, microphone, and hushfield – and I must add that I saw little of this bountiful junk in use; Dora made it unnecessary, being perfect secretary to all of us while also offering and serving refreshments.

(I could never get over the feeling that there was a live girl named Dora somewhere out of sight. But no mortal girl could have kept all the eggs in the air that Dora did.)

'Sit down anywhere,' Lazarus said. 'There is no rank here. And don't hesitate to ask questions and offer opinions. If you make a fool of yourself, no one will mind and you won't be the first to do so in this room. Have you met Lib?'

'Not formally.' It was the other strawberry blonde, the not-Deety one.

'Then do. Dr Elizabeth Andrew Jackson Libby Long . . . Colonel Richard Colin Ames Campbell.'

'I am honored, Dr Long.'

She kissed me. I had anticipated that, having learned in less than two days here that the only way to avoid friendly kisses was by backing away . . . but that it was better to relax and enjoy it. And I did. Dr Elizabeth Long is a pleasant sight and she was not wearing much and she smelled and tasted good . . . and she stood close to me three seconds longer than necessary, patted my cheek, and said, 'Hazel has good taste. I'm glad she brought you into the family.'

I blushed like a yeoman. Everyone ignored it. I think. Lazarus went on, 'Lib is my wife and also my partner starting back in the twenty-first century Gregorian. We've had some wild times together. She was a man back then and a retired commander, Terran Military Forces. But then and now, male or female, the greatest mathematician who ever lived.'

Elizabeth turned and caressed his arm. 'Nonsense, Lazarus. Jake is a greater mathematician than I and a more creative geometer than I could ever hope to be; he can visualize more dimensions and not get lost. I—'

Hilda's Jacob Burroughs had followed us in. 'Nonsense, Lib. False modesty makes me sick.'

'Then be sick, darling, but not on the rug. Jacob, neither your opinion, nor mine – nor that of Lazarus – is relevant; we are what we are, each of us – and I understand there is work to be done. Lazarus, what happened?'

'Wait for Deety and the boys, so we don't have to discuss it twice. Where's Jane Libby?'

'Here, Uncle Woodie.' Just entering was a naked girl who resembled – Look, I'm going to stop talking about family resemblances, hair red or otherwise, and the presence or absence of clothing. On Tertius, through climate and custom, clothing was optional, usually worn in public, sometimes worn at home. In the Lazarus Long household the males were more likely to wear something than the females but there was no rule that I could ever figure out.

303

Red hair was common in Tertius, still more common in the Long family – a 'prize ram' effect (as stockmen say) from Lazarus . . . but not alone from Lazarus; there were two other sources in that family, unrelated to Lazarus and unrelated to each other: Elizabeth Andrew Jackson Libby Long and Dejah Thoris (Deety) Burroughs Carter Long – and still another source that I was not then aware of.

People who favor the Gilgamesh theory have noted how redheads tend to clump, e.g., Rome, Lebanon, south Ireland, Scotland . . . and, even more markedly, in history, from Jesus to Jefferson, from Barbarossa to Henry Eighth.

The sources of resemblances in the Long family were hard to sort out, other than with the help of Dr Ishtar, the family geneticist – Ishtar herself looked not at all like her daughter Lapis Lazuli . . . not surprising once you learned that she was no genetic relation to her own daughter . . . whose genetic mother was Maureen.

Some of the above I learned later; all of it I mention now in order to dismiss it.

That panel of mathematicians consisted of Libby Long, Jake Burroughs, Jane Libby Burroughs Long, Deety Burroughs Carter Long, Minerva Long Weatheral Long, Pythagoras Libby Carter Long and Archimedes Carter Libby Long – Pete and Archie – one borne by Deety and the other birthed by Libby and these two women sole parents to both young men – Deety being the genetic mother of each and Elizabeth the genetic father . . . and I refuse to sort that one out at this point; let it be an exercise for the student. I would rather offer you one more; Maxwell Burroughs-Burroughs Long – then conclude by saying that all these weird combinations were supervised by the family geneticist for maximum reinforcement of mathematical genius and no reinforcement of harmful recessives.

Watching these geniuses at work had some of the soporific excitement of watching a chess match but not quite. Lazarus first had Gay Deceiver testify, bringing her voice through Dora's circuits. They listened to Gay, examined her projected tapes, light and sound, called in Zebadiah, took his testimony, called Hilda in, asked for her best estimate of Zebadiah's anticipation of the bomb.

Hilda said, 'Somewhere between a shake and a blink. You all know I can't do better than that.'

Dr Jake declined to express an opinion. 'I did not watch. As usual I was backing up the spoken orders by setting the vernier controls. The penultimate order, being a scram, aborted the run and then we went home. I did not set the verniers, so nothing more appears on my tapes. Sorry.'

Deety's testimony was almost as skimpy. 'The scram order preceded the explosion by an interval of the order of one millisecond.' On being pressed she refused to say that it was 'of the close order.' Burroughs persisted about it and mentioned her 'built-in clock.' Deety stuck out her tongue at him.

The young man (an adolescent, really) called Pete said, 'I vote "insufficient data." We need to place a rosette of sneakies around the site and find out what happened before we can decide how close to the tick we can set the rescue.'

Jane Libby asked, 'After the scram, was the nova bomb already visible from the new point of sight, or did it appear after Gay's translation? Either way, how does that fit the timing at Checkpoint Beta? Query: Is it experimentally established that irrelevant transportation is instantaneous, totally nil in transit time . . . or is it an assumption based on incomplete evidence and empirical success?'

Deety said, 'Jay Ell, what are you getting at, dear?' I was bracketed by these two; they talked across me, obviously did not expect opinions from me – although I had been a witness.

'We are trying to establish the optimum tick for evacuating THQ, are we not?'

'Are we? Why not pre-enact evacuation, time it, then start the evacuation at minus H-hours plus thirty minutes? That gets everyone back here with gobs of time to spare.'

'Deety, you thereby set up a paradox that leaves you with your head jammed up your arse,' Burroughs commented.

'Pop! That's rude, crude, and vulgar.'

'But correct, my darling stupid daughter. Now think your way out of the trap.'

'Easy. I was speaking just of the danger end, not the safe end. We finish the rescue with thirty minutes to spare, then move to any empty space in any convenient universe – say that orbit around Mars we have used so often – then turn around and reenter this universe at a here-now tick one minute after we leave for the rescue.'

'Clumsy but effective.'

'I like simple programming, I do.'

'So do I. But doesn't anyone see anything wrong with taking whatever length of time we need?'

'Hell, yes!'

'Well, Archie?'

'Because it's booby-trapped, probability point nine nine seven plus. How it is booby-trapped, depends. Who's our antagonist? The Beast? The Galactic Overlord? Boskone? Or is it direct action by another history-changing group, treaty or no treaty? Or – don't laugh – are we up against an Author this time? Our timing must depend on our tactics, and our tactics must fit our antagonist. So we must wait until those big brains next door tell us whom we are fighting.'

'No,' said Libby Long.

'What's wrong, Mama?' the lad asked.

'We will set up *all* the possible combinations, dear, and solve them simultaneously, then plug the appropriate numerical answer into the scenario the fabulists give us.'

'No, Lib, you would still be betting a couple hundred lives that the big brains are right,' Lazarus objected. 'They may not be. We'll stay right here and find a safe answer if it takes ten years. Ladies and gentlemen, these are our *colleagues* we are talking about. They are not expendable. Damn it, find that right answer!'

I sat there feeling silly, slowly getting it through my head that they were seriously discussing how to rescue all the people – and records and instruments – in a habitat I had seen vaporized an hour ago. And that they could just as easily rescue the habitat itself – move it out of that space before it was bombed. I heard them discuss how to do that, how to time it. But they rejected that solution. That habitat must have cost countless billions of crowns . . . yet they rejected saving it. No, no! The antagonist, be he the Beast of the Apocalypse, or Galactic Overlord (I choked!), or whatever – he must be allowed to think that he had succeeded; he must not suspect that the nest was empty, the bird flown.

I felt a remembered sensation in my left leg: Lord Pixel was again challenging the vertical front face. Furthermore he was driving in a fresh set of pitons, so I reached down and set him on the table. 'Pixel, how did you get here?'

'Blert!'

'You certainly did. Out into the garden, through the garden, through the west wing – or did you go around? – across the lawn, up into a sealed spaceship – or was the ramp down? As may be, how did you find me?'

'Blert.'

'He's Schrödinger's cat,' Jane Libby said.

'Then Schrödinger had better come get him, before he gets himself lost. Or hurt.'

'No, no, Pixel doesn't belong to Schrödinger; Pixel hasn't selected his human yet – unless he has picked you?'

'No. I don't think so. Well, maybe.'

'I think he has. I saw him climb into your lap this noon. And now he has come a long way to find you. I think you've been tapped. Are you cat people?'

'Oh, yes! If Hazel lets me keep him.'

'She will; she's cat people.'

'I hope so.' Pixel was sitting up on my scratch pad, washing his face, and doing a commendable job in scrubbing back of his ears. 'Pixel, am I your people?'

He stopped washing long enough to say emphatically, '*Blert!*'

'All right, it's a deal. Recruit pay and allowances. Medical benefits. Every second Wednesday afternoon off, subject to good behavior. Jane Libby, what's this about Schrödinger? How did he get in here? Tell him Pixel is bespoke.'

'Schrödinger isn't here; he's been dead for a double dozen centuries. He was one of that group of ancient German natural philosophers who were so brilliantly wrong about everything they studied – Schrödinger and Einstein and Heisenberg and – Or were these philosophers in your universe? I know they were not in all parts of the omniverse, but parallel history is not my strong point.' She smiled apologetically. 'I guess number theory is the only thing I'm really good at. But I'm a fair cook.'

'How are your back rubs?'

'I'm the best back rubber in Boondock!'

'You're wasting your time, Jay Ell,' Deety put in. 'Hazel still walks him on a leash.'

'But, Aunt Deety, I wasn't trying to bed him.'

'You weren't? Then quit wasting his time. Back away and let me at him. Richard, are you susceptible to married women? We're all married.'

'Uh – Fifth Amendment!'

'I understood you but they've never heard of it in Boondock. These German mathematicians – Not in your world?'

'Let's see if we're speaking of the same ones. Erwin Schrödinger, Albert Einstein, Werner Heisenberg—'

'That's the crowd. They were fond of what they called "thought experiments" – as if anything could be learned that way. Theologians! Jane Libby was about to tell you about "Schrödinger's Cat," a thought experiment that was supposed to say something about reality. Jay Ell?'

'It was a silly business, sir. Shut a cat in a box. Control whether or not he is killed by decay of an isotope with a half life of one hour. At the end of the hour, is the cat alive or dead? Schrödinger contended that, because of the statistical probabilities in what they thought of as science in those days, the cat was neither alive nor dead until somebody opened the box; it existed instead as a cloud of probabilities.' Jane Libby shrugged, producing amazing dynamic curves.

'Blert?'

'Did anyone think to ask the cat?'

'Blasphemy,' said Deety. 'Richard, this is "Science," German philosopher style. You are not supposed to resort to anything so crass. Anyhow Pixel got the tag "Schrödinger's Cat" hung on him because he walks through walls.'

'How does he do that?'

Jane Libby answered, 'It's impossible but he's so young he doesn't know it's impossible, so he does it anyhow. So there is never any knowing where he will show up. I think he was hunting for you. Dora?'

'Need something, Jay Ell?' the ship answered.

'Did you happen to notice how this kitten came aboard?'

'I notice everything. He didn't bother with the gangway; he came right through my skin. It tickled. Is he hungry?'

'Probably.'

'I'll fix him something. Is he old enough for solid food?'

'Yes. But no lumps. Baby food.'

'Chop chop.'

'Ladies,' I said. 'Jane Libby used the word "brilliantly wrong" about these German physicists. Surely you don't include Albert Einstein under that heading?'

'I surely do!' Deety answered emphatically.

'I'm amazed. In my world Einstein wears a halo.'

'In my world they burn him in effigy. Albert Einstein was a pacifist but not an honest one. When his own ox was gored, he forgot all about his pacifist principles and used his political influence to start the project that produced the first city-killer bomb. His theoretical work was never much and most of it has turned out to be fallacious. But he will live in infamy as the pacifist politician turned killer. I despise him!'

XXVI

'Success lies in achieving the top of the food chain.'

J. HARSHAW 1906–

ABOUT THEN the baby food for Pixel appeared, in a saucer that
rose up out of the table, I believe. But I can't swear to it, as
it simply appeared. Feeding the baby cat gave me a moment
to think. The vehemence of Deety's statement had surprised
me. Those German physicists lived and worked in the first half
of the twentieth century – not too long ago by my notions of
history, but if what these Tertians wanted me to believe were
true – unlikely! – a truly long time to them. 'A double dozen
centuries –' Jane Libby had said.

How could this easygoing young lady, Dr Deety, be so
emotional about long-dead German pundits? I know of only
one event two thousand years or more in the past that people
get emotional about . . . and that one never happened.

I had begun to make a list in my mind of things that did
not add up – the claimed age of Lazarus – that long list of
deadly diseases I was alleged to have suffered from – half a
dozen weird events in Luna – Most especially Tertius itself.
Was this indeed a strange planet far distant from Earth in
both space and time? Or was it a Potemkin village on a South
Pacific island? Or even Southern California? I had not seen
the city called Boondock (one million people, more or less, so
they said); I had seen maybe fifty people all told. Did the others
exist only as memorized background for dialog extemporized to
fit Potemkin roles?

(Watch it, Richard! You're getting paranoid again.)

How much Lethe does it take to addle the brain?

'Deety, you seem to feel strongly about Dr Einstein.'

'I have reason to!'

310

'But he lived so long ago. "A double dozen centuries" Jane Libby put it.'

'That long ago to *her*. Not to me!'

Dr Burroughs spoke up. 'Colonel Campbell, I think you may be assuming that we are native Tertians. We are not. We are refugees from the twentieth century, just as you are. By "we" I mean myself and Hilda and Zebadiah and my daughter – my daughter Deety, not my daughter Jane Libby. Jay Ell was born here.'

'You slid home, Pop,' Deety told him.

'But just barely,' Jane Libby added.

'But he did touch home plate. You can't disown him for that, dear.'

'I don't want to. As pops go, he's tolerable.'

I did not try to sort this out; I was gathering a conviction that all Tertians were certifiably insane by Iowa standards. 'Dr Burroughs, I am not from the twentieth century. I was born in Iowa in 2133.'

'Near enough, at this distance. Different time lines, I believe – divergent universes – but you and I speak much the same accent, dialect, and vocabulary; the cusp that placed you in one world and me in another must lie not far back in our pasts. Who reached the Moon first and what year?'

'Neil Armstrong, 1969.'

'Oh, *that* world. You've had your troubles. But so have we. For us the first Lunar landing was in 1952, HMAAFS *Pink Koala*, Ballox O'Malley commanding.' Dr Burroughs looked up and around. 'Yes, Lazarus? Something troubling you? Fleas? Hives?'

'If you and your daughters do not want to work, I suggest that you go chat elsewhere. Next door, perhaps; the fabulists and the historians don't mind chasing rabbits. Colonel Campbell, I think that you will find it convenient to feed your cat elsewhere, too. I suggest the 'fresher just clockwise of my lounge.'

Deety said, 'Oh, rats, Lazarus! You are a bad-tempered, grumpy old man. There is no way to disturb a mathematician who is working. Look at Lib there – You could set off a firecracker under her right now and she wouldn't blink.' Deety stood up. 'Woodie boy, you need a fresh rejuvenation; you're getting old-age cranky. Come on, Jay Ell.'

Dr Burroughs stood up, bowed, and said, 'If you will excuse me?' and left without looking at Lazarus. There was a feeling of edgy tempers, of a need to place distance between two old bulls before they tangled.

Or three – I should be included. Chucking me out over the kitten was uncalled for; I found myself angry with Lazarus for a third time in one day. I had not brought the kitten in, and it was his own computer that had suggested feeding it there and had supplied the means.

I stood up, gathered Pixel in one hand, picked up his dish with my other hand, then found I needed to hang my cane over one arm to move. Jane Libby saw my problem, took the kitten, and cuddled it to her. I followed her, leaning on my cane and carrying the dish of baby food. I avoided looking at Lazarus.

In passing through the lounge we picked up Hazel and Hilda. Hazel waved to me, patted the seat by her; I shook my head and kept going, whereupon she got up and came with us. Hilda followed her. We did not disturb the session in the lounge. Dr Harshaw was lecturing; we were barely noticed.

One delightful, decadent, Sybaritic aspect of life in Tertius was the quality of their refreshers – if such a mundane term can apply. Without trying to describe any of the furnishings strange to me, let me define a rich Tertian's luxury refresher (and Lazarus was, I feel certain, the richest man there) – define it in terms of function:

Start with your favorite pub or saloon.

Add a Finnish sauna.

And how about bathing Japanese style?

Do you enjoy a hot tub? With or without an agitator?

Was the ice-cream soda fountain a part of your youth?

Do you like company when you bathe?

Let's put a well-stocked snack bar (hot or cold) in easy reach.

Do you enjoy music? Three-dee? Feelies? Books and magazines and tapes?

Exercise? Massage? Sun lamps? Scented breezes?

Soft, warm places to end up and nap alone, or in company?

Take all of the above, mix well, and install in a large,

beautiful, well-lighted room. That list still does not describe the social refresher off Lazarus Long's cabinet, as it omits the most important feature:

Dora.

If there was any whim that ship's computer could not satisfy, I was not there long enough to discover it.

I did not sample at once any of these luxuries; I had a duty to a cat. I sat down at a medium-sized round table, the sort four friends might use for a drink, placed the kitten's saucer thereon, reached for the kitten. Instead Jane Ell sat down and placed Pixel at the food. Burroughs joined us.

The kitten sniffed at the food he had been greedily eating minutes earlier, then gave an inspired bit of acting showing Jane Ell that he was horrified at her action in offering him something unfit for cats. Jane Ell said, 'Dora, I think he's thirsty.'

'Name it. But bear in mind that the management does not permit me to serve alcoholic beverages to minors other than for purposes of seduction.'

'Quit showing off, Dora; Colonel Campbell might believe you. Let's offer the baby both water and whole milk, separately. And at blood temperature, which for kittens is—'

'Thirty-eight point eight degrees. Coming up pronto.'

Hilda called out from a plunge – no, a lounging tub, I guess – a few meters away, 'Jay Ell! Come soak, dear. Deety has some swell gossip.'

'Uh –' The girl seemed torn. 'Colonel Campbell, will you take care of Pixel now? He likes to lick it off your finger. It's the only way to get him to drink enough.'

'I'll do it your way.'

The kitten did like to drink that way . . . although it seemed possible that I would die of old age before I got as much as ten milliliters down him. But the kitten was in no hurry. Hazel got out of the lounging tub and joined us, dripping. I kissed her cautiously and said, 'You're getting that chair soaking wet.'

'Won't hurt the chair. What's this about Lazarus acting up again?'

'That mother!'

'In his case that's merely descriptive. What happened?'

313

'Uh – Maybe I reacted too strongly. Better ask Dr Burroughs.'

'Jacob?'

'No, Richard did not overreact. Lazarus went out of his way to be offensively difficult with all four of us. In the first place, Lazarus has no business trying to supervise the mathematics section; he is not a mathematician in any professional sense and is not qualified to supervise. In the second place each of us in the section knows the quirks of the others; we never interfere with each other's work. But Lazarus kicked me out, and Deety, and Jane Libby, for daring to talk a few moments about something not on his agenda . . . totally unaware, or at least uncaring, that I and both my daughters use a two-level mode of meditation. Hazel, I kept my temper. Truly I did, dear. You would have been proud of me.'

'I'm always proud of you, Jacob. I would not have kept my temper. In dealing with Lazarus you should take a tip from Sir Winston Churchill and step on his toes until he apologizes. Lazarus doesn't appreciate good manners. But what did he do to Richard?'

'Told him not to feed his cat at the conference table. Ridiculous! As if it could possibly harm his fancy table if this kitten happened to pee on it.'

Hazel shook her head and looked grim, which doesn't fit her face. 'Lazarus has always been a rough cob but, ever since this campaign – Overlord, I mean – started, he has been growing increasingly difficult. Jacob, has your section been handing him gloomy predictions?'

'Some. But the real difficulty is that our long-range projections are so vague. That can be maddening, I know, because when a city is destroyed, the tragedy is *not* vague; it's sharp and sickening. If we change history, we aren't truly undestroying that city, we are simply starting a new time line. We need projections that will let us change history *before* that city is destroyed.' He looked at me. 'That's why rescuing Adam Selene is so important.'

I looked stupid – my best role. 'To make Lazarus better tempered?'

'Indirectly, yes. We need a supervising computer that can direct and program and monitor other large computers in creating multiverse projections. The biggest supervising com-

314

puter we know of is the one on this planet, Athene or Teena, and her twin on Secundus. But this sort of projection is a *much* bigger job. Public functions on Tertius are mostly automated fail-safe and Teena steps in only as a trouble-shooter. But the Holmes IV – Adam Selene or Mike – through a set of odd circumstances, grew and grew and grew with apparently no one trying to keep his size down to optimum . . . then his self-programming increased enormously through a unique challenge: running the Lunar Revolution. Colonel, I don't think any human brain or brains could possibly have written the programs that Holmes IV self-programmed to let him handle all the details of that revolution. My older daughter, Deety, is a top specialist in programming; she says a human brain could not do it and that, in her opinion, an artificial intelligence could swing it only the way Holmes IV did it – by being faced with the necessity, a case of "Root, Hog, or Die." So we need Adam Selene – or his essence, those programs he wrote in creating himself. Because *we* don't know how to do it.'

Hazel glanced at the pool. 'I'll bet Deety could do it. If she had to.'

'Thank you, dear, on behalf of my daughter. But she is not given to false modesty. If Deety could do it, or thought she had even a slim chance, she would be hacking away at it now. As it is, she's doing what she can; she is working hard at tying together the computer bank we have.'

'Jacob, I hate to say this –' Hazel hesitated. 'Maybe I shouldn't.'

'Then don't.'

'I need to get if off my chest. Papa Mannie isn't optimistic over the results even if we are totally successful in retrieving all the memory banks and programs that constitute the essential Adam Selene – or "Mike" as Papa Mannie calls him. He thinks his old friend was hurt so badly in the last attack – I remember it to this day; it was dreadful – Mike was hurt so badly that he withdrew into a computer catatonia and will never wake up. For years Papa tried to wake him, after the Revolution when Papa had free access to the Warden's Complex. He doesn't see how bringing those memories and programs here will do it. Oh, he wants to try, he's eager to, he loves Mike. But he's not hopeful.'

'When you see Manuel, tell him to cheer up; Deety has thought of an answer.'

'Really? Oh, I hope so!'

'Deety is going to provide Teena with lots more unused capacity, both for memory and for symbol manipulation, thought – and then she'll shove Mike into bed with Teena. If that does not bring Mike back to life, nothing will.'

My love looked startled, then giggled. 'Yes, that ought to do it.'

She then went back to the pool and I learned from Jacob Burroughs why his daughter Deety spoke so emotionally about the Father of the Atom Bomb: She had seen – they had seen, all four of them, their own home wiped out by an atom bomb – a fission bomb, I inferred, but Jake did not say.

'Colonel, it is one thing to read a headline or hear a news report; it is something else entirely when it's your own home that has the mushroom cloud covering it.

'We are dispossessed, we can never go home. Eventually we were wiped completely off the slate. In our time line there is nothing to show that we four – myself, Hilda, Deety, Zeb – ever existed. The houses we once lived in are gone, never were; the earth has closed over them with no scars.' He looked as lonely as Odysseus, then went on:

'Lazarus sent a Time Corps field operative back – Dora? May I speak to Elizabeth?'

'Start talking.'

'Lib love? Place that rosette Pete wanted – or was it Archie? Spike the earliest date of surveillance. Go back three years. Evacuate.'

'Paradox, Jacob.'

'Yes. Place those three years in a loop, squeeze them off, throw them away. Check it.'

'I check you, dear. More?'

'No. Off now.'

Burroughs continued, '– sent a field operative to our time line to try to find us, anywhere in the fifty-year bracket from my birth to the night we ran for our lives. We are not there at all. We were never born. Both Zeb and I had military careers as well as academic ones; we are not in military records, we are not in campus records. There is a record of my parents . . . but they never had *me*. Colonel, in all the dozens, hundreds, of ways that citizens were recorded in the twentieth century in the United States of North America not one trace could be found that showed that we had ever been there.'

Burroughs sighed. 'The Gay Deceiver not only saved our lives that night; she saved our very existence. She took evasive action so fast that the Beast lost track – What is it, dear?'

Jane Libby was standing by us, dripping, and looking round-eyed. 'Papa?'

'Say it, love.'

'We need those sneakies Pythagoras wanted but they should go back much farther, oh, ten years or more. Then, when they spot the tick at which the Overlord or whoever started watching THQ, back off some and evacuate. Loop and patch, and they'll never suspect that we outflanked them. I told Deety; she thinks it could work. What do you think?'

'I think it will. Let me get your mother on line and we'll introduce it. Dora, let me have Elizabeth again, please.' Nothing in his face or manner suggested that he had just spoken to Libby Long, proposing what was (so far as I could see) the same plan.

'Elizabeth? A message from our table tennis champ. Jane Libby says to place that rosette at minus ten years, spike first surveillance, then go back – oh, say, three years – evacuate, squeeze off a loop and patch in. Both Deety and I think it will work. Please submit it to the panel, credited to Jane Ell, with Deety's vote and mine noted.'

'And my vote.'

'You have smart children, mistress mine.'

'Comes of picking smart fathers, sir. And good ones. Good to his offspring, good to his wives. Off?'

'Off.' Burroughs added, to the girl waiting, 'Your parents are proud of you, Janie. I predict that the maths section will produce a unanimous report in the next few minutes. You have answered the objection Lazarus raised – his quite legitimate objection – by producing a solution under which it does not matter who did this to us; we can repair it safely without knowing who did it. But did you notice that your method may also tie down who did it? With a little bit of luck.'

Jane Libby looked as if she had just received a Nobel Prize. 'I noticed. But the problem simply called for safe evacuation; the rest is serendipitous.'

'"Serendipitous" is another way of spelling "smart." Ready for some supper? Or do you want to get back in the bowl? Or both? Why don't you throw Colonel Campbell in with his clothes on? Deety and Hilda will help you, I'm certain, and I think Hazel might.'

'Now wait a minute!' I protested.

'Sissy!'

'Colonel, we won't do that to you! Pop is joking.'

'I am like hell joking.'

'Throw your pop in first, for drill. If it doesn't hurt him, then I'll submit quietly.'

'*Blert!*'

'You just keep out of this!'

'Janie baby.'

'Yes, Pop?'

'Find out how many orders there are for strawberry malted milks and hot dogs, or unreasonable facsimiles. While you are doing that, I will hang my clothes in the dry cabinet – and if the colonel is smart, he will, too; Colonel, this is a rowdy bunch, especially in this exact combination – Hilda, Deety, Hazel, and Janie. Explosive. Who takes care of the kitten?'

An hour later Dora (a little blue light) led us to our stateroom; Hazel carried the kitten and one saucer, I carried our clothes, the other saucer, my cane, and her handbag. I was pleasantly tired and looking forward to going to bed with my bride. For too long she had not been in my bed. From my viewpoint we had missed two nights . . . not long for old married couples, much too long for a honeymoon. And the moral of that is: Don't get yourself mugged on your honeymoon.

From her standpoint it had been . . . a month? 'Best of girls, how long has it been? That Lethe field has left me with my time sense fouled up.'

Hazel hesitated. 'It has been thirty-seven Tertian days here. But to you it should feel like overnight. Well, two nights . . . because, by the time I came to bed last night, you were snoring. I'm sorry. Hate me some but not too much. Here's our wee bunty ben.'

('Wee bunty ben' indeed! It was larger than my luxury suite in Golden Rule and more lavish . . . with a bigger and better bed.) 'Bride, we bathed in Lazarus's Taj Mahal playroom. I no longer have to remove my cork leg and I took care of everything else in that Taj Mahal. If you have anything to do, do it. But be quick about it! I'm eager.'

'Nothing. But must take care of Pixel.'

'We'll put his saucers in the 'fresher, shut him in, let him out later.'

So we did, and went to bed, and it was wonderful, and the details are none of your business.

Sometime later Hazel said, 'We've been joined.'

'We still are.'

'I mean, "We have company."'

'So I noticed. He climbed on my shoulder blades way back when, but I was busy and he weighs almost nothing, so I didn't mention it. Can you grab him and keep him from being rolled on and crushed while I get us untangled?'

'Yes. No hurry about it. Richard, you're a good boy. Pixel and I have decided to keep you.'

'Just try to get rid of me! You can't. Love, you phrased something oddly. You said it was "thirty-seven Tertian days here."'

She looked up at me soberly. 'It was longer than that for me, Richard.'

'I wondered. How long?'

'About two years. Earth years.'

'I be goddam!'

'But, dear, while you were ill, I did come home every day. Thirty-seven times I came to your hospital room in the morning, exactly as I promised. You recognized me every time, too, and smiled and seemed happy to see me. But of course the Lethe field made you forget every moment even as it happened. Each evening I went away again, and came back later that evening, having been gone, on the average, about three weeks each time. The schedule wasn't difficult for me, but Gay Deceiver made two trips every evening, with either the double twins or Hilda's crew making the runs. Let me up now, dear; I have the Pixel cat safe.'

We rearranged ourselves comfortably. 'What were you doing, gone so much?'

'Time Corps field work. Historical research.'

'I guess I still don't understand what the Time Corps does. Couldn't you have waited a month, then both of us could have done it, together? Or do I have my head on backwards?'

'Yes and no. I asked for the assignment. Richard, I've been trying to trace down what happens after you and I tackle rescuing Adam Selene. Mike the computer.'

'And what did you learn?'

'Nothing. Not a damn thing. We can find only two time lines from that event – it's a cusp event; you and I created both futures. I searched the following four centuries on both lines – on Luna, down dirtside, several colonies and habitats. They all say either that we succeeded . . . or that we tried and died . . . or they don't mention us at all. The last is the usual case; most historians don't believe that Adam Selene was a computer.'

'Well . . . we're no worse off than we were before. Are we?'

'No. But I had to look. And I wanted to check it out before you woke up. Out from under the Lethe field, I mean.'

'Do you know, small person, I think well of you. You are considerate of your husband. And of cats. And of other people. Uh – No, none of my business.'

'Speak up, beloved, or I tickle.'

'Don't threaten me. I'll beat you.'

'At your own risk – I bite. Look, Richard, I've been waiting for the question. This is the first time we've been alone. You want to know how horny old Hazel stuck it out in faithful chastity for two aching years. Or rather, you don't believe she did but you are too polite to say so.'

'Why, damn your eyes! Look, my love, I'm a Loonie, with Loonie values. Love and sex are ruled by our ladies; we men accept their decisions. That's the only happy arrangement. If you want to boast a bit, go ahead. If not, let's change the subject. But don't accuse me of groundhog vices.'

'Richard, you are your most infuriating when you are being your most reasonable.'

'Do you *want* me to quiz you?'

'It would be polite.'

'Tell me three times.'

'"'I tell you three times and what I tell you three times is true."'

'You peeked in the back of the book. All right, I'll cut to the chase. You are a member of the Long Family. No?'

320

She caught her breath. 'What caused you to say that?'

'I don't know. I truly don't because it's been many little things no one of which meant anything and mostly did not stick in my mind. But sometime this evening, while talking with Jake, I found that I was taking it for granted. Am I mistaken?'

She sighed. 'No, you're right. But I did not intend to load it onto you just yet. You see, I'm on leave of absence from the Family, not a member of it right now. And that was not what I intended to confess.'

'Wait a second. Jake is one of your husbands.'

'Yes. But remember, I'm on leave.'

'For how long?'

'Till death do us part! I promised you that in the Golden Rule. Richard, histories show that you and I were married at the time of the cusp event . . . so I asked the Family for a divorce . . . and settled for a leave of absence. But it might as well be final – they know it, I know it. Richard, I was here every night, every Tertian night I mean – thirty-seven times . . . but I never slept with the Family. I – Usually I slept with Xia and Choy-Mu. They were good to me.' She added, 'But not once with a Long. Not any of them, male or female. I was faithful to you, in my own fashion.'

'I don't see why you needed to deprive yourself. Then you are one of Lazarus Long's wives, too. On leave, but his wife. That ornery old curmudgeon! Hey! Is it possible that he's jealous of me? Hell, yes, it's not only possible but likely. Certain! He's not a Loonie; he is not conditioned to accept "Lady's Choice." And he comes from a culture in which jealousy was the commonest mental disorder. Of course! Why, the silly bastich!'

'No, Richard.'

'In a pig's eye.'

'Richard, Lazarus got all the jealousy leached out of him many generations ago . . . and I've been married to him thirteen years with plenty of chance to judge. No, dear, he's worried. He's worried about me and he's worried about you – he knows how dangerous it is – he's worried about all the Family and all of Tertius. Because he knows how dangerous the multiverse is. He's devoting his life and all of his wealth to trying to make his people safe.'

'Well . . . I wish he could be a little more urbane about it. Mannerly. Polite.'

'So do I. Here, take the kitten; I gotta pee. Then I vote for some sleep.'

'Me, too. Both. My, it feels good to get out of bed and stroll to the jakes without having to hop.'

We had cuddled up together, lights out, her head on my shoulder and the kitten wandering around the bed somewhere, both of us about to sleep, when she murmured, 'Richard. Forgot . . . Ezra—'

'Forgot what?'

'His legs. When . . . he first walked on them . . . with crutches. Three days ago I think . . . 'bout three months back for me. Xia 'n' I congratulated Ezra . . . horizontally.'

'The best way.'

'Took him to bed. Wore him out.'

'Good girls. What else is new?'

She seemed to have dropped off to sleep. Then she barely muttered. 'Wyoming.'

'What dear?'

'Wyoh, my daughter. Little girl playing in fountain . . . you 'member?'

'Yes, yes! Yours? Oh, grand!'

'Meet'r . . . 'n morning. Named for . . . Mama Wyoh. Lazarus—'

'She's a daughter of Lazarus?'

'Guess so. Ishtar says. Cer'nly had lots . . . opportunity.'

I tried to picture the child's face. A pixie, with bright red hair. 'Looks more like you.'

Hazel did not answer. Her breathing was slow and even.

I felt paws on my chest, then a tickle on my chin. 'Blert?'

'Quiet, baby; Mama's sleeping.'

The kitten settled down, went to sleep himself. So I finished the day as I had begun it, with a baby cat asleep on my chest.

It had been a busy day.

322

XXVII

'It's a poor sort of memory that only works backwards.'

CHARLES LUTWIDGE DODGSON 1832–1898

'GWENDOLYN MY love.'

Hazel stopped with a teethclean in hand, looked startled. 'Yes, Richard?'

'This is our first anniversary. We must celebrate.'

'I'm quite willing to celebrate but I can't figure out your arithmetic. And celebrate how? A fancy breakfast? Or back to bed?'

'Both. Plus a special treat. But eat first. As for my arithmetic, attend me. It is our anniversary because we have been married exactly a week. Yes, I am aware that you think of it as two years—'

'I do not! Doesn't count. Like time spent in Brooklyn.'

'And you tell me that I have been here thirty-seven, thirty-eight, thirty-nine days, more or less. But it is not thirty-nine days to me, Gwen Hazel, as Allah will not subtract from my allotted time those days spent in the Lethe field, so I don't count them. Hell, I wouldn't believe in them if it weren't that I now have two feet—'

'You're complaining?'

'Oh, no! Except that I now have to cut twice as many toenails—'

'*Blert!*'

'What do you know about it? You don't have toenails; you have claws. And you scratched me in the night, you did. Yes, you did – don't look innocent. Monday evening the thirtieth of June – of 2188, it was, though I'm not sure what year it is here – we went to see the Halifax Ballet Theater with Luanna Pauline as Titania.'

'Yes. Isn't she lovely?'

323

'Wasn't she! Past tense, dear. If what I've been told is true, her ethereal beauty has been dust for more than two thousand years. Rest in peace. Then we went to Rainbow's End for a late supper and a total stranger had the bad taste to get himself abruptly dead at our table. Whereupon you raped me.'

'Not at the table!'

'No, in my bachelor's apartment.'

'And it wasn't rape.'

'We need not fight over it since you repaired my tarnished reputation before noon the next day. Our wedding day, my true love. Mistress Gwendolyn Novak and Dr Richard Ames announced their marriage on Tuesday the first of July, 2188. Keep track of that date.'

'I'm not likely to forget it!'

'Me, too. That evening we got out of town fast, with the sheriff's hounds a-snappin' and a-yappin' at our heels. We slept that night in Dry Bones Pressure. Right?'

'Right so far.'

'The next day, Wednesday the second, Gretchen drove us to Lucky Dragon Pressure. We slept that night in Dr Chan's place. The following day, Thursday the third, Auntie drove us toward Hong Kong Luna, but not all the way because we encountered those eager agrarian reformers. You drove the rest of the way and we wound up at Xia's hotel so late at night that it was hardly worthwhile to go to bed. But we did. That puts us into Friday the fourth of July. Independence Day. Check?'

'Check.'

'We were roused out – *I* was roused out; you were already up – I was roused out too soon late Friday morning . . . and learned that City Hall did not like me. But you and Auntie sprung me – sprang me? – sprung me . . . and we left for Luna City so fast I left my toupee hanging in the air.'

'You don't wear a toupee.'

'Not anymore, I don't; it's still hanging there. We arrived L-City circa sixteen hundred that same Friday. You and I had a difference of opinion—'

'Richard! *Please* don't dig up my past sins.'

'– which was soon cleared up as I saw the error of my ways and craved pardon. We slept that night at the Raffles; it was still Friday the fourth of July when we went to bed. We had started that day many klicks west of there, with freedom fighters getting gay with guns. Still with me?'

'Yes. Somehow in my memory it feels much longer.'

'A honeymoon is never long enough and we're having a busy one. The next morning, Saturday the fifth, we retained Ezra, then we went to the Warden's Complex . . . came back and were waylaid at the entrance to the Raffles. So we left the Raffles hurriedly, in a cloud of corpses, escaping by courtesy of Gay Deceiver and the Time Corps. Most briefly we were in the land of my innocent youth, Ioway where the tall corn grows. Then we blinked to Tertius. Beloved, at this point my groundhog calendar becomes useless. We left Luna Saturday evening the fifth; we arrived here in Tertius a few minutes later, so for our purposes I designate the Tertian day of our arrival as equivalent to Saturday, five July, 2188, and I so name it. Never mind what Tertian citizens call it; it would only confuse me. Still with me?'

'Well . . . all right.'

'Thank you. I woke up the next morning – Sunday July sixth – with two feet. For Tertius the lapse of time was, I concede, thirty-seven days. You tell me that for you it was about two years, a most unlikely story – I'd rather believe in unicorns and virgins. For Gretchen it was five or six years, which I am forced to stipulate because she is now eighteen or nineteen and knocked up; I have to believe it. But for me it was just over one night, Saturday and Sunday.

'That "Sunday" night I slept with Xia, Gretchen, Minerva, Galahad, Pixel, and possibly Tom, Dick, and Harry and their sheilas Agnes, Mabel, and Becky.'

'Who are they? The girls, I mean; I know those boys. Too well.'

'You poor, sweet, innocent child; you are too young to know. Surprisingly I slept well. Which brings us to yesterday, designated by strict numbering as Monday July seventh. Last night we spent catching up on our honeymoon . . . and thank you bolshoyeh, mistress mine.'

'You are welcome, sirrah. But the pleasure was shared. I now see how you arrived at that date. Both by dirtside calendar and your biological clock – the basic clock, as every timejumper knows – today is Tuesday the eighth of July. Happy Anniversary, darling!'

325

We stopped to swap some spit and Hazel cried and my eyes got watery.

Breakfast was swell. That's all the description I can give it because Gwen Hazel decided to treat me to Tertian cooking and consulted with Dora under a hushfield, and I et what was sot before me, as the Iowa farmer had carved on his tombstone. And so did Pixel, who had some specials that looked like garbage to me but tasted like ambrosia to him, as proved by his behavior.

We had just finished our second cups of – no, it was not coffee – and were about to slip over to the Long mansion for my 'special treat,' i.e., for me to meet my new daughter, Wyoming Long . . . when Dora spoke up:

'Advisory notice: Time line, date, time, and location. Official. Please prepare to set your timepieces on the tick.' Hazel looked surprised, hurriedly grabbed her handbag, dug into it, pulled out a something I had not seen before. Call it a chronometer. 'We are in a stationary orbit around Tellus, Sol III, in time line three, coded "Neil Armstrong." The date is Tuesday the first of July—'

'My God! We're back where we started! Our wedding day!'

'Quiet, dear! Please!'

'– Gregorian. Repeat: Time line three, Sol III, July first, 2177 Gregorian. At the tick it will be zone five, oh nine forty-five. *Tick!* Those equipped to receive sonic close correction, wait for the tone—'

It started with a low note and squealed on up until it hurt my ears. Dora added: 'Another time tick and sonic correction will be offered in five minutes, ship's time or Tellus zone five time, which are now matched for local legal time designated "daylight time" for interception point on this time line. Hazel hon, private to you.'

'Yes, Dora?'

'Here are Richard's shoes –' (Plunk, they hit the bed. Out of nowhere.) '– and his other two suits –' (Plop.) '– and I packaged the small clothes and stockings with them. Shall I add a couple of jumpsuits? I took Richard's measurements while you slept. These aren't washables; these are Hercules cloth, won't take dirt, can't wear out.'

326

'Yes, Dora, and thank you, dear. That's thoughtful of you. I hadn't yet bought him anything but city clothes.'

'I noticed.' (Plop – another package.) Dora went on, 'We've been loading and unloading all night. The last of the stragglers left at oh nine hundred but I told Captain Laz about your anniversary breakfast, so she refused to let Lazarus disturb you. Message from Lazarus: If it suits your convenience, will both of you kindly get off your dead duffs and report to THQ. End of message. Transmission from the bridge, live.'

'Hazel? Captain Laz speaking. Can you two leave the ship by ten hundred? I told my hard-nosed brother that ten was the departure time he could expect.'

Hazel sighed. 'Yes. We'll leave for the car pocket at once.'

'Good. Felicitations to both of you from me and Lor and Dora. Many happy returns of the day! It has been a pleasure to have you aboard.'

We were at the car pocket with two minutes to spare, me loaded with packages and cat, and getting used to new shoes – well, one old, one new. I learned that the 'car pocket' referred to our old friend Gay Deceiver; the end of a short passage led right into her starboard door. Again I missed seeing those spacewarp bathrooms; Hazel's grandsons piloted us, and we were told to take the back seats. Pol got out to let us get in. 'Hi, Grandma! Good morning, sir.'

I said good morning and Hazel kissed both her grandsons in passing, no seconds lost, and we settled down and strapped in. Cas called out, 'Report seat belts.'

'Passengers' seat belts fastened,' Hazel reported.

'Bridge! Ready for launch.'

Laz answered, 'Launch at will.'

Instantly we were out in the sky and weightless. Pixel started to struggle; I caged him with both hands. I think it was weightlessness that startled him . . . but how could he tell? He didn't weigh anything to start with.

Earth was off to starboard, apparently full, although one can't tell that close up. We were opposite the middle of North America, which told me that Laz was a more than competent pilot; had we been in the usual twenty-four-hour orbit, concentric with Earth's equator, we would have been over the equator

327

at ninety west, i.e., over the Galapagos Islands. I guessed that she had selected an orbit tilted at about forty degrees and timed for ten hundred ship's time – and made a mental note to check it later, if and when I ever got a look at the ship's log.

(A pilot can't help second-guessing every other pilot; it's an occupational disease. Sorry.)

Then we were suddenly in atmosphere, down thirty-six-thousand klicks in a tick. Gay spread her wings, Cas tilted her nose down, then leveled off, and we again had weight, at one gee – and Pixel liked this change still less. Hazel reached over and took Pixel, soothed him; he quieted down – I think he felt safer with her.

With her wings raked in for hypersonic, the only way I had seen her, Gay is mostly a lifting body. With her wings spread, she has lots of lift area and she glides beautifully. We were a thousand meters up, give or take, and over farm country on a fine summer day – clear, save for anvil cumuli here and there on the horizon. Glorious! A day to feel young again—

Cas said, 'I hope that translation did not bother you. Had I left it up to Gay, she would have put us on the ground in one jump; she's nervous about anti-aircraft fire.'

'I am *not* nervous. I'm rationally careful.'

'Right you are, Gay. She does have reason to be careful. The Pilots' Precautionary Notice for this planet on this time line at this year states that one must assume AA weapons around all cities and larger towns. So Gay blinks down below the AA radar—'

'You hope,' said the car.

'– so that we will show up simply as a subsonic private plane on air-control radar, if there is any. None, that is, where we are.'

'Optimist,' the car sneered.

'Quit bitching. Have you spotted your squat?'

'Long since. If you'll quit yacking and give me permission, I'll take it.'

'At will, Gay.'

I said, 'Hazel, I had counted on getting acquainted with my new daughter about now. Wyoming.'

'Don't fret, dear; she will never know we were away. That's the way to handle it until a child is old enough to understand.'

328

'She won't know, but I will. I'm disappointed. All right, let's table it.'

The scene blinked again and we were on the ground. Cas said, 'Please check to see that you aren't leaving anything behind.' As we got out and stood clear, Gay Deceiver disappeared. I stared through the space she had occupied. My Uncle Jock's house was two hundred meters away.

'Hazel, what date did Dora say this is?'

'Tuesday July first, 2177.'

'That's what I thought I had heard. But when I thought it over I decided that I must have been mistaken. I now see that she wasn't fooling: '77. Eleven years in the past. Sweetheart, that ratty old barn there is standing where we landed last Saturday, three days ago. You wheeled me from there toward the house in Ezra's wheelchair. Hon, that barn we're looking at was torn down years back; that's just its ghost. This is bad.'

'Don't fret about it, Richard. In timejumping it feels that way, the first time you get involved with a loop.'

'I've already lived through 2177! I don't like paradoxes.'

'Richard, treat it just as you would any other place, any other time. No one else will notice the paradox, so ignore it yourself. The chance of being recognized when you are living paradoxically is zero for any era outside your own normal lifetime . . . but usually only one in a million even if you timejump close to home. You left this area quite young, did you not?'

'I was seventeen: 2150.'

'So forget it. You can't be recognized.'

'Uncle Jock will know me. I've been back to see him a number of times. Although not recently. Unless you count our quick visit three days ago.'

'He won't remember our visit three days ago—'

'He won't, huh? Sure, he's a hundred and sixteen years old. Or will be eleven years from now. But he's not senile.'

'You're right; he's certainly not senile. And Uncle Jock is used to time loops. As you have guessed by now, he's in the Corps and quite senior. In fact he's the major stationkeeper for North America in time line three. Last night's evacuation of THQ was made to this station. Didn't you realize that?'

'Hazel, I didn't even touch second. Twenty minutes ago I was sitting in our stateroom – Dora was parked on the ground on Tertius, so I thought – and I was trying to decide whether to have another cup, or to take you back to bed. Since then I've been running as fast as I can to try to catch up with my own confusion. Unsuccessfully. I'm just an old soldier and harmless hack writer; I'm not used to such adventures. Well, let's go. I want you to meet my Aunt Cissy.'

Gay had put us down across the road from Uncle Jock's place. We walked down the road a piece, me carrying packages and swinging my cane, Hazel with her handbag and carrying the kitten. Some years back Uncle Jock had placed a much stouter fence around his farm than was usual in Iowa in those days. It was not yet built when I left home and enlisted in 2150; it was in place by the time I visited in . . . 2161? That's about right.

The fence was heavy steel mesh, two meters high and with a six-strand cradle of barbed wire on top of that. I think the barbed wire was added later; I did not recall it.

Inside the cradle were copper wires on ceramic insulators. About every twenty meters there was a sign:

DANGER!!!
Do Not Touch Fence Without
Opening Master Switch # 12

At the gate was another sign, larger:

INTERBUREAU LIAISON AGENCY
Bio-Ecological Research Division
District Office
Deliver Radioactive Materials
To Gate Four – Wedns. Only
7-D-92-10-3sc
YOUR TAXES AT WORK

Hazel said thoughtfully, 'Richard, it does not look as if Uncle Jock lives here this year. Or this is the wrong house and Gay missed her clues. I may have to call for help.'

'It's the right house and Uncle Jock did – does – live here this year. If this year is 2177, on which I'm keeping an open mind. That sign smells like Uncle Jock; he always did have funny ideas about privacy. One year it was piranhas and a moat.'

I found a push button to the right of the gate and pressed it. A brassy voice, so artificial that it had to be an actor, announced, 'Stand one-half meter from pickup. Display your clock badge. Face pickup. Turn ninety degrees and show profile. These premises are guarded by attack dogs, gas, and snipers.'

'Is Jock Campbell at home?'

'Identify yourself.'

'This is his nephew Colin Campbell. Tell him her father found out!'

The brassy voice was replaced by one I recognized. 'Dickie, are you in trouble again?'

'No, Uncle Jock. I simply want to get in. I thought you were expecting me.'

'Anyone with you?'

'My wife.'

'What's her first name?'

'Go to hell.'

'Later, don't rush me. I need her first name.'

'And I won't play games; we're leaving. If you see Lazarus Long – or Dr Hubert – tell him that I'm sick of childish games and won't play. Good-bye, Uncle.'

'Hold it! Don't move; I have you in my sights.'

I turned away without answering and said to Hazel, 'Let's start walking, hon. Town is a far piece down the road but somebody will come along and give us a lift. People around here are friendly.'

'I can phone for help. The way I did from the Raffles.' She lifted her handbag.

'Can you? Wouldn't the call be relayed right back to this house no matter where or when or what time line? Or have I failed to understand any of it? Let's start hoofing it. My turn to carry that fierce cat.'

'All right.'

Hazel did not seem to be troubled over our failure to get into Uncle Jock's place, or Time Headquarters, whichever. As for me, I was happy, light-hearted. I had a beautiful, lovable bride. I was no longer a cripple and I felt years younger than my calendar age. If I still had a calendar age. The weather was heavenly in a fashion that only Iowa knows. Oh, it would be hot later in the day (it takes hot sun to grow good corn) but now, at about ten-fifteen, it was still balmy; by the time it was really hot I would have my bride – and the kitten – indoors. Even if we had to stop at the next farmhouse. Let's see . . . the Tanguays? Or had the old man sold out by 2177? No matter.

I was not worried by my lack of local legal money, my lack of tangible assets of any sort. A beautiful summer day in Iowa leaves no room for worry. I could work and would – spreading manure if that was the sort of work available. And I would soon spread manure of another sort, moonlighting nights and Sundays. In 2177 Evelyn Fingerhut had not yet retired, so pick some new pen names and sell him the same old tripe. The same stories – just file off the serial numbers.

File off the serial numbers, change the body lines a bit, give it a new paint job, switch it over the state line, and it's yours! – that's the secret of literary success. Editors always claim to be looking for new stories but they don't buy them; they buy 'mixture as before.' Because the cash customers want to be entertained, not amazed, not instructed, not frightened.

If people truly wanted novelty, baseball would have died out two centuries back . . . instead of being ever popular. What can possibly happen in a baseball game that everyone has not seen many times before? Yet people like to watch baseball – shucks, I'd enjoy seeing a baseball game right now, with hot dogs and beer.

'Hazel, do you enjoy baseball?'

'Never had a chance to find out. When the drugs against acceleration came along, I went dirtside for my law degree but never had time to watch baseball even in the idiot box. I worked my way through law school and was I busy! That was when I was Sadie Lipschitz.'

'Why were you? You said you didn't like that name.'

'Sure you want to know? The answer to "Why" is always "Money."'

'If you want me to know, you'll tell me.'

'Scoundrel. That was right after Slim Lemke Stone died and – What in the world is that racket?'

332

'That's an automobile.' I glanced around for the source of the noise.

Starting about 2150 or a little earlier (I saw my first one the year I signed up) supreme swank for an Iowa farmer was to own and drive a working replica of a twentieth-century 'automobile' personal transport vehicle. Of course not a vehicle moved by means of internal explosions of a derivative of rock oil: Even the People's Republic of South Africa had laws against placing poisons in the air. But with its Shipstone concealed and a sound tape to supply the noise of a soi-disant 'IC' engine, the difference between a working replica and a real 'automobile' was not readily apparent.

This one was the swankest of all replicas, a Tin Lizzy, a 'Ford touring car, Model T, 1914.' It was as dignified as Queen Victoria, whom it resembled. And it was Uncle Jock's . . . as I had suspected when I heard that infernal banging.

I said to Hazel, 'Here, you take Pixel and soothe him; he's certainly never heard anything like this. And ease well off to the side of the road; these wagons are erratic.' We continued on down the road; the replica pulled alongside us and stopped.

'Need a lift, folks?' Uncle Jock asked. Up close the racket was horrible.

I turned and grinned at him, and answered, mouthing my words so that they couldn't possibly be heard above the noise: 'Four score and seven years ago did gyre and gimble in the wabe.'

'How's that again?'

'Billiards will never replace sex, or even tomatoes.'

Uncle Jock reached down and switched off the sound effects. I said, 'Thanks, Uncle. The noise was scaring our kitten. It's mighty nice of you to turn it off. What were you saying? I couldn't hear you over the engine noise.'

'I asked if you wanted a lift.'

'Why, thank you. Going into Grinnell?'

'I planned to take you back to the house. Why did you run away?'

'You know why. Did Dr Hubert or Lazarus Long or whatever name he's using this week put you up to it? If so, why?'

'Introduce me first, if you please, nephew. And pardon me for not getting down, ma'am; this steed is skittish.'

'Jock Campbell you old goat, don't you dare pretend that

you don't know me! I'll have your rocks for castanets. Believe!'

For the first time that I can remember, Uncle Jock seemed shocked and baffled. 'Madam?'

Hazel saw his expression, said hastily, 'Are we inverted? I'm sorry. I'm Major Sadie Lipschitz, Time Corps, DOL, assigned to Overlord. I met you first in Boondock about ten of my subjective years ago. You invited me to visit you here, and I did, in year 2186 as I recall. Click?'

'Click, a clear inversion. Major, I'm happy indeed to meet you. But I'm happier still to learn that I will meet you again. I'm looking forward to it.'

Hazel answered, 'We had a good time, I promise you. I'm married to your nephew now . . . but you're still an old goat. Get down out of that toy wagon and kiss me like you mean it.'

Hastily Uncle unclutched his rotor and got down; Hazel handed Pixel to me, which saved his life. After a while the old goat said, 'No, I have not met you before; I could not possibly forget.'

Hazel answered, 'Yes, I have met you before; I'll never forget. God, it's good to see you again, Jock. You haven't changed. When was your last rejuvenation?'

'Five subjective years ago – just long enough to marinate. But I wouldn't let them youthen my face. When was yours?'

'Same subjective, about. Wasn't due for it yet but I needed cosmetic because I planned to marry your nephew. So I took a booster along with it. Turned out I needed it; he's a goat, too.'

'I know. Dickie had to enlist because they were closing in on him from all sides.' (An outright lie!) 'But are you sure your name is Sadie? That's not the name Lazarus gave me as a test word.'

'My name is whatever I want it to be, just as it is with Lazarus. My, I'm glad they moved THQ to your place last night! Kiss me again.'

He did and finally I said mildly, 'Not on a public road, folks, not in Poweshiek County. This is not Boondock.'

'Mind your own business, nephew. Sadie, headquarters was not moved here last night; that was three years ago.'

334

XXVIII

'The majority is never right.'

L. LONG 1912–

WE RODE back to the house, Hazel up front with Uncle Jock, Pixel and me back with the packages. As a favor to Pixel, the replica Model T moved as silently as a ghost. (Do ghosts really move silently? How do such clichés get started?) The gate opened to Uncle Jock's voice and no lethal defenses were actuated. If there were any. Knowing Uncle Jock I suspect that there were – but not the ones posted.

We were met on the front veranda by Aunt Til and Aunt Cissy. While Uncle Jock went inside, my aunts welcomed my bride into the family with all the warmth of country manners. Then I passed the kitten to Hazel and I was greeted by them much as Hazel had greeted Uncle but with no time loop to confuse us. Golly, it was good to be home! Despite my sometimes stormy adolescence the happiest memories of my life were associated with this old house.

Aunt Cissy looked older today, in 2177, than I recalled her looking the last time I had seen her – 2183, was it? Was this a clue as to why Aunt Til had always looked the same age? An occasional trip to Boondock could work wonders.

Were all three – no, all four, including Aunt Belden – serving fifty-year enlistments with the Fountain of Youth as one of the perks?

Was Uncle Jock metabolically about thirty while maintaining the face and neck and hands of an old man in order to support a charade? (None of your business, Richard!)

'Where's Aunt Belden?'

'She's gone to Des Moines for the day,' Aunt Til answered. 'She'll be home for supper. Richard, I thought you were on Mars?'

I consulted a calendar in my head. 'Come to think about it, I am.'

335

Aunt Til looked at me keenly. 'Are you looped?'

Uncle Jock came back out just in time to say, 'Stop it! That sort of talk is forbidden. You all know it; you are all subject to the Code.'

I said quickly, 'I'm not subject to the Code, whatever it is. Yes, Aunt Til, I'm looped. Back from 2188.'

Uncle Jock fixed me with a look that used to scare me when I was ten or twelve. 'Richard Colin, what is this? Dr Hubert gave me to understand that you were under orders to report to Time Headquarters. Just this minute I stepped inside and phoned him about your arrival. But no one goes to Headquarters who is not sworn in and ruled by the Code. Leastwise, if he did, he wouldn't come out again. You said earlier that you weren't in trouble but you can stop lying now and tell me about it. I'll help you if I can; blood is thicker than water. So let's have it.'

'I'm not in any trouble that I know of, Uncle, but Dr Hubert keeps trying to hand me some. Are you seriously suggesting that reporting to Time Headquarters could result in my not coming out alive? I'm not sworn into the Time Corps and I am not subject to its code. If you are serious, then I should *not* report to the Time Corps' headquarters. Aunt Til, is it all right for us to spend the night here? Or would that embarrass you? Or Uncle Jock?'

Without consulting Uncle Jock even by eye, Aunt Til answered, 'Of course you'll stay here, Richard; you and your darling bride are welcome tonight and as long as you'll stay and whenever you come back. This is your home and always has been.' Uncle shrugged, said nothing.

'Thanks! Where shall I drop these packages? My room? And I need to make arrangements for this fierce feline. Is there a sandbox around from the last litter? And, while Pixel has had his breakfast, I think he could use some milk.'

Aunt Cissy stepped forward. 'Til, I'll take care of the kitten. Isn't he a pretty one!' She reached for Pixel; Hazel passed him over.

Aunt Til said, 'Richard, your room has a guest in it, a Mr Davis. Mmm, I think, this being July, that the north room on the third floor would be the most comfortable for you and Hazel—'

'"Hazel"!' Uncle Jock interjected. 'That was the test word

Dr Hubert gave me. Major Sadie, is that one of your names?'

'Yes. Hazel Davis Stone. Now Hazel Stone Campbell.'

'"Hazel Davis Stone,"' Aunt Til put in. 'Are you Mr Davis's little girl?'

My bride suddenly perked up. 'Depends. A long time ago I was Hazel Davis. Is this "Manuel Davis"? Manuel Garcia O'Kelly Davis?'

'Yes.'

'My papa! He's *here?*'

'He'll be here for supper. I hope. But – Well, he has duties.'

'I know. I've been in the Corps forty-six years subjective and Papa about the same, I think. So we hardly ever see each other, the Corps being what it is. Oh, goodness! Richard, I'm going to cry. Make me stop!'

'Me? Lady, I'm just waiting for a bus. But you can use my handkerchief.' I offered it to her.

She accepted it, dabbed at her eyes. 'Brute. Aunt Til, you should have spanked him oftener.'

'Wrong aunt, dear. That was Aunt Abigail, now gone to her reward.'

'Aunt Abby was brutal,' I commented. 'Used a peach switch on me. And enjoyed it.'

'Should have used a club. Aunt Til, I can't wait to see Papa Mannie. It's been so long.'

'Hazel, you saw him right here – Right *there,*' I said, pointing at a spot halfway to the old barn, 'only three days ago.' I hesitated. 'Or was it thirty-seven days? Thirty-nine?'

'No, no, Richard! Neither. By my time, subjective, it's over two years.' Hazel added, to the others, 'it's all still new to Richard. He was recruited, his subjective time, just last week.'

'But I wasn't recruited,' I objected. 'That's why we're here.'

'We'll see, dear. Uncle Jock, that reminds me – I want to tell you something and I must bend the Code a bit to do so. That doesn't worry me; I'm a Loonie and never obey laws I don't like. But are you really so regulation that you won't listen to "coming attractions" talk?'

'Well –' Uncle Jock said slowly. Aunt Til snickered. Uncle Jock turned to her and said, 'Woman, what are you laughing at?'

'Me? I wasn't laughing.'

337

'Mmrrph. Major Sadie, my responsibilities and duties require a certain latitude in interpreting the Code. Is this something I need to know?'

'In my opinion, yes.'

'That's your official opinion?'

'Well, if you put it that way—'

'Never mind. Perhaps you had better tell me and let me be the judge.'

'Yes, sir. On Saturday the fifth of July eleven years forward, 2188, THQ will transfer to New Harbor on time line five. You will go along. All your household, I think.'

Uncle Jock nodded. 'That is exactly the sort of loop-derived information the Code is designed to suppress. Because it can so easily create positive feedback and result in heterodyning and possible panic. But I can take it calmly and make good use of it. Uh . . . may I ask why the move? As it seems unlikely that I would go along – and surely not my household. This is a working farm, no matter what it conceals.'

I interrupted. 'Uncle, I'm not bound by any silly code. Those West Coast hotheads finally quit talking and seceded.'

His eyebrows shot up. 'No – Really? I didn't think they would ever get off the pot.'

'They did. May Day '88. By the day Hazel and I were here, Saturday July the fifth, the Angeleno Phalanges had just captured Des Moines. Bombs were dropping all around here. You may think – today – that you wouldn't pull out. But I know that you were about to do so then; I was there. Will be there. Ask Dr Hubert – Lazarus Long. *He* thought this place was too dangerous to hang around any longer. Ask him.'

'Colonel Campbell!'

I knew that voice; I turned and said, 'Hi, Lazarus.'

'That sort of talk is strictly forbidden. Understand me?'

I took a deep breath, then said to Hazel, 'He'll never learn' – then to Lazarus, 'Doc, you've been trying to make me stand at attention ever since we first met. It won't work. Can't you get that through your head?'

Somewhere, somewhen, Lazarus Long had had some sort of formal training in emotional control. I could now see him calling on it to help him. It took him about three seconds to invoke whatever it was he used, then he spoke quietly, in a lower register.

'Let me try to explain. Such talk is dangerous to the person you talk to. Making predictions, I mean, from knowledge gained from a loop. It is an observed fact that, again and again, it turns out to be a disservice to the person you inform when you tell him something in his future that you have learned in your past.

'As to why this is true, I suggest that you consult one of the mathematicians who deal with time – Dr Jacob Burroughs, or Dr Elizabeth Long, or anyone from the Corps' staff of mathematicians. And you should consult the council of historians for examples of the harm it does. Or you could look it up in our headquarters library – file "Cassandra" and file "Ides of March," for starters, then see file "Nostradamus."'

Long turned to Uncle Jock. 'Jock, I'm sorry about this. I pray that you will not let the troubles of '88 make your household gloomy during the forward years till then. I never planned to bring your nephew here not yet trained in the disciplines of Time – I never planned to bring your nephew here at all. We do need him, but we expected to recruit him at Boondock with no need to bring him to Headquarters. But he refused to enlist. Do you want to try to change his mind?'

'I'm not sure I have any influence over him, Lafe. How about it, Dickie? Want to hear what a good deal a career in the Time Corps can be? You could say that the Time Corps supported you throughout your childhood – you could say it because it's true. The sheriff was about to auction this farm right out from under us . . . when I joined up. You were just a tad . . . but you may remember a time we ate corn bread and not much else. Then things got better and stayed better – do you remember? You were about six.'

I had some long thoughts. 'Yes, I remember. I think I do. Uncle, I'm not against joining. You're in it, my wife is in it, several of my friends are in it. But Lazarus has been trying to sell me a pig in a poke. I've got to know what it is they want me to do and why they want me to do it. They say they want me for a job with the chances only fifty-fifty that I get out of it alive. With those odds there is no point in talking about retirement benefits. I don't want some chairwarmer in Headquarters being that casual about my neck. I must know that it makes sense before I'll accept those odds.'

'Lafe, just what is this job you have for my boy?'

'It's Task Adam Selene in Operation Galactic Overlord.'

'I don't think I've heard of it.'

'And now you should forget it, as you don't figure into it and it has not been mounted as of this year.'

'That makes it difficult for me to advise my nephew. Shouldn't I be briefed?'

Hazel intervened. 'Lazarus! Knock it off!'

'Major, I'm discussing official business with the THQ stationkeeper.'

'Pig whistle! You are again trying to chivvy Richard into risking his life without his knowing why. When I agreed to try to do so, I had not yet met Richard. Now that I know him – and admire him; he is *sans peur et sans reproche* – I'm ashamed that I ever tried. But I did try . . . and almost succeeded. But you barreled your way in . . . and mucked it up, as was predictable. I told you then that the Circle would have to convince him, I told you! Now you are trying to get Richard's closest relative – his father in all that counts – to pressure him in your place. Shame on you! Take Richard to the Circle. Let *them* explain it . . . or let him go home! Quit stalling! Do it!'

What I had always thought of as a closet in Uncle's den turned out to look like an elevator inside. Lazarus Long and I went into it together; he closed the door and I saw that, where an elevator usually has floor numbers with touchplates for each number, there was a display of lighted symbols – signs of the Zodiac I thought, then changed my mind, as there is no bat in the Zodiac, no black widow spider, certainly no stegosaurus.

At the bottom, by itself, was a snake eating its own tail – the world snake, Ouroboros. A disgusting symbol at best.

Lazarus placed his hand over it.

The closet, or elevator cage, or small room, changed. How, I am not certain. It simply blinked and was different. 'Through here,' Lazarus said, and opened a door on the far side.

Stretching from that door was a long corridor that would never fit inside my uncle's house. But views I could see through windows that lined that long passageway did not fit his farm, either. The land looked like Iowa, yes – but Iowa untouched by the plow, never cleared for farming.

340

We stepped into this passage and were at once at its far end. 'Through there,' Lazarus said, pointing.

An archway melted out of a stone wall. The passage beyond it was gloomy. I looked around to speak to Lazarus; he was gone.

I said to myself, Lazarus, I told you not to play games with me . . . and turned around to go back down the long passage, back through Uncle Jock's den, find Hazel and leave. I had had it, fed up with his games.

There was no passage behind me.

I promised Lazarus a clop in the head and followed the only available route. It remained gloomy but always with a light a little farther ahead. Shortly, five minutes or less, it ended in a small, comfortable lounge, well-lighted from nowhere. A brassy uninflected voice said, 'Please sit down. You will be called.'

I sat down in an easy chair and laid my cane aside. A small table by it held magazines and a newspaper. I glanced at each one, looking for anachronisms, but found none. The periodicals were all ones that I recalled as available in Iowa in the seventies; they carried dates of July 2177 or earlier. The newspaper was the *Grinnell Herald-Register*, dated Friday, June 27, 2177.

I started to put it down, as the *Herald-Register* is not exactly exciting. Uncle subscribed to a daily printout from Des Moines and, of course, the *Kansas City Star*, but our local paper was good only for campus notes, local notices, and the sort of 'news' and 'society' items that are published to display as many local names as possible.

But an ad caught my eye: On Sunday, July twentieth, one night only, at Des Moines Municipal Opera House, the Halifax Ballet Theater will present *Midsummer Night's Dream*, with the sensational new star Luanna Pauline as Titania.

I read it twice . . . and promised myself that I would take Hazel to see it. It would be a special anniversary: I had met Mistress Gwendolyn Novak at Golden Rule's Day One Ball, Neil Armstrong Day, July twentieth a year ago (never mind that silly time loop) and this would make a delightful reprise of the gala eve of our wedding day (without, this time, some unmannerly oaf crashing our party and dying at our table).

Would a one-gravity performance be disappointing after

having seen the Queen of Fairies cutting didoes high in the air? No, this was a sentimental journey; it would not matter. Besides, Luanna Pauline had made (would make, will make) her reputation dancing in one gravity – it would be a fascinating contrast. We could go backstage and tell her that we saw her dance Titania at one-third gravity in the Circus Room of Golden Rule. Oh, certainly – when Golden Rule does not yet exist for another three years! I began to understand why the Code had limitations on loose talk.

Never mind. On Neil Armstrong Day I would gift my beautiful bride with this sentimental celebration.

While I was looking at the *Herald-Register*, an abstract design on the wall changed to a motto in glowing letters:

A Stitch in Time Saves Nine Billion

While I watched, it changed to:

A Paradox Can Be Paradoctored

Then:

The Early Worm Has a Death Wish

Followed by:

Don't Try Too Hard; You Might Succeed

I was trying to figure out that last one when it suddenly changed to 'Why Are You Staring at a Blank Wall?' – and it was a blank wall. Then on it appeared, large, the World Snake, and, inside the circle it made by its nauseating way of eating, letters were chasing themselves. Then they leveled out into a straight line:

Making Order Out of Chaos

Then under that:

THE
CIRCLE
OF
OUROBOROS

This was displaced by another archway; that brassy voice said: 'Please enter.'

I grabbed my cane and went through the archway and found myself translated to the exact center of a large circular room. There is such a thing as too much service.

There were a dozen-odd people seated around the room on a dais about a meter high – a theater in the round, with me in the leading role . . . in the sense in which an insect pinned to the stage of a microscope is the star of the show. That brassy voice said, 'State your full name.'

'Richard Colin Ames Campbell. What is this? A trial?'

'Yes, in one sense.'

'You can adjourn court right now; I'm not having any. If anyone is on trial, it is all of *you* – as I want nothing from you but you seem to want something from me. It is up to *you* to convince *me*, not the other way around. Keep that clear in your mind.'

I turned slowly around, looking over my 'judges.' I found a friendly face, Hilda Burroughs, and felt enormously better. She threw me a kiss; I caught it and ate it. But I was enormously surprised, too. I would expect to find this tiny beauty at any gathering requiring elegance and grace . . . but not as a member of a group that had been represented to me as being the most powerful council in all history and any universe.

Then I recognized another face: Lazarus. He nodded; I returned his nod. He said, 'Please don't be impatient, Colonel. Allow protocol to proceed.'

I said, 'Protocol is either useful or it should be abolished. I am standing and all of you are seated. That is protocol establishing dominance. And you can stuff it! If I don't have a chair in ten seconds I am leaving. *Your* chair will do.'

That invisible robot with the brassy voice placed an up-holstered easy chair back of my knees so fast that I had no excuse to leave. I sank back into it and put my cane across my knees. 'Comfortable?' Lazarus inquired.

'Yes, thank you.'

'Good. The next item is protocol, too – introductions. I do not think you will find it objectionable.'

The brassy voice started in again, naming members – 'Companions' – of the Circle of Ouroboros, governing body of the omniversal Time Corps. Each time one was named, my chair faced that companion. But I felt no movement.

'Master Mobyas Toras, for Barsoom, time line one, coded "John Carter."'

'Barsoom'? Poppycock! But I found myself standing up and bowing in answer to a gentle smile and a gesture suggesting a blessing. He was ancient, and hardly more than skin and bones. He wore a sword but I felt sure that he had not wielded one in generations. He was huddled in a heavy silk wrap much like that worn by Buddhist priests. His skin was polished mahogany, more strongly red than any North American 'redskin' – in short he looked exactly like the fictional descriptions in the tales of Barsoom . . . a result easy to achieve with makeup, a couple of meters of cloth, and a prop sword.

So why did I stand up?

(Because Aunt Abby had striped my calves for any failure whatever in politeness to my elders?

Nonsense. I knew that he was authentic when I laid eyes on him. That my conviction was preposterous did not alter it.)

'Her Wisdom Star, Arbiter of the Ninety Universes, composite time lines, code "Cyrano."'

Her Wisdom smiled at me and I wiggled like a puppy. I'm no judge of wisdom but I am certain that males with high blood pressure and any history of cardiac problems or T.I.A. should not be too close to her. Star, Mrs Gordon, is as tall or taller than I, weighs more and all of it muscle but her breasts and that slight layer that smooths female body lines. She was wearing too little for Poweshiek County, quite a lot for Boondock.

Star may not be the most beautiful woman in all her many universes but she may be the sexiest – in a sultry, Girl Scout fashion. Just walking through a room she is in should change a boy into a man.

'Woodrow Wilson Smith, Senior of the Howard Families, time line two, code "Leslie LeCroix."' Lazarus and I again exchanged nods.

'Dr Jubal Harshaw, time line three, code "Neil Armstrong."'

Dr Harshaw raised his hand in a half salute and smiled; I answered the same way – and made a note to buttonhole him, back in Boondock perhaps, about the many legends of the 'Man from Mars.' How much was truth, how much was fiction?

'Dr Hilda Mae Burroughs, time line four, code "Ballox O'Malley."' Hilda and I exchanged smiles.

'Commander Ted Smith, time line five, code "DuQuesne."' Commander Smith was a square-jawed athlete with ice-blue eyes. He was dressed in an undecorated gray uniform, carrying a holstered hand gun, and wearing a bejeweled heavy bracelet.

'Captain John Sterling, time line six, code "Neil Armstrong alternate time line."' I looked at my boyhood hero and considered the possibility that I was asleep and having a vivid dream. Hazel had told me and told me again that the hero of her space opera was real . . . but not even the repeated use of the code phrase 'Operation Galactic Overlord' had convinced me . . . and now here he was: the foe of the Overlord.

Or was it he? What proof?

'Sky Marshal Samuel Beaux, time line seven, code "Fairacre."' Marshal Beaux was over two meters tall, massed at least a hundred and ten kilos, all of it muscle and rhinoceros hide. He was dressed in a midnight black uniform and a frown, and was as beautiful as a black panther. He stared at me with jungle eyes.

Lazarus announced, 'I declare quorum. The Circle is closed. Dr Hilda Burroughs now speaks for the Circle.'

Hilda smiled at me and said, 'Colonel Campbell, I have been conscripted to explain to you our purposes and enough of our methods to enable you to see how the job you are being asked to do fits into the master plan, and why it must be done. Don't hesitate to interrupt, or to argue, or to demand more details. We can continue this discussion from now until lunchtime. Or for the next ten years. Or for a truly long time. As long as necessary.'

Sky Marshal Beaux cut in with: 'Speak for yourself, Mrs Burroughs. I'm leaving in thirty minutes.'

Hilda said, 'Sambo, you really should address the chair. I can't let you leave until you speak your piece, but, if you need to leave, you can speak now. Please explain what you do and why.'

'Why is this man being coddled? I've never been asked to

explain my duties to a raw recruit before. This is ridiculous.'

'Nevertheless I ask you to do so.'

The sky marshal settled back in his chair and said nothing.

Lazarus said, 'Sambo, I know this is without precedent but all the Companions including the three who are not here have agreed that Task Adam Selene is essential to Operation Galactic Overlord, that Overlord is essential to Campaign Boskone, that Boskone is essential to our Plan Long View . . . and that Colonel Campbell is essential to Task Adam Selene. The Circle is closed on this, no dissent. We need Campbell's services, given fully and freely. So we must persuade him. You need not go first . . . but, if you expect to be excused from the Circle in thirty minutes, you had better speak up.'

'And if I don't choose to?'

'Your problem. You are free to resign; all of us are, anytime. And the Circle is free to terminate you.'

'Are you threatening me?'

'No.' Lazarus glanced at his wrist. 'You've stalled for four minutes against the unanimous decision of the Circle. If you expect to comply with the Circle's decision, you are running out of minutes.'

'Oh, very well. Campbell, I am commanding officer of the armed forces of the Time Corps—'

'Correction,' Lazarus Long interrupted. 'Sky Marshal Beaux is the chief of staff of—'

'It's the same thing!'

'It is not the same thing and I knew exactly what I was doing when I set it up that way. Colonel Campbell, the Time Corps sometimes intervenes in key battles in history. Histories. The Corps' board of historians seeks to identify cusps where judicious use of force might change history in fashions that we believe, in our limited wisdom, would be better for the human race – and this policy strongly affects and is affected by Task Adam Selene, I must add. If the Circle closes on a recommendation by the historians, military action is mounted, and a commander in chief for that operation is selected by the Circle.'

Lazarus turned and looked directly at Beaux. 'Sky Marshal Beaux is a highly skilled military commander, perhaps the best in all history. He is usually selected to command. But the Circle picks the commander of each task force. This policy keeps ultimate power out of the hands of military commanders. I must add that the Chief of Staff is an auditor without a vote; he is not a Companion of this Circle. Sambo, do you have anything to add?'

'You seem to have made my speech.'

'Because you were stalling. You are free to correct, amend, and elaborate.'

'Oh, never mind. You should give elocution lessons.'

'Do you now wish to be excused?'

'Are you telling me to leave?'

'No.'

'I'll hang around a while as I want to see what you do with this joker. Why didn't you simply conscript him and assign him to Task Selene? He's an obvious criminal type; look at his skull, note his attitude toward authority. On my home planet we never use anything as sloppy and unreliable as volunteers . . . and we don't have a criminal class because we draft them into the forces as fast as they show their heads. There are no better fighters than the criminal type if you catch 'em young, rule them with iron discipline, and keep them more scared of their sergeants than they can possibly be of the enemy.'

'That will do, Sambo. Please refrain from expressing opinion uninvited.'

'I thought you were the great champion of free speech?'

'I am. But there is no free lunch. If you want to make a speech, you can hire your own hall; this one is paid for by the Circle. Hilda. Speak up, dear.'

'Very well. Richard, most interventions recommended by our historians and mathematicians are not brute force, but actions far more subtle, carried out by individual field operatives . . . such as your gal Hazel, who is a real fox when it comes to robbing a henhouse. You know what we are trying to do in Task Adam Selene; you don't know what it is for, I believe. Our methods of prognosticating the results of a change introduced into history are less than perfect. Whether it's digging in on one side in a key battle, or something as simple as supplying a high school student with a condom some midnight and thereby avoiding the birth of a Hitler or a Napoleon, we can never predict the results as well as we need to. Usually we have to do it, then send a field operative down that new time line to report the changes.'

'Hilda,' said Lazarus, 'may I offer a horrible example?'

'Certainly, Woodie. But make it march. I plan to finish before lunch.'

'Colonel Campbell, I come from a world identical with yours to about 1939. Divergence, as usual, showed most at the start of space flight. Both your world and mine showed a tendency toward religious hysteria. In mine it peaked with a television evangelist named Nehemiah Scudder. His brand of fire and brimstone and scapegoatism – Jews of course; no novelty – peaked at a time when unemployment also peaked and public debt and inflation got out of hand; the result was a religious dictatorship, a totalitarian government as brutal as my world has ever seen.

'So this Circle set up an operation to get rid of Nehemiah Scudder. Nothing as crass as assassination; the specific method Hilda mentioned was used. A high school boy without a rubber was provided with one by a field operative, and the little bastard who became Nehemiah Scudder was never born. So time line two – mine – was split and time line eleven was created, allee samee but without Nehemiah Scudder, the Prophet. Bound to be better, right?

'Wrong. In my time line World War Three, the nuclear war – sometimes known by other names – badly damaged Europe but did not spread; North America under the Prophet had opted out of international affairs. In time line eleven the war started a little sooner, in the Middle East, spread to all the world overnight . . . and a hundred years later it was still impossible to find any life superior to cockroaches on the land masses of what had once been the cool green hills of Earth. Take it, Hilda.'

'Thank you, too much! Lazarus leaves me with a planet glowing in the dark to show why we need better prediction methods. We hope to use Adam Selene – supervising computer Holmes IV known as "Mike" – the programs and memories that make him unique – to tie the best computers of Tertius and some other planets into a mammoth logic that can correctly project the results of a defined change in history . . . so that we won't swap Nehemiah Scudder – who can be endured – for a ruined planet that cannot be endured. Lazarus, should I mention the super-snooperscope?'

'You just did, so you had better.'

348

'Richard, I'm way out of my depth; I'm just a simple housewife—'

A groan went up in that hall. Lazarus may have led it but it seemed to be unanimous.

'– who lacks a technical background. But I do know that engineering progress depends on accurate instruments, and that accurate instruments ever since the twentieth century – my century – have depended on progress in electronics. My number-one husband Jake Burroughs and Dr Libby Long and Dr Deety Carter are whipping up a little doozy combining Jake's space-time twister with television and the ordinary snooperscope. With it you will be able not only to watch what your wife is doing while you are away overnight but also to watch what she will be doing ten years from now. Or fifty. Or five hundred.

'Or it could let the Circle of Ouroboros see what would be the result of an intervention before it is too late to refrain. Maybe. With the unique power of Holmes IV – maybe yes. We'll see. But it is as certain as anything can be in this quicksand world that Mike Holmes IV can improve the performance of the Circle of Ouroboros enormously even if the super-snooperscope never comes on line.

'Since we are trying hard to make things better, more decent, happier for everyone, I hope that you will see that Task Adam Selene is worth doing. Any questions?'

'I have one, Hilda.'

'Yes, Jubal?'

'Has our friend Richard been indoctrinated in the concept of the World as Myth?'

'I barely mentioned it, once, in telling him how we four – Zeb and Deety, Jake and I – were hounded off our planet and erased out of the script. I think Hazel has done better. Richard?'

'Not anything I could get my teeth into. Nothing that made sense. And – forgive me, Hilda – I found your story hard to swallow.'

'Of course, dear; I don't believe it myself. Except late at night. Jubal, you had better take it.'

Dr Harshaw answered, 'Very well. The World as Myth is a subtle concept. It has sometimes been called multiperson solipsism, despite the internal illogic of that phrase. Yet illogic may be necessary, as the concept denies logic. For many centuries religion held sway as the explanation of the universe – or multiverse. The details of revealed religions differed wildly but were essentially the same: Somewhere up in the sky – or down in the earth – or in a volcano – any inaccessible place – there was an old man in a nightshirt who knew everything and was all powerful and created everything and rewarded and punished . . . and could be bribed.

'Sometimes this Almighty was female but not often because human males are usually bigger, stronger, and more belligerent; God was created in Pop's image.

'The Almighty-God idea came under attack because it explained nothing; it simply pushed all explanations one stage farther away. In the nineteenth century atheistic positivism started displacing the Almighty-God notion in that minority of the population that bathed regularly.

'Atheism had a limited run, as it, too, explains nothing, being merely Godism turned upside down. Logical positivism was based on the physical science of the nineteenth century which, physicists of that century honestly believed, fully explained the universe as a piece of clockwork.

'The physicists of the twentieth century made short work of that idea. Quantum mechanics and Schrödinger's cat tossed out the clockwork world of 1890 and replaced it with a fog of probability in which anything could happen. Of course the intellectual class did not notice this for many decades, as an intellectual is a highly educated man who can't do arithmetic with his shoes on, and is proud of his lack. Nevertheless, with the death of positivism, Godism and Creationism came back stronger than ever.

'In the late twentieth century – correct me when I'm wrong, Hilda – Hilda and her family were driven off Earth by a devil, one they dubbed "the Beast." They fled in a vehicle you have met, Gay Deceiver, and in their search for safety they visited many dimensions, many universes . . . and Hilda made the greatest philosophical discovery of all time.'

'I'll bet you say that to all the girls!'

'Quiet, dear. They visited, among more mundane places, the Land of Oz—'

I sat up with a jerk. Not too much sleep last night and Dr Harshaw's lecture was sleep-inducing. 'Did you say "Oz"?'

350

'I tell you three times. Oz, Oz, Oz. They did indeed visit the fairyland dreamed up by L. Frank Baum. And the Wonderland invented by the Reverend Mr Dodgson to please Alice. And other places known only to fiction. Hilda discovered what none of us had noticed before because we were inside it: The World *is* Myth. We create it ourselves – and we change it ourselves. A truly strong myth maker, such as Homer, such as Baum, such as the creator of Tarzan, creates substantial and lasting worlds . . . whereas the fiddlin', unimaginative liars and fabulists shape nothing new and their tedious dreams are forgotten. On this observed fact, Richard – not religion but verifiable fact – is based the work of the Circle of Ouroboros. Hilda?'

'Only a short time until we should break for lunch. Richard, do you have any comment now?'

'You won't like it.'

Lazarus said, 'Spill it, Bub.'

'I not only will not risk my life on wordy nonsense, I will do all that I can to keep Hazel from doing so. If you really want, and need, the programs and memories of that out-of-date Lunar computer there are at least two better ways to get them.'

'Keep talking.'

'One way simply uses money. Set up a front organization, an academic fakery. Funnel money into Galileo University as grants, and walk in the front door of the computer room, and take what you want. The other way is to use enough force to do a real job. Don't send an elderly married couple to try to watergate it. You cosmic do-gooders have not convinced me.'

'Let's see your ticket!'

It was Little Black Sambo, the sky marshal. 'What ticket?'

'The one that entitles you to unscrew the inscrutable. Show it. You are just a lily-livered coward, too yellow to do your plain duty.'

'Really? Who appointed you God? Look, boy, I'm mighty glad that your skin color matches mine.'

'Why so?'

'Because, if it didn't, I would be called a racist for the way I despise you.'

I saw him draw his side arm, but my cane, damn it!, had slid to the floor. I was reaching for it when his bolt hit me, low on the left.

As he was hit from three sides, two to the heart, one to the

351

head, by John Sterling, by Lazarus, by Commander Smith – three crack gunmen, where one would have sufficed.

I didn't hurt yet. But I knew I was gut-shot – bad, final bad, if I didn't get help fast.

But something was happening to Samuel Beaux. He leaned forward and fell off his chair, dead as King Charles – and his body began to disappear. It didn't fade out; it disappeared in swipes, through the middle, then across the face, as if someone had taken an eraser to a chalkboard. Then he was gone completely; not even blood was left. Even his chair was gone.

And the wound in my gut was gone.

XXIX

'There may come a time when the lion and the lamb will lie
down together, but I am still betting on the lion.'

HENRY WHEELER SHAW 1818–1885

'WOULDN'T IT be better,' I objected, 'to have me pull a sword
out of a stone? If you really want to sell the product? The
whole plan is silly!'

We were seated at a picnic table in the east orchard, Mannie
Davis, Captain John Sterling, Uncle Jock, Jubal Harshaw, and
I – and a Professor Rufo, a bald-headed old coot introduced to
me as an aide to Her Wisdom and (impossible!) her grandson.
(But having seen with my own bloodshot eyes some of the
results of Dr Ishtar's witchcraft, I was no longer using the
word 'impossible' as freely as I did a week ago.)

Pixel was with us, too, but he had long since finished his
lunch and was down in the grass, trying to catch a butterfly.
They were evenly matched but the butterfly was ahead on
points.

The bright and cloudless sky promised a temperature of
thirty-eight or forty by midafternoon; my aunts had elected to
eat lunch in the air-conditioned kitchen. But there was a breeze
and it was cool enough under the trees – a lovely day, just
right for a picnic; it reminded me of our conference with Father
Hendrik Schultz in the orchard of Old MacDonald's Farm
just a week ago (and eleven years forward).

Except that Hazel was not with me.

That groused me but I tried not to show it. When the Circle
opened for lunch, Aunt Til had a message waiting for me.
'Hazel left here with Lafe just a few minutes ago,' she told me.
'She asked me to tell you that she will not be here for lunch
but expects to see you later this afternoon . . . and will be here
for supper without fail.'

A damned skimpy message! I needed to discuss with Hazel all the talk and happenings in the closed Circle. Damn it, how could I decide anything until I had a chance to talk it over with my wife?

Women and cats do what they do; there is nothing a man can do about it.

'I'll sell you a sword in a stone,' said Professor Rufo, 'cheap. Like new. Used just once, by King Arthur. In the long run it didn't do him any good and I can't guarantee that it will help you . . . but I don't mind turning a profit on it.'

Uncle said, 'Rufo, you would sell tickets to your own funeral.'

'Not "would." Did. Netted enough to buy a round toowitt I badly needed . . . because so many people wanted to be certain I was dead.'

'So you cheated them.'

'Not at all. The tickets did not state that I was dead; they simply called for "admit bearer" to my funeral. And it was a nice funeral, the nicest I've ever had . . . especially the climax when I sat up in my coffin and sang the oratorio from *The Death of Jesse James*, doing all the parts myself. Nobody asked for his money back. Some even left before I reached my high note. Rude creatures. Go to your own funeral and you'll soon learn who your real friends are.' Rufo turned to me. 'You want that sword and stone? Cheap but it has to be cash. Can't let you have credit; your life expectancy isn't all that good. Shall we say six hundred thousand imperial dollars in small bills? No denomination higher than ten thousand.'

'Professor, I don't want a sword in a stone; it's just that this whole silly business sounds like the "true prince" nonsense of pre-Armstrong romances. Can't do it openly with money, can't do it safely with enough force to hold the losses down to zero, has to be me and my wife with nothing but a scout knife. That's a crummy plot; even a confessions book would reject it. It's logically impossible.'

'Five hundred fifty thousand and I pick up the sales tax.'

'Richard,' Jubal Harshaw answered, 'it is logic itself that is impossible. For millennia philosophers and saints have tried to reason out a logical scheme for the universe . . . until Hilda came along and demonstrated that the universe is not logical but whimsical, its structure depending solely on the dreams and nightmares of non-logical dreamers.' He shrugged, almost spilling his Tuborg. 'If the great brains had not been so hoodwinked by their shared conviction that the universe must contain a consistent and logical structure they could find by careful analysis and synthesis, they would have spotted the glaring fact that the universe – the multiverse – contains neither logic nor justice save where we, or others like us, impose such qualities on a world of chaos and cruelty.'

'Five hundred thousand and that's my last offer.'

'So why should Hazel and I risk our necks?' I added, 'Pixel! Leave that insect alone!'

'Butterflies are not insects,' Captain John Sterling said soberly. 'They are self-propelled flowers. The Lady Hazel taught me that many years ago.' He reached down and gently picked up Pixel. 'How were you getting him to drink?'

I showed him, using water and my fingertip. Then Sterling improved on it, offering the kitten a tiny puddle in the palm of his hand. The kitten licked at it, and then was lapping cat-properly, curling his dainty tongue down into the spoonful of water.

Sterling bothered me. I knew his origin, or thought I did, and thus had trouble believing in him even as I spoke with him. Yet it is impossible not to believe in a man when you see him, and *hear* him, crunching celery and potato chips.

Yet he had a two-dimensional quality. He neither smiled nor laughed. He was unfailingly polite but always dead serious. I had tried to thank him for saving my life by shooting what's-his-name; Sterling had stopped me. 'My duty. He was expendable; you are not.'

'Four hundred thousand. Colonel, are there any deviled eggs down there?'

I passed the stuffed eggs to Rufo. 'Shall I tell you what to do with your sword in a stone? First, pull out the sword, then—'

'Let's not be crude. Three hundred and fifty thousand.'

'Professor, I wouldn't have it as a door prize. I was simply making a point.'

'Better take an option, at least; you'll need it for the boff opening when they shoot this as a stereoseries.'

'No publicity. That's one of the conditions imposed on me. If I do it.'

'No publicity until *after*. Then there has to be publicity; it must wind up in the history books. Mannie, tell 'em why you have never published your memoirs of the Revolution.'

Mr Davis answered, 'Mike sleeping. Not have people bother him. Nyet.'

Uncle Jock said, 'Manuel, you have an unpublished auto-biography?'

My stepfather-in-law nodded. 'Necessary. Prof dead, Wyoming dead, Mike dead maybe. Am only witness true story of Loonie Revolution. Lies, lots of lies, by cobbers not there.' He scratched his chin with his left hand, the one I knew to be artificial. Or so I heard. This hand looked just like his right hand. A transplant? 'Stored with Mike before out to Asteroids. We rescue Mike – then publish maybe.' Davis looked at me. 'Want to hear how I met my daughter Hazel?'

'Yes indeed!' I answered, and Sterling strongly agreed.

'Was Monday thirteen May, 2075, in L-City. Talk-talk in Stilyagi Hall, how to fight Warden. Not revolution, just sad stupid talk-talk, unhappy people. Skinny little girl sat on floor down front. Orange hair, no breasts. Ten, maybe eleven. Listens every word, claps hard, dead serious.

'Yellow Jackets, Warden's cops, break in, start killing. Too busy to keep track of skinny redheads, Jackets kill my best friend . . . when see her in action. Throws self through air, rolled in ball, hits Yellow Jacket in knees, down he goes. I break his jaw with left hand – not this hand; number-two – and step over him, dragging my wife Wyoming – not wife then – with me. Skinny flametop is gone, don't see her some weeks. But, friends, hard rock truth, Hazel as little girl fought so hard and smart that she saved her Papa Mannie and her Mama Wyoh both from Warden's finks long before she knew she was ours.'

Manuel Davis smiled wistfully. 'Did find her, Davis Family opted her – daughter, not wife. Still a baby. But not baby when counts! Worked hard to free Luna every day, every hour, every minute, danger don' stop her never. Fourth o' July, 2076, Hazel Meade Davis youngest comrade signing Declaration of Independence. No comrade rated it more!'

Mr Davis had tears in his eyes. So did I.

Captain Sterling stood up. 'Mr Davis, I am humbly proud to have heard that story. Mr Campbell, I have enjoyed your hospitality. Colonel Campbell, I hope you decide to fight with us; we need you. And now, if I may be excused, I must leave. As the Galactic Overlord does not take long lunch hours, I must not.'

Uncle Jock said, 'Shucks, John, you've got to have some R and R now and then. Come go dinosaur hunting with me again. Time spent in the Mesozoic won't affect your quest; the Overlord will never know you're away. That's the greatest beauty of timejumping.'

'*I* would know that I was away. But I do thank you. I enjoyed that hunt.' He bowed and left.

Dr Harshaw said quietly, 'There goes real nobility. When at last he destroys the Overlord, he will be erased. He knows it. It doesn't stop him.'

'Why must he be erased?' I demanded.

'Eh? Colonel, I know that this is new to you . . . but you are, or have been, a fabulist yourself, have you not?'

'Still am, as far as I know. Finished a long one and sent it off to my agent just ten days ago. Must get back to work soon – got a wife to support.'

'Then you know that, for plot purposes, especially in adventure stories, heroes and villains come in complementary pairs. Each is necessary to the other.'

'Yes, but – Look, lay it on the bar. This man who just left is truly the character that Hazel – and her son, Roger Stone – created for their series *The Scourge of the Spaceways*?'

'Yes. Hazel and her son created him. Sterling knows it. Look, sir, all of us are fictions, someone's fabulist dreams. But usually we do not know it. John Sterling knows it, and is strong enough to stand up to it. He knows his role and his destiny; he accepts it.'

'He doesn't have to be erased.'

Dr Harshaw looked puzzled. 'But you are a writer. Uh . . . a literary writer perhaps? Plotless?'

'Me? I don't know how to write literature; I write stories. For printout or three-dee or even bound books, but all sorts. Sin, suffer, and repent. Horse opera. Space opera. War. Murder. Spies. Sea stories. Whatever. Hazel and I are going to revive her classic series, with Captain Sterling in the lead role. As always. So what's this noise about "erasing" him?'

'You are not going to let him destroy the Galactic Overlord?

357

You should, you *must*, as the Overlord is every bit as evil as Boskone.'

'Oh, certainly! First thirteen weeks. Should have happened years back.'

'But he *couldn't*. The series was dropped with both hero and villain still alive. Sterling has been forced to fight only a holding action ever since.'

'Oh. Well, we'll fix that. *Overlord delenda est!*'

'Then what does Sterling do?'

I started to answer, suddenly realized that the question was not inquiry but Socratic. For each fine cat, a fine rat. A hero of Sterling's stature must oppose a villain as strong as he is. If we kill off the Overlord, then we must dream up Son of Overlord, with just as many balls, teeth just as long, disposition just as vile, and steam coming out of his ears.

'I don't know. We'll think of something. Age him, maybe, and put him to pasture as commandant of the Star Patrol Academy. Some such. No need to kill him off. A job like that would not require a villain as horrendous as the Overlord.'

'Wouldn't it?' Harshaw asked quietly.

'Uh – Maybe you would like to take over the series?'

'Not me. I'm semi-retired. All I have now is *The Stonebender Family*, a series strictly for laughs, no substantial villain required. Now I know the truth of the World as Myth I will never again create a real villain . . . and I thank Klono that I never have, not really, as I have only a limited belief in villainy.'

'Well, I can't answer without Hazel anyhow; I'm the junior writer, in charge of punctuation and filling in weather and scenery; she controls plot. So I must change the subject. Uncle Jock, what was this you were saying to Captain Sterling about hunting dinosaurs? One of your jokes? Like the time you sawed off ten square klicks of the Ross Ice Shelf and towed it to Singapore, swimming sidestroke.'

'Not sidestroke all the way; that's not possible.'

'Come off it. Dinosaurs.'

'What about dinosaurs? I like to hunt them. I took John Sterling with me once; he got a truly magnificent tyranno-saurus rex. Would you like to try it?'

'Are you serious? Uncle, you know I don't hunt. I don't like to shoot anything that can't shoot back.'

'Oho! You misunderstood me, nephew. We don't kill the poor beasties. Killing a dinosaur is about as sporting as shooting a cow. And not as good meat. A dinosaur more than a year old is tough and tasteless. I did try them, years back, when some thought was being given to using dinosaur meat to quench a famine on time line seven. But the logistics were dreadful and, when you come right down to it, there is little justice in killing stupid lizards to feed stupid people; they had earned their famine. But hunting dinosaurs with cameras, that's real fun. It even gets sporting if you go after the big carnivores and happen to flush a bull who is feeling edgy and sexy – it improves your running. Or else. Dickie, there is a spot down about Wichita where I can promise you triceratops, several sorts of pterodactyls, duckbills, thunder lizards, and maybe a male stegosaurus all in one day. Once this caper is over we'll take a day off and do it. What do you say?'

'Is it that easy?'

'With the installed equipment the Mesozoic is no farther away than is THQ or Boondock. Time and space are illusions; the Burroughs irrelevancy gear will plunk you down in the middle of a herd of feeding and fornicating flapdoodles before you can say sixty-five million years.'

'The way you phrased that invitation seemed to imply that you assume that I have closed on Task Adam Selene.'

'Dickie, the equipment does indeed belong to the Time Corps . . . and it is expensive, how expensive we don't discuss. It was built to support Plan Long View; its recreational use is incidental. Yes, I implied that. Aren't you going to do it?'

Mannie Davis looked at me, with no expression. Rufo stood up, said loudly, 'I've got to mosey along; Star has a chore for me. Thanks and thanks for the last time, Jock. Nice meeting you, Colonel.' He left quickly. Harshaw said nothing.

I let out a deep breath. 'Uncle, I might do it if Hazel insists. But I'm going to try to talk her out of it. Nothing has been offered me that convinces me that I am wrong about the two options I offered. Either of them is a more sensible approach to recovering the programs and memories that embody Holmes IV or Mike . . . and I am glad to stipulate that they should be recovered. But my methods are more logical.'

Harshaw said, 'It is not a matter of logic, Colonel.'

359

'It's my neck, Doctor. But in the long run I'll do what Hazel wishes . . . I think. It's just—'

'Just what, Dickie?'

'I hate to go into action with inadequate intelligence! Always have. Uncle, for the past week or ten days – hard to figure it, the way I've bounced around – I've been haunted by unexplained and, well, *murderous* nonsense. Is the Overlord you talk about after me? Does the fact that I'm mixed up in this account for the endless near misses? Or am I getting paranoid?'

'I don't know. Tell me about them.'

I started to do so. Shortly Harshaw took out a pocket notebook, started taking notes. I tried to remember all of it: Enrico Schultz and his weird remark about Tolliver and his mention of Walker Evans. His death. If it was his death. Bill. The curious behavior of the management of Golden Rule. Those rolligons and the killers in each. Jefferson Mao. The muggers at the Raffles—

'Is that all?'

'Isn't that enough? No, not quite. What cargo was Auntie carrying? How did we get chivvied into flying a heap that durn near killed us? What were Lady Diana and her fat-headed husbands doing away out there in the wilds? If I could afford it I would spend endless money on sherlocks to dig out what was going on, what was truly aimed at me, what was just my nerves, what was simply coincidence.'

Harshaw said, 'There are no coincidences. One respect in which World as Myth is far simpler than earlier teleology is the simple fact that there are *no* accidents, no coincidences.'

Uncle Jock said, 'Jubal? I don't have the authority.'

'And I do. Yes.' He stood up. 'Both of us, I think.'

My uncle stood up, too. 'Dickie boy, you wait right here; we'll be gone five minutes or so. Errand to do.'

As they left, Davis stood up. 'Excuse, please? Need change arm.'

'Sure, Papa Mannie. No, no, Pixel! Beer is not for baby cats.'

They were gone seven minutes by my Sonychron. But not, quite apparently, by their time. Uncle had grown a full beard. Harshaw had a new, pink knife scar across his left cheek. I looked at them. 'Ghosts of Christmas past! What happened?'

'Everything. Is there any beer left there? Cissy,' he said, not raising his voice, 'could we have some beer? And Jubal and I have not eaten in some time. Hours. Days, maybe.'

'Right away,' Aunt Cissy's disembodied voice answered. 'Dear? I think you ought to take a nap.'

'Later.'

'Just as soon as you have eaten. Forty minutes.'

'Quit nagging me. Could I have tomato soup? For Jubal, too.'

'I'll fetch soup and more of your picnic. Forty-five minutes until your nap; that's official. Til says so.'

'Remind me to beat you.'

'Yes, dear. But not today; you're exhausted.'

'Very well.' Uncle Jock turned to me. 'Let's see, what'll you have first? Those rolligons? Your friend Hendrik Schultz handled that one; you can be sure it's thorough. He has turned out to be an ichiban field investigator. You can forget paranoia on that one, Dickie – two opponents, the Time Lords and the Scene Changers . . . and both of them after you as well as each other. You have a charmed life, son – born to be hanged.'

'What do you mean? – Time Lords and Scene Changers? And why me?'

'May not be their own names for themselves. The Lords and the Changers are groups doing the sort of thing the Circle does . . . but we don't see eye to eye with them. Dickie, you don't think that in all the universes to the Number of the Beast or more, we of the Circle would be the only ones to catch on to the truth and attempt to do something about it, do you?'

'I don't know anything about it, one way or another.'

'Colonel,' put in Dr Harshaw, 'a major shortcoming of World as Myth lies in the fact that we contend with . . . and often lose to . . . three sorts of antagonists: villains by design such as the Galactic Overlord, and groups like us but with different intentions – bad in our opinion, perhaps good in theirs – and the third and most powerful, the myth makers themselves – such as Homer and Twain and Shakespeare and Baum and Swift and their colleagues in the pantheon. But not those I have named. Their bodies have died; they live on by the immortal corpus of myth each has created . . . which does not change and therefore does not imperil us.

'But there are living myth makers, every one of them dangerous, every one of them casually uncaring as he revises a myth and erases a character.' Harshaw smiled grimly. 'The only way one can live with the knowledge is to realize first that it is the only game in town and second that it does not hurt. Erasure. Being X'd out of the story.'

'How do you know that it doesn't hurt?'

'Because I refuse to entertain any other theory! Shall we get on with our report?'

'Dickie boy, you asked, "Why me?" For the same reason Jubal and I left a pleasant lunch to work our tails off and to set many others to arduous and dangerous investigation in several time lines. Because of Task Adam Selene and your key part in it. Near as we can tell, the Time Lords want to kidnap Mike while the Scene Changers want to destroy him. But both groups want you dead; you're a menace to their plans.'

'But at that time I had not even heard of Mike the Computer.'

'Best time to kill you, wouldn't you say? Cissy, you are not only beautiful, you are pleasant to have around. Besides your hidden talents. Just put it down; we'll serve ourselves.'

'*Blagueur et gros menteur*. You still must nap. Message from Til. You are not to come to the dinner table until you shave off that beard.'

'Tell that baggage that I will starve before I will be hen-pecked.'

'Yes, sir. And I feel the same way she does about it.'

'Peace, woman.'

'So I volunteer to shave you. And to cut your hair.'

'I accept.'

'Right after your nap.'

'Begone. Jubal, did you have any of this jellied salad? It is something Til does exceptionally well . . . although all three of my owners are fine cooks.'

'Will you put that in writing?'

'I told you to disappear. Jubal, living with three women takes fortitude.'

'I know. I did so, for many years. Fortitude plus angelic disposition. And a taste for lazy living. But a group marriage, such as our Long Family, combines the advantages of bachelorhood, monogamy, and polygamy, with the drawbacks of none.'

362

'I won't argue it but I'll stick with my three Graces as long as they'll let me hang around. Now let' see – Enrico Schultz. No such character.'

'So?' I answered. 'He made some horrid stains on my tablecloth.'

'So he had another name. But you knew that. Best hypothesis makes him a member of the same gang as your friend Bill . . . who was a smiling villain if one ever smiled, as well as a consummate actor. We call them The Revisionists. Motivation had to be Adam Selene. Not Walker Evans.'

'Why did he mention Walker Evans?'

'To shake you up, maybe. Dickie, I didn't know about General Evans until you brought the matter up, since that debacle is still in my future. My normal future. I can see how it weighs on your mind. Will weigh on your mind. Remember, I didn't know that you had been invalided out of the Andorran Contract Crusaders until you told me.

'Anyhow – All of the "Friends of Walker Evans" are dead except you and one who went to the Asteroids and can't be found. This is as of July tenth, 2188, eleven years forward. Unless you want to talk to any alive on some date not quite so forward.'

'Can't see any reason to.'

'So it seemed to us. Now Walker Evans himself. Lazarus handled this . . . and a spot of world-changing, partly to show you what can be done. No attempt was made to revise the battle. It would be difficult, in 2177, to revise a battle in 2178 without utterly changing your life. Either kill you that year, or not lose your leg and you stay in the service – yes, I now know about your leg although it's forward from here. Either way, you don't go to Golden Rule, you don't marry Hazel . . . and we aren't sitting here, talking about it. World-changing is touchy, Dickie – best done in homeopathic doses.

'Lazarus has two messages for you. He says that you should feel no personal guilt over that debacle. To do so would be as silly as a subordinate of Custer feeling guilty over Little Big Horn . . . to which he adds that Custer was a far more brilliant general than Evans ever was. Lazarus speaks as one who has held every rank from private to commander in chief, in experience spread over many centuries and seventeen wars.

'That's the first message. The second is this: Tell your

363

nephew that, yes, it horrifies nice people. But it happens. Only those who go out beyond the end of street lights and of pavements know how such things can happen. He says that he is certain that Walker Evans would not hold it against you. Dickie, what's he talking about?'

'Had he wanted you to know, he would have told you.'

'Reasonable. Was General Evans a man of good taste?'

'What?' I stared at my uncle – then answered reluctantly: 'Well, no, I would not say so. I found him tough and a bit stringy.'

'Now we have it out in the open—'

'Yes, damn you!'

'– and I can tell you the rest, the world-changing. A field operative hid a couple of ration packs under the General's body. When you moved the body, you found them . . . and it was just enough that none of the Friends of Walker Evans ever reached that degree of hunger necessary to overcome the taboo. So it never happened.'

'Then why do I remember it?'

'Do you?'

'Why—'

'You remember finding jettisoned field rations under the body. And how good you felt!'

'Uncle, this is crazy.'

'That's world-changing. For a time, you have a memory. Then a faded memory of a memory. Then nothing. It never happened, Dickie. You went through one hell of an ordeal and lost a leg. But you did not eat your commanding officer.'

Uncle went on, 'Jubal, what do we have left that's important? Dickie, you can't expect to have all your questions answered; no man can expect that. Mmm, oh, yes, those diseases – You had two of them; the rest was hype. You were cured in three days; then they kept you in a controlled-memory field and put a new leg on you . . . and did something else. Haven't you felt better lately? Brisk? More energetic?'

'Well . . . yes. But it dates from the day I married Hazel, not from Boondock.'

'Both, probably. During the month they had you available Dr Ishtar gave you a booster. I learned that they shifted you from the rejuvenation clinic to the hospital just the day before they let you wake up. Oh, they really swindled you, boy; they gave you a new leg and made you thirty years younger. I think you ought to sue them.'

'Oh, knock it off. How about that heat bomb? More hype?'

'Maybe, maybe not. Not decided, just the time tick spiked. The thing is—'

Harshaw intervened. 'Richard, we think now that we may be able to finish Task Adam Selene before a heat bomb would be necessary. There are some plans. So the heat bombing right now is in the status of Schrödinger's Cat. The outcome depends on Task Adam Selene. And vice versa. We'll see.'

'These plans – You're assuming that I'll come around.'

'No. We're assuming that you won't.'

'Humm . . . If you are assuming that I won't, why are you two bothering to tell me all this?'

Uncle said in a tired voice, 'Dickie boy, thousands and thousands of man-hours have gone into satisfying your childish demand to have the veil lifted from the unknown. You think we are simply going to burn the results? Sit back down and pay attention. Mmm, stay out of Luna City and Golden Rule after June of 2188; there are warrants out for you for eight murders.'

'Eight! Who?'

'Mmm, Tolliver, Enrico Schultz, Johnson, Oswald Progant, Rasmussen—'

'Rasmussen!'

'Do you know him?'

'I wore his fez for ten minutes; I never laid eyes on him.'

'Let's not waste time on these murder charges. All they mean is that someone is out to get you, both in L-City and in Golden Rule. With three timejumping groups after you, that's not surprising. You want them cleared up; they can be cleared up later. If needed. If you don't just go to Tertius and forget it. Oh, yes – those code groups. Not a message, just a prop to get you to open that door. But you didn't let yourself be killed quietly the way you were supposed to. Dickie, you're a troublemaker.'

'Gosh, I'm sorry.'

'Any more questions?'

'Go take your nap.'

'Not yet. Jubal. Now?'

'Certainly.' Dr Harshaw got up and left.

'Dickie.'

'Yes, Uncle.'

'She loves you, boy; she really does. God knows why. But that does not mean that she will tell you the truth or always act in your interest. Be warned.'

'Uncle Jock, it never does any good to warn a man about his wife. Would you accept any advice from me about Cissy?'

'Of course not. But I'm older than you are and much more experienced.'

'Answer me.'

'Let's change the subject instead. You don't like Lazarus Long.'

I grinned at him. 'Uncle, the only thing that persuades me that he might be as old as he is reputed to be is that it would take more than one ordinary lifetime to grow as cantankerous and generally difficult as he is. He rubs me the wrong way every time. And the bastard makes it worse by putting me under obligations to him. This foot – From a clone of his – did you know that? And that dustup you heard about this morning. Lazarus shot that bloke what's-his-name who tried to kill me. But Captain Sterling and Commander Smith did, too, and probably quicker. Or maybe not. Either way I had to thank all three of them. Damn it, I'd like to save his life just once to balance the books. The bastard.'

'No way to talk, Dickie. Abby would have trounced you.'

'So she would have. I take it back.'

'Besides – Your own parents never were married.'

'So I've often been told. Colorfully.'

'I mean it literally. Your mother was my favorite sister. Much younger than I. Pretty child. I taught her to walk. Played with her when she was growing up, spoiled her every way I could. So, naturally, when she was in what used to be called "trouble" she came to her big brother. And to your Aunt Abby. Dickie, it was not that your father wasn't around; it was that your grandfather disliked him, disliked him as intensely as – well, as you dislike Lazarus Long.

'I don't mean Mr Ames. You got his name but he met and married Wendy after you were born. And we took you and raised you. Your mother was going to come for you, after a

366

year – she said Ames deserved that much – but she didn't live that long. So Abby was your mother in every way but biology.'

'Uncle, Aunt Abby was the best mother a boy could want. Look, those peach switchings were good for me. I know it.'

'I'm pleased to hear you say so. Dickie, I love all your aunts . . . but there will never be another Abby. Hazel reminds me of her. Dickie, have you made up your mind?'

'Uncle, I'll fight it all the way. How can I okay letting my bride risk a caper that she stands only a fifty-fifty chance of coming out of alive? Especially when nobody has even tried to show me why my ways aren't better?'

'Just asking. The mathematicians are testing another team – since you're unwilling. We'll see. Your father was stubborn and your grandfather was stubborn; it's no surprise that you are stubborn. Your grandfather – my father – said flatly that he would rather have a bastard in the family than Lazarus Long. So he had one. You. And Lazarus went away and never knew about you.

'Not surprising that you and your father don't get along; you're too much alike. And now he's going to take your place, on the team for Task Adam Selene.'

XXX

'Our revels now are ended.'

WILLIAM SHAKESPEARE 1564–1616

DYING ISN'T difficult. Even a baby kitten can do it.

I'm sitting with my back to the wall in the old computer room of the Warden's Complex in Luna. Pixel is cradled in my left arm. Hazel is on the floor, by us. I'm not sure Pixel is dead. He may be asleep. But I am not going to disturb him to find out; he's a badly hurt baby at best.

I know Hazel is still alive because I'm watching her respiration. But she is not in good shape. I do wish they would hurry.

I can't do much for either of them because I don't have anything to work with and I can't move much. I'm shy one leg and I don't have a prosthetic. Yes, that same right leg – Lazarus's leg – burned off just about at the transplant line. Guess I shouldn't gripe – being a burn job it's cauterized, not much blood. Hasn't really begun to hurt much yet, either. Not that white pain like a blow torch. That comes later.

I wonder if Lazarus knows he's my father? Did Uncle ever tell him?

Hey, this makes Maureen, that wonderful, beautiful creature, my *grandmother!*

And – Maybe I had better back up.

I'm a bit light-headed.

I'm not even sure this is being recorded. I'm carrying a battle recorder but it's a tiny Tertius type I'm not familiar with. Either it was on and I turned it off or it was off and I turned it on. I'm not sure Pixel is dead. Did I already say that? Maybe I had better back up.

*   *   *

It was a good team, the best, with enough fire power that I felt that our chances were good. Hazel was in command, of course—

Major Sadie Lipschitz, strike team leader

Brevet Captain Richard Campbell, XO

Cornet Gretchen Henderson, JO

Sergeant Ezra Davidson

Corporal Ted Bronson aka W. W. Smith aka Lazarus Long aka Lafayette Hubert, MD – additional duty, medical officer

Manuel Davis, civilian special field operative

Lazarus insisted on being called 'Ted Bronson' when he was designated a corporal for this task force. It's an insiders' joke, I think; I was not let in on it.

Cornet Henderson had been back on duty several months after having her baby boy. She was slender-solid and tan and beautiful and the combat ribbons on her pretty chest looked at home there. Sergeant Ezra always did look like a soldier, once he had legs, and his ribbons showed it, too. A good team.

Why was I breveted to captain? I asked that question right after Hazel swore me into the Corps – got a silly or reasonable answer depending on your bias. Because (said Hazel) in every history book in which this was mentioned, I had been second in charge. The histories did not name others, but they did not say that we acted alone, so she decided on more fire power and picked her team. (She decided. She picked. Not Lazarus. Not some THQ brain trust. That suited me.)

Gay Deceiver was manned by its first team, too – Hilda, commanding; Deety, XO and astrogator; Zeb Carter, chief pilot; Jake Burroughs, copilot/irrelevancy gear – and Gay herself, conscious, sentient, and able to pilot herself . . . not true of any other irrelevancy craft except Dora (who was too big for this job).

The skipper of the car, Hilda, was under the command of the strike force team leader. I would have expected a hitch here . . . but Hilda had proposed it. 'Hazel, it's got to be that way. Everybody must know who's boss. When it hits the fan, we can't stop to chat.'

A good team. We had not trained together but we were professionals and our CO made everything so clear that we didn't need drill. 'Attention to orders. The purpose of this force is to capture items selected by Davis, and to return them and Davis to Tertius. *There is no other purpose*. If we have no casualties, fine. But if all of us are killed while Davis and his selections reach Tertius, our task is accomplished.

'This is the plan. Hilda places us at the north wall, starboardside to, on the tick, after THQ advises that warp is ready to activate. Leave car in this order: Lipschitz, Campbell, Henderson, Davidson, Bronson, Davis. Place yourselves fore and aft in the bathrooms to exit in that order.

'The computer room is square. Lipschitz to southeast corner, Henderson to southwest corner, Campbell to northwest corner, Davidson to northeast corner. Diagonal pairs cover all four walls, so two such pairs doubly cover all walls. Bronson is bodyguard to Davis, no fixed post.

'As Davis works, filled boxes will be placed in car. Henderson and Davidson will move items to car as directed by Davis, and assisted inside by Deety. Car commander and pilots will remain ready to scram and will assist only by passing items back. Bronson will not repeat *not* move baggage; his sole task is bodyguard to Davis.

'When Davis tells me task is finished, we return to the car with all speed, in reverse order – Davis, Bronson, Davidson, Henderson, Campbell, Lipschitz. Hilda, you will give order to scram anytime after Davis and the stuff he came for is aboard, depending on tactical situation. If there is trouble, don't wait for anyone. Use your judgment, but your judgment must tell you to save Mannie and his items no matter who gets left behind.

'Questions?'

How long have I been doping off? My Sonychron was an early casualty. The team Hazel picked was – No, I said that. I think I did.

What happened to Tree-San?

The time tick selected was right after Hazel left the computer room on Saturday July fifth. The group picking the tick reasoned that if they were laying for us to arrive at the Raffles, then that antagonist (Time Lords?) would not be looking for us in the computer room. No way to do it earlier than that;

Hazel had reported that 'Adam Selene' was in the computer room when she was there.

We cut it mighty sharp, almost too sharp; when Hazel was getting out of Gay, she stopped suddenly with me right behind her – waited briefly, then moved out.

She paused because she saw her own back, leaving the room:

I must get word to Aunt Til that Hazel and I can't make it home for supper.

My head aches and my eyes bother me.

I don't know how Pixel got aboard Gay. How that baby does get around!

Jubal Harshaw says, 'The only constant thing in these shifting, fairy-chess worlds is human love.' That's enough.

Pixel moved a little.

It's been nice to have both feet for a few days.

'Richar'?'
    'Yes, beloved?'
    'Gretchen's baby. You his fathe'.'
    '*Huh?*'
    'She tol' me, mon's ago.'
    'I don't understand.'
    'Par'dox.'
    I started to question her about it; she was asleep again. The compress I had placed on her wound was seeping. But I didn't have anything more, so I didn't touch it.

* * *

Won't see Aunt Belden this trip. Too bad.

What happened to my files? Still in my other foot?

Hey! Tomorrow is the day 'we're all dead' if Tolliver isn't.

The first hour went by with no incident whatever. Mannie worked steadily, changed arms once, started filling boxes. Gretchen and Ezra carried them to the car, passed them in, resumed their posts between trips. Most of this seemed to be programs that Mannie was bleeding off into his own cubes, using equipment he had fetched. I could not see. Then he started filling boxes more quickly, loading them with cylinders. Adam Selene's memories? I don't know. Maybe I watched too much.

Mannie straightened up, said, 'Does it! Done!' I heard an answering, '*Blert!*'

And they hit us.

I was down at once, lower leg gone. I saw Mannie fall. I heard Hazel shout, 'Bronson! Get him aboard! Henderson, Davidson – those last two boxes!' I missed the next, as I was firing. The whole east wall was open; I traversed it with my heater at full power. Somebody else was firing, on our side, I think.

Then it was quiet.

'Rich'r'?'
    'Yes, dearest?'
    ''S been fun.'
    'Yes, love! All of it.'
    'Rich'r' . . . that light, end tunnel.'
    'Yes?'
    'I'll wait . . . there.'
    'Honey, you're going to outlive me!'
    'Look for me. I'll—'

*　　　*　　　*

When that wall opened, I think I saw what's-his-name. Could the bloke who erased him write him back into the story? To clip us?

Who was writing *our* story? Was he going to let us live?

Anyone who would kill a baby kitten is cruel, mean cruel. Whoever you are, I hate you. I *despise* you!

I dragged myself awake, realized that I had fallen asleep on watch! I had to pull myself together, because they might be back. Or, Glory Be! Gay Deceiver will be back. I couldn't figure out why Gay wasn't back. Trouble spiking the right time tick? Could be anything. But they won't just leave us here.

We saved Mannie and the stuff he picked out. We *won*, damn you all!

Had to see what weapons, ammo, were left. I didn't have anything more. My beam gun was exhausted, I knew. But my side arm? Don't remember firing it. All gone. Must look around.

'Dear?'

'Yes, Hazel?' (She's going to ask me for water and I haven't got any!)

'I'm sorry people were eating.'

'What's that?'

'I had to kill him, dearest; he was assigned to kill you.'

I placed the little cat on Hazel. Maybe he moved, maybe not – maybe both of them were dead. I managed to pull myself up onto my foot, by holding on to a computer rack, then let myself down again. Despite long practice in hopping at one-sixth gee I found that I was neither strong enough nor did I have good balance – and I was separated from my cane, for the first time in years. It was, I thought, in Gay's forward bathroom.

So I crawled, careful of my right leg. It was beginning to hurt. I found no weapons with charges. At painful last, I was back with Gwen and Pixel. Neither stirred. I couldn't be sure.

A week isn't a long honeymoon and it's an awfully short married life.

I explored her handbag, which I should have done earlier. She had carried it, slung over one shoulder to the other hip, even into battle.

That handbag was much bigger inside than out. I found twelve chocolate bars. I found her little camera. I found her deadly little lady's gun, that Miyako – fully loaded, eight in the clip, one in the chamber.

And, down in the bottom. I found that dart projector that had to be there. I almost missed it, it was styled to look like a toilet kit. Four darts were still in it.

If they come back – or a fresh gang, I don't care – I'm going to get us a baker's dozen.